Sundown Apocalypse: Homeland Defense

Sundown Apocalypse series

Book 3

By Leo Nix

In the post-apocalyptic Australian desert, a small band of survivors wage a desperate battle against ruthless religious terrorists.

The city survivors have set out to join Sundown's Commando on the edge of the Simpson Desert, but Sergeant Nulla and his motley group soon find that the trek to sanctuary is not as safe as they had hoped.

Forced to defend their friends against a brutal assault and confronted with certain death, they react with ferocious brutality of their own.

Despite the vicious fire fights between the terrorists and the survivors, love finds a way to flourish like the desert sands after rain.

In the unforgiving Australian deserts and the fractured city of Adelaide, Sundown and his commando seek to survive any way they can.

Book 3 continues the Sundown Apocalypse series.

"What a refreshing, exciting, fast paced, action novel that shows the possible realities of the near future. Lots of gun fighting and sudden battles blend with full bodied characters that will stir your heartstrings. Leo Nix has the ability to write most convincing dialogue... His world building is superb giving the reader the opportunity to experience the outback... In this book I laughed, snickered, cried and sighed. That's pretty darn good for a post-apocalyptic novel." K

Other books in this series:

Sundown Apocalypse – book 1

Sundown Apocalypse: Urban Guerrilla – book 2

Sundown Apocalypse: Homeland Defense – book 3

Sundown Apocalypse: Desert Strike – book 4

Sundown Apocalypse: Special Ops – book 5

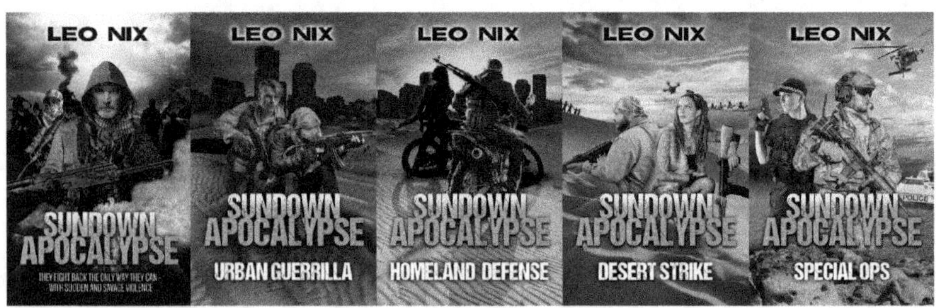

Sundown Apocalypse series is now in audiobook

I would like to take this opportunity to acknowledge and show respect, to the first Australians, our land's traditional custodians, the aboriginal people.

Copyright (C) 2017 Leo Nix

This book is a work of fiction. Names, characters, places, and incidents are the product of the author's imagination or are used fictitiously. Any resemblance to actual events, locales, or persons, living or dead, is purely coincidental.

All rights reserved. No part of this book may be reproduced or transmitted in any form or by any means, electronic or mechanical, including photocopying, recording, or by any information storage and retrieval system, without the author's permission.

Contact the author, Leo Nix

Email: leo@leo-nix.com

Web: http://www.leo-nix.com/

Cover art: Stephen Kingston

Web: http://www.wingtipdesign.com.au/

A special thank you to Marja, Peter and Bruce for your proof reading and ongoing support.

Dedication: To my wife Marja, see, I told you I could write.

Contents

Chapter 1 - Sundown - Pedro

Shadow held Pedro's limp, moist hand in both of hers and looked up at Lorraine.

"Is he going to die?" she asked softly.

Lorraine was sitting beside them both and nodded. "If we don't get some antibiotics or penicillin into him soon, he won't last the week."

McFly entered to find his wife and Lorraine crying at Pedro's bedside. "What? Is he dead already?" he blurted out when he saw the two girls in tears.

"Darn it, McFly, not so loud, he'll hear you!" whispered Lorraine. "Can you please sit with Shadow and Pedro for a while?" A sob suddenly escaped her lips but she managed to continue before she fled the room in tears. "I've got to speak to Sundown about that drug order he's sending Fat Boy to collect."

"I'm not bloody dead yet, you boofheads," croaked Pedro, his eyes still shut, "and I can hear every word, McFly."

Shadow almost leaped out of her chair when she heard him, "Pedro," she yelped as she hugged his emasculated body, "you scared the living daylights out of us."

"Just keepin' you's on yer toes, me little missie," he whispered.

"Pedro, hey." McFly leaned over almost touching Pedro's ear with his lips. "Do you need anything? A drink, a beer, a smoke or something?"

"Get out of me ear hole, yer boofhead! And yes to all of those. I'm bloody parched, I need a beer." Pedro moved a little as he tried to sit up. "And not one of that bludger Andy's warm, fruity piss he passes off as beer, I need a real beer. Get me a cold one from Harry's secret stash." The old man had a bit more force to his voice now as he slowly forced open his eyes. His skin was hot to the touch and yellowish, his eyes bloodshot.

"On my way old man," said McFly with a grin. "And boofhead yourself, you old bastard, I thought you were dead."

"I'll bloody go when I want to bloody go! The old scythe-master ain't tapped me on the shoulder yet." Pedro lay back panting as Shadow propped him up with some pillows. "Shadow, me little girlie, can you push me up a bit more? I need to get into action when McFly brings me that cold beer. You can't drink beer through a straw you know."

McFly excitedly told everyone in the kitchen that Pedro was awake. When Billie heard he ambled himself into Pedro's room like he owned the place.

"Hey, me ol' son, Pedro, how's it goin'?" he said sitting on Pedro's bed, his skinny legs swinging back and forth like pantyhose on a clothes line.

"Hi Billie, got that hip flask on you, mate? I could do with a drop of the ol' mountin' dew." Pedro smiled for the first time in quite a few days.

Gail was just on her way to Andrew's office when she spied Billie entering Pedro's room. She suspected what he might be up to, so she followed him.

"Billie!" she called through the open door in her proper British nurses voice, reserved for troublesome patients. "I can see you, and put that rum flask back in your pocket, or I'll tell Tricia. She'll cut your rum ration if your not careful."

Billie stopped with his flask in his hand half-way to Pedro's lips. "I'll be damned! That woman has eyes in her backside I'm sure of it," he said as he eased his flask back into his pocket. "Sorry, Pedro me ol' son, that woman scares me, her and that damn Tricia. They remind me of me childhood in the convent school. Bleeding nun's tortured the living daylights out of us kids, and I was one of them goody two-shoes too."

Pedro pushed himself up into an awkward sitting position. He tried to yell but he only managed a whisper in retaliation. "Look wot you done, Gail, you big bully! You frightened me ol' mate, Billie. It's unfair scaring that nice old man." He paused for a second then called, "Ya boofhead!" Then he eased back into the fluffed-up pillows.

"Darn it, Pedro," said Shadow as she settled him in again, "just ease up a bit will you. McFly's going to find a way through that incoming fire with your beer so just relax." She wiped his sweaty face with the wet cloth.

Lulu and Donna came in with some soup and another jug of water. Pedro groaned, "Shit, not another bloody bucket of water. I'm up to me back teeth in water. Now ya's have to add soup to it. I'm already farting like Niagara Falls," he complained.

"Pedro, Lorraine said you have to have it, it flushes the muck out of your system she said. Come on, sit up and let us pretty, young girlie's feed yer proper," said the ever bright Lulu. For once she was almost serious. Like all of them she was afraid Pedro would soon pass away. "You're sick Pedro so just let us help you." She turned away and a tear escaped from the corner of her eye to drip onto her t-shirt.

"OK, but only if ya help McFly bring me a cold beer, or I won't drink a drop o' that butt fountain-water." Pedro was slowly coming back to his old cantankerous self.

"Lorraine, for the tenth time we've given the list of medications to Fat Boy and Blondie, it's safe in their hands. We've given them a list of Cessna parts too. They're heading off in just a few minutes." Andrew was sitting in his office with Sundown studying the maps for the two biker's rescue trek. It was just on dawn and the place was starting to crawl with soldiers and Sundown's commandos.

A head poked in through the office door. "Sundown, ah, Andrew, you don't mind me joining you for a minute?" It was Captain Lewis' smiling face. "We'll soon be heading back to Alice Springs but we've just heard that there's a bit of a crisis happening. Do you need some help?"

Sundown looked across at him and nodded. "We sure could do with some extra fire support, Captain."

"So what's this about, Sundown? We heard Pedro was dying or something." The captain's face was now serious.

"Yeah, he took a turn during the night. Lorraine and Tricia said that he needs penicillin or antibiotics but we've got nothing like that here so we're sending Fat Boy to Mount Isa for it. It's the closest large town and it should have what they need," replied Sundown. "You're saying that Major Thompson wants to help?"

The captain's face lit up in a smile that threatened to break his face in two.

"Yes he bloody-well does!" he almost yelled. "I was praying that something like this would happen. We've not had a proper stand up stoush - ever! Me and the boys were hoping that meeting you lot would give us somewhere to point our 25 mm guns." He let out a little 'whoop!' and then stopped, calmed his face and continued. "Sorry, Sundown, I got a little carried away with myself. Right, what do you have planned? I'm sure the major will permit you to advise us."

"Thanks, Captain Lewis, we certainly do appreciate this," said Sundown smoothly. "OK, we've got Fat Boy and Blondie heading into Mount Isa in about five minutes. They'll be riding their Harley-Davidson. I was planning to send Wiram and an armed squad with our two machine guns to set up an ambush about three hundred click's from here and another just outside

Mount Isa itself. But if you can take your ASLAV, and we include one of our commandos, that should be enough. What do you think?"

"They've got, what, six hundred kilometres to Mount Isa? Fat Boy should be able to do that in a day, even though it's mostly dirt, hmm." The captain rubbed his chin, thinking. "Our intelligence tells us the terrorists have multiple road blocks and the township's controlled by them and the local bikie gang. We've had the town under surveillance for months and every exit and entry point is covered. They've started preparations to move against you lot too." The captain nodded guiltily at Andrew and Sundown, then continued quickly. "We weren't going to tell you until we knew for certain that you were with us, but you might as well know now."

"Thanks for telling us, Captain," said Andrew drily. "We will need your ASLAV to run up there in about an hour, do you think you could manage that?"

"Better than that, we'll send two bushmasters and the ASLAV and hit them up the arse once we get Fat Boy out of there." The captain was almost salivating. "Leave it to me, I'll get it sorted out right now." The captain paused, "so, who did you want to send with us from your commando?"

Andrew looked at Sundown and said, "Assassin hasn't had much time on patrol and he's been pestering to get away from the CB listening post again. Not McFly, he's asked to have a break from patrolling to spend more time with his missus,

Shadow. Not Wiram, I want him here to run the Birdsville Track and Marree patrols. What about Cambra and Donna?"

Sundown ran his fingers through his thick, greying hair as he assembled his thoughts. He really wanted to go with the patrol himself. A ride in one of those Bushmasters at one hundred kph would be fun, he thought.

"Yeah," he said at last. "Send Cambra and Donna, she deserves a break. Oh, hang on, Lulu and Danni might get upset. Hmm, OK, Cambra and his girls, Lulu and Danni, they work well together. I know the girl's are busy fussing over Pedro but I'll offer it to them anyway." He was thinking out loud, something he did a lot these days. "OK, I'll get them in here and ask them."

The captain headed out to his crews while Sundown went to find Cambra and his fan club. He knew Cambra looked after the two teenagers like they were his daughters and they adored him in turn. The problem, he realised, could be with those hot blooded soldiers all crammed into the vehicles for several days. But then on second thoughts he was sure the girls could handle themselves well enough, he'd seen them in action enough times to know that. Besides, he thought, if they could handle the terrorists at the mines they can handle our own soldiers.

Sundown knocked as he walked into Pedro's room. McFly was trying to hide Pedro's beer behind his back.

Shadow innocently said, "Hi, Sundown," as she looked around nervously to see if Lorraine was behind him. Lulu and Donna's face had flushed a bright red.

"It's OK everybody it's only me for crying-out-loud." Sundown nodded to McFly who quickly brought the bottle out from behind his back and handed it to Pedro.

"Ahhhhh," sighed Pedro taking a long pull on the bottle, "give me that any day! Sundown, me ol' matey, what's happening? I can hear footsteps racing everywhere, are we under attack or something?"

"Nope, not that I know of, except for your legs and blood poisoning we're just dandy." Sundown smiled brightly as he clasped his friend's proffered hand. Pedro pulled his friend in close to his mouth.

"I'm not well, matey, when I fart me butt squirts and it's damn embarrassing. Can you tell the girls to leave off with the water and just give me beer?" He winked at his friends around him. Just then he loudly passed wind, and what may have been a bit more than wind. "Sorry, can someone get that for me?" He let out a soft laugh. "I never knew what a relief it would be to let someone else clean me arse for me." He chuckled again but Sundown and everyone else knew that those tears weren't necessarily happy ones, the poor old warrior was in a lot of pain.

"OK, everyone out," announced Lorraine as she and Tricia entered. They could smell Pedro's latest production from the other room. "We'll look after this, we've done it a million times before. Just give us a moment and then we'll leave you in peace."

"Thanks ladies, and please be gentle with him, I need him back on deck by the weekend. And Lorraine, while you're wiping his butt please don't wipe his smile away?" Sundown tried to make a joke but not even Pedro responded. "Well, that sure went down like a lead balloon," he said as he walked out with the others.

The break gave Sundown the opportunity to sort out what he was really there for. "Lulu, go and get Danni and Cambra, please. Bring them to Andy's office, pronto. I need you all there five minutes ago," he said.

Lulu looked up realising something exciting was in the air. She raced away, her wide smile shone bright against her dark skin.

"Sundown," said Captain Lewis, "Major Thompson is now free to see you about our patrol to Mount Isa."

"Fine," said Sundown. He unconsciously scratched his ear lobe as he replied, "tell the major I'll meet he and his crew leaders in a few minutes." He turned and quickened his pace as he walked back to Pedro's room.

As Sundown entered he saw Pedro patting Fat Boy on the back as the giant of a man leaned over his bed hugging the withered old warrior. Pedro looked up at Sundown with worried eyes.

"Sundown, me big boofheaded friend here won't stop crying." He turned back to Fat Boy, "Now stop that and let me up, yer squashing me." He patted Fat Boy on the back some more. . Blondie stepped over and pulled Fat Boy off him.

"Hell, you'd think I was already dead the amount of people who've come in here crying. Now stop it, it's upsetting me." He turned to Sundown again. "Fat Boy says he's on a 'Mission from God' to get some drugs for me. Mount Isa is it? I know I'm crook but that's a long ride to fetch a bottle of pills for someone old and decrepit like me." Sundown noted that Pedro's voice was stronger than it was earlier.

Fat Boy sniffed and wiped the back of his hand across his face. "You're worth it mini-me, me skinny little brother. I might not come back though, that's what's worrying me and Blondie. We, ah, we don't really have a good reputation in Mount Isa but if anyone can pull it off it's Blondie. I'm just the driver this time." Fat Boy pulled off his bandanna and wiped at the remaining tears on his face.

"Pedro, say your good-byes. I've got to get these two on their way. I'll be back in a half hour." Sundown lowered his face to hide his sadness then turned to lead the two adventurers off to Andrew's office. He caught up with Jenny who was walking along the corridor. "Jenny, can you sit with Pedro for a while, please, until I finish sending Fat Boy and Blondie off?"

Jenny nodded, "Sure, Sundown, I was just dropping in for a yarn with him anyway. I'll wait for you."

The bikers took off in a cloud of dust and were well on their six hundred kilometre journey of salvation not long after the sun had risen above the horizon.

It was a crazy morning. Everyone was awake and had said their farewells to Fat Boy and Blondie earlier. Now they were ready to wish good luck to the armoured patrol.

The three vehicles were being checked over by their crews while the crew chiefs busily sorted out supplies. With three extra crew members, Cambra elected to go with the ASLAV while Lulu and Danni happily put their kits in with the soldiers of Bushmaster One One Bravo under the rapid-speaking Sergeant Ahmet.

Sundown went back to talk with Andy. He needed to get his head around what was happening and he found Andrew was the only one who could do that for him.

"We've got Chan and John on patrol with the other Bushmaster down south. Sergeant Doff and his One One Charlie isn't it?" asked Sundown. In answer Andrew pointed to the wall map covered in pins and then to the enormous wall calendar next to it.

"Ah, good, and we've got Cambra, Danni and Lulu with the armed patrol.... McFly, Shadow, Pinkie and myself will be taking one of our four-wheel drives with Major Thompson's cavalry across the Simpson Desert to the Alice..." Sundown paused while he tried to remember everything he needed to discuss with Andy. "I've been thinking I might take Billie as guide and interpreter. He's from the region we'll be crossing, he knows this country and the local language. If we get into strife and need help from the local aborigines they'll be more inclined to talk to Billie than us."

Andrew nodded assent and Sundown continued. "I need Bill and Wiram to get that aeroplane fixed and running. If the drugs don't help Pedro, I want him flown to Alice Springs, pronto." Andrew nodded once again and pointed, it was all up there on his pin board and wall calendar.

"Good, yeah, now for Donna. I want her and Wiram to work together from now on. He's managed the commando by himself up to now. Halo has helped but I really want him to focus on training. Besides, I think Wiram fancies Donna." Sundown looked at Andrew and winked, a light smile on his face.

"Matchmaker now are we?" Andrew grinned. "I've noticed, and so have Jeda and Bill. Donna never misses an opportunity to be around Wiram too." The wily old administrator continued. "What do you think of this major organising the armoured patrol to Mount Isa? Do you think he can control himself? I'd prefer the captain to run it but…"

"He reminds me of Captain Mainwaring from that British home-army show," interjected Sundown his thoughts racing. "A doddery old beggar but his heart's in the right place I think. He certainly seems to be keen enough. You know how Beamy told us of his conversation with the Bushmaster crew?" Andrew nodded. "Well, this is exactly what they need, a proper contact. I'll tell Cambra to make sure it happens. We've got to let these soldiers know what we've been doing all this time. Besides, they really need blooding. It might as well be on our watch with some of our best commandos. I think Lulu and Danni will make it easy for the boys to side with us when the time comes."

"You think of everything, Sundown. Just don't get too clever or it might blow up in your face," warned Andrew.

"The way I see it, Andy, this is our best and only opportunity to bond the two officers and their crews to us. My thoughts, and this is confirmed by what Beamy said, is that this mob in Alice Springs are a bunch of yobbos who couldn't organise a root in a brothel." Sundown chuckled, there was no way he would ever have said that out loud a year ago. "We bind them to us now, through blood, sweat and tears. Then we'll call on their loyalty when we need it."

The major spoke to Sergeant Ahmet, "Sergeant, gather the men, thank you." He then turned to Sundown. "Sundown, would you like to say a few words before we leave?"

"Thank you, major, yes, I would." Sundown stood beside Major Thompson and Captain Lewis while the three armoured cavalry crews gathered together.

"Squadron, attention! Stand at ease!" cried Sergeant Ahmet in his rapid-fire high pitched voice. He spun on his heels and saluted the major. "All present, sir."

The major saluted smartly and stepped forward to claim the command position, which was one step in front of Sundown.

"Men, today we go on a special mission. We have all spoken with Sundown's Commando over the past few days and know the burden they have carried as front line fighters against these terrorists. They've been at it since the beginning of the apocalypse." He looked up into the sky for a moment then continued. "Our commander has ordered that we avoid conflict at all costs." The major's voice rose in anguish, "and we have followed his orders to the letter for months!"

He stopped and looked back at the faces of his command and smiled. Speaking softly now he continued. "Well men, today I am going to tell my commanding officer, General Hughes, Alice Springs Command, Third Australian Army, that we have been informed of a strong Revelationist Church force, moving down from Mount Isa, and that we intend to intercept it."

"Silence in the ranks, please!" commanded Sergeant Ahmet as several of the cavalrymen swore excitedly.

"Thank you, Sergeant Ahmet. I know you lot think that we have run like cowards at every contact. That's not quite correct though, is it. We have preserved the only armoured military force still operating on the Australian mainland, beside the Abrams of 1st Cavalry." He again looked upwards as if expecting something to appear in the skies above him. "Today we go forward into enemy territory to assist in the rescue of one of our own, Lance Corporal Pedro Owens, formerly of 3rd RAR, Vietnam, Laos, Thailand, Cambodia, Burma and anywhere the CIA and ASIO sent him. He needs medications that we simply can't get here in Birdsville." Again he paused, then looked at his men's excited faces. "Are you with me?" he asked quietly.

With a roar the three crews cheered. They fought the urge to break ranks and rush to embrace their major. Sergeant Ahmet called them back to order.

"Cavalry of the Third Army, the major would like a simple 'yes' or a 'no', thank you."

"YES!" came their impassioned answer.

The two officers smiled proudly as Captain Lewis stepped forward to speak. "Before we rush off to prepare for the patrol we would like to extend our gratitude to Sundown's Commando for their hospitality these past few days. We now look forward to a successful patrol and safe return. Sergeant Ahmet, before you dismiss the men, Commander Sundown would like a word. Commander?" He stepped back conceding the dominant position, reluctantly, to join the major, one step behind Sundown.

"Thank you. Major Thompson; Captain Lewis; members of Alice Springs Command." He nodded respectfully to the two officers. "Our commando would like to thank you for accepting our invitation to join us on what will probably be a fighting patrol. As you know, Pedro has been the solid rock upon which we've built our commando and he is very precious to us. Those not going with you extend our wishes for your safe return." Sundown waved at Cambra, Lulu and Danni to stand beside him.

"I am handing these three warriors over to you for the duration of this patrol. Please take good care of them, just as they will take good care of you. Good luck and…" but before he could finish he saw Halo running towards him. He looked comical with his camouflage jacket twisted awkwardly around his shoulders, his AK47 in one hand and his precious Deaths Head knife gripped firmly in his free hand. Halo pushed politely through the ranks of the armoured cavalry to stand at attention beside his three commando mates.

Sundown looked quizzically at him, Halo smiled brightly back.

"Forgetting someone, Sundown?" announced Halo in a loud voice for all to hear.

"Um, no. Halo, what's this about?" asked Sundown. His creased brow made his weathered face look more confused than it already was.

"Major Thompson asked if I would like to go with him in his ASLAV. I had to get my gear. I'm sorry I'm late, boss." He nodded to Major Thompson who smiled broadly back at him. Sundown looked across at the major noting his grin and realised that he'd been played.

"Well… this does leave us short manned." Sundown wasn't going to take this lying down. "What about the patrol down south, who's going to support them if things fall apart?"

"Beamy said he'd take my place," said Halo quickly. His face revealed that he hadn't really thought of that through properly.

Fortunately for Halo, Major Thompson cleared his throat and said, "Ah, Sundown, I am very sorry but Halo was so keen to participate and he will be of great value to us as one of your original hero's. Besides, he swore you wouldn't mind." The major couldn't keep the smile off his face as he spoke. He almost snorted trying to choke back a laugh.

"This is a bloody conspiracy! Bugger!" Sundown almost stamped his feet in frustration. He stared firmly at Halo. "Right mate! Go and get Beamy, if he can hold a rifle and hit that post there with a three round burst you can go." There was no way Sundown would let the major put one over him. '*You smart arsed, Dad's Army sod*', he thought to himself.

Halo sped off and brought Beamy from the CB room where he'd been all morning.

"What's this then?" Beamy asked Sundown and the troops. "Who said I was taking Halo's place on patrol? I'm too busy flirting with the nursie girls, I've got no time for patrolling." Beamy's grin caused a ripple of muffled laughter among the soldiers and spectators watching with growing interest.

"Last time Halo tried to trade places with me I got shot up and damn near died. Bugger that," he said as he lifted his AK47 and sighted at the post Halo had pointed out.

"Kids! Everyone! Cover your ears," he called and then fired hitting the post twenty metres away fair in the middle. Beamy and Halo both turned to see Sundown's look of resignation, he'd been played all right.

With his face a crooked image of loss and defeat Sundown said softly, "OK, you can go, Halo."

He drew in a deep breath to regain his composure. "Beamy, you come with me when we finish here because I'm putting you on the next bloody patrol down south now that you've managed to heal up so bloody fast."

The group in front of the officers were smiling behind their faces at this display. They loved the affection that was such an obvious part of the Sundown's Commando community.

"Squadron!" called Sergeant Ahmet at a nod from the major. "Attention! You've got jobs to do boys, go do them. Dismissed!" The soldiers slapped each others backs as they laughed and joked all the way back to their vehicles to begin their preparations.

"Major," Sundown smiled over at the Dad's Army captain look-alike. "That was, well, cleverly done. I do expect results now that you that have my four best soldiers. Look after them for me." They shook hands, Sundown turned and walked back to the hotel.

It slowly dawned on him that this was probably Andy's idea. Sundown smiled then laughed out loud as he realised he'd been out manoeuvred by just about everybody.

Chapter 2 - Sundown - Prospector's Hideaway

By the time Riley made his way back to the bushman's hut his wife was asleep. Roo and Bongo were wide awake. Even though both were sorely wounded they were the only ones who could entertain Elle, all of four years, and two year old Harry. Katie was up all night tending to the two wounded men. She had collapsed with welcome relief when Bongo said he and Roo would look after the kids while she grabbed some sleep.

Katie knew plenty about nursing from helping her father tend his livestock and a multitude of sick neighbours. It seemed everyone preferred to drop in to see her father rather than go to the 'quack' in town. Her father had been an army medic during the Vietnam war. He had returned there after the war to do voluntary work in hospitals up and down the country. His skill with wounds, broken bones and simple aches and pains was legendary.

Riley chuckled when he saw his wife asleep and the two young men groaning as little Harry climbed all over them, he was like a hyperactive caterpillar. Roo in particular struggled to keep his broken arm free of little Harry's squirming arms and legs. Elle, ever the responsible eldest child, fretted when she couldn't slow Harry's enthusiastic play. The two men could only grunt in pain at the infant's every twist and turn.

"Hey, fella's, how're you feeling?" Riley asked as he collapsed exhausted onto the low bed next to his sleeping wife.

"Hi, Riley," answered Bongo as he dragged Harry away from Roo again. He then pushed one of the dogs off his own leg which was swollen and felt like it was on fire. "As you can see we're doing fine but poor Katie's bushed. Sorry we kept you both awake last night."

"No worries, Bongo, you pair were prepared to give your lives to save my family's, we owe you." As an afterthought he added, "Oh yeah, you killed the lot of them. Brad and Ferrie and even some of my old mates from school, the traitorous bastards." He now sat up, his face clearly showing the strain of his nights toil. "I hid the Rovers and I've found another safe place to shack us up. It's a bit of a trek but we can use the horses to take us there."

Roo was sitting with his back to one of the old tree posts supporting the bark roof. He looked at Bongo and nodded.

"Roo says we should get the hell out of here. At least you, Katie, and the kids should. Maybe take your truck and head off to Birdsville and hook up with our lot." He looked back to Roo who nodded again.

"Bongo, you're both pretty badly wounded. Any travel is going to make you worse, just look at you." He waved his hand at them. "Neither of you can stand up and Roo can't even hold a knife and fork. Nah, we stay here until we're all fit enough to travel. It will take a few days before you two will be well enough to move from here."

"Riley, they'll hunt you down. They'll do bad things to Katie and the kids. Those Wilson's are bad, real bad." Riley now noticed Bongo's bruised and swollen face as his new friend pushed one of the dogs off his injured leg.

Riley shook his head in resolve, he would stay and look after his injured mates. The two commandos brightened a little when he told them of the weapons he'd collected from the dead Wilson's and then of his plans to move them deeper into the Arkaroola wilderness. He knew of an old prospectors hut that lay among the wild gully's several kilometres away.

"That sounds fine but you're handicapped, Riley. Neither Roo nor I can do much more than hold a rifle. We can't go out on patrol, we're useless. Please, just leave us, we can hide then in a few days we'll be strong enough to fight back," argued Bongo who was starting to fret, worrying about Katie and the kids again.

"No way, Bongo. Roo's my cousin and you're his mate, that makes you family too. We don't leave family behind," said Riley, his face firm. Bongo could see that the conversation was over.

Katie was up by lunch time and took the kids with Riley as they transported their gear over to the new hiding place. This gave Bongo and Roo time to settle down on the rough ground-sheets and sleep. They'd eaten a meal of porridge and that was all. Katie said she'll do better once they moved to 'grander lodgings'.

By evening Riley and Katie had moved everything to the old prospector's hut. Bongo suggested they should leave he and Roo there to get some sleep, then pick them up the next morning. Riley looked carefully at both men, then nodded. He wished them a good night sleep as he climbed on the back of one of the horses and headed off to be with his wife and kids.

The prospector's hut was hidden deep at the end of a gully, heavily overgrown with bushes. It once housed a lone gold prospector many years ago. Riley said he and his brothers brought food and a few bottles of beer to his camp on weekends. The boys listened to his stories of the early days of prospecting when the local aboriginals lived there in much larger numbers. He told of the violent clashes between the aboriginals and the farmers who had settled the region. Those were bad times when farmers would shoot and poison any aborigines on their land.

The old prospector said there were many times he would swap tobacco, flour and sugar for a leg of kangaroo meat from the surviving tribesmen. Both of Riley's parents had a soft spot for the quiet old man and looked after him as best they could. The old prospector eventually passed away when Riley was still a kid, he said.

The hut was big enough for the family to sleep at one end and it had a fireplace and table at the other. The dogs and the two wounded men would sleep outside under a bark lean-to. By lunch time the next day, the cattleman had finished building the lean-to and added two bench seats and sleeping mats, making it quite cosy. The dogs loved it.

When they arrived at their new lodgings, Katie asked the men to be careful with their rifles around the children. Both Bongo and Roo refused to leave their weapons beyond their reach. Having lived as warriors for so long now they felt uncomfortable without them.

Roo eventually asked Riley with 'mmm's' and gestures to oil his Gewehr and place it in a bag for him. It was useless now that he'd run out of ammunition for it. Instead he lay next to his artistically decorated AK47 with its replica Mrs. Sow and her piglets carved into its wooden stock.

Riley displayed his collection of captured kangaroo rifles. Roo carefully examined then picked one, a hard-hitting Ruger fitted with an expensive scope.

Although both men were wounded and needed plenty of rest and recuperation they insisted on doing their part. Each took turns to keep watch while Riley and Katie set up camp.

The next morning Riley was up before dawn taking his dogs to patrol the surrounding bush and to set rabbit traps on the approaches to the hut. That first day he kept watch from a hilltop that overlooked their hiding place. His traps were well hidden and he made sure the dogs stayed well away from them.

The following morning at their new camp, Bongo woke with a heavy head. His leg was so swollen that he couldn't move it. From the skills she'd learned from her father, Katie recognised what the problem was immediately.

"I'm sorry, Bongo, but that's blood poisoning. I've got no medicines for it so I'll have to use an old aboriginal remedy for it. My dad learned this from working on the aboriginal missions. There's a special bark that can penetrate the skin and counteract the poison. Then there is some clay in the creeks nearby that will draw the pus out." She looked for Roo who was now able to walk around without feeling dizzy.

"Roo, can you and Bongo look after Elle and Harry for me again? I'll take the horse to gather what I need and be back in about two hours. There's plenty of tucker for the kids, just don't let Harry out of your sight for a minute."

Roo nodded but Bongo was just too sick to care. Katie rounded up the mare left behind by Riley and set out into the desert scrub with a machete, shovel and some leather saddle bags.

By the time Katie returned, Riley was back at camp. He was talking with Roo and Bongo.

"I looked all over the place but saw no signs of them. I even went part way back to my farm, nothing there either. I don't like it one bit. Those Wilson's are up to something."

"Riley, darling, I need your help," Katie called. "I've got a sick fellow here and I need you to roast these bark pieces. Don't let them burn, just dry them out until they're brittle. I'll mix this clay up and then we can spread it over Bongo's leg."

Katie had been trying to hide just how serious Bongo's injury really was. She had seen grown men and women die from injuries as small as a pimple that had turned septic. Bongo's blood poisoning was one that could easily kill him if not treated immediately. At her feet she could clearly see that Bongo was in severe pain. The commando scout's face was bathed in sweat and he was becoming delirious.

Katie pounded the dried bark and the clay into a fine powder. She added the ingredients to warm water then mixed it into a muddy paste.

"Bongo, this is going to feel nice and soothing so don't rub it off. I'll need to change it every hour so lie back and try to get some sleep." The bullet had gone through his lower calf which was black and blue all the way down to his toes. A red line now travelled from his wound to the swollen gland in his groin. Katie gently applied the clay and wattle bark mixture to his hot and angry leg. She let it dry then eased his leg onto the blanket.

"Now just lie back and let it do it's job. I'll keep changing it until the swelling's gone." Her eyes looked carefully at Bongo's bruised, fevered face then unconsciously leaned across to wipe the perspiration from his forehead. By evening the swelling was down and Bongo was asleep.

"Riles?" called Katie, brushing a wisp of stray hair from her face. "I'll need to stay up tonight to change Bongo's mud pack. Will you be OK tomorrow to let me sleep in?" She tried to sound pleasant but she was so tired that it sounded more like a demand.

"Sure, just don't wake me." Riley smiled warmly at his wife. It wasn't the first time she'd done this for some poor stockman and his family. Many injured and sick visitors stayed overnight at their home while Katie treated them.

Although he'd never met her father, he'd sadly passed away when Katie was in her late teens, he accepted her healer role as part and parcel of who she was.

"Besides, Roo here is well enough to take on tomorrows patrol for me."

Roo nodded, "Mm, yeah," he said clearly, causing both Katie and Riley to stop and stare at him.

"Blimey, Roo, we're not used to you talking," Riley said. He slapped him on the back as Katie left to put the children to bed. "Roo, do you want to sleep in here with me tonight? Katie is going to be busy and she'll wake you every time she puts mud on Bongo's leg. She'll want to sleep in the lean-to next to Bongo and the dogs anyway."

Roo grabbed his sleeping gear in his one good hand and dragged it into the hut itself. He nodded to Katie, "Ta," he grunted and smiled his thanks.

Katie looked at Riley and they raised their eyebrows in shared surprise. After twenty years without uttering a word of speech what on earth had changed in Roo to make him want to start now?

Both men were up at dawn. It was cold, mist lay across the hills and they could hear Katie talking softly to Bongo.

"How's he going, Katie? How's the swelling?" asked Riley rubbing the sleep from his eyes.

"The swellings gone down nicely," replied Katie. She noticed that Bongo was stirring so asked, "How does it feel, Bongo? Is it still on fire?"

Bongo was clearly tired but he replied in the positive. "I feel a lot better, Katie, and I'm hungry. That lump in my groin's better but my leg's still a bit stiff and sore. I think I can do the mud packs myself now too, thank you."

"I'll put the mud bowl within reach," Katie said, the relief obvious in her voice. "Riles, when the kids wake up don't let them jump all over me or Bongo, we both need our sleep now," she said as she went straight to the warm bed Riley and Roo had just vacated.

Over breakfast Roo indicated he would do the first watch. He had his pistol in it's holster at his waist and his AK slung over his good arm. There was a set of binoculars slung around his neck and food in a small back pack which he had awkwardly dragged onto his back.

"Roo, I'll come out and relieve you at exact midday. Take Black Dog, he knows the way and he's the most reliable," said Riley. "And stay off the path when you come to the big rock. I've hidden some rabbit traps in the grass there. Black Dog knows where they are, but just be careful."

Roo grunted a primitive reply then clicked his fingers at Black Dog. Together they set off at a slow walk. It was a cool morning and Roo was excited to get back to the solitude of the bush once again.

"That Roo surprises me, Bongo. He hasn't spoken a word in twenty years and now he's chattering like a monkey. I wonder what it means?" Riley scratched his head as he began to prepare breakfast for his children, who were just starting to wake up.

Chapter 3 - Nulla - Out Of The Frying Pan

The dwellers were completely exhausted as they pulled into an abandoned motel outside the city suburbs.

"Squelch, click, click," came the coded call as the boys gave the 'all clear'. Nulla and Phil switched off their engines and proceeded to climb from their vehicles.

"I've had it!" groaned Phil, he sagged onto the car bonnet and looked around to check that they were concealed from the main road. The motel units opened up right next to where they'd parked.

"Nice work boys, you've brought us right to our bedroom doors," Nulla called to their motorcycle escort.

Nulla helped Glenda out of the car but she refused his offer to carry her. "No, I can do it, don't spoil me," she said and hobbled with her AK47 over one shoulder and her backpack on the other.

"I'm sorry everyone but I have a blinding headache from these night vision goggles," Glenda mumbled. "I really need to get a cup of tea, and then some sleep. Now, is anyone going to open a door for me?" She looked at the two boys who were just pulling off their helmets. Glenda softened when she saw that they were so exhausted they could barely climb off their bikes.

"I'll do it," said Nulla. His face reflected the same strain from peering through the distorted image of night vision goggles for six hours straight. He kicked at the first unit door. When it wouldn't budge he tried the handle, it opened smoothly.

"Huh! Well I guess this is ours," he said to Glenda. "You go and lie down while I get everyone sorted out then I'll put a brew on for us."

The sky was starting to colour as the clouds shifted from a violet pink into a range of red and orange as the sun slowly rose above the horizon.

By the time Nulla had the billy boiled and eleven cups of tea and coffee made the group had settled into their units and most were nodding off to sleep. He chatted with Phil for a while but the old man kept squinting to keep his eyes open. Nulla knew he was simply too exhausted to listen.

"Sorry, Phil," said Nulla, "I guess I pushed things a little too hard last night. Those night vision goggles are hard work."

"I think we need to take a break tonight, Nulla. I don't think anyone can go through that again until their headaches clear. I've got a migraine and I don't normally get migraines. I think from now on we stick to four hour runs, no more. Last night was just murder. If we didn't pull over when we did I think I would have crashed into something." Phil finished his cup of tea and waved in Nulla's direction as he headed towards his unit. Fatima was already sound asleep.

With his head in his hands Nulla pondered what he should do.

'Surely everyone realises the importance of getting out of the city as fast as possible? I guess we won't have to push so

hard now that we're almost clear of it,' Nulla thought as he leaned back in his chair to drink his third cup of black tea. Slowly he closed down his mind and built his sanctuary of calm and harmony. He placed the dilemma inside his mind palace and disappeared into a deep sleep, but not for long.

"Nulla, boss, wake up." Nulla looked up, it was Luke. "I've checked the motel rooms and we're safe and secure. What do you want me to do now?"

Nulla rubbed at his gritty eyes and got up, turned on the tap and splashed his face with cold water. *'This must be fed by a rain-water tank,'* he thought absently.

"You'd better go and have a sleep, mate. You look bushed too. You and the boys did a great job last night too, well done. Hey, how's your head feeling?" he asked as an afterthought.

"Head? Dunno. I'm tired but otherwise I'm OK. Everyone else has headaches but all I got was bored. Doing sixty k's an hour is way too slow boss. We should be flying along…" he trailed off when he saw Nulla looking at him. "Yeah I know, safety first. But…" again came Nulla's look and he stopped, turned and went off to his room.

At midday Simon was up and cooking a meal for himself. No one else was there except Nulla who was listening to the CB. Simon brought him some tinned salmon and some of Fatima's flat bread with curry powder, his favourite condiment.

"Thanks, Simon," Nulla said, as he took the tin without looking. After his first spoonful he gagged. "Hey what is it with you and this blasted curry powder? I'm going to have to explain to Glenda why I smell so bad now."

The teenager just smiled, he was tired and his eyes rimmed by a flaming redness. "What are we going to do now? Everyone's exhausted. I don't think we can do another night like that, Nulla, my head's like cotton wool and my eyes are sore."

"I was thinking that too..." Nulla suddenly stopped talking. From the road came the clear sounds of laughter.

"Terrorists or looters! Simon, wake everyone up and have them weapons-ready," whispered Nulla grabbing his assault rifle. "And Simon, do it quietly."

As he peered around the edge of the motel wall he saw a patrol of five terrorists walking in the middle of the road. They were laughing and singing, obviously quite drunk. Nulla tracked them with his scope and watched as they disappeared in the direction he had planned to lead his small group the following evening.

"Nulla, what's happening?" asked Simon, crawling up beside him. Luke was there too putting his webbing and cartridge belt around his waist. Heidi and Arthur were pulling on their boots and he could see Charlene with a 9mm pistol in her hand. She flicked her tussled hair away from her face with it's barrel.

'Strewth!' Nulla exclaimed softly to himself, *'I'd better teach her to be more careful with that blasted pistol, she's way too casual with it and sure to blow her head off.'*

"Looks like terrorists out for a stroll." Simon's voice brought him back to the present.

"Drunk too," Nulla replied. "I'm going to follow and see where they're going. You stay here on guard, Simon. Luke, you get everyone packed and ready to run if we need to. I'll be back within the hour." He looked at his watch. "At this point there's no reason to panic. They don't know we're here." Nulla looked at the boys. "Simon, post Arthur in a sniping position upstairs too."

Crouching low he headed towards the fading sound of voices.

They continued walking for a hundred metres where they stopped at a road block of sandbags. In front were four or five cars parked in such a position to slow any approaching vehicles. It was just as well he'd stopped his group when he did, he thought. There was one thing he forgot to do when they arrived, he reminded himself, and that was to reconnoitre their extended environment.

He scoped out the guards, their weapons, and looked for any other support in the vicinity - he saw none. It looked like a single roadblock on the main road. A machine gun and small arms surrounded by sandbagged walls. It was a solid-looking stockade. There was a roof to keep the sun and rain off and right opposite was their living quarters.

Nulla noted four guards inside the post. They didn't move when the group waved to them and entered the house opposite. The four guards appeared to be well disciplined and stayed at their posts. Nulla then noticed there were bullet holes in the cars and the stockade sandbags were peppered with holes as well. He looked further down the road and saw two cars severely damaged by rifle fire, another looked like it had been hit by an RPG.

The group he followed were now sitting on camp chairs at the front of the house drinking. Some were setting up a table with food and drinks. He could still only see the five terrorists he saw earlier, he didn't see any new faces exiting the house itself. Nulla stayed in the area to scope out as far as his binoculars could see in each direction. It appeared to be an outpost as well as a well prepared road block. Music came blaring from the house and Nulla decided he could safely head back to the group.

"What did you see, boss?" asked Simon.

"It's an outpost with a road block. It cuts us off from the Murray River but we can get around that if we want to. You'd better call everyone into the motel office where we can watch the road - and tell Fatima and Heidi to bring some food. We'll eat then we need to move out," answered Nulla, the tension in his jaw and neck muscles betrayed his fears.

"Will do, boss." Simon ran off on his errand.

When they were gathered Nulla called to Arthur, "Arthur, did you see anything while I was gone?"

"Nothing, Nulla, no more people, not even dogs or cats," he replied.

"Good, looks like that's the lot of them. They don't know we're here and that's the way I want it to stay. They've got a heavy machine gun at their post and it appears they've had contacts in the past. Perhaps my cavalry unit visited or perhaps it's another local group of civilian resistance.

"I've thought a lot about where we should be heading and I think the Flinders Ranges is our best bet. Although there are reports that there are plenty of Revelationists there and the locals are on their payroll. We might not have friends there but the Murray River plan I was working on is now out."

Glenda spoke up quickly, she sounded irritated. "Since when have we been going to the Murray River? I thought it was always going to be the Flinders Ranges?"

"I've been talking to our friends in Birdsville and to Sydney Charlie, they both said to be careful in the Flinders." Nulla stood up and placed his big road map on the table and waved for everyone to gather around it.

"They didn't know much about anything else though, not in our region. I really think we should get to Birdsville and meet up with this Sundown's Commando mob. They're the one's we've heard so much about from listening in on the Revelationist's radio calls. I think they have the kind of civil resistance I've been wanting to organise since the day of the apocalypse."

Charlene and Heidi spoke at once, "Nulla, what the hell is going on with you? You shouldn't be making plans without advising us first," said an irritated Charlene. "If you've changed plans then we need to be involved too. I'm not budging one inch until you come out with everything that's in your head." She defiantly folder her right arm over her left resting in its sling.

"Hey, hey girls," stuttered Nulla putting up his hands in surprise. "I'm sorry, my bad. I spoke to Birdsville and Sydney Charlie on HF only yesterday and that's when I found out about the terrorist activity in the Flinders Ranges. I thought about what to do next while we were driving last night. I started to form a loose plan to see what was out towards the Murray River. I was going to talk with you all today but everyone fell asleep."

He ran his finger over their original route which Heidi had drilled into everyone and then showed an alternative route that avoided all the townships between where they were now and Arkaroola.

Heidi excitedly said, "Arkaroola is a wild place. I've been out there with my family. We spent a whole week in the bush prospecting for gold with grandma and grandpa, they used to have a farm somewhere in the Flinders Ranges. There's a small village at Arkaroola, it's got a hotel and a beaut camping ground and cabins... it's perfect for what we want. Oh Nulla, can we stay there?"

"Whoa, slow down there, Heidi. It's probably quite a safe place but the Birdsville commando said the farmers around the

Flinders Ranges were sympathetic towards the crusaders." He looked at the small group gathered around him and continued.

"We need to take these back tracks here." He pointed to the faint lines on the map. "They'll become rougher the closer we get to the village. At night and with our night vision we'll need to be careful, especially the bikers."

He looked around at his friends then asked for their thoughts.

"Boss, we can do it but not six hours straight like last night. I think we should stick to four hours of driving and as we get better we can stretch it out," Luke said. Then he pointed to their proposed trek. "All of this is off the main roads, that should be safe shouldn't it?"

Phil, who'd been quiet throughout Nulla's presentation, now spoke up. "I know these roads pretty well, Nulla. They pass through a lot of properties and vineyards, sheep and cattle stations and across some irrigation canals. I wouldn't expect the terrorists to have many outposts out there. It's dry, it's hot and it's boring. Most of the terrorists appear to be youngsters and like that noisy patrol we just heard they prefer having fun to soldiering."

"If we travel by night, hole up by day and keep a low profile we'll make it easily," said Simon. "If we get hit by terrorists it's more likely right here than anywhere in the countryside." Phil and Nulla nodded in agreement.

"OK, thanks everyone, it's a done deal then. We now need to keep watch until midnight. Arty, how's your leg, are you good enough to stay upstairs here and keep watch? I'll send Heidi with you to help." He winked at them but they knew he wasn't playing match-maker, this was serious.

Just then the rooster in the chicken pen crowed - loudly. It crowed again and then again.

"Shit!" spluttered Nulla. "Luke, grab that damned rooster and shut it up. Put the cage inside one of the rooms and shut the door," ordered Nulla, he almost tripped over his chair getting up.

Luke waved for Simon to come with him to help. They ran out of the room together.

Again the rooster crowed and Nulla looked at everyone. "That rooster is going to ruin my bloody day! Grab your weapons and prepare for action!"

Charlene hurriedly spoke up. "Nulla, there's a back exit around there. We should jump into our cars and drive away. Maybe we could go somewhere and hide till dark. What do you think?"

Their worried leader looked at Charlene then at everyone else "Good idea, let's do it. Now!" He gathered the map while everyone ran off to their vehicles.

"Change of plans!" called Charlene softly to Luke. "We're leaving out through the back exit right now." She pointed to the winding driveway leading out from the back of the motel. "Tie the chicken pen back onto the trailer and let's go."

As Luke and Simon were tightening the ropes of the chicken pen the rooster began crowing again.

"That frigging thing's going to get us frigging killed!" cried Simon. In frustration he banged his fist on the pen which started the hens clucking and the rooster crowed even louder. "I'm going to kill that friggin' rooster!" he cried in frustration.

"Get on your bikes, let's go, now!" called Nulla from his four wheel drive just as two terrorist heads came around the side of the motel.

Arty was sitting on his bike when he saw them. He swung his Steyr around but they were just as fast and fired exactly at the same moment Arty fired. One of the terrorists swung back behind cover while the other slowly slid face down onto the ground.

"Go! Go!" cried Nulla and the two drivers slammed their feet on the accelerator while Simon and Luke sped ahead on their bikes to lead the way. None of them saw Arty lean forward and collapse beside his bike.

Phil was the last in line. As he looked in his rear-view mirror he saw Arty lying on the ground.

"Oh no!" he cried into his CB forgetting their safety protocols. "Arthur's been hit and he's on the ground!" He stepped on the brakes causing the chicken pen to jerk forward and start the rooster and hens fussing and crowing again. Heidi was riding guard in Phil's sunroof. When she heard his cry she looked back.

"Stop! Stop the car! Arty's wounded!" she screamed and immediately opened the door to sprint towards her partner. There came a shattering roar as an assault rifle opened up forcing her to leap behind a brick wall. She looked around and saw Lucy running towards her, rifle in hand and firing from the hip. Behind Lucy she could see Luke and Simon race their bikes back to the motel. They all leaped behind the brick wall and joined her.

"Squelch click, squelch click," came through their headphones - *'danger escape'* - but none of the teenagers obeyed. Their mate was down and they wouldn't leave him. Simon signalled back that they were staying to fight it out.

Luke nodded for Simon to get behind the terrorists and then opened fire with Heidi to keep their enemy distracted. Lucy saw what Simon was doing so she ran to join him. The combined fire of Luke and Heidi forced the enemy to retire behind the cover of the building.

Simon and Lucy ran around the side of the motel complex to come up behind their enemy. They saw the feet of one terrorist lying on the ground but now there were two others. They were looking back towards their armed outpost where Simon could now see two more terrorists sprinting towards them.

"Damn!" he breathed deeply then set himself for a fight - to the death if need be. He and Lucy were the best positioned to take the enemy out but only if they weren't discovered.

Nulla had ensured the boys were well versed in the famed Sun Tsu philosophy of the art of warfare. One thing that stuck in Simon's mind was, *'when you make a decision to fight it is always to the death'*. Every contact should be approached with this in mind Nulla reiterated time and again.

This was one of those moments when he clearly heard Nulla speaking: *'When you decide to fight you give it everything you have. If you're conviction is less than your enemy's then they will win. If your conviction is equal to theirs then you might win; but if your conviction is greater than your enemy's then you will win. Just make sure you cover your arse, be strategic in your approach, be patient and strike the decisive blow when it presents itself.'* That decisive blow had now presented itself and Simon knew it.

Simon looked at Lucy and whispered for her to wait for him to fire first. Tight lipped she nodded back at him. Simon held up three fingers and mouthed, *'Three round bursts.'* Lucy nodded as she checked her assault weapon to see if the fire mechanism was set correctly.

'OK, this is time for the 'decisive blow,' Simon whispered to himself as the two terrorists now joined the others. He could hear Luke and Heidi's fire answer the terrorist's increased fire-power.

The terrorists now had a leader. She was tall, solid and had strategically placed her squad for a frontal assault. Just as the terrorists prepared to skirmish forward Simon pulled the trigger of his Steyr.

Of their group Nulla was the best marksman followed by Simon close behind. Simon had a talent for patience and he always fired cleanly. Luke, on the other hand, usually became excited and frightened the enemy more than doing them any harm.

Lucy now joined Simon and together their bullets hit the squad just as they took their first steps towards Luke and Heidi's position. Simon made sure he hit the leader first and then raked the others hitting all four.

Simon continued to fire until his magazine was empty then brought himself back from where he'd sent his mind. All was quiet except for the squealing of one of the wounded. Simon automatically reloaded with a fresh magazine.

Lucy looked at Simon and nodded. Her face was white and beads of sweat dripped down her forehead. They could now hear Heidi screaming for Phil and Nulla to help her get Arthur into their car.

Simon called out loudly, "All clear! Cease firing!" Just as Nulla had done the day they took out the scavengers at the shopping mall car park.

He stood up and looked at the work they'd done. He felt no emotion, rather, he felt revulsion and disgust. Taking each step as though he was walking on egg shells he walked to the pile of dead and dying.

A particularly young terrorist looked up and called to Lucy, sobbing. "Mum, help me. I can't feel my legs," he cried. "I can't feel my feet. Something's wrong… please, mum, help me." He sobbed uncontrollably. His condition was partially caused by alcohol, the dope and the shocking impact of the bullets.

Lucy looked briefly at Simon then walked over to the young man lying on the ground. She stopped and stared at the bodies for a long moment. Leaning over the youth she forced the young terrorist to look at her.

"Why don't you just die? I tried to kill you but you're still alive. That's not good is it?" She nonchalantly checked her AK and cocked it like she had done a dozen times in training. Simon had never seen Lucy so calm and focused. He stood mesmerised as she aimed and fired.

"I, I don't know if we're allowed to do that, Lucy. You know, to kill the wounded…" Simon mumbled in shocked bewilderment.

"They killed my husband so I kill them," replied Lucy. Her face remained serene but now exhibited what appeared to be pleasure. With a look at the other bodies to make sure they were dead she left the scene of violence.

Simon kicked the weapons out of reach of the newly dead hands just as he was taught then called to Luke, "Luke, come and help me collect the weapons and ammo!"

Luke looked up when he heard his friend and ran forward. He didn't stop to check on Arty, Heidi was already dragging him towards Phil's four wheel drive. Together the two boys collected as much as they could carry in their arms and ran back to the vehicles.

Nulla was only now running towards them with Charlene, her pistol in her good hand pointed to the ground. Nulla looked at his young warriors and nodded.

"Good work everyone, good work. Righto, Simon, get back to the motel entrance and watch for enemy reinforcements. I'm sure they'll want to see what the fire fight was all about. Luke, help Heidi get Arthur into the car and tie his bike on top of the chicken pen. We leave in sixty seconds."

The aboriginal cavalry sergeant didn't move, he stood there breathing deeply. The fact was that he had miscalculated the danger they were in. As their leader he had failed them and now one of their group was badly injured.

"Nulla? Nulla?" called Charlene leaning over Arthur in the back seat. Nulla came back from his reverie and walked briskly towards her.

"Arthur's OK. He's got a bullet wound to his arm. Heidi's finished bandaging it and now we really need to get moving." She looked at his far-away eyes and said with some force. "Come on, lead us!"

With a look of surprise Nulla turned to reassure her. "I'm OK, Charlene, honest, I'm OK. I just wasn't prepared for this." Nulla then called to his troop, "Righto, let's get moving, times up."

He waited for Simon to get back onto his bike before moving them out of the motel heading towards Arkaroola. The adventurous nature of the road trip had now gone sour.

There was no terrorist activity behind or in front so Nulla steered back onto the main road. He put on speed to get as far from the terrorist stockade as possible. A few hours later he pulled over. It was now just on dark and he reminded everyone to put on their night vision goggles. The groans of complaint at having to use night-vision so soon certainly didn't do his mood any good.

All around them stood scraggly, stunted bushes and patches of desert sand. They were well into flat desert country now. Nulla peered through his binoculars in both directions.

"We'll be pulling off the main road in a few minutes. We should be quite safe then and I'll slow down once we hit the dirt." He then climbed back into his vehicle and accelerated on the bitumen road wanting to get to the turn off as quick as possible.

Nulla hadn't spoken since the ambush, but now, turning to Glenda, he said angrily, "That blasted rooster is going into the pot tonight. I don't care what anyone says, his name is now 'dinner'!" He continued to fume until he had rebuilt his mind palace and replaced the image of Arthur's slumped body lying on the motel car park. with the road map of where he intended to stop that evening.

His task right now was to guide his group carefully along the dusty dirt roads to Arkaroola without mishap.

They didn't eat the rooster that night. Fatima put her foot down and said that it belonged to her and she needed it for her hens. If they wanted eggs then they just had to let the rooster live. Arthur said that he liked the rooster and he'd be upset if Nulla killed it. That settled that matter and so they ate Fatima and Heidi's spiced lentil soup with flat bread and a hot chilli sauce.

Nulla was experienced in using compass and map, orienteering was his strong point. Every track on the map was dirt, some had hidden patches of sand which were almost impossible to follow in the dark with their headlights covered. They made sure to avoid as many farm houses as possible too. It took four nights of painful night-vision driving before they were within striking distance of the Flinders Ranges.

The two boys rode up front only stopping for wash outs, dips and cutaways. They soon got tired of the novelty of guiding Nulla and Phil along the many criss-crossing tracks in the darkness. It seemed that the farmers and country folk simply drove anywhere they liked. Often they had to use Nulla's compass to navigate when the tracks simply disappeared.

By dawn they had covered the final leg and entered Arkaroola village. It appeared to be completely deserted as they pulled up in front of the hotel.

Heidi was the first to leap from the cars delightedly showing the troop where they should park their vehicles. She pointed to the best cabins for each of them then arranged for Arthur to go to the hotel where he could relax in the comfortable lounge chairs. In her enthusiasm Heidi told Nulla how to organise the guard duty roster. She joyfully took control just as she had done when Charlene and Arthur had joined her.

Nulla shook his head thinking that he might have to claw back control from this attractive little dynamo. But for now he was too tired and simply couldn't be bothered playing games. With a soft chuckle to himself he decided to let Heidi have her day at the top. It was, after all, her special place so why not let her enjoy herself for a while, he thought.

"Arty, are you OK sitting there?" asked Heidi as she fussed over him. Everyone was tired, grumpy and the aches and pains of sitting and standing in the cars for such an arduous trek had taken its toll on everyone's good humour. The night-vision goggles didn't seem quite so bad after wearing them for only five nights. The one advantage was that their night driving sessions were only four hours long. Once they had stopped the teenagers got to sleep most of the day while they waited for evening to resume their journey.

Heidi satisfied herself that Arthur was comfortable then began moving food from the vehicles into the hotel kitchen. She had already lit the fire in the enormous hotel fireplace before turning to help Fatima cook a giant hot meal for everyone. Action Heidi was back in control and she loved it.

"Simon, before you relieve Nulla on duty, can you help Fatima and Phil settle into their cabin? They're exhausted and Phil might want to have a nap before breakfast is served, thanks sweetie." She smiled up at him and, of course, Simon did as he was bidden.

Even though the two boys were only a year younger than Heidi they absolutely adored both her and Charlene. They loved the attention and acceptance they got from any of the females, but especially the two youngest. Even if they were in a bad mood they would always leap up and do whatever the girls wanted of them. Glenda told Nulla that the boys were 'simply smitten' with the two pretty young girls.

"Smitten?" grinned Nulla. "Bullshit, that's what we call 'blue balls'."

The next morning they sat around the fireplace and decided it was safer to set up their cooking and eating quarters in the caravan park. Nulla's reasoning was that it would attract less attention from anyone dropping in unannounced. It was most probable that new arrivals wouldn't bother with the caravan park and instead they would go straight to the hotel. They could easily hide their vehicles behind the vans and cabins too.

"Nulla, I've found a deserted stone building not far from here, it's huge. We could even hide out there if we need to," said Luke as he held a burning branch out for Annie to play with. Annie thoroughly enjoyed the freedom of the caravan park after many months stuck indoors in Adelaide city.

Charlene looked up excitedly and called across the fireplace, "Luke, do you and Simon want to take us there for target practice? It sounds perfect, no one would hear us firing in there."

Nulla nodded affirmative so Luke went to find Simon.

"Sounds like a great place for target practice," said Simon when he heard Luke's plan.

Arthur was sitting outside his cabin when he saw Luke walking towards his van. Luke stopped when he heard Arthur's shout then walked over to greet his new friend.

Arthur had heard from Charlene that they were planning to do some target practice. "Luke, I need to get some more target practice in too."

Luke laughed, "You don't need more practice, Arty, you knocked down one of them terrorists without even aiming. You're a hero, mate, a legend."

"That's crap, Luke," replied Arthur, but his face brightened. "I'm sure I pulled the trigger accidentally when I slipped off the safety. If anything, I'm an accidental hero."

"How's the arm going, Arty?" Simon heard them talking and had wandered over. His Steyr was always in his hands now.

Arthur lifted his arm and unwrapped the bandage to reveal a long, thick scab. "Yeah, it's OK, burns a bit though. That castor oil Nulla had must have helped because it looks pretty good doesn't it. Charlene said the burning feeling is just the nerves settling in. My elbow's sorer though. I must have banged it when I hit the ground. Look at the bruise."

The boys mouthed words of adulation and wonder as Arty showed his war wounds. "It's worse than the bullet wound you know. That's the second time the bastards have had a go at killing me. I think it's time they picked on someone else."

"You sure are lucky, Arty. That bullet could have gone in through your arm and then come out just about anywhere," said Simon, as he touched the scab that ran from Arthur's wrist to his elbow.

Arthur smiled then pulled down his trousers to reveal his bare backside. "Look!" he said, splitting his buttocks apart. "This is the hole the bullet made on it's way out!" he giggled and the three almost busted their insides laughing.

"I wish I'd seen you take them out though, Simon." Arthur continued a little more seriously. "I missed that part. I heard the firing, lots of it, then it stopped. When I looked up I saw Luke running towards you and then Heidi screaming. My leg was sore from the fall too. Poor Heidi, I think she thought I was dead." The two boys nodded sagely as they listened to the older boy.

"Luke's firing must have stopped them shooting at me again. Those terrorists enjoy killing. They would have used me for target practice you know. I've seen them do it."

"Arty, even though Luke and I have been with Nulla, had some fire-fights and learned all these things about warfare, you're a real hero and have the scars to prove it." Simon was thinking of Arthur's story about the terrorist ambush at the university. "You've been blown up, burnt alive, shot twice and now a little bruise on your elbow puts you out of action."

Simon jabbed Arty in the ribs, "Come on, come with us and we'll go check out that stone building Luke found." With that the three boys walked off to collect the girls and head-out to this special stone building of Luke's.

Chapter 4 - Sundown - Wilson's War - Arkaroola

In the Wilson's camp there were only enough men left to look after the cattle mustered inside the compound itself. As members of the Revelationist Church the Wilson's were obliged to send the church one tenth, a tithe, to fight or work whenever they were called upon. General Himmler needed horsemen for his cattle stations yet the Wilson's had taken nearly every man in the entire Flinders Ranges, and beyond, to work on their own properties.

"Damn it, Kelvin! You've got every horseman in the whole damn country. I've said this before and I'll say it again: if you don't share your cattlemen I'm going to have your properties impounded and absorbed into the churches estates!" Himmler slammed his fist on the table. "Since the apocalypse I've given you control over every property in this region. They now call you the 'Cattle King of the Flinders' because of me and this is how you treat me? It's like you've spit in my face, Kelvin!"

Kelvin Wilson, the patriarch of the Flinders Ranges cattle industry, was used to getting his own way and felt outraged, betrayed by the general's demands. "I've damn well pandered to your whims for too many years now, Russell! Who the hell would have allowed you to fire weapons all over their properties like I've done for you? I've had to pay off politicians, police, wildlife rangers, the neighbours, you name it I damn-well paid for it! Without me you'd be a nobody with no-one to command and in no shape to run this stupid war! You're here because of me and my boys! You owe me, brother!" stormed Wilson, standing what looked like an entire metre higher than the Revelationist Army Alpha general.

Colonel Rommel, the mastermind of the Revelationist Alpha Army and the single most experienced soldier in their military, knocked on the door forcefully and walked in.

At sight of the colonel, Kelvin thought, *'Bloody idiots think they're Nazis, jokers is what they are.'* Kelvin often laughed about them behind their backs to anyone who would listen.

"What the hell is going on in here? Do you want the troops to hear you arguing?" he said pushing the door firmly shut behind him.

Himmler deliberately stood still and closed his eyes. He began counting backwards from ten to zero eventually feeling himself calm down. Old man Wilson continued to fume though.

"Rommel, this bastard boss of yours wants me to send more of my men to work your properties. He no doubt wants to send them to fight those mongrels at Birdsville too. As if I want my horsemen killed by you incompetent morons!" spat the fire-brand.

"Those 'incompetent morons' made you rich Kelvin. They handed the entire Flinders region to you on a platter, you ungracious prick. Without us you'd be dead or working on one of our farms so get over it."

Rommel stared venomously at the shrewd cattleman with the beady red eyes and blotched face. "I've just about had a gut-full of you, Kelvin. My men have been itching to teach your bully boys a lesson for years. I've heard that you've lost some of them already to some farmer in Arkaroola. If you can't handle a few dirt-poor farmers then don't come whining to us. You have your duty to your church now do it and stop your sniveling and whining."

Rommel continued to stare down the fiery old man who eventually turned his eyes to blaze his own fury at General Himmler.

"I don't take orders from your lackey, Russell, call your dog off." He knew that he couldn't dominate Colonel Rommel but he had been bullying the general and everyone else who stood in his way for years. He hadn't become the King of the Flinders Ranges by backing down every time someone tried to prevent him from getting what he wanted.

"Don't look to the general for support, Wilson, he's the one who gave you the orders." Rommel snapped to attention as his general opened his eyes and saluted with the stiff armed Nazi salute. "Begging your pardon, sir! I've forgotten my manners but it seems to me that these Wilson's need to be taught a lesson, sir."

By now General Himmler was back in control of himself. Kelvin Wilson always got under his skin. "Thank you, Colonel, I'll take it from here." He paused and drew a deep breath. "Kelvin, the Revelationist Church requires you to fulfill your obligations and to present one tenth of your cattlemen to my farm managers in Hawker. You are hereby ordered to produce thirty cattlemen, with two horses apiece and their gear, by lunch time tomorrow. Any more arguments and I'll include you and your family in the call-up to fight against the Birdsville commando."

The general turned his back and walked out of the door followed by Colonel Rommel. They left Kelvin Wilson alone in the church presbytery fuming with rage.

The Wilsons received only the single radio call from Brad's vengeance squad. He had called to say that they were following Riley's tracks into the Arkaroola wilderness. When he heard that Brad hadn't returned home or answered any of the Wilson's radio calls, his cousin Greg lost it.

"I bet that scum Riley has ambushed them. They're probably all dead," he cried in despair at the night sky.

'He's drunker than a priest,' thought Laurie as he awkwardly tried to avoid eye contact with his boss.

"Laurie, mate," said Greg, as he sidled over next to the cattleman by the camp fire. "You know that Riley bloke pretty well. Maybe you know where he might be hiding out, what do you reckon? Do you think you could show me?" Greg's words were slurred and his breath stank of whiskey.

"Tomorrow we're going there, just you and me. We're going to find my cousins and then we're going to fix Riley and his missus up good and proper."

Laurie shivered in the cool night air before answering. "Sure, Greg, tomorrow we'll go and visit Riley at his property."

They were up by dawn. Jack had already sent his ten cattlemen to the church collection point in Hawker and was now trying to muster his cattle and sheep with the absolute minimum staff he needed. Not only did he have to move his animals onto fresh pastures but he needed men to hunt down the wild dogs that killed his calves and lambs. Jack was in a foul mood and waved Greg away with his hand.

"Piss off, Greg. I don't care, just do whatever you want. And yes, you can take Laurie with you. Just make sure you're back by tomorrow night." He had a sudden idea and turned back to his nephew. "That Katie's a good sort. Kill Riley and the kids but bring her back. I'll make good use of her myself. If she doesn't cooperate I can use her for trade. And Greg, don't let me down now will you?" He lifted his eyebrows, a cruel smile played across his lips.

"I sure won't, uncle. You don't mind if I take care of that Katie myself before I pass her over?" He chuckled as he climbed into his truck and signalled for Laurie to join him.

"Just don't damage the goods," Jack called then turned back to his men and continued giving out the orders of the day.

The two cattlemen made good time and were at Riley's burnout farm house by lunch time. They took a break in the shade where Greg pulled out a bottle of whiskey and put it to his lips.

"Here Laurie, help yourself. I brought enough for the two of us." He handed the bottle over to Laurie who took a pull then handed it back.

"I'd better not drink any more, Greg. I've got an ulcer and it's merry hell inside my guts," he said softly.

"Yeah, whatever, all the more for me." Greg continued to drink heavily while Laurie built a fire and cooked some bacon and eggs.

"We'll follow the tracks and find where Brad headed off to. Then we'll search Arkaroola village. I have a feeling Riley might have hidden his family there." Having made his plans Greg lay back and pulled his hat over his face. Within the minute he was snoring, sound asleep.

Laurie was in a quandary. He hated Greg, hated his brothers and cousins too. He had a deep desire to kill this Wilson and escape with his family, to go somewhere safe where they'll never find them. But the Wilson's had his wife and three children prisoner. Everyone who worked for the Wilson's had their family brought into the compound. Not that Jack Wilson said they were prisoners as such, they still attended school and church services every day. But if he walked in there and packed them into his truck and tried to drive out they'd stop him. There was no way he could escape the Wilsons without help or without killing everyone.

He fingered his knife as he looked across at Greg, snoring, not two metres away. *I could easily slit that pig's throat right now.*

It'd save me doing it later,' he thought. But Laurie wasn't a murderer, he'd never harmed anyone in his life.

Laurie hated bullies having been the victim of the Wilson family since childhood. The only way he survived was by rolling over and doing everything they asked of him. He made a good 'yes' man and was ashamed of himself. *'What sort of man am I to let these bastards bully me, my family and my friends?'*

His only friend during childhood was a lonely kid that the Wilsons bullied mercilessly. They made fun of him and called him Fatty. Laurie had a crush on his cute, blond haired little sister, and had even tried to befriend her. He still felt the terror of the time Fatty turned on him and ordered him to stay away from her. Not long after that his puppy-love was crushed when Fatty bashed Brad senseless and escaped into the Northern Territory taking his sister with him.

It was only a week later that he met another beauty, his wife. They'd been married twelve years now and he still felt a warmth flow into his chest at the very thought of her.

In resignation he finished eating and cleaned up. Laurie then pulled his hat over his face and joined Greg in their siesta.

They followed the Range Rover tracks to the gully and like most outback cattlemen, Greg expertly interpreted the story the tracks told. They went up onto the rock ledge and saw the empty cartridges and dried pools of blood. Greg thought long and hard.

"Bastards ambushed our boys, look at the number of cartridges here. See, AKs and these big bastards, what sort of rifle is that?" he asked of no-one in particular. "Must be a hunting rifle, maybe one of those expensive Belgian ones." He continued walking around the rock ledge then finally examined the fireplace and the horse tracks.

"These horses are ours. Look that's Patsy's tracks and there's Domino's. Maybe it wasn't Riley that ambushed Brad, maybe it was those two mongrel cousins of his. OK, come on back down and we'll look for bodies. It shouldn't be too hard to find, there's plenty of drag marks to follow."

Laurie saw where the drag marks converge and called Greg over. "Look, they've been dragged over that ridge there. We'd better prepare ourselves, Greg."

When they topped the rise they looked down and saw the bodies. Some had been badly mauled by wild dogs.

"Bastards, they killed the lot of them!" Greg roared at the now darkening sky.

"Come on, Greg, we'll head back to the car and set up camp. We can bury them tomorrow. It's too dark to do it now," suggested Laurie, his hand on Greg's shoulder.

"No!" Greg shouted, flinging Laurie's hand away. "We'll bury them now. Tomorrow we'll go hunt down those pricks and screw them over like Jack said. Get the shovels."

The next morning they rose to frost on the ground. Laurie had the fire lit and was boiling the billy for tea. He noticed Greg was unsteady on his feet as he staggered over to sit heavily in his camp chair.

"We'll have something to eat then head straight to Arkaroola village. I'm pretty certain they're hiding out there. It's the best place around, no one's there now so they'll feel safe." He dragged out another bottle of whiskey and started drinking.

Greg continued to drink as they drove towards Arkaroola village. He held his powerful hunting rifle between his legs.

"This little beauty will do the trick." He held up his Ruger American bolt action. "Uncle Jack gave this to me when I took care of a bunch of rustlers with Brad. Some of the boys from up the Northern Territory way thought they could help themselves to our cattle. Brad and I caught them skinning one. While Brad kept an eye on them with his rifle I busted them good with me fists. You should have seen the state of their faces when I'd finished with them."

Greg laughed a cruel laugh. "They never came anywhere near the Flinders after that. I heard they went back to Darwin, or somewheres." Greg had a gleam in his eye and looked at Laurie who carefully kept his eyes steady on the washed-out dirt track.

"When we get that honey, Katie, I'll hand my rifle over to you. You do what Brad did for me and I'll look after you, mate,"

Greg said smiling. He took another drink and emptied the bottle. Laurie didn't reply.

It was just on midday when they saw Arkaroola in the distance, nestled in a small valley among the wild, tortured ranges. Laurie stopped the car and they both looked around.

"OK, drive right up to that junction behind the rocks there. We'll get out and walk the rest of the way. We don't want to telegraph we're visiting especially if Riley and his cousins are there waiting for us," ordered Greg.

As they approached, Greg cried softly, "Stop!" he grabbed at his rifle and climbed unsteadily out of the car. "I saw someone over there, near the old copper smelter. It looked like a girl, come on."

Laurie froze. His eyes glazed as he began to hyperventilate in fear. 'Was *it Katie? This can't be happening.*' he said to himself in a rising panic. *'I can't let him do it. I can't let him kill and rape my friends.'*

They quietly walked towards where Greg had seen the girl. As they closed on the abandoned stone building they could hear rifle fire.

"Huh? They're firing automatics. They must have some assault rifles in there. We'd better find a sniping position and wait it out." Greg looked around and saw a perfect position beside a rocky outcrop and waved for Laurie to follow.

Laurie's ears were ringing. His blood pressure was up and his blood sugar crashing as he entered a full-blown panic attack.

It was only a matter of minutes before the firing stopped and a group of teenagers walked out of the old stone building. Each had a bandoleer of ammunition and automatic rifles slung over their shoulders. Neither Laurie nor Greg recognised any of them but Greg settled down to kill them anyway.

"Oh, yeah!" he whispered in pleasure as he leaned his rifle barrel on the rock to steady it. "I reckon we can take out those three boys and then we run up and grab the girls while they're still in shock. Get ready."

Again Laurie felt a wave of nausea and dizziness as he began to dissociate. A state of panic and disbelief washed over and into him.

'This is not happening!' His head began to spin as in sheer desperation he threw himself at Greg. The sound of a heavy calibre rifle shot suddenly crashed against the rocky walls of the gully.

The two men wrestled to the ground. Laurie was like a madman fighting with a lifetime of humiliation behind his drive to kill this rotten man. But Greg had years of fighting experience. The bully's urge to have those teenage girls drove power into his limbs.

At the sound of the rifle shot the group jumped in fright. Luke immediately leaped behind a large rock with his rifle ready. Simon waved for the girls and Arthur to get into the scrub and to run back to the village.

"Heidi, you look after them! Move up the hill and get to high ground as fast as you can." When Heidi hesitated he said, "Don't worry about us, we're trained for this."

Simon crouched behind one of the large rocks strewn around the landscape like a child's lego set.

"Heidi! Take Annie, I'm staying!" cried Lucy as she flicked the safety off her AK and slipped in a fresh magazine. She crouched down beside Simon and leveled her weapon to peer through its scope.

After a few seconds Luke called out, "Look, down there, there's someone fighting. They're wrestling on the ground. You stay here Simon, I'll check it out. Cover me." Simon nodded and set his sights on the two he could now clearly see in his scope.

Lucy looked and she too found the fighters amongst the dust cloud they had made. They continued to wrestle locked together like two gladiator bull-ants.

The two men struggled on the ground kicking up dust and stones with their flailing feet until Laurie finally forced one hand free and clawed at Greg's face. Greg twisted his torso and together they rolled over and over among the sharp rocks and spinifex grass. Luke could now hear their heavy breathing and muted grunts as he carefully edged closer.

The fighter's heaving lungs desperately tried to suck in enough oxygen to propel their limbs in the dry heat. In a single moment of opportunity Laurie swung his fist at his enemy's head. But Greg had fought a hundred battles each just as vicious as this one. His knife was already in his hand.

As Laurie lifted his fist Greg plunged his blade into his back with such force that it penetrated between his ribs and into his heart.

Laurie stiffened then groaned as he collapsed onto his murderer. The Wilson bully shook him off then stood up. As he did so he saw Luke walking carefully towards him.

Jack Wilson's nephew was fast. In a single fluid movement he reached for his rifle, brought it to his shoulder and fired.

Chapter 5 - Sundown - Blondie's Revenge

The morning ride would normally be an enjoyable one for the two bikers. The air was cool and there was no wind. The road surface, though dirt, was reasonably compact and still good enough to ride on at speeds up to a hundred kph. Fat Boy had been riding bikes since childhood and rode like he was on the Dakar Rally. In fact, he and Blondie were raised riding bikes doing petty crime and trafficking drugs through deserted state border crossings.

Their father was a patched member of an outlaw bikie gang in Queensland. He often enjoyed the spoils of his gang's plunder be it bikes, women, drugs or other pleasures. But one thing he never took for granted was his children, he loved them with a passion.

When their father died his two children were not yet in their teens. They were callously dumped on the doorstep of their father's family by the local community services. There they fell victim to the abuse and brutalisation at the hands of their beloved cousins, the Wilsons of the Flinders Ranges.

Fat Boy was forced to protect his little sister from the predators within their own family. At the age of fourteen, already six foot tall and the same wide, he was pushed too far and beat cousin Brad, to a pulp. That put a sudden stop to the Wilson's sexual assaults on himself and his little sister.

When he joined his father's bikie gang not even the members of higher rank messed with Fat Boy or his 'girlfriend' Blondie.

He had a nasty temper and when he cracked it no one was safe.

The siblings found that the best way to stop any unwanted attention for Blondie was to pretend to be lovers.

Fat Boy developed a reputation as an enforcer and earned the rank of Sergeant-at-arms in his father's old gang. When things went bad at the club he bashed a few heads as payback and joined another gang in Darwin.

Blondie took to loathing men after her experience with the Wilsons and their friends. She hated the men she was forced to hang around with in the bikie gangs too. For the siblings to act like lovers was easy enough, they really did care for each other. The two were as close as siblings could be. The only stability they had in life was each other. Where Fat Boy went Blondie followed.

It didn't hurt when Blondie scored some modeling work and started to make a decent income but once again the advances from the *'arse-holes I work for'* meant she was forever changing jobs.

Many a time Fat Boy would step in to advise would-be admirers to back off. Now at six foot four inches tall and the same wide, Fat Boy rarely had problems with men trying to bully him or his sister.

Every year they would travel to another town and another job until one day they met a Revelationist church representative, Walter. Like most other criminals Fat Boy recognised a fellow conman in his church contact and they hit off a strong friendship.

One day Walter told him that he needed to find an isolated farm property for his church to lease for some very special training requirements. Fat Boy soon learned what those training requirements were. But heck, who cared anyway, these idiots wouldn't amount to much more than a nuisance, or so he thought.

Walter introduced them to the *Tajna Služba*, the church's secret service who were considered akin to the Nazi Gestapo of the Second World War. This was their big break. It gave Fat Boy and Blondie leverage and access to the hard hitting church leaders, politicians and the circle of power controlling the world-wide Revelationist Church.

They were inducted into the secretive Tajna Služba and quickly gained a reputation as the go-to's when the church needed dirty deeds done. Neither backed away from extortion, kidnapping, prostitution, assassination… you name it Blondie and Fat Boy did it and they did it properly.

Blondie excelled in this corrupt underworld and was soon called upon to run missions of a political nature. With her attractive model looks and her analytical brain Blondie worked her way to the top of the Tajna Služba in Australia. Her reputation within church circles was a hushed secret and the name 'Tajna Služba' eventually became synonymous with a beautiful, blond-haired assassin in the night.

Church preachers would threaten their congregation that if they didn't participate willingly in their training this mythical 'Tajna Služba' would drop in to visit them one night. The vision of a gorgeous blond-haired assassin became a titillating tradition within the church.

Fat Boy specialised in organising special training venues in outback Australia. He enjoyed convincing farmers and local politicians to cooperate. It helped when he could easily conjure willing women, boys and girls, money and anything else he needed to get the job done. Fat Boy was often seen riding his Harley-Davidson along outback roads to spend a few nights with his many friends. Even the Wilson's of the Flinders Ranges willingly participated by offering their properties for the church's use.

The Wilson's had taken up the church doctrine very early in it's inception recognising the power it afforded them. They enjoyed the churches protection and the contacts and wealth it easily provided. The Wilson family profited from the favours Fat Boy so willingly gave them.

Recognised as a valuable church salesman, Fat Boy was paid handsomely for the first time without having to run drugs. Finally he and his sister could live without having to worry about someone trying to take what wasn't theirs. The siblings became the church's preferred negotiators, setting up meetings between willing property owners and church leaders in every state.

Their extensive gang connections proved even more useful and they soon had a network to procure weapons, drugs and sex. They also managed protection and even blackmailing uncooperative church members, civil authority administrators, police and politicians. Blondie and Fat Boy were soon making millions.

They had their own property outside Mount Isa in north-west Queensland, a palatial mansion. That was where they were heading now, home. Unfortunately both the church and the bikie gang running Mount Isa had a price on their heads.

Every year the church held a rally and conference in Mount Isa. The local bikie gang made a lot of money selling drugs and prostitution throughout the week long conference. Fat Boy and Blondie always attended. This was where they brought their contacts for sex and drug parties, essential for good business.

Before the apocalypse was announced Blondie was called upon to 'work' one of the church fathers, Reverend Albert, for the Tajna Služba. Albert was the head of the church in the southern hemisphere. With her sex appeal, model looks and charm she could pull anyone she wanted.

After an evening of banquets and meetings Blondie was invited by Reverend Albert to be his personal escort. She knew that the church planned to bring on the apocalypse soon but the Tajna Služba needed more information. There was a wide rift between the top echelon and their secret service which needed a little help to breach. The Tajna Služba believed that Blondie could build that bridge.

Although she and Fat Boy often discussed church politics as part of their business neither showed any interest in this mythical 'apocalyptic revelation' the church worshiped. This banquet was the one that made them think that these idiots really might destroy the world.

That night Blondie spoke with her brother and they talked into the early hours of the morning. Not that it really bothered them, they believed that they would be safe enough in Mount Isa. None of the church members ever tried to force them to adopt the churches cannon, ethics, rules or moral codes, they were Tajna Služba, they were protected. The siblings decided that they would just sit tight, keep their mouths closed, and see what happened.

The next day the entire tone of the church changed. The date was set and every member was given a role to play. Around the world there were millions, hundreds of millions, some said a billion followers of the Revelationist Church. They would all step out and proclaim the beginning of the Apocalypse foretold in the Book of Revelation on the appointed day.

The conference over the loyal members left for home and the Reverend Albert decided it was too close to the apocalypse to fly back to Sydney. He told the press that it was because he was unwell but the truth was that a SARS corona virus was soon to be released in every international airport in the world. So he shacked up in the church's penthouse and called on Blondie each night for entertainment.

Blondie came home the night before the apocalypse to tell Fat Boy to stay away from the tap water and not to leave the property. She made him collect his weapons from under the house and together they prepared to defend themselves.

That night the Revelationist Church announced the Apocalypse. Immediately Revelationist fanatics began to slaughter civilians and military personnel across the globe. Water sources were poisoned and people died in their houses, front yards, even on their way to work. In some parts of the country bikie gangs were elected to control their local towns as was the case in Mount Isa.

The church were now free to run their programs of extermination. The Raven's Claw and their sister battalion, the Crusaders of Light in Longreach, now controlled central Queensland. Their role was to exterminate the non-believers and create a slave class to serve the church.

The problem was that Fat Boy had morals, not many, but strong enough to know that what the church were doing was wrong. By the end of that first month he had worn out his welcome at both the church palace and the bikie gang headquarters. They threatened to kill him if he showed his face one more time.

Blondie was ordered to stay in touch with the church hierarchy by the Tajna Služba and so continued playing her game with Reverend Albert. But he had began to tire of her beauty and sex appeal.

Then came the night Blondie was assaulted on her way home from the Reverend's apartment - or perhaps he had set her up. The boys dragged her back to the club house where they bashed and raped her. This was the first time anyone had assaulted her since Fat Boy had beaten up Brad - it nearly destroyed her. It nearly destroyed Fat Boy too. He wasn't there to protect his beloved little sister.

The giant of a man stormed into the gang clubhouse and with his bare hands he killed three gang members. They forced him out with a baseball bat blow to his skull. It should have killed him but he was made of tougher stuff than most men.

Fat Boy took his sister and escaped to Birdsville where he met the only bloke he had ever truly trusted. And now that man was dying and he was devastated.

Blondie and Fat Boy stopped twice during the six hundred kilometre trip. Once to fill up from the fuel cans strapped to their bike and the other time to eat the sandwiches Pinkie had packed for them. They were starved and were grateful to the 'little pink lady' as they liked to call her. Blondie was quiet for most of the trip and Fat Boy knew why. They had discussed strategy but in the end they knew that if it worked it worked, if it didn't... then... well... it didn't.

Fat Boy slowed to a stop in front of the teenager with his AK47 pointed directly at his chest. The boy's over-sized uniform was nonetheless immaculate, pressed and starched.

"Who are you and what do you want?" the youth asked the huge biker. He twitched his gun twice for Fat Boy and Blondie to dismount. His off sider was in a fortified stockade casually leaning on a machine gun that was also pointed at the bikers. The entire fortified position was well presented and built to withstand heavy incoming fire.

"And who the hell are you, boy?" asked Fat Boy already feeling irascible and annoyed from the long ride. He remembered to give the secret Revelationist hand signal for the regions army corps, the Raven's Claw Battalion of Mount Isa.

"No one rides through here 'boy'," replied the teenager sarcastically, "unless we permit them to. I won't ask you a second time, mate. Who are you and what do you want here?" With that he cocked his rifle, the bolt action was loud in the still evening air.

Blondie stepped forward and raised her hand to show she was unarmed. It was also another of the Raven's Claw hand signals.

"Lord be praised, we've finally gained ascendancy over the heathen masses. The God of the Revelations can now descend to take that which is rightfully His," she said trying to remember the rhetoric she'd heard and recited a million times over the years.

"You's Revelationists?" asked the youth now lowering his rifle to point at the ground.

Fat Boy exploded. "Of course we fuckin' are! Can't you tell? You boofheaded moron! You didn't even bother to check to see if we gave the correct hand signs, you dick head!"

 The teenager took a step back. "I, I…" He wasn't so smug now. Turning to his mate in the fortified bunker he called out, "Corporal, what's the officer's secret hand signal for the Raven's Claw Battalion?"

The corporal called back. "You idiot. It's a hooked claw with the ring finger pointing down."

"See, dickhead! You don't even know you're own battalion's secret hand signals. What sort of God loving Claw are you?" Fat Boy didn't let up.

"I'm sorry, sir!" He stood to attention and saluted, stiff armed like the Nazi salute. "I didn't recognise it in the darkness. We've been ordered to escort officers to the Casa Grande…" before he could finish Blondie spoke.

"Private, I'd be careful if I were you. We're secret service officers - Tajna Služba." Blondie looked at Fat Boy who leaned over the now shaking youth.

"Private, you will let us through and you will not go mouthing off that you saw the Tajna Služba pass through here. You do know who the Tajna Služba are, don't you?" she added.

"Sir, yes madam, sir! Yes I know who the Tajna Služba are, well, I've heard of them. You may proceed. Sorry, sirs." Once again he stood to attention and saluted stiffly.

"One more thing, private," Fat Boy said as he heaved one enormous leg over the seat of his bike. "We'll be needing supplies. Which of you will be coming with us to arrange our house and provide fresh food and entertainment? You didn't think we'd come all this fucking way through enemy territory just to be pissed on by the likes of you - did you?"

"Sir, we aren't allowed to leave our post..." The private swallowed so loudly they could hear it.

"What's your name, private?" asked Fat Boy softly.

"Private Brinley, sir." He saw Fat Boy begin to raise his leg to get back off his bike. "It's all right," he said hurriedly. "I'll escort you and arrange food and supplies. Please give me a few seconds and I'll get my car keys." He leaped into the stockade and came straight out with the keys to his car. "Sirs, follow me. I'll lead you to where ever you need to go."

Blondie called to the other guardsman. "We'll be taking your Private Brinley for the next few hours. We'll bring him back unharmed."

The guardsman nodded. "Got that, Tajna Služba, sir," and he saluted, but it was a little too casual.

The entire township was silent except for one place in the centre of town where the bikie gang were throwing their usual party. Fat Boy and Blondie passed it on their way to find the pharmacy. Fat Boy flashed his headlights and stopped his bike, waving for the youth to pull over. He needed to distract his old gang and now was as good a time as any.

"Private Brinley, I'm heading into the club house. I've got a mighty thirst and I'm feeling pretty darn crook." He turned to Blondie. "Tajna Služba, do you have that list of medications I need? Give it to the private and make sure he gets them for me." He turned back to the frightened young man.

"If I don't get my medications I'll get very sick. If I get sick I get mad and when I get mad I rip people's heads off their shoulders." He looked at the private and bent his head down level with his face. "Are you going to make me sick, boy?"

The private's eyes opened wide and he shook with fear. "No, sir!" Then his eyes looked from side to side. "Sir, the chemist's been closed for months. What should I do?"

"Do you know where any of their medications are?" asked Blondie.

"They should still be in the chemist shop. I think so anyway," he replied.

"Then take me there and help me find Fat Boy's medicine, now," ordered Blondie.

"Madam Tajna Služba, I'll meet you at the safe house in two hours. If not, send Private Brinley to find me," said Fat Boy mounting his bike and revving it back into life.

Turning to Blondie, Private Brinley said, "Come with me, madam Tajna Služba." Together they walked the half block to the pharmacy.

While Blondie and the private were going through the myriad drugs on the pharmacy shelves and store room, Fat Boy was entering the gang's strip club only one block away.

"Well I'll be hogtied and stripped naked! It's Fat Bastard! Hey everybody, look who's here!" shouted the doorman shaking Fat Boys hand and walking him into the lounge area. Some of the gang members came over to shake his hand and some held back unsure how to greet him. Others fingered the knives in their belts or the pistols in their pockets. One went upstairs to call down Iceman Ed, their Sergeant-at-arms.

Iceman Ed was busy. Trixie was on her knees giving him a head-job when the messenger entered. Ed listened careful not to break the rhythm of the girl at his waste.

"Hurry up, Trixie, darling," he grunted, "I've got business downstairs."

While Fat Boy waited for the Iceman to show his face he called for a beer - a long, cold beer. "I need to get one of them real beers in me belly!" he roared at the barman, "and if it's not here in three seconds I'm climbing over this bar and jamming your head up my arse!" The barman shrugged as with a laugh he poured the beer, slamming it down on the bar-top.

"There ya go, Fat Bastard!" announced Smiley. "I never thought to see you again, mate. Where's the missus? Where's Blondie?" he asked.

"I sent her home, she'll be warming me bed tonight." He roared as he downed the beer in one gulp. "Another, Smiley, make it a full one this time, no bubbles or bullshit!" The second didn't touch his insides either. By Fat Boy's third beer Iceman Ed was on his way down the stairs and took the stool next to him.

"Hey, Fat Bastard, how's they hanging?" asked the gang's tough-man. He wasn't afraid, in fact he'd never known fear except the night Fat Boy took out three of his henchman.

"Iceman! Well I'll be bashed with a broken beer bottle!" Fat Boy slapped him on the back amicably. "I'm good, mate. So how is the old dung-house going? Anything new since I've been gone?" asked Fat Boy just as calmly.

The Iceman nodded at Smiley who magically produced crack pipe and lighter. Iceman Ed lit up and sucked the fumes till he was red in the face. He held the smoke deep in his lungs while his eyes dilated. Slowly he released his breath.

"You knocked us up pretty bad before you left, Fat Bastard. But that's sweet now, we don't hold grudges. Those Raven's Claw pricks give everyone the shits these days. Hey, I've got some good ganga upstairs and some more of this if you want it. You're old favourite's here tonight too. You haven't forgotten Mary-Theresa?" Iceman Ed's head lolled a little as he spoke.

"Smiley, grab me a beer too will you, mate." He grabbed Fat Boy by the arm. "Come on upstairs me ol' son and join me in some fun. I've still got Trixie waiting to finish me off."

He stood and called to Smiley, "Hey Smiley, call Mary-Theresa, tell her Fat Bastard's here and wants to give her something special." Iceman stopped and looked at his old mate. "Fat Bastard," he said warmly, "I missed you old buddy."

Fat Boy loved the gang life, he really did. He could feel the atmosphere of the strip club soaking into his cells like insulin to a diabetic. He let the Iceman walk him up the stairs where they shared a couple of bongs. That, the ice and the beers went down nicely after his long ride. Mary-Theresa sat on his lap and twirled his beard in her fingers like she did before things had gone pear-shaped. It was all so familiar and pleasurable. Fat Boy began to slide backwards in time and morality.

It was midnight and both Iceman Ed and Fat Boy were laughing and drinking. Trixie sat astride Iceman while Mary-Theresa was riding Fat Boy like only a country cowgirl could. All too soon he'd forgotten about his 'mission from God'. He once was in hell but now he was in heaven - and he loved it.

Blondie sat quietly with Private Brinley in their mansion, the drugs were in her bag ready to go. They had lighting and electricity from the town's generator and the Raven's Claw had cooked a meal and prepared the bed for his superiors.

But Brinley was frightened. Blondie was so beautiful he was certain she was evil incarnate sent by the devil to tempt him. Beauty was a crime, a crime against the Lord.

'Always watch out for temptation, it leads to sin,' and a beautiful woman, the Tajna Služba, was temptation itself.

"Damn bastard!" Blondie exploded looking at her watch for the hundredth time. "Private Brinley, go to that damn clubhouse and bring that fat bastard back here! Don't fail me or I will hang you up by your balls!" Her face was strained and despite her fuming anger the private felt a special warmth flood his being. He was head-over heels in love.

"Yes, madam, sir! I'll do that right now. But.. what if he refuses to come with me?" he asked, his head bobbed nervously.

"Tell the club Sergeant-at-arms that Tajna Služba demands Fat Bastard come home. NOW!" she screamed at him. Brinley startled so badly his head nearly left his shoulders as he spun around and raced for the door.

"Fat Bastard? Iceman?" Smiley held the door open as he called softly. He raised his voice a little. "Iceman? Fat Bastard?" but still there was no answer. He walked in and saw the girl's naked bodies draped across the two men. They were all sound asleep. "Come on mate, help me carry the fat bastard down the stairs and I'll help you put him in your car."

Smiley had to call down for help. It took four of them to put some clothes on the fat man first, enough to preserve his modesty. They struggled awkwardly down the stairs bashing his head several times on the walls and stairs. Finally they dumped his unconscious body into the back seat of the car.

"Mate, good luck, you might have to leave him in the car though. I suggest you not be around when he wakes up, he's a right bastard after a night like this." Smiley chuckled and waved the frightened youth off.

Blondie met them in the driveway and saw her brother in his usual pose - asleep and drugged to the eyeballs.

"Bastard!" she said out loud. Turning to the private once more she spoke to him. "Private Brinley, I'm impressed with your manner and I'll soon be making a favourable report to your superior. I have one more task I need you to complete for our glorious church. I need aeroplane parts for our Tajna Služba team, they're waiting just out of town. Right now we're preparing for a secret mission to attack and annihilate the Sundown's Commandos. This bastard here was supposed to collect the parts tonight but just look at him!"

And the private did look, at her breasts which bounced up and down as she moved. Blondie had deliberately changed into a seductive see-through blouse. She moved in such a way that the private couldn't help but notice her pert nipples. He tried not to stare but failed miserably.

"Private Brinley! You're not looking at my tits are you?" she asked icily, the friendliness suddenly disappearing from her face.

"No, Tajna Služba, madam, I mean…" he gulped, "No, sir!" She knew she had him completely in her power now.

"I need you to take me to Iggy, the aircraft mechanic, in two hours. Go and get some sleep and I'll call you when I'm ready." The private headed off to the spare bedroom, exhausted and as nervous as hell. Private Brinley didn't think he could fall asleep in that state but he did.

Blondie lay back in her four thousand dollar lounge chair and sipped on a fresh pineapple juice while waiting for the sun to rise. She knew she was cutting it fine. The church would surely come down on her and Fat Boy if they knew they were there. But she needed time to unwind and think.

Just as the sun touched the eastern horizon Blondie woke Brinley. He dressed and went to splash his face. By the time he was ready Blondie had made him breakfast. She changed back into fatigues but despite her attempt to blend in and look unattractive beauty simply radiated from her.

"Private. You've an important mission to perform for me and the Tajna Služba. Today you'll either make it or you won't. Fail me and you'll be cast into the pits of damnation. Succeed and you'll be promoted and invited to join us, the Tajna Služba. What is it to be?"

"The Tajna Služba?" His face beamed. "Madam, sir! I'm with you. I'll do whatever you want me to do," he said overawed with the promise of joining the famed Revelationist secret service.

"OK, finished? We'll go to the mechanic's workshop and wake Iggy. I do believe Iggy still lives in his workshop at the airport?" Blondie lifted one eyebrow.

Brinley stood staring at her, he couldn't stop himself. Blondie's body pulled at him like a sexual magnet. Finally he stuttered, "M, Madam, y, yes he does. I mean, yes, sir."

Fat Boy snored loudly in the back seat while Private Brinley parked his car right next to the aerodrome shed.

"Private, go and wake up Iggy, I'll follow you inside in a moment." Blondie then leaned over and checked her brother. He stirred and told her to 'bugger off'. Yes, she thought, he's fine.

There was now another problem - how to get back to Birdsville. Fat Boy was out of it for the next twenty four hours. There was no way she could ride his Harley-Davidson with him unconscious behind her. She knew that the only way home was in Private Brinley's car, she saw no other options. Blondie looked up when she noticed Iggy at the door rubbing the sleep from his eyes.

Not wanting Iggy to say anything to arouse suspicion she called Brinley over. "Private, get this car filled with fuel and check the oil. You're to come with us on our rendezvous with the Tajna Služba team. Get moving, we only have a few minutes."

Blondie walked over to her old friend, Iggy. She quickly pushed him inside and told him what she needed as she passed over Bill's hand-written note.

"What the hell, Blondie? You're crazy coming back here." Iggy reached across his messy desk for his glasses then glanced at the note. "OK, I've got all these parts. I'll be as fast as I can. Give me a minute." He wandered off into his workshop where Blondie could hear noises of movement as he collected the vital aircraft parts.

She looked outside and saw Private Brinley filling the car from one of the aerodrome's fuel tanks. She wished everyone would move faster. It was nearly an hour since sunrise and the stockade guard was due to be relieved. She was afraid that she might have to fight her way out and she was hopeless with an automatic assault rifle.

"Here you are, luv," called Iggy as he sauntered in with a duffel bag containing the plane parts. "Got them all. Some are new and the rest are reconditioned." He looked at the boy beside the car, Brinley was replacing the nozzle in the tank. "Good luck, darling. Sorry I can't help you out more."

Blondie reached up and kissed him. "You've always been a darling, Iggy. Look after yourself and your grandkids. Maybe one day this madness will be over and we can pay you back for this." They stood for a moment and embraced, Blondie didn't want to let go fearing what was ahead of her.

There came the sound of Brinley's car crunching on the gravel outside Iggy's shed and Blondie stepped back.

"Until next time, Iggy." She ran out of the shed and jumped into the driver's seat.

"Private Brinley, this is your day to prove if you're one of us or one of them. I'll drive you just get us through the road block by charm, persuasion or by force." She looked deeply into his eyes as she spoke.

Brinley no longer saw a beautiful woman. Instead, he saw a determined secret service agent who had braved the horror of war and was in need of his help. An image of the Revelationist Crusader icon, a knight in full armour, sword drawn, protecting a semi-naked woman flashed into his mind. His heart beat faster.

"Madam, Tajna Služba, I won't fail you. If I need to kill my own kind I will." The private cocked his assault rifle, checked its firing mechanism, pulled three spare magazines from his webbing belt and nodded.

"I'm with you, Tajna Služba." His face was aglow in adulation, a state of spiritual bliss. He was her saviour, her Knight Crusader.

Blondie put her foot down on the accelerator in a desperate bid to beat the change of guard at the stockade. She spun the back wheels of Brinley's battered Ford and sped as fast as the road allowed.

The blond secret agent had no time to look beyond the road in front of her. But if she did she would have noticed that Private Brinley had his eyes closed, his lips slightly parted in a smile and he was shaking. Brinley was in ecstasy imagining that he was fighting heroically to protect the sexual goddess seated beside him. The image suddenly shifted to reform into the adolescent fantasy frequently shared among his sexually frustrated Revelationist friends. For that single moment he could actually feel the naked temptress, the Tajna Služba, mounting his rigid maleness.

Chapter 6 - Blood Brothers

The commando wished the patrol good luck as the ASLAV armoured vehicle led the two Bushmasters towards Mount Isa. The spectators then turned away and walked back into the hotel.

Although it was winter the temperatures still fluctuated. Some days were freezing and some were stinking hot and Sundown never got used to it. He wandered into the kitchen and made himself a cup of Mel's bush coffee and a cup of tea for Pedro. He carried them into the first aid room.

"Hi Jenny, you missed saying goodbye to the boys," he said as he watched her finish her cup of tea.

"Nah, there's not much joy for me in fighting, Sundown. I've got little Lenny breaking his neck to join up and then it'll be Liam. A mother's curse is having beautiful sons only to watch them go off to war to die," she mused almost to herself.

"You's right you know," said Pedro, sitting propped up with his pillows. "War is hell and watching youngsters die is sometimes worse than dying yerself," he said matter-of-factly.

"Maudlin lot we are this morning then," said Sundown as he passed Pedro his cup of tea and sat beside Jenny.

"I miss Shamus, you know," Jenny said as she leaned forward resting her hands on her waist to ease her aching back.

"Pedro and Shamus would come into our shop and chat the whole day away. Then we'd all go to the Marree pub for a meal and chat some more. Shamus always had a lot of stories. He'd travelled the world and done a lot of things and not once did he think he was better than anyone else."

"Yeah, I miss him too. He never let an opportunity pass when he could help someone. Hey, Jenny, remember when little Lenny got his toe stuck in the bathtub at your old house outside Marree? I think it was yer old pa's house," said Pedro starting to pick up again.

"Yeah, I do, poor little fella. We had to chop the tub up from around his foot. He must have been five or six then," replied Jenny, remembering the pain as mother's do.

"Remember what Shamus done?" Pedro asked her.

"Yes, I do, Pedro, he picked him up and you two drove all the way to Alice Springs, a thousand kilometres away with his bleeding foot wrapped in a rag." She looked at Sundown and explained.

"We couldn't get onto the Flying Doctor so Shamus just grabbed Lenny and told Pedro to get the truck. They drove all the way in one go. I'll never forget it and neither will Lenny. I was pregnant with Liam and had to stay home with Danielle. Harry was away with the mustering, that was before he had his accident." Jenny looked at Pedro again. "You blokes were there at the right time and place, you always were."

Turning back to Sundown she continued with the story. "Those two blokes wouldn't leave Lenny, oh no. Those lousy hospital people told the boys to leave Lenny by himself in the room, alone. The poor kid must have been terrified. Shamus and Pedro stood up to them bully's. There was no way they would leave Lenny by himself among strangers."

Sundown nodded in understanding. "You know what I miss about Shamus? His mind. Just about every question I asked he had an answer for. When he didn't know the answer he would help me find it," added Sundown. They continued chatting away like this until Tricia came in to look in on Pedro.

"How are you feeling, Pedro? Did that beer taste good?" she smiled.

Pedro, was about to say something then stopped. "What? Damn! What bastard told you. I bet it was that boofhead, McFly! Bloody boofheaded, whiskey drinking, silver-tail!"

"Well, actually, between you and me, it wasn't McFly." Tricia giggled.

"Whoever it was I'll kick his butt with me tin legs when I gets them back on," said Pedro halfheartedly.

"I guessed by that guilty look on your face and knew someone had done something naughty." She giggled again then bent over to check his vitals. "Have you moved your bowels today?" she asked as she read his pulse.

"Moved me damn bowels?" he gasped. "I've moved me entire intestines inside out!" cried Pedro with emotion. "Every time I fart I shed tears and they ain't tears of joy neither. I've drunk so much water I've flooded the bed and backed up the toilets!"

The three of them nearly gagged with laughter. Tricia stopped laughing then said with a more serious tone. "Let's see. You're colour is good, your eyes are clear and your nose is wet, all good vital signs for a cattle dog. All we need do now is find some very slow cattle for you to chase." Tricia had so few opportunities these days to stop and have a joke and was actually enjoying herself.

"Harrumph," said Pedro. "I'm glad those water-bucket twins of Cambra's went on patrol with him, the damn boofheads." He stopped, looked quizzically at Tricia. "Can girlies be boofheads do ya know?" he asked. Tricia stared blankly at him and shrugged her shoulders. "Doesn't matter. Those boofhead girlies haven't stopped pouring water down me gullet all week. But now I see Lorraine has set Donna to take their place. What is it with nurses and water?"

"Aha, it's our trade secret. If I tell you, then I'll have to kill you," said Tricia with a wink.

Sharp as ever Pedro came back. "Kill me? Isn't that what you're doing with the water? I'll be the first person who has ever died in the desert from drinking too much water."

"I've got to get back to work," said Sundown getting up off his seat. "Pedro behave yourself. I'll drop in and see you later. Tricia when you've got time after lunch can you organise a meeting with Wiram and Assassin in Andy's office? We've got to talk supplies and hygiene before summer hits. If we don't shift out of Birdsville before then we need to do something to keep the oldies and injured out of the heat. I really need to get these things organised before I head off to Alice Springs."

Six hundred kilometres is a long way on a dirt road even when you're vehicle is a first-class Bushmaster six wheel drive light armoured protection vehicle.

Bushmaster One One Bravo, commanded by Sergeant Ahmet, carried the extra fuel for the other two and stopped at the three hundred kilometre point. There they would set up an ambush with land mines and Javelin in case the two assault vehicles, the ASLAV commanded by Major Thompson and the second Bushmaster, commanded by Captain Lewis, were pursued.

Sergeant Ahmet and his crew took Lulu and Danni under their wings and made them feel part of the team. While the ASLAV and the other Bushmaster refueled and headed off to protect Fat Boy and Blondie at Mount Isa, Ahmet's crew made their ambush site as inconspicuous as possible. The men and girls dug fire pits for their single FN Mag machine gun and Javelin then positioned their Bushmaster with it's mounted machine gun to cover the road.

Everyone pitched in and by mid afternoon they were ready to set up their bivouac and sleep arrangements. The boys did the cooking and the girls sat back and soaked up the attention. They made Cambra's girls feel like royalty, they loved having them around. It wasn't every day the armoured cavalry had two pretty teenagers sharing a bivouac with them on patrol.

While Bushmaster One One Bravo was setting up their ambush site, Major Thompson's ASLAV and Captain Lewis' Bushmaster were just preparing to move into position two kilometres out from the Mount Isa roadblock. As Captain Lewis prepared their ambush Major Thompson discussed strategy with Cambra, Halo and Corporal Hassam.

"Boys, quite simply we don't know what to expect. Corporal Hassam knows this area well so I'll send you three as a forward post to reconnoitre the road block," said the major.

Corporal Hassam nodded. "Sir, what's the plan if we are engaged?"

"The captain and I have been planning for this and that's why you three experienced soldiers will go. One Zero Bravo and One One Alpha will move forward the moment there is activity and take out the road block. Our intelligence says they only have the single mounted machine gun and there is generally a small guard, sometimes two sometimes four in a stockade style post."

The major looked at his men. "We'll bring the two armoured vehicles to about one hundred metres from you, just around the bend here." He pointed to his map. "Just before dawn."

Cambra and Halo smiled, they were going to have ringside seats to the fire-fight. "You bet major, we'll be there," said Halo.

They set out at midnight and took turns to keep watch. An hour before dawn Corporal Hassam woke the two commandos as arranged. A half hour later the corporal jumped on the radio to inform the major of peculiar activities at the road block. Now all three looked through their binoculars as several loaded cars pulled up swelling the armed terrorist numbers, something was up.

Blondie was only a few hundred metres from the roadblock when she realised things were not going to be easy. She noticed a number of cars and Ravens Claw troops gathered at the stockade. The Tajna Služba was distracted by a groan from the back seat. In her rear-vision mirror she saw Fat Boy lift his head.

"Uh, where are we? Who's that bloke? What's going on, Blondie?" he grunted.

"Get your head down Fat Boy. We're approaching the road block then we're heading out to rendezvous with our Tajna Služba. Private Brinley here is going to provide fire support to make sure we get through." She turned and looked at the now frightened youth. "That's right isn't it private? You are one of us now aren't you?"

With the sudden realisation that this could easily turn into a firefight, Brinley's mind immediately dumped all notions of teenage love.

In a voice a little too loud for Fat Boy's headache he said, "I'm with you. I'm ready to defend you, madam, Tajna Služba." Clearly fighting to contain his terror Private Brinley puffed up his chest as he sought to gather the scattered remains of his earlier bravado.

Blondie slowed down as she approached the road block. There were about a dozen armed terrorists milling around the stockade and they turned to look at the car as she approached.

"Private, you know what you need to do if they try to prevent us leaving don't you." It was a statement that he well understood. As she spoke she pulled her 9mm Heckler and Koch pistol from inside her blouse and cocked it. She held it loosely in her right hand steering with her left. The car was now almost level with the first few terrorists who were lazily smoking and talking among themselves.

"Private Brinley, if the officer approaching us now tries to stop us I will take him out. You will then open fire and engage the closest terrorists. Then you will take out the machine gunner. Do you copy that?"

She saw the look of horror on his face as he mouthed some words but nothing came out. Blondie leaned across and slapped his face, hard. The private pulled his head back and looked at her in shock. It now dawned on him that they all might die.

"I need you to focus! Are you with me or not?" she asked once more. Private Brinley focused on her beautiful face, he was both aroused and terrified.

Private Brinley swallowed hard then said with quiet conviction, "I'm with you, Tajna Služba."

The teenage Raven's Claw solemnly cocked his weapon, the safety was off and he was ready for whatever eventuated. He carefully leaned it against his door as the officer walked to Blondie's side.

"Good morning, missus. What do we have here then?" the lieutenant said then visibly balked. "Private what are you doing in this vehicle?"

"Lieutenant, look at me, please," said Blondie quietly yet firmly. "I am on a mission for the Tajna Služba." She stopped and let that sink in. "I ordered this young man to attend me on secret service business last night. I now have what I need and I will be on my way. I will be taking the private to assist me and then return him. Now step away from the vehicle or you will have to answer to the Tajna Služba, personally. I can assure you they will not be happy with you interfering with secret service business."

The lieutenant looked carefully at Blondie and then noticed the weapon in the private's hands. "I see a woman, a naked fat man and one of my men who is armed. I have no information of any Tajna Služba dropping by. Stay there while I radio through to Casa Grande headquarters to confirm your story." He stood up and said forcefully. "Do not move from here."

The officer was about to call to his second in command when Blondie lifted her pistol and fired. The bullet hit him in the cheek and went through his skull exploding from the side of his head in a spray of blood and brains.

"Private Brinley, if you don't mind!" shouted Blondie as the terrorists momentarily froze at the sudden turn of events. They now readied their weapons to return Blondie's fire. "For fuck-sake fire your weapon!" She stamped her foot on the accelerator knocking two of the terrorists to the ground. The welcome sound of Brinley's AK47 put a ghost of a smile on Blondie's lips. Her hasty plan might work - *with a great deal of good luck*,' she thought.

Cambra cried out, "It's Blondie and she's got a stranger in the front seat with her! Hassam, tell the major to get his ass here now! Halo, grab your weapon and come with me!"

The two commandos leaped to their feet and raced to the edge of the bush where they immediately engaged the enemy with their captured AK47's. They were just as proficient with the terrorist's assault rifle as they were with any other.

"I'll take out the machine gunner, Cambra, you focus on that bunch over there!" said Halo excitedly. He was still that same Xbox gamer at heart and every fire fight was like a video game to him.

Blondie planted her foot down on the accelerator but lost control of the car slamming it heavily into the stockade. The car hit with such force that the raised platform and the machine gunner toppled to one side.

"Out! Get out! Everyone out of the car!" she screamed. Blondie opened the rear door and reached in to grab at Fat Boy. He was wide awake now and crawled to join her at the side of the car just as a stream of bullets blasted glass and debris over them.

Private Brinley continued to fire through his open window into a group of terrorists opposite him. The force of the car's impact with the stockade had trapped his legs between a pile of sandbags and his car seat.

"Brinley, get out!" cried Blondie firing her pistol. She had yet to notice the incoming fire from Halo and Cambra.

"I can't get out! My legs are stuck!" As Brinley turned to face Blondie he was hit in the cheek by a bullet and his head flicked to the side. "Leave me, madam Tajna Služba! I'll go to blessed paradise protecting you! Leave me and run!" he called back over his shoulder as a bullet struck him in the stomach then another just below the collar bone.

"I'm with you," he moaned as he tried to slip a fresh magazine into his rifle but his hands failed to perform the simple task they'd done a thousand times before.

"Fat Boy! Stay next to me. We have to make a run for the bush. Here, hold this bag it's got the medicines and the aircraft parts. Don't drop it!" she yelled above the noise. Blondie put her head inside the open car door while she slapped a fresh magazine into her pistol.

She looked at Brinley and realised that he was not going to survive regardless of what orders she gave him. "We're going to run across to the bushes, cover us!" she yelled at him.

Brinley heard her voice as though it came from the end of a long tunnel. His attention was now a laser-point of awareness as he fought the pain and creeping numbness from his injuries and loss of blood.

"Go now my beautiful… Tajna Služba… my love… I'm with you." It was so soft that Blondie never heard a word.

As she turned to her brother a burst of automatic gunfire hit the young man in the chest flinging him across the front seat. His head lay where Blondie's lap had been only seconds earlier. His eyes were open but there was no breath of life in his lungs. Brinley had kept his promise, he was with her.

Grabbing Fat Boy's arm in her free hand, Blondie leaped towards the bushes just as Halo and Cambra stepped out firing their assault rifles. The two commandos sudden gunfire forced the enemy to duck behind cover long enough for Blondie and Fat Boy to notice their rescuers. When Blondie saw them she cried out with joy and changed course to join her commando friends.

Halo pointed behind him directing her towards the corporal. Slipping in another magazine he continued to fire giving the two time to escape.

At that moment Cambra saw in Blondie something more than just another bottle blond. There was no doubt that Blondie was as dry as a martini in a Bond movie but what he now saw struck him dumb – she was simply stunning. It might have been the dawn light that highlighted her blond tipped hair or it could have been the body-hugging uniform she was wearing. Whatever it was it forced Cambra to stop firing and stare.

A burst of gunfire struck the ground at his feet. The thoughts forming in his mind immediately evaporated as he swung his AK in the direction of the terrorists now recovering from the Sundown Commando assault. His instincts suddenly kicked in and Cambra was back to being the fierce fighter he was known for in the commando.

The ASLAV and Bushmaster skidded to a halt as Halo and Cambra decided it was wise to retreat back to the cover of the bush as well. They were now under heavy fire, the terrorist bullets caused leaves and dirt to spray all around the two fleeing commandos.

From out of the two armoured vehicles leaped a squad of Alice Springs Command soldiers busting for a fight. They'd been waiting for this very moment. After almost a year of running from conflict they were desperate to prove that they were as good as, if not better, than their enemy.

Two men raced to set up the FN Mag machine gun while the others opened up with their Steyrs, skirmishing forward to engage with their enemy. They swapped bullet for bullet with the Ravens Claw terrorists and some of the Alice Springs Command soldiers fell to the ground. The fire slackened for a few seconds when the machine gun came to life and pounded the enemy stockade.

The ASLAV's 25 mm cannon opened fire a second later directing it's exploding shells to decimate the stockade while the 7.65 mm machine guns from both armoured vehicles knocked most of the remaining enemy to the ground.

Corporal Hassam now had the opportunity he was waiting for and dragged Blondie and Fat Boy into the ASLAV. He then turned yelling for Cambra and Halo to jump into the Bushmaster as well.

Around the corner now sped four trucks loaded with more terrorists, the Mount Isa Talons, elite commandos of the Raven's Claw Battalion. These terrorists trained with similar intensity as the Deaths Heads and had a fierce reputation for their fighting prowess.

"Major, incoming vehicles, four. Firing now," informed the gunner. He pulled the trigger on his 25 mm cannon and destroyed the lead truck but the other three made it through the hail of fire to dump their crusaders in a series of trenches overlooking the stockade. Their automatic fire stopped the Alice Springs assault in it's tracks and more soldiers fell.

Corporal Hassam saw the grenade fly through the air and fall beside the machine gun crew. In that split second he knew his mates would be killed if he didn't do something. Instinctively he sprinted across the ground and kicked it like a football. Just as he dropped to the ground it exploded spraying metal shards over the machine gun crew and himself.

"Captain, this is serious! Even the machine gun won't cut it against their trenches. Look, they've dropped smoke on the ASLAV, clever bastards!" cried the Bushmaster driver watching through his view finder.

Halo heard the staccato of rifle fire on the armoured sides of the Bushmaster and instinctively ducked down. When the grenade exploded he realised his new-found friends were in big trouble.

"Fuck this!" he yelled and reached over to grab Cambra by the shirt. "Cambra, our mates need us, come on!"

Together they leaped back outside and opened fire on the enemy in their trenches. They tried to hold back the overwhelming tide of incoming fire.

By now the Alice Springs Command assault had stalled. Both the Raven's Claws and elite Talons began to stand up and direct their RPGs at the armoured vehicles. Before the driver had managed to back out from the smoke cloud two RPGs exploded under the ASLAV. It savagely rocked the armoured vehicle. But it also blew some of the smoke away allowing the

25 mm turret gunner to see the enemy standing in their trenches.

"Gunner, would you care to direct your fire on those terrorists firing their RPGs. It looks like they're gaining the upper hand against our troop," said Major Thompson as calmly as he could. "And don't let up until they're all frigging dead! If you don't mind."

"Firing!" replied the gunner. He could now see his own comrades lying flat on the ground. Some were still firing at the terrorists but there were many casualties among the Alice Springs Command in front of him. The gunner then noticed his best mate lying on the ground with blood pooling beside him.

"Take that, you pricks!" he cried as he watched his cannon shells completely obliterate a section of trench. Then he walked the rounds into the next one. He continued firing until the Talons platoon ceased to exist.

The major called over his radio, "This is Sunray Actual, One One Alpha, move up and secure this stockade. Collect our wounded, Sunray Actual will provide cover." His face was a sheen of sweat, he knew his troop had taken heavy casualties and it hurt.

Both vehicles now moved forward while the machine gunners continued to rake the enemy position. Any movement received special attention. The major inquired of his gunner if he could see any movement towards town.

"No movement, sir, all clear. I think we've done what we needed to do," he replied but his face was tight and his voice caught a little as he strained to control his emotions.

Captain Lewis cut in on the radio. "I'll see to the wounded, Sunray. My men are loading your ASLAV now." There was sound behind him and the major saw several of the wounded men being brought inside. He watched as their medic busily staunched the blood from one of the soldiers wounds.

Incredibly there were only two killed outright, but of the ten who hit the ground only one remained free of wounds. Halo and Cambra raced over to the corporal they had shared their watch with. Corporal Hassam lay still on the ground covered in blood. Halo thought his friend was dead until he heard him grunt. They watched as his hand reached for the weapon he'd dropped at the moment the grenade detonated.

"Halo, he's alive!" the two reached down and carefully sat him up.

"I've got him, boys," said the Bushmaster medic. "Corporal, can you see me?" Hassam nodded. "Good, you can hear and you can see. We're going to get you inside and patched up." He nodded to the two commandos and together the three carried the corporal into the crowded Bushmaster.

There was blood and shattered bone, there were sobs of pain and cries of anguish. One of the dead men was Captain Lewis' brother, the captain cradled his head in his lap. He turned to Cambra who was beside him looking to see if he could help in any way.

"Poor bastard, only joined up because of me. I told him I'd look after him - it looks like I didn't do too well." He leaned into his brother's chest his body racked by sobs of pain.

Halo heard the machine gun open fire again and he looked up to the Bushmaster's gunner. "What's happening, Noddy?"

"More vehicles incoming, trucks with troops, they probably have Javelins," replied the gunner who continued to steadily swap fire with the enemy.

Just then the call came through from the major. "Sunray Actual, OK boys, let's get these medicines and parts back to where they belong. One One Alpha, you lead, let's move out at speed, if you will." The driver released his brakes and accelerated causing some of the wounded to groan in pain.

The major handed the radio mic to his crew chief, Sergeant Tobi, and crawled carefully between the wounded to speak with his visitors.

"Thanks Major, and just in time. I thought we were going to die back there," panted Blondie, gulping water from the bottle a soldier now handed her. "I've got the medicines and parts in this bag here but you'd better check to see they're not damaged."

The major took the bag she held out to him. He found a seat and inspected its contents.

"What numbers do you think the enemy have in Mount Isa, Blondie? Do you think our little raid will cause a retaliation any time soon?" the major asked.

"I have no idea, major," she replied. Blondie really didn't care right then. They had done what they said they would do and that was that. The exhausted Tajna Služba lay back against her big brother and snuggled her head into his chest and closed her eyes. Fat Boy leaned into his sister and did the same. Within seconds they were both sound asleep.

The major decided not to stay and engage the enemy they had left behind. He wanted to give his wounded the best chance of survival he could. The only way to do that was to get back to Birdsville where the nurses were already preparing their first-aid room to receive them.

They arrived at the ambush site three hundred kilometres north of Birdsville and pulled into the bush clearing just as lunch was made ready. The medics exited their armoured vehicles and gathered the wounded around the camp fires. The One One Bravo medic had already prepared stretchers and bush beds for their wounded mates. Those in need of more extensive medical attention now received it. Despite the ferocity of the fire-fight most of the men had only minor injuries.

The Alice Springs Command, Third Australian Army, were now well and truly blooded. They had finally shown the enemy they could stand up and fight like men.

Major Thompson personally directed the troops to prepare their ambush in case the terrorists were following behind. Their radio operator reported that the chatter from the Mount Isa Claws dropped out some hours ago suggesting that they had decided they had enough fighting for one day. They were most likely licking their wounds at the ruined stockade wondering what had hit them.

As soon as Cambra exited the Bushmaster, Lulu and Danni raced across to leap into his arms. They had been crying and now wouldn't let him go. Sergeant Ahmet laughed and asked if they wanted a hotel room. Lulu turned to him and giggled but didn't say what she normally would in such circumstances. Instead the girls led Cambra to the camp fire and made sure he was given the best food their own hands could prepare for their returning hero.

Halo walked Corporal Hassam over to the first aid post where the medics could do a thorough assessment of his wounds. Once the blood was cleaned from his face he didn't look too badly injured, *just a few scratches'* he said.

As he passed Blondie the corporal called out, "Blondie, who was that young man we saw riding shot gun in your car? He was covering you all that time, a good soldier. I'd be proud to have someone like him at my back."

Blondie looked at him blankly. "Who?" she asked. "Oh him. Just one of the terrorists, an enemy." She reached out and took a sandwich as a plate was passed around. "Thanks," she said to the soldier and started eating. Private Brinley's brave sacrifice already forgotten.

The corporal looked over at Fat Boy now tucking into his meal as well.

"OK, yeah, sure, enjoy your meal," he said, then went with Halo to sit and stare into the fire.

Chapter 7 - Cain and Abel

Greg almost dropped his rifle as the incoming fire splintered the rock beside him. He crouched down then fled back to his car.

'That's not Riley or his mates, just some tourists, probably. I'd better head back to the farm house and search that gully where we found the bodies. I should be able to find Riley's tracks easily enough,' he thought to himself.

On reaching his car he pulled the top off his whiskey bottle and finished half in one go. Not that he was stressed, not at all, he was feeling quite aroused after knifing Laurie. He relived the fight, the man-on-man brawl. Greg felt pumped recalling how he managed to pull his knife and stab the coward in the back. He could still feel Laurie's life slipping away.

Greg remained on a high and on his way back to the gully he started singing.

It was heading towards dark when he pulled up at Riley's burnt-out farm house. Parked in the yard was his cousin, Joey, so he tooted his horn and called him over. Joey had his jaw wrapped in a bandage and walked gingerly towards Greg's car.

"What took you so long, cuz? I needed you yesterday you lazy bastard!" yelled Greg into his cousin's bandaged face.

"D'yer geg 'm?" mumbled Joey through his broken jaw. It sounded horrible but Greg didn't care, he was still on a high and drunk.

"No, I didn't get them. I killed Laurie though. Coward turned on me. Just as I was going to grab some cute girls up at Arkaroola. We had a great fight too, it was a beauty. He's tough that Laurie but I managed to pull my knife and stabbed him clean in through the back and right into his heart. I felt him die right on top of me. Man, that was so good. Here, grab a slug of this." He handed Joey his bottle of whiskey.

Joey drank a little through the side of his mouth and chuckled deep in his throat. "Asad hd kow ow," he said and laughed.

Greg looked at him in bewilderment. He nodded as if he understood then told him they were going to spend the night there and follow up in the morning.

"Tomorrow, Joey, we'll go hunting Riley and his mates. Uncle Jack told me we could have Katie to ourselves and then bring her back for him." Greg smiled to himself as he imagined what it would be like to have her.

"Jack said as long as we don't damage the merchandise we could take her. What do you reckon?" He slapped Joey on the back completely ignoring his mumbled reply. Together they took their swags and made camp ready for the morrow.

The next morning Greg was in a foul mood. He felt crook in the stomach and his head was sore from failing to hydrate. Joey started to mumble through his broken jaw.

"Don't fuckin' talk to me, Joey!" he yelled, "I can't understand a word you say! So shut up and just follow my orders!"

Their breakfast now finished the two drove silently into the gully. Greg showed his cousin the tracks of the fight and where the bodies were buried.

"Right, we separate and start tracking. They've taken the two Rovers and there's horse tracks plus Riley's truck tracks. It should be easy enough. If we lose the tracks we'll get out and walk. Is your rifle loaded?" Joey nodded. "Have you got enough ammo for a fight?" Joey nodded again. "OK, jump in the car, we'll follow as far as we can then you climb onto the bull-bar and point the way. We should be right until it gets too rough for the truck."

They did a quick tour of the battlefield then drove forward. Within fifteen minutes the ground became too rocky to continue and Greg was forced to stop the truck.

"Joey, grab your gear we're walking. If you see anything call me. No, come and get me. I can't stand the sound of yer grunting shit."

Greg was in one of his moods again. Joey had seen this before. Whenever Greg drank he became a real psycho. When they went out partying there were times Brad or Ferrie had to knock him out to stop him spoiling their drinking and whoring. Of the four cousins, Greg was the worst. Joey remembered Brad saying many a time that Greg couldn't handle his grog, how true it was.

It was now a few hours after dawn and Roo was on the hill overlooking the Arkaroola wilderness. He knew the Wilsons would come looking for them and he also knew he might not see them coming. The wilderness was a jumble of gullies and scrub, a hell-hole for walking or riding. It was dry, dusty and once you found yourself in the scrub you couldn't see more than ten or twenty metres. The only way to find your way was by map or by standing on a hill, like he was doing now.

Bongo could barely walk. With the mud packs and herbs he'd improved but at night he was restless and barely slept. He still suffered fevers and hot sweats, by morning he was exhausted. Fortunately Katie didn't need to stay up all night any more because her patient was out of danger. She was busy enough with the kids and cooking the emu and kangaroo meat Riley brought in.

Riley was on his knees carefully cleaning the kangaroo he'd shot that morning. His children watched in fascination, as he skinned, gutted and cut slabs of meat for Katie's cooking pot.

"Daddy?" asked Elle, "what's that?"

He answered, "That's the kangaroo's kidney." Then she asked the same question for every part of anatomy she could see coming out of the kangaroo's abdominal cavity. Harry held the pieces of meat as his father carved them then carefully took them over to his mother. Then she sliced them into fine strips and lay them on a stick platform to dry. She made broth from the bones, organs and brains, the smell was not at all pleasant.

Bongo moaned as he almost vomited up his breakfast when she started cooking in the confined space of the hut. He crawled into the fresh air to join the kids and Riley.

"I know it's going to taste good," he called to Katie, who now stood outside carefully placing a handful of sliced kangaroo steak on the thin branches, "but boiled brains is not my favourite meal. I'm not real keen on eating what some animal has used to think with. I hope you brought some chili or herbs to make it taste decent," he chirped hopefully.

"Bongo, you saw the mess at our farmhouse, what do you reckon? No, I've only got the bush herbs and most of them aren't ready so you'll just have to do with what you're given." She was too busy to even look at him.

Katie casually added, "Apparently one of the mines around here has radioactive water in it. What about we get some and see if that makes it taste any better?"

"That's seriously bad form, Katie. I hope they marked the mine properly so we don't go in there looking for kangaroos or something," Bongo said.

Riley commented, "One of those city companies went looking for uranium. They found it, dug it up, then dumped the toxic waste all over the blasted bush killing everything. The government wouldn't do a damn thing about it until us locals kicked up a stink. Bloody useless politicians," he said, then added darkly, "bloody useless politicians and damn religion!"

"And damn Wilsons!" added Bongo grimly.

While Riley and his family were doing their domestics Greg and Joey left their vehicle in the bush and began tracking the horse prints deep into the wilderness. They found the bushman's hut the family had first stayed in and sat there to drink more whiskey and eat some food. Joey sipped on the soup he'd brought in a canteen. He mumbled something but shut up when Greg flew into him.

"Are you a nob-head or something, Joey? I can't understand a word you're saying so shut up! Open your mouth again and I'll break the other side of your face!" His mood grew worse as they continued into the jumbled hills and gullies of the Arkaroola wilderness.

Sitting on a hill top just on dusk they saw Riley returning from one of his patrols. He was a long way off but the direction he was walking indicated their new hideout was further up in the mountains.

Greg put down his binoculars. "You bloody beauty, we've got them! They're holed-up in that direction and it looks like he's going back for dinner. I'll bet they have their lookout on that hill. If we make our way over there now, before it becomes too dark, we'll be ready for them at dawn. We can stretch out there tonight and be ready for them when they come out tomorrow."

They pulled on their jackets and hitched their rifles over their shoulders carefully fixing the position of their destination by the landmarks around them. It would be dark when they got there so they needed to orient now while there was enough light.

That night Roo sent his dream body out as he did every night, but it was restless. All night he saw images of the Wilsons. He struggled to sleep but every hour his dream body came back to wake him. By dawn he was edgy, irritable and exhausted.

"Mm," he said when he and Riley were making breakfast. Riley looked at him and noticed Roo had a serious frown on his face.

"What is it, Roo?" he asked.

"Mm, ah..." Riley could see he was struggling to find words and sounds, he could tell his cousin was clearly worried.

Bongo was awake so he came over to listen to the noises Roo was making then said, "Roo, did you have one of your dreams?"

Roo nodded forcefully, "Mm, yeah."

"So it was a bad dream?" Bongo asked and Roo nodded.

Riley watched as Bongo and Roo went through their twenty-question routine. It was fascinating, especially as Roo was now adding sounds to his nods.

"Riley, it sounds like Roo's dream showed him the Wilson's are out there, close." Roo nodded again without hesitation. "And if we go out it might mean we get shot at." Roo nodded again even more forcefully.

"Blimey," said Riley. "We've got the kids and Katie here. Are they coming for us now?"

Roo nodded but this time it was slower. He lifted his eyes, thought for a moment, and finally said, "No."

Bongo and Riley were shocked, the word he had spoken was as clear as a gun shot.

"Shit!" said Riley, "did you hear that, Bongo? He said, 'No' as clear as day." He smiled despite the seriousness of their situation. "Right, what should we do?" He sat quietly to think things through.

The rugged cattleman piled the three plates with food and poured three mugs of tea while he considered his plan. Both men watched and waited for him to say something while they all tucked into their breakfast.

"This is what we need to do. We move Katie and the kids out of here and up into the mountains proper. There's a cave up there I know of. They might be able to track us and they might not. None of them are as good as Roo here but us cattlemen are crafty. I wouldn't be surprised if they do find us, they've already done it from what Roo's saying. We'll need supplies and water, that's what we'll need the most of up there."

Riley scratched his head. "Bongo, you and Roo stay here and cover the approaches to our hut. I'll start moving Katie and the kids then take up our supplies with the horses. It's not a great plan but it's better than nothing. They must know we're in the scrub here somewhere."

Riley looked up as Roo nodded then continued. "Roo, you keep Black Dog with you, he seems to think you belong to him anyway. I'll get the horses, load them up and take the other two dogs with me."

Roo and Bongo filled in time by cleaning the rifles that Riley had collected. Bongo had a little more movement in his leg now. It wasn't as stiff as it was earlier that morning. He was pleased because now he might be able to help Riley some.

'I'm a bit like Pedro. We're both too proud to sit and do nothing while everyone else is working,' Bongo thought to himself.

The two scouts were a good team, Roo needed Bongo for his hands and Bongo needed Roo for his legs. They would laugh together each time they found themselves in a tangle of arms and legs barely able to move from the pain of their injuries.

Roo stopped what he was doing and stood up. He sniffed the air and reached for his pistol. Bongo saw him and immediately grabbed his assault rifle. Black Dog pricked up his ears as he noticed the two humans in a state of alertness but didn't move.

"What is it, Roo? Did you hear something?" asked Bongo quietly.

Roo was silent, his dream body had already begun to meld into the trees and hills searching for whatever it was that disturbed his highly refined instincts. A few moments later they could hear the sounds of Riley's pack horses returning to camp.

Roo smiled at Bongo, shrugged his shoulders and sat back down to help Bongo reassemble the last rifle. The two prepared to help Riley load the horses. At least they intended to help but neither could actually do much more than watch Riley do all the work.

"Riley, Roo and I are going to stay here, if we bump into the Wilsons we'll stay and fight. We don't want you leaving your family to help us either. We've fought them before and we can do it again, even if we do lack arms and legs." He made a wry smile despite his obvious pain.

"If they get through us they'll come after you. They'll track you up into the mountains." He paused for a moment. "Roo and I need you to stay and protect your family, Riley. Don't come and help us because we'll not be able to focus on fighting if we have to worry about Katie and the kids sitting up there unprotected."

Bongo's face was drawn and his eyes were sunk deep into his head. He'd lost weight these past few days and was looking gaunt. Roo didn't look much better. It struck Riley that he might look much the same.

"Yeah, I've got that Bongo. You guys just be careful. You've got plenty of captured ammunition and a choice of weapons here. Pick your ambush and pick your targets. Most importantly pick your battle, make them come to you." He shook their hands firmly.

"I'll drop the horses and gear off at the cave then head half way down. There's a saddle-back, a narrowing on the track up where I can ambush them. There's no other way up except across the saddle. Don't worry about me, I'll be fine." He paused as a fleeting feather of fear crossed his mind. "Good luck cousin, good luck Bongo. I'll wait till dusk to come back for you and lead you up into the cave. I'll meet you here, got it?"

Riley turned around and began the slow trek back up the mountain to be with his wife and children. He told Black Dog to stay and with a wag of it's tail it ran back and leaned protectively against Roo's leg.

Greg and Joey had spent a miserable night on the hilltop. It was freezing and they only had their jackets and whiskey to keep warm. They had picked a bad place to sleep, right next to a water soak where the large mosquitoes continued to breed right through winter. All night they were buzzed and bitten by myriads of mosquitoes.
The men had lit a small fire on the other side of the hill around midnight. They kept it going all night for warmth and to try to

make just enough smoke to keep the vicious mosquitoes away.

Greg's mood shifted for the worse after a sleepless night soaking himself in liquor. He was down to his last bottle and he swore that if they didn't find Riley today he would leave Joey there and go back for more supplies.

"Get yer hands off me drink, ya bastard," slurred Greg, he was plastered. "You come near my boddle and I'll kill ya just like I did that prick… what's 'is name." He waved his knife in front of Joey who easily moved back a few steps. "And don't even think 'bout mumbling shit at me or I'll smash yer head in." He staggered and fell across the fire barely able to roll off it.

"Bastard, yer pushed me didn't ya!" he yelled as he stood back up and lunged at Joey who again side-stepped. Greg tripped and collapsed unconscious to the ground. Joey decided to leave him there while he heated up his soup. He took his meal and his rifle to the top of the hill and prepared for Riley and his cousins to show themselves.

That morning Roo and Bongo searched the tracks and gullies with their binoculars. They saw nothing out of the ordinary but Roo was uneasy and so was Black Dog. Black Dog kept looking beyond the bush screen they were hiding behind staring at the lookout hill.

"There's something up there. Any chance we could get around the back of the hill and come up behind? What do you think, Roo?" asked Bongo.

Roo looked at Bongo's leg and smiled, he shook his head and tapped his rifle. It was one of the Wilson's, a nice bolt-action hunting rifle. Roo said he had enough rounds to kill a hundred kangaroos with this one. It had a high-powered scope and was in immaculate condition, obviously someone's prized possession.

Bongo noticed that Roo had already begun to sketch some kangaroos on its wooden stock. His AK assault rifle was now always slung across his back and an ammunition bandoleer over his shoulder.

"Roo! Look, movement!" whispered Bongo and Black Dog straightened and stood up. Bongo put his hand on it's back and shushed it back down. "Not now Black Dog, if the Wilsons see you they'll shoot you."

Roo had his binoculars up, Bongo joined him and together they watched as two men began arguing then fighting on the top of the lookout hill. One unsteadily swung his fist and punched the other man in the face. They now recognised the taller man, it was Joey. Joey collapsed as he clutched at his newly broken jaw. The other one turned towards them for a split second and they noticed it was Joey's cousin, Greg. They watched in amazement as Joey stood up and fought back. It was like watching a comedy act or perhaps it was just a pair of drunks fighting.

Joey hadn't seen Greg stagger to a standing position and move towards him. His attention was fixed on the bushes towards the end of the gully where he thought he saw movement. He was completely taken by surprise as Greg king-hit him in the side of the face. Joey fell to the ground blood streaming from his mouth. A searing pain lanced through his entire body and he clutched at his broken jaw trying to sooth the pain.

Joey could see Greg out of the corner of his eye, there was a knife in his hand again.

'Damn idiot, I should have hidden his knife and rifle while I had the chance!' The thought of what a fool he was for turning his back on his mad cousin slammed into his brain with each shuddering pulse beat.

Neither of the Wilsons were in a state to fight. They were both handicapped by injuries: self inflicted in Greg's case and the other inflicted by Bongo at the Wilpena Pound camp-fire a week earlier. They staggered towards each other like drunken lovers. As Joey dodged Greg's knife blade he reached for his own knife.

They collapsed together and wrestled on the ground. Joey's jaw was an agony of pain and he could feel the calcium which had begun to seal the break, crack open when Greg's shoulder slammed into him.

"Mmnneerrrargh!" he screamed in pain, tears sprang into his eyes momentarily blinding him.

"You prick! I know yer trying to do me out of having Katie. I'm having her first you bastard!" cried Greg as he slashed his knife across Joey's back slicing deeply into the muscle. Joey screamed and tried to turn to face his enemy. Greg had his knee in Joey's back pinning him to the ground beneath him. Joey was in a panic, he knew he would die if he didn't get up soon.

"I'm gonna do you, Riley, ya bastard! I'm gonna do you with me knife just like I did with that coward Laurie!" He lunged at Joey's back again. But Joey had managed to catch his foot against one of the myriad rocks strewn on the hilltop and pushed himself out from under his cousin's knee. The knife cut deeply into his flesh as it glanced off his shoulder blade.

"Mmmnnrrragh!" sobbed Joey in pain still unable to stand up fully. Greg grabbed Joey's shirt with one hand and stabbed upwards with his knife into his cousin's side.

"Yer bastard! She's mine! Get off her!" Greg was screaming at Joey who now saw the spectre of death in his cousin's face. There was so much blood pouring out of Joey's wounds that he was starting to feel faint.

Greg still had hold of Joey's shirt and wouldn't let go. Joey swung his fist as hard as he could and hit Greg in the nose. A lucky shot that allowed him to stagger several paces away. His cousin collapsed to his knees holding his bloody nose making grunting noises, he was clearly psychotic and beyond all reason. Joey saw Greg's knife on the ground. He kicked it away then lurched towards his own rifle leaning against the rock.

"Mnyayer! Yer fn gog!" Joey cried as he cocked, aimed and fired his rifle in one flowing movement.

The two men hidden in the bushes at the end of the gully saw the spray of blood and brains. This was soon followed by the sound of a rifle shot which echoed around the hills and gullies. Black Dog's ears pricked up and he growled.

"Steady boy. It's OK, Cain has finally killed his brother Abel. I don't think Cain is going to make it home for lunch either," Bongo said, sickened by what he'd just witnessed.

Roo looked at Bongo for a moment then reached one-handed for his rifle. Bongo instinctively knew what Roo was doing. He cocked Roo's rifle, handed it back, then leaned forward allowing Roo to place the rifle barrel on his shoulder.

With only one arm in working condition, Roo still managed to sight on the standing man and pull the trigger. He immediately dropped the Ruger and drew his pistol from its holster at his belt. He then leaped up and raced towards the top of the hill at full speed. Black Dog barked excitedly racing alongside.

Bongo picked up Roo's new rifle, pulled the bolt back and slammed in a new cartridge. He then carefully watched through the scope to cover his mate.

'You dope, Bongo,' he sighed to himself. *'One has his brains spread all over the ground and the other Roo took out - and you know what that means.'*

Roo and Black Dog dodged the traps and made it to the top of the hill breathing hard. Roo summed up the situation in one glance, then waved to Bongo giving the *'all clear'*.

Chapter 8 - Arkaroola Wilderness

Simon and Lucy fired just as Greg pulled the trigger of his rifle. From that distance they didn't truly expect to hit the enemy but were more than happy when they saw him drop and duck behind the rock he was standing beside. Luke had thrown himself to the ground, his weapon at the ready aimed at where the man had been standing. He looked around then called over his shoulder.

"Hey, where is he, is he dead?"

Simon answered, "No, stay still. He's run behind the rock. We're covering you. You know the drill so just don't move."

Luke knew that Simon and Lucy had both fired from the sound of the two different sounds: an AK47 and a Steyr. They were all waiting to see what the stranger did. Luke knew that Simon would want to get around behind the enemy's flank. Simon was strategic at all times, '*a natural warrior,*' Nulla often said.

They waited but nothing happened. Simon decided to move and motioned for Lucy to cover him just as she'd been taught by the boys while in Adelaide. By the time he'd made his move there was no one there, just Laurie's dead body lying on the ground now covered in flies.

Simon believed that the man who had fired at them had run away. Peering around the big rock he could see a track that wound it's way through the scrub. Making sure it was safe he called for Luke to cover Lucy while she ran up to him. Luke then followed on Simon's next call.

"He's run away up along that track. Lucy, you cover from here while I go around the rocks and Luke you…" Just then they could hear a diesel engine start up and the sound of tyres spinning on gravel. "Well, I guess he's escaping. We'll continue the drill. Lucy, you stay here and cover the centre. Luke you go right and I'll go left and meet where we heard the car drive off. And let's not shoot each other because Nulla will take our Steyrs off us." He flashed a smile at his mate and they quietly headed off.

Heidi had her AK47 armed and ready as she squatted at Arthur's side. The young hero was still suffering bouts of exhaustion and had yet to fully recovering from his leg wound. Right now his injured elbow and scarred forearm were throbbing. Nulla said that maybe he'd chipped the bone in his elbow because it just wouldn't stop giving him trouble.

Charlene had automatically continued on to the camp site with Annie. She had a head for direction, fortunately, and watched for landmarks she'd noted on the way in. Sticking to the faint track she finally led Annie to Nulla and the others.

Heidi decided she would stay with Arthur until things had sorted themselves out and everyone was safe. As she hadn't heard any more sounds of fighting after Simon and Lucy's automatics replied to Greg's heavy calibre rifle, she presumed they had killed the stranger.

"Hey, Simon! What's happening?" she shouted at the top of her voice. Her words echoed back and forth among the rock strewn hills.

Lucy's reply was faint but clear. "We're all safe. The enemy has gone so come down and join us."

Walking hand in hand Heidi led Arthur down the hill. Arthur was tired but curious. He'd inherited Nulla's Steyr which was slung over his good shoulder. Heidi had unslung hers in case she had need of it. At the bottom of the hill they met up with Lucy.

Lucy hadn't moved nor had she turned to watch Heidi and Arthur. Her attention remained focused on her role as guard for the two boys in front of her.

"Lucy, what happened? Is the rifleman still here?" Arthur asked, now crouched beside her, staring at Laurie's dead body.

"No, he's gone, but Simon and Luke are scouting out the situation. We heard a car drive off from behind those rocks. The boys should be returning from their patrol soon. Find a position to cover them just in case it's a trap," said the warrior woman as she shifted her position to a more comfortable one easing the ache in her calves.

The three dwellers were formed up around the rock beside the dead body and tried not to think about it. Flies buzzed about them to settle on the still-wet blood on the ground.

"I wonder what happened here?" said Arthur looking down at the man who saved their lives. "That bloke must have been trying to stop the other one from shooting us. He deserves to be buried, I reckon. We should go back and get some shovels."

"Lucy!" called Simon, who had taken command of the squad. "Lucy, all clear, come over and have a look."

"OK," she called back. "I've got Heidi and Arthur with me. I'll bring them."

They all gathered around the fresh skid marks on the dirt track. There was a single empty bottle of whiskey lying on the ground.

Luke said, "They must have been drinking and got into a fight. The one who fired at us must have wanted to kill us and the other one tried to stop him. I don't understand what they would have been doing out here though. We're in the middle of a desert, a wilderness for crying out loud." He scratched at a mosquito bite on his face and looked at the others.

"We should bury that man over there. He saved our lives and deserves some sort of recognition," piped up Arthur.

"You're right, Arty," replied Simon. "I'll stay here with Lucy while you three go back and tell Nulla what happened. Come back with some of those fold-up shovels and some food and water."

Lucy and Simon decided to climb one of the hills close by. It was bare of scrub and had a clear view for miles. When they made it to the top they noticed a dust cloud some distance away and Simon quickly pulled out his binoculars.

"Look at this Lucy, I bet it's that bloke who tried to kill us," said Simon handing his binoculars to Lucy.

"We should watch where he goes and tell Nulla. He's always on about intelligence." She kept the glasses to her eyes making comment as he disappeared and reappeared through the rugged gullies.

Some hours later Luke arrived with the shovels. He called out when he couldn't find them. Simon replied from the top of the nearby hill. Leaving Lucy to stay on watch the two boys buried the brave Laurie. They didn't even know his name.

"Nulla said we need to stay out here and keep watch while he works out what to do. He said that bloke might have been on his way to Arkaroola village. I've got some supplies here too. The tent and some food. Fatima gave me some eggs and flat bread so we won't starve," Luke said.

"Did she give you some curry powder to go with those eggs?" asked Simon.

"No, no curry powder, thank goodness, it makes me fart, and you don't want that near a naked flame do you?" They both chuckled. Lucy just rolled her eyes. "Nulla said to stay out here until he relieves us. He's studying the map trying to figure a way to get to Birdsville without heading into the Flinders Ranges. He's been on the CB with Birdsville and they said the Flinders people were dangerous and that we shouldn't trust anyone. Funny he should say that because we've just met one of their friendly locals.

"Anyway, Nulla said that he's going to bush-bash through the desert and get to Birdsville that way. He and Phil are working on the Toyota's now doing repairs and modifying them for the trip. Nulla said that we might have to leave the trailer behind but Phil said as long as we don't hit too much sand we should get through." Luke suddenly became animated. "Hey, guess what? They found a fuel dump! One of the houses had a dozen drums of diesel and some with petrol for our bikes in a shed!"

"So we get to ride our bikes in the desert? Woohoo!" called Simon with a grin on his face.

The teenagers carried their camping gear up the hill to set their tent up just below the top. They lit a fire for dinner and began preparing their meal. It was starting to get dark by the time they were ready to eat. It was a pleasant night and fortunately the tent had a fly screen to keep the mosquitoes out. They deliberately kept the fire making smoke throughout the night so the mosquitoes didn't annoy them while on watch.

It was just on dawn and the thought of food and the smell of eucalyptus smoke from the camp fire made the boy's stomachs grumble. Lucy poked at the fire to boil the billy so that she could make herself a cup of tea. For a teenage male the thought of food was almost as good as a threat from Nulla to get out of bed.

"What's for grub?" asked Simon scratching his back while looking for a suitable site to poop. "I've got to dump last night's dinner. I'll be back in a minute." He wandered off into the bushes.

Luke was just crawling out of the tent and called out, "Simon, find some ants, they might like some of that for dessert." He smiled when he heard Simon laugh in reply.

"You boys are disgusting. Dessert? Really? Where did you get such an idea from, Luke? And don't go peeing or pooping on ants while you're out here, that's just plain wrong!" complained Lucy stirring the eggs in the pan while toasting the flat bread on a stick.

"Well Lucy, did you know that ants will eat anything? And out here in the desert wilderness, well, there's not much of anything. So, therefore by simple deduction they must be starving. Simon's just giving them some nice dessert for after they've eaten some stale seeds or something boring like that." He couldn't stop himself from giggling as he spoke, it sounded ridiculous even to his own ears.

"Boys!" she said but it lacked conviction. They'd been together for some time now and she was almost as immodest as everyone else. "I often wonder how Glenda ever put up with you boys." She turned away so Luke couldn't see her smile. Lucy had grown fond of these two rascals, they reminded her of Tony and helped ease the constant pain in her chest.

The following morning Nulla arrived. They were sharing a cup of bush tea when they heard the sound of a single rifle shot. All four of them stopped, mugs half way to their mouths, listening. Some seconds later there came a second shot and it wasn't all that far away either.

"Righto, I think we now know where that bloke went to." Nulla stood up, pulled out his binoculars and looked in the direction he'd heard the noise come from. "Righto, how far is it and from what direction?" He turned to his warriors and they saw that this was another lesson.

"Ah," Simon spoke first, "over there towards the mountain ridge, probably that hill." He now had his binoculars out as well.

"Nulla, I can see smoke on that hill Simon pointed at. It must be a camp fire. I bet that's where they are," said Luke.

"Mm, so what is he shooting at? What's the story of these clues?" came Nulla's next question.

The three looked and wondered until Lucy spoke and broke the silence.

"Maybe this man has a camp out there and he's shooting kangaroos for food?" she said.

"Good Lucy, you're thinking. But if you were all listening those were two different weapons and from different directions. What could that mean?" The experienced aboriginal cavalry sergeant continued.

"That means there's at least two of them. Probably from a camp nearby. They might be survivors hidden in the wilderness? I think they're out shooting for food," said Simon.

Luke chimed in and said, "or they're fighting, shooting at each other. Maybe these two blokes who were fighting are from two different groups, one terrorists and the other a band of survivors. Maybe they met by accident and fought it out and maybe they're still fighting."

"Righto, all good points. I like how you're all thinking strategically. Next question is: what are the risks to our people and what do we do about it?" continued Nulla.

Lucy looked at him. "We should investigate. If we're going to stay here we need to know who is nearby, friend or foe. If we're about to head into the desert we need to know if our route passes near them and if it puts us all in danger."

The two boys looked at each other and nodded. "That's real good, Lucy," said Luke seriously and Lucy's face cracked into a smile, the first the boys had seen.

"This is what we're going to do," said Nulla finally. "I'll take Simon with me on a patrol to that hill. Luke, you stay here and wait for us. You'll also back us up if there is a fire-fight. I think it's not much more than a half kilometre away, not far at all. Watch our every step as we approach the hill... and put dirt on that fire!"

Turning to Lucy he said, "Go back to the cars and tell everyone to pack up and be ready to roll. Phil and I have already planned our route but it passes that hill. It's the only track out of this wild country. Get everyone armed, even Fatima and Phil… and Annie too, she's keen to do something. I'm putting you in charge of the dwellers, Lucy. Tell Heidi and Arthur they will be riding shotgun together in Phil's vehicle. The two boys here will ride their bikes as they did before. You'll ride shotgun with me, Glenda and Annie."

Nulla stopped for a moment to think. "And Lucy, if anything should happen to us, if we're not back in twenty four hours, leave without us. You'll then take command of our group, you'll be in charge. Got that?"

Lucy looked at him in shock, this was something she certainly didn't expect. Up till now she was just one of the dwellers, a parasite, a drain on everybody, she thought. No one really liked her and now this beautiful man made her feel like someone special.

"Thanks Nulla, I'll do my best. If there's no news by this time tomorrow, I'm coming out here to find out what happened. If I'm satisfied you lot are gone, then I'll take us across country to Birdsville myself." She reached up and kissed him on the lips, a kiss that was a bit more than a friendship kiss.

"Whoa there Lucy, I'm taken," he laughed with embarrassment as he pulled away. Nulla then deliberately caught her up in his arms and hugged her close before sending her on her errand. "Lucy, you're my main backup girl for our people, be careful. OK boys, let's do it."

Simon and Nulla crept as stealthily as they could up the hill. They couldn't see much, visibility was difficult once they struck the scrub. Simon tried to keep as quiet as he could but it was hot hard work with the sun beating down and the air so dry that his lungs felt like they were on fire. The path Nulla had chosen could not avoid the myriad slippery slope and the loose gravel hidden among the prickly desert shrubs.

They were almost at the top when they heard a firm voice. "Stay there, don't move! Put your weapons on the ground and your hands in the air. Walk slowly to the top of the hill. If you do anything we don't like we'll shoot you dead," came the simple command.

The two Adelaide dwellers looked at each other incredulously. *'How did we just walk into an ambush so easily?'* their faces said. Nulla nodded to Simon to follow their captors instructions. One small advantage that made them feel a sense of security was that they both had their .38 pistols, the small 'Saturday night specials' holstered inside their shirts.

As instructed Nulla and Simon stepped out of the bushes and walked up to the top of the hill where they saw two men. One was a lithe, part aboriginal and part something else that gave him the appearance of an Afghan warrior from the days of the British Raj. He had his arm in a sling and was pointing a M1911 pistol at them held steadily in his left hand. He looked serious and his eyes didn't waver from theirs.

The other was a younger man, tall, well built with sandy coloured hair. His eyes were tired and gaunt like he had been sick for some time. He sat on a log with an AK47 pointing at them. His position looked down into the gully below. He was probably the one who had spoken.

"Who are you and what are you doing here?" the grim faced man sitting on the log said. They then noticed he had his leg bandaged and it stuck out in front of him like a stick. His face squished up when he moved, obviously he was in pain.

"Who are you? And what are you doing up here shooting people?" answered Nulla looking at the two dead bodies.

Bongo smiled. "We've got the upper hand here, mate, or haven't you noticed? And don't try to play games with us we aren't in the mood. Just answer or die, it's as simple as that." He nodded towards the two dead bodies to press his point.

Nulla sighed, he had a sixth sense, a natural instinct about people and what he felt about these two gave him the confidence to take a punt.

"We heard firing and investigated." He looked at the two bodies again, turning to Simon he asked, "Are any of these the bloke who fired at you, Simon?" He looked at the man on the log to see if he would let Simon move towards the bodies. Bongo nodded, Roo continued to keep his pistol on Nulla while Bongo covered the youth.

"That one," said Simon pointing to Greg, "the one with half his head shot off. That's the bloke that fired on us. I don't recognise the other one though," he said as he walked back to Nulla his hands still in the air.

"Now answer our questions. Who are you and what are you doing here?" Bongo was uncomfortable and exhausted from the climb to the top of the hill. It had taken him ages to climb up on one leg and no sooner had he sat down to inspect the bodies than these interlopers turned up.

Trusting his instincts Nulla continued. "We've come up from Adelaide with a group of civilians. We're on our way to Birdsville to join up with Sundown's Commando and..." He stopped talking because both Bongo and Roo had their mouths open in astonishment.

"Say that again?" said Bongo wanting to hear a bit more before he let on that he knew what this bloke was talking about.

"You are from Sundown's Commando aren't you? Bloody beauty!" Nulla dropped his hands and squatted on his haunches. As he spoke he pulled out his tobacco pouch and began making himself a cigarette to put the two riflemen at ease, and because he needed a smoke. It also gave him the opportunity to go for his pistol if his instincts were wrong. Simon sat down too but he just sat there not knowing what to do.

Bongo looked at Roo who nodded but kept his weapon pointed in their general direction. Bongo now rested his AK on his knees.

"You those blokes we've been chatting with from down south? OK, what's the name of the old man in your group?" he asked.

Simon's eyes brightened. "That's easy, his name is Phil. He's an old historian or something, but he can do magic in his workshop."

Nulla hadn't taken his eyes off Roo nor had Roo taken his eyes off Nulla. The two warriors were rightly very wary of the other. It was the black border-collie who ended the stand-off. At the very moment Simon answered the dog stepped up to Nulla and licked his hand. Black Dog then sat on Nulla's foot reaching his head up to the aboriginal cavalry sergeant for a scratch.

"Well, if Black Dog says you're welcome, then who am I to say otherwise. I'm Bongo, this is Roo, he doesn't talk much." Bongo tried to stand but his leg was now so stiff he had to sit back down. "As you can see we've had a run in with these two bastards here and are a little shot up."

Nulla forgot about his pistol, drew deeply on his cigarette and stood up, slowly. He and Simon walked forward to shake hands with the two wounded commandos.

"What happened here Bongo? I can see the marks on the ground that tell me there was a fight. There's an awful lot of blood spread around here too." He stopped talking and waited for an explanation that would answer the story of the tracks.

To the trained bushman any footprint or mark on the ground told a story that rarely lied and he now wanted to know what was going on. Each new piece of information he saw written on the ground just led to more confusion. Two very wounded men, on the top of a hill with two very dead men and yet the story of the tracks was that the two dead men had killed each other.

"Roo and I had a bit of a fight with the Wilpena Pound mob run by the Wilson family. They turned out to be part of the terrorists in this area, they run the whole Flinders Ranges. We met up with Roo's cousin, Riley, you'll meet him tonight. Riley and his family are hidden in the mountains behind us because these two bastards were trying to kill them, and us. These two have been looking us for the past week or so and we've finally met up. When we saw them this morning it appears they'd rather kill each other than kill us."

Bongo pointed to the bodies individually. "That's Greg, one of the Wilson bully boys, and apparently you know him already. He attacked this bloke, Joey, his cousin. Joey then shot Greg while we watched from the scrub down there. We decided to finish the fight for them and shot Joey. Not bad for a days work. Two arse-holes no longer stealing oxygen from good folks like us." He stopped speaking to ask, "So what's your connection with them?"

Nulla nodded for Simon to tell his story. "Me and my friends were doing some target practice near Arkaroola village, inside a big stone building just over that hill. When we came out we were fired at. There was no warning just a single shot that just missed us. When we looked to see where the shot came from we saw two men fighting. One of them, this bloke here," Simon nudged Greg's body with the toe of his boot, "stabbed the man he was fighting then he stood up and fired at us again. We skirmished forward like Nulla showed us and he ran away. Looks like he came here."

Bongo asked about the other man who had stopped Greg from shooting them. Simon described him and both Bongo and Roo stared at each other.

"Laurie? That's bad, really bad. Laurie was a gentleman," said Bongo his face showing the pain he felt for the loss of another good man. "The bloke who saved you was our friend. He's got a wife and kids, poor things. I'd better mention it to Riley, they were mates from way back."

While this was all happening Luke had been watching through his binoculars. He started freaking out when he saw Nulla and Simon put their hands in the air and walk to the top of the hill. His first thought was to prepare to assault the hill and rescue his friends but when he checked a moment later he noticed them all shaking hands and sitting together like old mates.

'This is outright confusing,' he thought to himself. *'My orders were to wait here unless Nulla and Simon were attacked. But they aren't being attacked... not now, so... I'll just stay here I guess.'*

Luke scooped some of the dirt off the fire and blew on the ashes, it roared back into life. He put the billy on to make a cup of tea to calm his nerves.

Nulla looked carefully at the two wounded men in front of him. "I think you'd better tell us a bit about what you think we should do next. My mob are on our way to Birdsville. I just spoke to your fellows and they're expecting us. But they didn't tell me they had some of you here in the wilderness. In your current condition I guess you might want a lift back home?"

"We'll meet with Riley tonight and discuss what to do, Nulla. But I have a feeling our stay here is over. The Flinders Ranges are out of contention as our new home. The whole damn place is riddled with Revelationists and I'd give a million dollars to be back at Birdsville right now," said Bongo. "What I would like though is for one of you to help me get back down to the bottom of this hill. We can build up our fire and make some lunch and a billy of tea. It took me all morning to climb this darn hill and I really don't want to bum-hop down on these sharp stones and spinifex spines."

"Yep, no worries. If you don't mind I'm sending Simon to collect the weapons we dropped back there. He can then go back and tell everyone we've made contact with the Birdsville commandos. That'll certainly cheer everybody up I can tell you. I'll stay here tonight and meet this Riley friend of yours and we'll work out a plan." Nulla saw the three men nod then spoke to Simon. "Simon, grab my AK for me then take Luke back to the vehicles. Tell everyone to prepare to leave first thing tomorrow. I'll stay here and come back for you in the morning."

"Yes, boss," said Simon. He retrieved Nulla's weapon then headed back to Luke and the group at the caravan park to deliver the news. They had finally met up with the Birdsville commando and were soon to be on their way to freedom and safety.

That night Riley sat with the three men and they came up with a simple plan: they would pack up and head out at first light for Birdsville. Riley knew there was no future for he and his family hiding in the mountains like this. It was just a matter of time before the Wilson's found and executed them. Riley and his group were now responsible for the deaths of all four of Jack Wilson's henchmen. All were related to the Wilson clan and there was no way old man Kelvin Wilson, the clan patriarch, would let that go unpunished.

"Nulla, you've come at the right time. I'll be spending the night with my wife and kids up in the cave, I'll then come down here at dawn. We can get my truck and meet everyone on the track at the bottom of the hill. I just hope the Wilson's haven't found it already and aren't waiting for me to collect it," said Riley.

"Why don't I go with you? I've got arms and legs," he smiled at Roo and Bongo, "and can provide support if anything goes wrong."

Riley looked at him. "Thanks Nulla, yes, that would be good. I don't think they have anyone here otherwise Greg and Joey wouldn't have been by themselves. I've hidden the truck pretty well but these bastards, well, you just never know."

Nulla looked at the sky, it was getting close to sunset. "We can go and get it now if you want, before full dark. It'll give us a head start in the morning," he suggested.

"Yep," said Riley, "let's do it. An extra hour in the morning will mean I get to spend a bit more time in bed with the missus."

While Roo and Bongo set up their prospectors hut for one extra visitor and prepared dinner from the food Riley had brought down for them, Nulla and Riley rode the horses to where the truck was hidden. Riley took Red Dog and Blue Dog to be his scouts while they picked up his truck.

The group arrived at the vehicles just on dark. Riley sent the dogs ahead to make sure there were no visitors. It was then a long circuitous route back to the base of the lookout hill where they parked their vehicle ready for the morrow.

While the three ate their meal Riley headed back to his family for the night.

"What about those bodies up there, did you want to bury them in the morning?" asked Nulla.

Bongo looked at Roo then at Nulla. "Nah," he said trying to talk while shoveling in spoonfuls of Katie's delicious brain and organ stew. "Let the dingo's eat them. They and their cousins were the most evil men I've known and I've known a few. I just hope the poor dingoes don't choke on their filthy hides."

Chapter 9 - Blondie's Secret

When the two Bushmasters and the ASLAV arrived back at Birdsville they were all treated as hero's. Tricia and Lorraine met the wounded at the front door while Gail took delivery of Pedro's medicine. Bill, Wiram and Cambra left straight away to start work on the Cessna repairs. Once in the shed they began what they had been waiting to do: fix that aeroplane.

Pedro had remained quite well the day Fat Boy and Blondie left on their mission but then he had slipped back into a light coma, everyone was worried. With the return of the Mount Isa fighting patrol there had formed a small group of visitors in Pedro's room. Gail had to 'shoo' everyone out while she and Tricia prepared him for his injections.

Fat Boy wasn't impressed. "Me and Blondie and the boys wanted to wish Pedro good luck. Why can't we go in?" he asked, his voice subdued for once. He was still recovering from his binge with Iceman Ed and wasn't in the best of moods either.

"Fat Boy, bringing the dead back to life isn't easy. Please, just let us do our job," whispered Lorraine as she stepped in to collect more bandages for the wounded in the 'hospital wing'.

Her eyes were gentle as she added, "Pedro's really sick right now, Fat Boy. These medicines you brought back should help a lot but we need just a half hour to sort them out. Once he's had his meds then we'll let you in." She'd come a long way with her bedside manners from the time Cambra had words with her in the Marree hotel – it now seemed a lifetime ago.

Tricia was standing behind her and together they ushered everyone back into the corridor. She told them to go and get some lunch. That should give them enough time to find out if the drugs worked or not she said.

"Sundown, can't you make them let me stay? That's my little brother in there," said Fat Boy sounding like a little boy himself.

"Mate, Fat Boy, one day these nurses may need to save your butt and then they'll do the same thing - what's best for you not you're friends," said Sundown putting his hand on Fat Boy's shoulder and directing him to the dining room. "Even though we all love Pedro we need to give him every chance to recover. If that means we go and eat some lunch then so be it. Besides, in our hospital room Tricia, Gail and Lorraine outrank us all."

The nurses and the two army medics were busy. They didn't lose anyone and only four stayed in the hospital wing over-night. The others were allowed to recover as out-patients.

The two soldiers killed were prepared for burial while the riggers went for a walk with Sundown and the major to select their grave sites. Only last week the commando had buried the two Birdsville oldies on a slight rise above the flood line. This was where they headed now.

"You know what, Sundown," said Major Vic Thompson, "our boys fought like true warriors. I'm proud of them. Now I know how you feel about your commando. I'd like to thank you for letting us participate in this action. I have decided to leave Bushmaster One One Bravo and One One Charlie behind with your commando to strengthen your force."

At that Sundown stopped walking, Assassin and Beamy stopped too. All three turned to look at the major. "Major Thompson, that's welcome news. We sure could use the additional fire power," said Sundown nodding his head as he thought of the possibilities this presented his community.

"Sundown," said Assassin, "that means we can keep an eye on the north and south routes into Birdsville. It's going to ease the workload for our boys." Turning to the major he extended his hand. "Major Thompson, thank you and welcome to Sundown's Commando. I think we have a better chance at kicking the terrorist's arses all the way out of here with the joint Alice Springs and Sundown's Commando."

The major's face lit up. To be accepted by these rugged fighting men was reward enough for his men's efforts, a sublime pleasure. The major finally found the heroes he was looking for in Sundown and his commando.

"Well boys, if I hadn't gone on that patrol with Cambra and Halo and witnessed their bravery against the Ravens Claws myself I wouldn't have bothered coming back here today." Turning back to Sundown he said, "Sundown, your commando is what Australia needs right now and I aim to make sure the government recognise that. I'd like to leave for the Alice in a few days time. That should give my boys a bit of a break and time to recover from their wounds. We certainly took a bit of a pasting against those terrorists yesterday." He paused for a moment to wipe the back of his hand across his moist eyes.

"My boys took it to them too, I can assure you. They walked into the enemy fire like, like…" He closed his eyes as his head swam in heroic images, "like the ANZACs at ANZAC Cove. My goodness they were a sight to inspire the hearts of every Australian." He stopped talking to pull out his handkerchief so that he could wipe his eyes properly and then he blew his nose loudly.

"Major, we heard how well your troops fought. They gave covering fire for Cambra and Halo, it got them out of a sticky situation. Cambra said your boys didn't flinch even when the Raven's Claw second wave arrived and began cutting them down," said Assassin. Even the cherub faced commando had a tear in his eye watching the emotions criss-crossing the major's face.

Sundown leaned across and put his arm around the majors shoulders as they walked. "You're now blooded to us and we to you. Our community proudly accepts Alice Springs Command as our brothers-in-arms."

They held the funeral that afternoon, everyone attended including the wounded.

Before dinner that night Sundown and Major Thompson called a meeting to debrief everyone. Only the front line warriors were invited to attend. Once the debrief was over everyone went in to the main lounge for dinner and drinks. Stories were told, the beer flowed and the guitars came out.

As the dinner plates were cleared away Lulu and Danni shyly entered. Each carefully carried something of what appeared to be of great value in their hands. The girls called for everyone to be quiet.

Halo stood and accepted the first flag from Lulu. He invited Major Thompson and Sundown to come to the front of the room. Everyone sat expectantly, even Fat Boy was quiet.

"Sundown. Our fighting girls have stitched the *Mount Isa* battle honours onto our flag and we ask that you accept it on behalf of our commando." Halo held the flag out for all to see. In big letters was stitched: '*Mount Isa*'. Below were written: *The Mines*, *Marree* and *Birdsville*.

Halo then solemnly took the next valuable object from Danni. He stepped solemnly across to address Major Thompson.

"Major Thompson," Halo began, "a few days ago we set out together as separate commands. Together we contacted the enemy and fought a vicious battle. Our casualties were high and sadly two of our Alice Springs Command brothers died protecting Cambra, Blondie, Fat Boy and myself. We bear witness to the bravery of your troops as they stood tall against overwhelming odds. Not a one shirked their duty despite the incredible volume of incoming enemy fire. We saw acts of heroism above and beyond what is expected of front line troops in any war and in any army. We are proud and honoured to be called your friends and comrades. Please accept this Alice Springs Command battle flag as a small gift of appreciation for your sacrifices."

The major pulled out his now well-used handkerchief and blew his nose. With tears in his eyes he proudly accepted the flag.

Halo saluted the major then turned to face the assembled members of Alice Springs Command and Sundown's Commando.

"Please, be upstanding." The lounge room was immediately filled with the sound of people respectfully standing at their tables. Some remained seated because of their injuries.

"Attention!" barked Halo. As one the joint command slid their feet together. In a loud voice he announced, "May God bless us here today because he has certainly stopped blessing the Revelationists! Now drink up!" He paused, a confused look spread across his face when everyone remained standing. His eye's flashed bright as he remembered. Bellowing like a parade ground sergeant he called, "Dismissed!"

There were some chuckles from the hardened men and women as they settled down to their drinking and bonding. Wiram couldn't stop smiling as he walked over and put his arm around Halo's shoulders.

"You dopey prick, Halo, military protocol will never be the same from now on. But by hell you sure made me shed a tear." He gave Halo a 'noogy' putting him in a headlock and bending his head down to rub his knuckles into his scarred scalp.

McFly called out, "Halo, since when does a civilian give parade ground orders in a hotel lounge room?"

"Don't worry about him, Halo, we're damn proud of you and the girls. I wish I'd thought of doing something like that," called Shadow offering to put McFly in a headlock to give him a noogy too.

Sundown was impressed, actually, he was quite overwhelmed. He nodded to Halo acknowledging his service to them all. Handing the major a beer he asked him what he would do with the flag.

"I'm not sure. It isn't official until its approved, in triplicate, by our commanding officer, but I'd like to have it here on the wall beside yours, if I may. And can I ask the girls to make a separate one for my ASLAV?" He stood at just below Sundown's height and looked like a little boy for just that second.

Sundown grinned. "You bloody-well can," he said and called out to the teenagers, "Danni, can you and Lulu come over here for a moment, please?"

"Yes, boss?" asked Danni as the two skipped across like school girls, their faces beaming.

"First of all, from myself and the commando, thank you for a wonderfully prepared and presented surprise. Secondly, Major Thompson has a request of you." He looked to the major who leaned forward so they could hear him above the noise of the lounge room.

"Danni and Lulu, from the bottom of my heart, thank you. That is the most wonderful thing I have ever set eyes on. I would like to have our flag up on the wall there next to yours. And if you don't mind, would you be so kind as to make me a smaller one that I can pin up inside my command vehicle?" He blinked as more tears flowed.

"Sure major, we can get that done tomorrow for you. Can we say that it was fun and a pleasure to be with your One One Bravo fellers on patrol, they were real gentlemen. What your troop did was very brave. You saved our Cambra and we won't ever forget that. We're real sorry for your losses, and poor Captain Lewis, losing his brother was horrible. We wish we could do something for him," said Danni, who was no longer the shy little teenager the commando rescued so long ago that it seemed like forever.

"Thanks girls and I'm sorry for the captain too. His brother was a hero and gave his life for all of us here. But now is not the time for tears, this is his wake and we celebrate his life, not his death. Come on, share a drink with me girls," offered the major brightening and feeling a little frisky as he grabbed their arms in his and walked towards the bar.

"Major, we're only a tiny bit under age, but if Pinkie says we can have one of Andy's shandies then we'll drink you under the darn table!" laughed Lulu.

After they'd had a few drinks Bill, Cambra and Wiram headed off with Beamy in tow to continue their work on the aeroplane. They looked in on Pedro on their way out where Gail told them that they had better work fast because he didn't appear to be responding to the medication.

Sundown tried to talk with Blondie and Fat Boy about the Mount Isa terrorists but they kept putting him off. Neither were in the mood to talk or mix with the others. He put it down to the stress of their ordeal but he wasn't going to give in.

"Fat Boy, for Pete's sake what happened. I haven't had a chance to debrief either of you and now is as good a time as any. Neither of you are interested in partying and I've got work to do so come into my office and we'll get this over and done with." He walked towards his office and the two obligingly, though reluctantly, followed.

"Sundown there's not much to say really. We got in, made contact with the bikie gang and Fat Boy kept them occupied while I sorted out the medication and saw Iggy for the aeroplane parts. It was quick 'n easy and then we hit the road block and it nearly fell apart on us. If it wasn't for the army boys we'd not be here." Blondie flicked the hair out of her eyes and stared at Sundown.

"Blondie, I know something's fishy when I smell fish. My demon is restless and he recognises a fellow demon in you." Sundown finally said what he'd wanted to say since he first laid eyes on Blondie and Fat Boy. "I want to know who you really are and we aren't leaving here until you tell me."

They sat quietly sipping their beers for a good minute when Fat Boy looked up at his sister then back again. She nodded so he began to talk.

"Sundown, first of all we aren't husband and wife - Blondie's my little sister. We've been playing the game of lies for so long it's hard to stop." He spoke softly and slowly, his vibrancy lost, for the time being at least.

Fat Boy looked at Blondie again, she was calm and in control as always. "I got smashed off my face at the strip club with my old mates in the gang while Blondie did all the work. We've got this down pat you know. I keep the opposition busy while my sister gets on with the job." He stopped to allow Blondie to take over.

"Sundown, I don't want you talking about this to anyone, we've still got unfinished business with the Revelationists." She paused and a funny smile played across her lips as she looked deeply into his soul. "My demon says I can trust you so I will tell you everything."

Sundown nodded in acknowledgment, waiting silently.

"I'm one of the Tajna Služba, the church's secret police. I've been working under-cover with them for years. I've killed, I've done a lot of bad things to survive. If the people here knew the truth they'd turn against us. Fat Boy and I don't want that, we need you." She stopped talking to look at him with a frankness that he knew expressed total honesty and respect, "We need your friendship," she said simply.

"After our little trip up north it's unlikely the church will be very kind to us, at least those in Mount Isa won't be. They're feuding with the other churches, that lot always did, so it's unlikely word has gone out about our raid. Anyway, I can pull rank with some of the big boys, they like my, um, good looks and bubbly personality."

She smiled a bitter smile and continued. "If ever we need to draw the Tajna Služba card it's still there. I can say that I was on Tajna Služba business that day in Mount Isa and leave it at that. But the Tajna Služba are a dying breed. Last count there's only a half dozen or so of us left alive in Australia. The church elders will be more than happy when we're all gone. We're now of little use to the church, their membership and their Priests. The Tajna Služba have done what we were created for and our time is almost over."

Their commander nodded and asked quietly, "What were you created for, may I ask?"

"When we were young we lived all over South Australia where ever our father could find work. We're Wilsons so we were given preferential treatment where ever we went in these parts." Blondie looked across at Fat Boy who laughed harshly.

"Sundown, my little sister and I were abused and brutalised by our own family. When we were old enough to fend for ourselves we left the Flinders Ranges and travelled around Australia. To stop the attention we were getting, me, the tough fat bastard and Blondie, the gorgeous model, pretended we were husband and wife. It helped stop the unwanted attention and it stuck." He nodded at Blondie to continue.

"We joined a few bikie gangs and then the church. We were popular with everyone. Fat Boy and his charming ways attracted the tough boys and my looks opened doors to the church elders and their bank accounts. We ran drugs and information all around the country. We were indoctrinated into the Tajna Služba and continued with what we did best: running people and weapons, setting up meetings, organising training on selected farms and outback properties throughout Australia.

"You could say we helped make the Ravens Claws, elite Talons, Crusaders and the Deaths Heads what they are today, the best. We handled the money and the contracts. We made a fortune Sundown, the church made us filthy rich." She eased back in her seat and stopped talking. Blondie finished the rest of her beer. "And that, Sundown, is our story. Tell anyone and I'll have to kill you." A demonic smiled crept across her face.

"If I tell anyone it will be because I've already sliced your beautiful throat," he replied with a matching demonic smile.

Sundown forcefully stopped his demon playing Blondie's game. He cleared his throat, "What I need from you is information on every Revelationist battalion surrounding us. I need to know everything you didn't tell Major Thompson in your debrief. I don't give a rat's arse what you did before the apocalypse, you probably already know that. When you put your lives on the line for my best mate, Pedro, it made you my blood brother and sister." He put out his hand to grasp theirs and they repeated, "Blood brothers and sisters."

"If you need me or my brother to kill for you, all you need do is ask, Sundown. You're someone we can trust and my instincts tell me you are just like us, ruthless. Us demons are always true to our word," she added with a slight smile.

"That we are," he answered. He took a deep breath to clear his mind to prepare for the detailed work ahead of them. "OK, let's get down to the details shall we." Sundown pulled out a note pad and began writing as they spoke of what they'd held back from the major.

Captain Lewis was in a bad way after losing his brother. He struggled to mix with the rest of the boys, even the alcohol did nothing to ease his grief. Pinkie was watching and at a nod from Tricia they both settled down and spent most of the night talking with him. Every now and then one of the soldiers would come over to lend a kind word and there was not a moment where he felt left out.

The wake continued long into the night. Andy kept the diesel generator on for the lights and the beer in the freezer was just cold enough to satisfy even the thirstiest digger.

Assassin and Beamy swapped CB duty so that they could both enjoy the party. The boys had their guitars out and Lorraine played piano. Even Billie did a little entertaining, playing the spoons. When his rum ration ran out Andy gave him credit for another which made the old timer's grin broader than a wide-mouthed desert frog.

Ever the entertainer he prattled to his growing audience. "I thought me spoons were out of tune but yer know wot? The more rum I drink the more in-tune they sound!" He smacked his gums together and sang another bush ballad keeping time with his spoons a'tapping.

Towards midnight Gail came in to get Tricia and Lorraine. Together they quietly left to look in on Pedro. The aged warrior was having a bad reaction to the drugs Blondie and Fat Boy had brought from Mount Isa. Beamy was off duty at the time and was soon sent to the mechanics shed to tell them to get a move on.

"You'd better have the Cessna ready by first light, because Pedro might not make it past tomorrow."

Chapter 10 - Crossing the Simpson Desert

The morning was chilly but it didn't stop Bill and his crew from firing up the engine on the Cessna 172. It made a sputtering noise and at first the mechanics thought it would die on them. But, with a chug and a puff of smoke it burst into a full throated roar. The three men looked at it in amazement and slapped each other on the back laughing. They'd been up all night and were exhausted, but this made up for it.

Lorraine hurried in when she heard Sundown wanted to talk to her. "What's wrong, did you need something urgent?" she asked slightly out of breath.

"I sure do Lorraine. I want you to escort Pedro in Bill's plane to Alice Springs - right now. I need Gail to stay here on the CB and Tricia is busy with the wounded. I know you've been flat out with the wounded too, but you know Pedro's condition better than anyone else." He looked at the dark circles under her eyes and her untidy hair. "You've been up all night haven't you?" he asked kindly, knowing she was extremely competent and completely dedicated to their little community.

"I'm exhausted, Sundown, but Pedro's sick, very sick. The drugs Fat Boy and Blondie brought back have been out of cold storage for nearly a year and they're useless. In fact they appear to have made him sicker than he already was. The only thing of any use are the pain killers. If we can get him to the hospital in Alice Springs he has a chance," said the tall, peaches-and-cream faced British nurse.

"I'll just check with Bill to find out when he's ready to go. He's out at the aerodrome running it in now. Are you OK about flying in that patched up contraption?" asked Sundown with some concern in his voice.

"If Bill's brave enough to fly it I'm brave enough to go with Pedro in it. Yes, count me in." As tired as she was Lorraine scurried out to prepare Pedro for the trip.

"Hey, Beamy, is it all go-for-launch with the repairs?" Sundown asked as he wandered out to the shed and met with Bill's assistants.

"Hi, Sundown," replied a very tired Beamy. "It sounds like Bill's got the thing going well enough to fly. As far as we can tell it's in reasonably good nick. Bill said the plane was an expensive one and had all the bells and whistles. It's been kept in good condition, he said. Better wish him luck because he's not a pilot but a mechanic," said Beamy with a wry smile. Sundown wasn't sure if it was in fear or joy.

Bill told everyone to step away while he tried to get the Cessna into the air. The One One Alpha communications operator had radioed Alice Springs to keep an eye out for the Cessna, they gave the aeroplane's call sign and details. Bill set his radio to the correct frequency and spoke to the command centre in Alice Springs himself.

With a nervousness he'd not felt for some years Bill crept the plane out on to the recently repaired runway and taxied to the end. He put the plane's nose into the slight morning breeze, kicked up the revs and the plane responded beautifully. The boys on the ground cheered as Bill raced down the runway, lifted off the ground and into the air like he was born with wings.

"Holy crap! Look at that, Beamy, he can really fly that thing," called Cambra in amazement.

The boys hung around for five minutes but got bored watching Bill loop the loop and spin, slip and slide like a pro. They brought up several aviation fuel drums and prepared to fill the tank when he came back down.

Captain Lewis had his Bushmaster on the side of the airfield. He called out letting the boys know that Bill was coming in to land.

Slowly, gently, Bill eased his plane on to the runway and taxied over to the fuel drum. He climbed out after switching off and going through his checks. He hadn't spoken a word and everyone was politely waiting. There was now quite a group of spectators from the hotel who'd heard the noise and had come out to see the spectacle.

"What?" Bill asked when he noticed the crowd. With a slightly startled look on his face he asked again. "What's everyone staring at?"

Wiram stretched out his hand and they shook. "You, that's what! You did it Bill, you did it!"

Sundown had Pedro and Lorraine sitting in the four wheel drive waiting to get in the plane. He called to Bill, "Nice work mate, when you're ready we'll load you up. Pedro's awake but he doesn't quite know where he is."

After the plane had lifted off and was just a speck in the sky Pinkie leaned on Sundown's shoulder and with a worried voice said, "Sundown, what if the plane doesn't make it? What if Pedro, you know, gets to Alice Springs and they've got no more medications?"

"Pinkie, I don't want to think of that." He paused for a second. "Hey, I thought we agreed, no more worries because we're about to head off on our own adventure. It's our second honeymoon, remember?" He grabbed her hands and did a little jig.

"I know but last time we went on a honeymoon the world ended. What will we find when we get back from this one I wonder," she said, looking into his now closed face.

"Pinkie, you sure know how to put a damper on things don't you." He dropped her hands and walked away to the hotel by himself.

Shadow was watching and walked over to Pinkie. "What's wrong with him?" Shadow asked.

"Hi, Shadow. He's worried about his mate, Pedro. I should have been a bit more sensitive, silly me." Pinkie looked thoughtful. "Poor Sundown, he takes things so seriously sometimes," she said and the two headed back to the hotel to pack their gear.

When they got there Billie was already sitting in the front seat of the four wheel drive.

"Hi missus! Hi Shadow! Come on, hurry up, I'm bored and I want to get on me way. I've got family out there and I'm in a hurry to see them," he called while fumbling to hide his stolen bottles of rum under the seat.

The major had spent many hours with Sundown, Wiram and Andy the previous night discussing the trip across the Simpson Desert. Captain Lewis was back from the dark place he had been and was now organising the departure of their small convoy. Sergeant Ahmet was called in for his briefing and things began to fall into place for their trip to visit the Australian Third Army Headquarters in Alice Springs.

The three vehicles were now ready for their trek across the desert. The Bushmaster led the convoy followed by Sundown's four wheel drive and the major brought up the rear with his ASLAV. Although the going was rough everyone was in high spirits even the soldiers who were sadly leaving their new friends and heading back to the boredom of the Alice. They had some stories to tell their mates though and that was something they looked forward to.

Major Thompson had his mini-flag stuck up inside his ASLAV and every now and then he caught himself admiring it. The night before he did have a few drinks with the two aboriginal teenagers and they did drink him under the table, well sort of, he admitted. Andy's home brew had a kick and the major resorted to cutting it by half with some of Mel's lemonade made from bush fruits, fermented to bring out the citrus flavours. It wasn't alcoholic but it tasted nice and even nicer mixed with Andy's home brewed beer.

The whole exercise of finding, meeting and mixing it with the Birdsville commando had been an incredibly moving experience for the major. He came from a family of soldiers who could trace their lineage back to the Crimean War and the charge of the Light Brigade. He wasn't one hundred percent certain that his ancestor was part of the charge but the information he had uncovered suggested he most likely was. To have been in a similar situation, leading his men into battle against overwhelming odds and against a well trained enemy was the highlight of his career.

The second highlight was Halo handing him the flag and battle honours for his squadron. The major felt a few tears form in the corners of his eyes as he remembered how he felt accepting the flag. He wiped them away with the back of his hand so no one would see.

Each troop carrier now consisted of driver, communications operator, gunner and troop commander plus himself in One Zero Bravo and Captain Lewis in One One Alpha. Five in each armoured carrier plus the five civilians.

Major Thompson smiled to himself as he watched the landscape change from arid dirt and stones to the soft sands of the true desert. He was looking forward to every day of this trip with his troops. The major was in command once again and he felt comfortable, confident and wildly courageous.

That night they parked on the edge of the Simpson Desert almost on the Northern Territory border itself. The troopers had prepared the evening's meal and everyone was relaxed. As it grew dark the boys began talking of the contact they had with the Raven's Claws in Mount Isa.

"Sundown, what does it mean when there's two companies in the one town? I've never heard of that before," asked the captain.

"I spoke to Blondie and Fat Boy and they said they were from the single Raven's Claws battalion but it was split into two," replied Sundown. "One is their specially trained Talons, they've had specialised commando training, they run to about company strength. The other is the basic soldier and they form the Ravens Claw Battalion. Sometimes they're posted in the Longreach area to support the smaller force there. The soldiers in Longreach are called the Crusaders of Light to distinguish themselves from the Ravens Claw of Mount Isa. The two churches compete against each other too." He reached for his tobacco pouch but realised he'd given up smoking months ago.

"They compete with each other to exterminate prisoners," he continued." Can you believe that? They go out and raid some poor bastard's farm then set them free in the scrub. They give them a gun or two and a head start. The Revelationists send out a squad from each company. Whoever brings back the most heads wins. They call it the 'Thunderdome Cup'."

"What is it about these terrorists, Sundown? We've been fighting them for nearly a year now and they still keep coming at us. They've got the whole country at their feet yet they want to exterminate us - we're in the middle of the darn desert. It's just too strange to believe." McFly said while sipping on his cup of tea.

Billie found he could easily sneak into his tent and put a few drops of his precious 'mountain dew' into his tea and was feeling quite cheery.

"McFly," Billy said, "back in me dad's day anyone who acted like these terrorists do now, they'd go out to their house, take them outside and give them a floggin'. That's what these bastards need, a good floggin'."

"It's not that easy, Billie," added Shadow. "This is a world-wide organisation that have billions of dollars to play with. Millions of members handed over their entire pay each week to support this apocalypse. With that amount of money comes power and with power there's always corruption. They corrupted their way into positions of power."

The major had his say too. "You're right, Shadow. It takes a lot of money to persuade people to look the other way. I'd say they had this prepared for years."

"At least ten years we've heard, major," said McFly who had many a chat with Chan and John over the past months.

Dinner was served and the group eased back in their deck chairs eating, smoking and talking in small groups leaving the discussion to those interested in politics. Someone pulled out a harmonica and began playing softly. By late evening everyone was asleep except the communications operator and the dingoes yapping in the distance.

They were well into their trip when the four wheel drive's axle broke and they spent two days repairing it. That first night Billie was restless, he just couldn't sleep and lay outside in his swag beside the fire looking up at the stars. The Milky Way's light was almost as bright as the moon's.

McFly was up late seated by the fire too, he didn't notice Billie lying next to him. He nearly leaped out of his skin when he heard the old man's voice coming from beside him.

"Hey, McFly," said Billie.

"Shit, Billie! You scared the daylights out of me! What are you doing down there? I thought you were in bed," he said in a startled voice.

"Can't sleep. Me heads full o' songs and tribal stuff. The land's calling me." He sat up and found a chair to sit next to the desert fisherman. "This is my tribal country and it's making me restless. I need to go off tomorrow to be with me people and talk to the spirits. I'll be back the next day. But right now I'm feeling the land. That's why I'm laying here on the ground. I can feel the spirits of me people, me blood, it's here in the earth itself," Billie explained.

McFly thought for a while. "Billie, I thought your father was Afghan, like Roo's grandfather," he spoke softly so as not to disturb those trying to sleep.

"He was. Me dad and Roo's grandfather came from the same village in Afghanistan and they travelled to Australia together after the war was over. This is from me mothers side. Like Roo me mother was from here and me uncles and aunts, me cousins and grandparents are all tribal. When we visited our cousins they'd always want to take me away to learn men's business. But me mum and dad always tried to stop them. They said I was going to be raised like a white fella and have opportunities. I think they were afraid that if they didn't do what the white missionaries told them they'd take me and me sister away to live in the city. They took a lot of my cousins away back in those days." Billie mused for a while before continuing.

"When I was twelve I was taken one night by my mother's father and me uncles. I was terrified but curious. I was gone for a week and went through their initiations. See these scars?" He opened his shirt to show a series of scars on his chest and arms. "That's to show I'm an initiated warrior. Bloody scary bastards that lot are. I think that's what me body is telling me. I'm in their country now and they want me back. They're calling me."

McFly shivered in the cool night air and pulled his jacket closer around his shoulders. "Billie, if you go walkabout tomorrow can you take me with you?"

Billie looked carefully at McFly. He liked this bright young man and knew him to be honest and staunch.

"OK, but you do as I say and nothing else. If we meet my people out there don't you do or say anything. Let me talk because we're on their land now. This is their sacred ground and your feet don't belong here. You white fella's ain't their blood. When we get away from here I'll need to do a ceremony to introduce you to my tribal spirits - otherwise they might kill you."

Once again McFly shivered but at the same time he sensed an adventure that he wouldn't miss for the world.

That morning the boys were up early to get started on the repairs. Billie and McFly had a quiet word with Sundown and the major. McFly mentioned to Shadow that Billie was taking him for a walk in the desert with Billie. She positively encouraged him to explore the desert with their friend.

He took his sniper rifle in case he saw some kangaroos for meat. Billie had a bag with food and tobacco, he also hid a bottle of rum in his bag as a gift for his people.

By mid morning Billie found what he was looking for. It was a shallow depression in the sandy landscape that contained a circle of spinifex grass. While they were walking Billie had collected various barks, herbs, grasses and resins that he'd found in the desert scrub.

In the middle of the depression Billie lit a fire. Every now and then he threw this mix of plant material to make smoke which he directed McFly to breathe in. Then he began a ceremony to ask permission for this white man to walk upon tribal country.

Billie stood naked and danced while singing a strange song that numbed McFly's mind. Billie told his friend to sit quietly throughout the ceremony. Each time he began to nod off Billie would hit him with a whisk of grass stems to keep him awake. The smoke from the hallucinogenic herbs and resins and the drone of the song had their effect and McFly soon entered an altered state of consciousness.

Billie kept on dancing and stamping his feet to the rhythm of the song that soon made McFly float out of his body. McFly felt more alive than he had ever felt before in his life. The next moment he awoke to see two strangers had joined them. McFly now felt afraid, very afraid.

One was an old woman and the other an old man, neither wore clothing and neither spoke. He intuited they were spirit people, custodians of the land.

They warned him that he should go no further, this was as far as he was permitted. McFly asked them why and they explained that this was not his country, that he was the wrong blood. To wander beyond, like he wanted to do, would be disrespectful. McFly felt disappointed but agreed to return to the vehicles.

Before he woke he saw a group of people, fighting, vicious hand to hand fighting and the old woman said, very clearly, "*It is out of your control. Duck, don't forget, duck, then leave it be, walk away.*" She said this twice and then he awoke with a sudden startle.

'Billie! Billie?!" he said reflexively still in a light trance.

"I'm here, mate. Did you see?" asked Billie, looking into McFly's eyes to make sure he was fully back and not still hallucinating.

"I saw an old man and an old woman. They were your people. I was flying and saw the desert and people fighting…" he talked quickly trying to fit everything in before he forgot it. "And the old woman said it wasn't my fault and I had to duck then let it go, let it be." He shook his head in bewilderment.

"Yes, sometimes they talk and sometimes they don't. Did they invite you to walk their country?" asked the old warrior.

McFly paused and looked carefully at Billie for the first time since the ceremony. "No, they told me I had to go back, now. If I stay I'll die. Something about the land was in your blood and not mine. The land would kill me if I continued."

Billie nodded looking at the young man with a frown on his aged, weathered face. "Hmm, OK, get up off yer arse and come with me." He stood and led McFly to the top of a nearby sand dune. "See there?" he pointed to a speck on the horizon.

"That's the convoy. Just follow yer tracks back to the trucks and don't look back." Billie stopped talking to see if McFly was listening. McFly nodded, he understood.

"Mate," he repeated, "if you don't start out now and keep movin', the land will kill you. The spirit people told you what you needed to do to survive your encounter with the land. Don't disrespect them or you'll pay fer it. It could be a snake; you could trip over and break yer neck; you could have one of them strokes... McFly, don't think this is a game now, it's serious. Those old folks rarely talk to strangers. You're the first white fella I know of that has ever seen them and I've taken a few on that same journey I just took you on. They showed you enormous respect now show them the same. Just don't look back if you want to stay alive."

The old man held McFly's arm and guided him back to their tracks coming into the circle. "Walk. If all goes well I'll be back with you's tomorrow night." He smiled at McFly. "I saw my spirits in the dance too," he said excitedly. "They told me where I needed to go and what to do when I get there. I have tribal business and you have yours. I'll see you tomorrow." Billie stepped off in one direction while McFly fearfully stepped off in the other.

Chapter 11 - Sundown Dreamer

The following evening Billie stepped into the firelight and collapsed into one of the camp chairs. McFly was silent, he hadn't spoken of what he'd experienced to anyone, he simply didn't know how to put it into words. He nodded at Billie who smiled back and took the cup of tea one of the soldiers handed him.

"Are you all right, Billie?" asked Pinkie, handing him a plate of food.

"Sure missus. I visited me folk out there and had a grand time of it. But I'm a bit tuckered out right now so I'll just have a feed and a drink and get some shut-eye," he replied soberly and did just that. Billie was already asleep when the group began their regular camp fire discussions.

Conversation around the camp fire that night was lively. The axle was now repaired and the vehicles were given a good overhaul and service by the crew mechanics. Everyone was well rested and ready to continue. Some had wives and girlfriends in Alice Springs and the thought of being back with their loved ones began to excite them.

"Excuse me, Sundown?" asked Sergeant Tobi, the crew master of the ASLAV. "I was wondering if you could walk us through some of the engagements you've had with the Revelationists. You know, what things helped form the decisions you made. I was thinking you could help educate the boys in fighting the terrorists."

Sundown sipped at his port, the bottle at the major's side was almost empty. It too was one of Andy and Fat Boys inventions. Brew up the mash, distil the spirits, add cordial and you had Birdsville Gutrot Port. It was rough though, not as nice as Andy's home brewed beer.

"Tobi, I'm not the brilliant strategist of Sundown's Commando, that was Shamus and Pedro. I just pay attention to my betters and try to do my best. Shamus, now he was my hero. He lived his entire seventy odd years studying warfare and when he couldn't lead from the front he taught his art. Pedro was a sniper, a commando, he joined the CIA after the Vietnam war. Those two were my mentors so my successes are only because of them. As they say, I stand on the shoulders of giants."

He stopped and waved his empty mug at the major. Major Thompson looked at his own mug, topped it up and deliberately tipped the final dribble into Sundown's mug. The major smiled one of his endearing smiles of, *'got ya!'*.

"Major," said Sundown looking at the miserable few drops sitting in the bottom of his mug, "it seems your appetite for grog exceeds your good manners." He leaned across to the box containing a dozen bottles of Gutrot Port and pulled out a full bottle. He filled his mug then passed the bottle to Pinkie beside him. It went around the circle in the opposite direction to the major - *'got ya back!'* chuckled Sundown quietly to himself.

"Sorry, Tobi, I was distracted by my impolite friend here." He smiled to show he was having a little joke with the major. Everyone noticed how the major and Sundown competed with each other ever since the arrival of Alice Springs Command, and they quite enjoyed the entertainment too.

"When Pinkie and I met with Shamus and Pedro in Birdsville we talked of what we wanted to do, where we wanted to live. The world had just ended, there was no law or organised force to stop louts and terrorists doing whatever they wanted. So Shamus, Pedro and I chatted of the options presented to us. I asked questions and listened to their answers. Much like we're doing now."

One of the soldiers called out softly in the dark, "Who's this Shamus fella you're always talking about. I didn't see him at the Birdsville camp."

Pinkie looked up and spoke. "He was Pedro's friend. They lived out here for twenty or thirty years shooting kangaroos, selling the skins and doing odd jobs like that. Shamus was in the IRA and taught war things. I'm not sure what he actually did, but Pedro and Sundown seem to think he was an adviser for armies all around the world. He was the most beautiful person I've met but I get the feeling he was also responsible for a lot of horrible acts of terrorism." She stopped to wonder how she would reconcile the good and the bad of someone she loved so much.

"Shamus was a warrior through and through, you wouldn't want to be up against him that's for sure. I learned a lot and you know what, even though he died at our very first contact with the terrorists, I still talk to him," said Sundown easily.

Some of the men looked at each other confused. The same soldier went on, "Sundown, did I hear right? You talk to a dead man?"

Sundown chuckled. "Yep, you did hear me right. I dream him. Sometimes I deliberately dream him before I fall asleep at night and when I'm meditating I'll talk to him about the issues I've got. I've done that all my life - if I've a problem I meditate or dream the answer."

There were a few comments and the soldier went on. "Sundown, is Shamus like a ghost then?" He sounded a little spooked.

"I don't really know the answer to that question. You might just say he's a figment of my imagination. Sometimes it's real and sometimes it's like a dream. But what I learned from him before he passed on was more than enough for a lifetime of study. It's all inside my head and I access it by dreaming it, by bringing back conversations we had around the camp fire, at the bar or map room in the Marree Hotel. It's all inside my head. I add a few of the things I learn from Pedro and it forms, or solidifies, while I meditate or while I sleep."

Captain Lewis shifted his chair around to move out of the smoke from the fire. "So Sundown, let me get this straight, you dream your strategies?"

"Yes and no, captain. I deliberately dream conversations with Shamus. But when I'm in a contact I set it into action. I just act. I guess that's the best way to describe it. I know what to do and then I let go of thinking and just do it." He stopped talking because he didn't want to talk about his berserker demon, that was special.

The same young soldier spoke again. "Sundown, sorry to ask another question but there's two types of action: one is leadership and directing your troops; and then there's your own actions during the contact. Can you describe both for us?"

Sundown looked at the soldier and recognised him as the pimply-faced teenager who always asked questions so that if he died he wouldn't regret not asking that last one.

"OK, I'll try to describe what happens. First is information, intelligence. I need to know what's happening and that's not always easy, just ask your officers. Once I get the big picture I consider my troop strengths and weaknesses and position them as best I can. At the Marree Hotel fight we were outnumbered and out gunned. We had four and they had nearly thirty but we were resolute and our morale was high from knocking the stuffing out of their mates at the mines that morning. Even though our morale was high we were also exhausted. We had a sniper rifle, an old Lee Enfield 303, two AK47's and some sweaty dynamite. They had two machine guns and they sent two, eight man squads, against us." He paused to fill his mug again.

"We were lucky that Pedro and McFly here, kept knocking off the machine gunners while Halo and myself kept the two squads off our women folk." Sundown stopped and went quiet. No one interrupted but the pressure of the silence mounted forcing Sundown to continue. "You want to hear about my berserker don't you?"

There were nods and '*yes sirs*' around the camp fire, even the major and captain leaned closer to hear.

"Ah, I really don't like talking about it so I'll just say I learned kung fu as a teenager. I never stopped learning and still do my patterns and breathing even today. When I saw those bastards beating up on Beamy and they had the girls and my wife, Pinkie, by the throat, I lost it. I left and the demon stepped into my body.

"My AK was empty and Halo was knocked unconscious, the terrorists were right in my face. When I came back those leering bastards were all dead. I thought I was psycho until Pedro took me outside and explained I went berserk, I was a berserker. But I frightened everyone and that really upset me. I frightened my wife, Tricia, Gail and McFly here. I didn't frighten Halo though."

Sundown smiled and the tension broke, they all knew Halo was made of tough stuff. "He saw the demon at the mines and sort of expects it every time we fight now." He stopped and drank the rest of his port. Pinkie put her hand over his mug and stopped him pouring himself another drink.

That same voice spoke once more, "Sorry to ask you Sundown, I know it's painful, but what's the demon like?" There were a few chuckles from out of the darkness but the major decided enough was enough. He could see the distress on Pinkie and McFly's face and spoke up.

"I think it's time for bed, boys. Sundown's had enough. Maybe he'll talk more some other night but not now." He turned to Sundown. "Thank you Sundown for explaining a few things our boys were dying to ask you." To his troop he said, "We'll be up early and we'll be on the track before dawn. We still have a few days driving ahead of us. From our latest reports Pedro is making a good recovery in hospital, annoying the nurses and almost back to his old self. Alice Springs Command told me they had to take his tin legs away because he kept escaping to the pub." The major laughed and stood up, indicating it was time for sleep.

As they were settling into bed Pinkie rolled into Sundown's arms and said, "Sundown, you know what? That major's grown up hasn't he. Have you noticed how his men have accepted him now? They're showing him the respect they didn't have when they first arrived."

Sundown was almost asleep when he replied, "Yeah, you're right, he's quite a character," he sighed. "I like him, the boys like him. All he needed was blooding. Now that he's my blood he'll follow wherever I lead him." He kissed her good night and they fell asleep in each others arms.

The next few days were rough going as they hit patches of soft sand followed by clay pans that appeared solid but the vehicles sunk to their axles in mud which lay just below the salt-crusted surface. It gave McFly time to go for walks into the bush with Billie. The two spent every free minute talking about Billies tribal world and the desert.

"Billie," McFly asked, "what was that smoke made of, the one you used for that ceremony?"

"Don't go thinkin' I'm gonna show ya, those herbs could kill ya, they're poisons. I learned when I spent all those years living with me mother's people. They taught me things only a nangarri, a sorcerer, should know. Did you know we have three languages?" Billie liked to go off on a tangent with McFly.

"Ah, no, I didn't know that." McFly replied, and he was hooked once again.

"One is our tribal language, another is finger talk, and the other one is what men talk doing secret men's business. That's how me people talked when the whites rounded us up to take us away. They told us to shut up and be quiet, so we finger talked and they didn't even know it." Billie chuckled and smacked his gums. "You know what? Me mother's people were clever, they could talk without making a noise." He laughed loudly as they walked across the salt pan and back to the vehicles ready to set out again.

"But, Billie, I thought you said you had to stay home so the police and aboriginal affairs people wouldn't take you away from your parents?" asked McFly, confused.

"They never did 'cause I was smart and 'cause I could speak good English. But when I was with me tribal family, them bastards would come out and raid us for no reason. I was just a hot headed youngster then and I'd give it to 'em. I stood up for me cousins and got a lot o' hidings for it too. Some of them police were good and kind, some were bastards. The worst were the white women who came and pointed out who they were going to take back to the city. They had hearts of stone they did." Billie stopped talking and wouldn't open up on the matter again.

They arrived at Alice Springs in the evening and settled into the military camp for the night. They'd driven hard the final two days only breaking for meals and toilet stops. The group were cranky and short tempered, all they wanted was a drink and bed, which is what they got.

The next morning Major Vic Thompson found Sundown and McFly and took them across the parade ground to see

General Hughes, the commanding officer, Australian Third Army.

Throughout their trip Sundown milked the major to learn what type of person the general really was. He wanted to be fully prepared before he shared his plans. He had dreamed the meeting many a time but it was always inconclusive, even his Shamus specter didn't help much.

The sun was shining, the day cool and the Nissen hut was warmed by a cheery fireplace. The general met them at the door and shook their hands.

"Welcome to Third Army, Sundown. And so this is McFly?" He hesitated, "that strange name reminds me of someone…"

McFly decided to help him out. "It's a nickname from a science fiction film of the 1980's. Apparently my interest in fly fishing had something to do with the name."

"Of course, of course! Now I remember, Marty McFly, yes!" the general said enthusiastically while shaking McFly's hand a second time. "Please, come in and take a seat. I hope you've all had a safe drive across the Simpson?" he asked a little more soberly as he invited the three visitors to be seated.

The rotund general sat behind his enormous desk on a raised chair, his little legs dangled without touching the floor. The three were seated in chairs that set them below the level of the general.

"Before we get started, General Hughes," began Sundown, "I would like to thank you for providing support to our community at Birdsville. You're men performed admirably against the terrorists at Mount Isa. They prevented the enemy from mounting a full scale assault against us. I would like to commend Major Thompson and Captain Lewis for showing initiative and bravery against a foe many times their number. Fortunately we hit them before they were ready for us. Your command certainly took them down a few notches. I don't expect they'll be coming our way for some months while they regroup and reinforce their battalion."

The general smiled with delight. "That's brilliant news Sundown, absolutely brilliant!" He almost bounced up and down in his chair. "I told the major that if he could manage a contact or two while on patrol then he should hit them where it hurts."

Sundown saw the opportunity to take and hold the initiative so he drove forward. "General," he began formally. "I believe you are the highest ranking officer in the Australian armed forces. It is appropriate that I place myself under your command as head of the Australian Third Army." The general's grin was a mix of amazement and delight. He hadn't expected this tough, successful warrior to be so easily manipulated.

"General," continued Sundown fully aware of the impact he was having on the man. "Major Thompson is a competent officer whom I am quite prepared to work alongside." Major Thompson didn't flinch, he knew what was coming. They'd spoken about this moment at length over the past week.

"I would like to offer you Sundown's Commando and to join your contingency. I, myself, will remain it's commander and I'm prepared to take on the task of organising other commando's in our region to come under you as part of Third Army."

He stopped when he saw he had made an impression. Now he waited to see which way the general would swing. Sundown had learned in his years as a scientist in organisations where ego's ruled above and beyond the science, that silence was power.

The general nodded to himself. His little legs swung back and forth under the table. The three visitors could clearly see the emotions of joy, lust, pleasure, fear and cunning play across his face like a light show.

General Hughes finally stopped moving and bobbing about. "Sundown, I take it you wish to be my second in command? My 2IC?" Sundown nodded. "I could do with a real live hero by my side." The general paused and again the emotions played havoc with his face. "Commander? That is ambitious and it's not even a rank. Why not Lieutenant Colonel? No?" Sundown shook his head, he wouldn't settle for less than Commander even though he knew it was a rank that didn't even exist in the Australian army.

"I was thinking Brigadier General but thought one general in the army was enough, you don't need another." Sundown said what General Hughes wanted to hear: confirmation that this was not just a grab for his title and position.

"Done! As improper as it is you have now become Commander Sundown!" He banged his fist on the table and leaning forward as far as his girth allowed he shook Sundown's hand. "Well I must say, I didn't expect a complete capitulation from you. This is just marvellous!"

The general's head bobbed up and down again as he spoke, "Tomorrow we'll parade and appoint you as Commander Sundown, second in command of the Australian Third Army." He called to his duty sergeant and rattled off a set of orders for the day and to prepare for tomorrow's formal announcement.

"Gentlemen, would you care to remain with me a little longer?" He walked around to McFly and shook his hand as he ushered him out the door, then paused.

"McFly, how would you care to be adjutant to Sundown's Commando? We'll need someone bright and brave. I hear you served with distinction in most of the battles your commando have won. What say I give you the rank of captain? Captain McFly?" General Hughes was on a roll and reveled in his power at the head of an organisation that now held the most successful civilian-soldier on Australian soil.

McFly stood still, turned, then held out his hand. He knew he had been offered a gem of a deal. "General Hughes, Captain McFly at your service." They shook and McFly turned to Sundown and the major. "Sir, I shall inform the men and start the ball rolling from our end. I'll speak with the duty sergeant on the way out to see how I can be of assistance."

Sundown nearly choked as he held back a laugh, *'smart-arse,'* he thought to himself.

The day was a whirlwind of activity as news spread of Sundown's arrival and his appointment as 2IC to Third Army. Within twenty four hours of arrival Sundown had achieved what he and Andy had hoped for ever since Major Thompson set foot on their door step.

At the Alice Springs reception on the evening of his appointment Commander Sundown took Major Vic Thompson aside and spoke to him.

"Vic, we've got work to do. I need you to look after the general. Keep him busy, happy and informed of everything we do - except certain things of course." The major nodded careful not to spill his red wine.

"I'm going to commandeer the Cessna and head out with McFly to every survivor community we know of and spread the word that Sundown's Commando is now fighting with Third Army. Do you think you can keep the general amused and compliant while we are away?"

The major tipped his head back and downed the rest of his wine before stepping back into the reception room to bring back another two. He downed the second before answering.

"Damn it, Sundown, I was hoping to go flying with you but I know what you mean. Hughes now sees me as another of his heroes. It means that myself, you or one of your boys have to be on call to cater to his whims. But yes, I'll do it."

"Vic, I've got to get back to the reception, I can see Pedro annoying the crap out of Lorraine and Shadow. But I'll meet with you and the general in the morning and we'll nut this out. Thanks, mate, I owe you."

It was way past midnight when the party ended and Sundown invited his commando friends to walk with him along the Todd River road back to their motel rooms. It was quiet and the air cool. When almost at their motel Shadow called for them to stop.

"Shh! There's noises down in the riverbed, it sounds like screaming... or crying." They all stopped and listened. The moon was out shedding an eerie glow as the noises now became louder. Someone was screaming in pain and there were more voices, shouting…

"There's a fight or something happening down in the river," said McFly.

Lorraine's voice was strained as she stated, "I know that voice, the one yelling. That's John, the rigger who started the fight at the Marree Hotel the day you arrived. I heard he brought his boys to Alice Springs and it seems he's still here."

Together they walked down into the dry river bed to see if they could help. Pedro was asleep in his wheelchair. A combination of drugs and alcohol was needed to achieve that feat.

Sundown was grateful because he knew the old man would want to stay and fight.

"It's certainly those rigger boys, Sundown, it sounds like they're killing someone down there, be careful," said Pinkie as she hurried with Lorraine to help her push the wheelchair to a safer position. Sundown told Lorraine and Pinkie to stay with Pedro while the rest of them carefully walked towards the sounds of violence.

The funny thing about the desert under a full moon is that it can sometimes appear to be as bright as daylight. Combined with the white river sand it was bright enough for the four commando's to see John and two of his boys beating up two young aboriginal youths. The three men were dressed in military police uniforms using their batons to viciously bash the two boys.

"Hey! Stop that you bullies!" yelled Shadow as they approached closer.

The three MP's recognised Sundown's group immediately. They stopped beating the teenagers and stepped forward together, their batons at the ready.

"Piss off, Sundown!" said John clearly. "We're Military Police now and we caught these arse-holes stealing chickens." He looked at the uniforms on McFly and Sundown. "You have no jurisdiction here, we're the police, you're just grunts, piss off."

"Leave the boys alone. Go on your way, John, and you won't be placed under arrest for assaulting civilians," replied

Sundown as he unconsciously put his arm out to stop Shadow stepping closer.

John raised his baton and stepped forward. "You just don't listen do you? I said piss off and leave us to do our job!" he hissed and took another step forward.

"I said leave off, step back corporal, stand down and you will live to enjoy another day. If you want to face off with me you will lose, I promise you that." Sundown's voice was menacing, cold, his demon straining to break free of the tight reins that held it at bay.

Shadow settled it when she ducked under Sundown's arm to kick at one of the MP's just as John swung his baton at the kung fu champion of Marree Hotel fame.

Unfortunately Shadow mistimed her kick in the moonlight. The heavy baton struck her on the side of the head and she went down with a cry. McFly immediately ran to her side and Bill stepped forward to cover her body. Another blow was aimed at her head but it struck Bill on his arm and he yelped. The blow fractured his wrist causing him to collapse to the ground in pain.

All this happened in a split second which was enough time for Sundown's demon to slip its reins - and Sundown was powerless to control it.

Sundown never left Shamus' knife more than a few feet from his knife hand since the mines fight. He usually had it strapped to his calf. He now reached down and pulled it free.

A flood of heat and power hit his chest and the knife in his hand felt soothing, arousing, it was almost sexual. It drove a lust for blood exploding inside his brain. The demon stood over Bill and Shadow's bodies as McFly stood beside him to protect his partner.

"McFly, leave it, just leave this to me," wheezed Sundown, consciousness was almost beyond his reach. "This is out of your control, you're not responsible." But McFly stood his ground as the other two MP's started to surround the small group. There was no way McFly would run and leave his friend alone.

"Leave it be, McFly! Take Bill and Shadow and walk away. You haven't seen a thing." Then Sundown was gone. Gone into dreamland, a space where he felt nothing, no tension just a pure form of joy. Then he felt pleasure, the blood lust of his demon and he smiled deep inside. '*Oh, yes! Let me release my power!*' his demon's voice screamed inside his head.

Chapter 12 - Alice Springs Demon

Lorraine and Pinkie were struggling to get Pedro's wheelchair upright. The wheels got stuck in the sand and it tipped over spilling poor Pedro to the ground. There they wrestled with the inebriated old hero. Pedro grabbed at the girls as though he was dancing with them, his legs whole and his body forty years younger.

But only a dozen metres away lives were about to be snuffed out.

The demon was in control at last, its power released it launched itself at it's nearest enemy. As the man brought his baton down the demon easily blocked and struck in a single movement. There was a rapid blur of hands and elbows as the demon's left forearm knocked the MP's baton arm off its line of destruction and the pommel of Sundown's commando knife slammed upwards crushing the man's larynx.

The demon's first victim collapsed, clutching at his throat, choking his life away. His soul was released to find another expression in the universe its current one now ended. Neither John nor the other MP noticed.

McFly was now busy throwing Shadow over his shoulder to move her away from the fight so that he could return to help Sundown.

John, like his two mates, had been drinking. He had a knife in one hand and his police baton in the other. "Come on Sundown I've got something for you. And where's that whore girl who was here a minute ago? I've got something quite different for her!"

The heavily built ex-rigger took one step too close to the demon who, with a swinging kick took his front leg out from under him. As John staggered backwards on his one leg the big man used the momentum to flip into a defensive position and stood back up. His baton raised above his head he came at Sundown with renewed vigour.

John's crazed look reminded McFly of a madman, he saw that John had the clear intention of killing Sundown.

McFly was now quite defenceless. He had Shadow on his shoulder and he hadn't had time to stand up and move her away from the fight.

There came a voice in his mind: "*Duck!*" it said but instead of ducking he stood up wondering where the voice had come from. The second MP had run the few metres separating them and smashed his baton down onto McFly's shoulder. The blow was so fierce that it knocked him back to the ground and Shadow tumbled heavily onto the sandy riverbed.

Bill was crouched holding his broken arm but when he saw the MP beat McFly to the ground he immediately stood back up. He placed his good arm and shoulder between the MP and McFly to protect his mate's exposed head. The MP swung his baton again and again trying to break through Bill's defences. Despite the vicious blows Bill refused to step back.

With one eye on John now screaming as he raced towards him, the demon lightly kicked the other MP's knee drawing the man's attention away from Bill and McFly. In that split second the demon was able to grasp the MP's raised baton arm. The MP tried to change his angle of attack to free his baton and strike Sundown. To do so he had to tilt his head back a little to maintain balance. This presented the demon with an opportunity to slice the man's throat.

Sundown liked to keep his knife razor sharp just for this reason. A gush of hot blood erupted from his enemy's wound and the MP collapsed to the ground. The man only had time for a gurgled groan before his life slipped into the next dimension.

Just as Sundown began to straighten his back John was on top of him. Slightly off balance Sundown dodged the swinging baton. He immediately stepped sideways as John's knife blade swung at his stomach. John saw an opening and quickly twisted his torso to bring his knife around in a figure of eight to slice at Sundown's throat.

Sundown now popped into semi-consciousness to briefly witness time slow almost to a stop. He saw the demon flip his commando knife and hold it by the blade, but then he disappeared again. Ducking John's swinging knife the demon bent and side-kicked John knocking him backwards several metres. The MP doubled over and let out a 'whoosh' sound, but the kick was easily absorbed by John's over-sized gut.

"You feeble old bastard!" grunted John. "I'm going to carve you up for dinner, military uniform and all. I've jurisdiction, civilian and army! I rule! I'll kill you and your missus and these little toadies right here. This is where you'll die." He let out a maniacal laugh then began to swing his baton around and around above his head. John advanced the single step that now sealed his fate.

The demon opened it's mind again. As he pulled back his right arm he allowed Sundown to watch. With his knife blade between his finger tips he threw the perfectly balanced World War Two commando knife. Inside his mind Sundown observed, fascinated, as his knife left his fingers turned once then entered John's eyeball. It pierced the MP's brain with a wet 'thunk'!

Sundown watched as John stopped moving. John stood dead still, not a muscle moved for several seconds. Then, like a ruined marionette, its strings cut, John's soulless body collapsed in a heap of senseless limbs to the ground.

"Sundown! Sundown!" he heard Lorraine and Pinkie crying his name. He pulled himself back from the edge of darkness.

"What?" he was lost in his mind not wanting to leave this wonderful feeling of pure ecstasy.

"We've got to leave here… there's three dead MP's… we have to get away… now!" said the voices around him. In a daze Sundown let them lead him away. Soon after he noticed that he was in a soft bed and allowed himself to drift into a deep sleep.

They were seated at the kitchen table in Sundown's motel room trying to work out how to manage this disaster.

"Damn it, how good is this! He's second in command of the Australian Army for half a day and already he's committed three murders." Captain McFly was severely bruised and in considerable pain. Bill was sitting beside him at the motel kitchen table while Lorraine bandaged his fractured wrist. Shadow was nursing a sore head and Pinkie was fretting as she made tea and coffee for everyone. Pedro was asleep in the other bedroom snoring loudly.

"What are we going to do, McFly?" asked Pinkie, struggling not to cry.

"We're all wounded and we'll be out of action for weeks now. Shit!" he swore again starting to feel himself losing control. The frustration, disappointment and fear pressing to get the better of him. "Curse that moron, John! The bloody psychopath! He's spoiled everything!"

Shadow sat up and looked at McFly.

"Calm down and think, McFly! Why don't we get Major Thompson and Captain Lewis in here so that we can explain everything. Maybe they'll do something. All of our troops will jump through fire to help us. What about we go and find Sergeant Tobi or Corporal Hassam and get their advice?"

"Hey yeah! Yeah, that's a great idea!" McFly now began to settle down and his head started to clear. "Pinkie, can you run around to the camp and get one of our men, anyone, to go and find Sergeant Tobi? I'm sure that he'll help us. Tell him everything and do what he says, please," said the newly appointed Captain McFly, Adjutant to the second most powerful man in Australia.

Pinkie didn't say another word. She wiped her eyes then ran out of the room.

"Oh, thank God!" said Pinkie as she almost collapsed at the guard post. "I need Sergeant Tobi, now. It's an emergency," she told the soldier on duty. In her panic she didn't recognise that it was Corporal Hassam, their friend from the major's own ASLAV.

"What's happened, Pinkie? Talk to me while we go and grab the sarg." They walked hurriedly to the sergeant's room and banged on his door. A tired but awake Sergeant Tobi answered. In a flood of tears Pinkie repeated the story.

"Strewth," he sighed in resignation, he couldn't believe what he had just heard. However, when he saw the state Pinkie was in he instinctively responded driven by the positive warmth he held for Sundown's commando. He pulled Pinkie into his chest and hugged her tightly. "It's OK, Pinkie, stop crying. Sundown's in safe hands with us, you can bet on that."

"Corporal, grab three of our boys. Go out to the river bed and collect the bodies. If you can try to find the two teenagers the

MP's were bashing then head out to the aboriginal camp and find Billie, tell him what just happened. Ask him to get their boys to bury the bodies. We'll disappear those pricks once and for all. And good riddance to them too." The sergeant turned to hug Pinkie again. "Don't worry darling, we're all one blood now, remember?"

The next morning McFly, Shadow and Bill were sitting in Major Thompson's office. It looked like a war zone with their bruises and bandages. The major had resumed his position as adjutant to the general and was back to running the army as usual. Nothing got to the general except through the major. Major Thompson asked Sergeant Tobi and Corporal Hassam to invite Captain Lewis to join them.

The major told Pinkie and McFly not to bring Sundown to the company headquarters that morning, not until he'd sorted things out. Sundown decided it best to return Pedro to his hospital room with Lorraine. Pedro was unwell, he'd drunk too much and was very hung over.

The major discussed the situation at length with the captain. They had the two teenage boy's statements and statements from the commando victims. It was a clear-cut case of self defence and it appeared that the three MP's had decided to escape into the bush rather than face a court martial.

Major Thompson, with Captain Lewis as his second, announced the verdict; all three were guilty of assaulting both civilian and military personnel, with intent to kill. If they returned to the camp they would be arrested and shot under military law.

When Billie arrived with an elder from the local tribe they drew them into their circle of chairs. Billie spoke for them both.

"Seems them rigger fellas have been bashing my people since they got 'ere. No one would complain because they'd be beaten. Our elders were powerless to stop the kids getting their heads bashed in. Those bastards killed thirteen of my people. Can yer believe that, thirteen!" Billie sighed and a tear dripped down his dark weathered face.

He looked at the officers. "The bodies are gone major, no one will ever find them now. My people are grateful they're gone too. Now that those blokes are gone I would like to ask if we can appoint our own law and work together now?"

"Billie, thanks mate, I'm sure we can work together," said Captain McFly. He looked at the major and captain, they both nodded.

"Thirteen? I'm sorry, we never knew, Billie," said Captain Lewis.

"We was too afraid to say anything," replied the aboriginal elder sitting beside Billie.

Early the next morning General Hughes met with Sundown, Captain McFly and his own adjutant, Major Thompson. This was their first formal meeting to discuss strategy moving forward. It was eye-opening for the two commandos.

"What? You've only got three hundred soldiers? In the entire Third Army?" McFly was incredulous, he couldn't believe his ears. "What the hell happened? They couldn't have all been killed?"

The general was quiet for a moment then courageously went on. "Actually, we had twice that number at the beginning. Over the first few weeks when people realised this was not a drill they... just sort of drifted away."

The major picked it up. "Sundown, I didn't want to tell you all this before you formally joined us, but that's the truth of it. Once everyone woke up to the fact that there was no more government and no more law and order things broke down. A lot of our troops came from Darwin and the north-west after the bombing and terrorist attacks and headed here. They expected central command in Alice Springs to be well managed and resourced. We weren't. We had the entire central Australian desert to rescue. In that first week we were completely overwhelmed with a flood of refugees. Then we lost almost all of our food and supplies. Looters got into our depot and stole everything they could get their hands on. We had to adopt a 'shoot on sight' policy to stop it."

He paused and pulled out a note pad and continued. "We now have two hundred and eighty-odd personnel. Of those only half arrived with weapons and supplies. Most of the Darwin and north-west cape military, and even some from Pine Gap, got out with their clothes on and just about nothing else. They were actually the most orderly of the new arrivals.

"Captain Walker brought the armoured cavalry from Darwin, bless his soul. He fought a valiant rearguard action as he pulled what he could away from the terrorists and came down to Alice. Our own mob from Alice Springs Command were staunch in their actions and controlled the township extremely well but some elements crept in with the refugees. We tried to sort out the good from the bad but we couldn't, it was impossible. Some we thought would be useful turned out to be liabilities."

McFly butted in once again. "Like John and some of those riggers?" he asked.

The general answered, "Yes, McFly, we thought they would work out just fine but they ended up terrorising our community, right under our noses." He stopped, wanting to move the conversation to safer ground.

"Some civilians joined up with us and they've turned out to be some of our best soldiers. Many joined our scouting platoon, experienced in working in the desert as cattlemen, shooters and riggers with the oil companies. Many of our own troops have also stepped up. Captain Lewis' brother joined as a civilian and proved to be one of our best. Blasted pity he was killed, I really miss him. He had a certain flare for humour and was a most welcome member at our official functions."

General Hughes looked out of the window at the storm clouds hanging over the township.

"General," said Sundown turning the conversation back to where he needed it. "I'm here to support you in every way possible." The general looked back at Sundown, waiting. "My commando have proved their worth for nearly a year against odds no other party have survived against. But we're small, we're poorly resourced and we need heavy weapons to hold our own. I propose we send two more armoured carriers to Birdsville with a platoon of our best. Then I want to take a few of our heroes with me to visit the outlying townships in the desert regions. I think we can double our numbers here and train them ready for the big push."

"Commander," said the major. "I agree we should try to find more soldiers and fighters but it's going to be tough. We have so little resources that we'll need to do some subtle juggling just to feed them. Remember, we lost most of our gear and stores to looters in those first few days of the apocalypse. We can send out parties to ransack the farm houses and sheds but this is the poorest region in the country. We tried to head into Darwin and the larger towns but were beaten back by the terrorists."

He paused and wiped at his eyes as he remembered his time in Birdsville with the commando. "Commander, before we hurry off to find more mouths to feed we really need to be self sufficient. In short we need to grow our own food. I suggest we get some of your boys here to help us build the vegetable gardens like you have. You know, divert the sewerage as food and water for the gardens. Like Birdsville we have plenty of subterranean water here, it'll never go dry, but we're struggling. If we can build up our own supplies we have a chance of strengthening our numbers. We'll attract them because we'll have plenty of food."

Sundown smiled. "That is exactly what I was thinking, major." He turned to McFly. "Captain, how long did Lorraine say it would take for Bill's wrist to heal? We need him to fly all over the centre with us to find more men and women who are prepared to fight."

"Lorraine said six weeks and it should have healed well enough. No sooner though," replied McFly.

"Good, I knew it was a month or so, OK," he turned once more to the general. "General, I'd like to add Shadow, to my team here, promote her to lieutenant. I need people who know how I think. I'd like to appoint her as my aide to your office."

Major Thompson quickly spoke before the general had a chance to gather his thoughts. "Excellent idea, Sundown!" he launched into a description of how well she helped organise the services in Birdsville and her courage on the battlefield. "General, Shadow knocked out John in the Marree fight you know. Took out eight of those riggers who were beating up Sundown and Pedro." He looked at McFly. "Why, she even rescued her boyfriend here, three times I heard." He winked and chuckled lightly.

"Twice I think it was, major. I got a few shots in too you know," said McFly defensively.

"Well, yes... I agree, we need more soldiers and growing our own food must be a priority." The general tried to regain control. He tapped his fingers on the desktop impatiently. "And by the way, Major Thompson, since we're restructuring our organisation, I am promoting Captain Lewis to Major and you to Colonel, as of now, congratulations."

General Hughes called out to his orderly to serve breakfast as he tried to gather his wits and unravel Sundown and Major Thompson's coordinated onslaught.

"Gentlemen, today I wish to see our final arrangements for your Commando's official entry into our command here, then we'll work on plans for the coming spring and summer offensives." He stood as the orderly announced that breakfast was ready.

The meal was a time for everyone to exchange stories but one story was waiting to be told.

"Commander" said the general sitting at the end of the table in the officers mess. "I believe you took out a group of MP's last night after our welcoming dinner party?" Sundown noticed Hughes was smiling but he didn't know how he should explain such a horrendous event especially when he missed most of it himself.

"I'm sorry about that, General. As you know we were walking back to our hotel beside the Todd River and went to investigate a fight in the river bed. It was John and two others of his patrol. Apparently they have a reputation for assaulting civilians and members of the aboriginal community here, just as they had in Marree. They trade food and petrol on the black market and had turned themselves into the underground rulers of Alice Springs." Sundown wanted to hit hard and fast. It worked, the generals eyes bulged somewhat as he listened.

"We went to investigate and were assaulted by these men. You have no doubt heard of the injuries: a broken wrist, multiple bruising and Shadow was knocked unconscious while McFly here is still black and blue." McFly nodded but declined to interrupt so Sundown continued. "I stepped in and that's when John and his mates bolted."

Sundown waited for a moment to see if Colonel Thompson would speak, but he didn't. He decided to step deeper into the hole he worried he might be digging for himself. "I can't remember what actually happened general. I lost consciousness and woke this morning. I have next to no memory of the events after I saw Shadow knocked down by John. Sorry."

"Blasted brutes that lot," agreed the general. "Major Lewis appointed them to patrol the township and at first they did a good job but we kept getting reports of assaults and black marketing of supplies." Finishing the last of his steak he heaped some mashed potatoes onto his fork then tried to balance more peas than would fit. He managed to get some of them into his mouth.

"I'm glad they've disappeared. If they come back we'll hang them for assault, black marketing and desertion." He signalled for the others to tuck into their meal.

The general paused with his next forkful of potatoes and peas. "Commander, one day you'll have to tell me about this demon of yours. I've heard so much about it, and then it leaps out right from under my nose. That would have been quite a fight between you and those three I imagine."

Sundown went slightly pale but at this distance he hoped it wouldn't show.

"I missed it too, General."

The game was interrupted when Corporal Hassam raced in, stepped back out and knocked, then re-entered. He walked straight to General Hughes but spoke directly at Commander Sundown.

"Sir, comms reports One One Charlie have contact with the Marree Revelationists, north of the Marree township. Patrol One have also relayed that Charlie and your bike squad, Commander, appear to have been ambushed. Birdsville base report they are preparing a patrol to support them. Wiram asked permission for One One Bravo to come off their northern post to support him."

Corporal Hassam paused to look at everyone seated around the general's table. "Sir, Wiram said it's a serious situation, very serious."

Chapter 13 - To Sanctuary

In Arkaroola the dwellers were up before dawn and still half asleep. Phil fussed with the grass protector for his radiator; Heidi argued with Lucy and Glenda about who would drive Nulla's Toyota first; and the boys were annoying Fatima as she tried to organise breakfast. Not that the boys actually did any of the cooking, they were just there to help her decide what she should cook for them. Fatima loved having them fuss around her, she sometimes even created special meals just for the two boys, they loved her for it.

The girls always argued over who got to choose the music in Nulla's four wheel drive. They were sick to death of his country music. But Nulla had a rule, whoever drove had first choice of music. Lucy won the fight to drive the Toyota first being the eldest and most experienced driver. It helped when Phil backed her. Lucy's smug face soon changed though.

"Lucy!" called Luke striding purposefully towards the vehicles, his hands in his pockets. "Have you got any toilet paper? My butt's full and I've got some Christmas pudding to feed the ants."

Annie reacted immediately, swinging around to look up at her mother. "Mum, how come Luke's got Christmas pudding? And why is he going to give it to the ants?"

Lucy looked at her daughter first then looked blankly at Luke. "Luke, since when have I become the toilet-paper lady?"

"Since you read all those books and have lots of spare paper. Better hurry though, the ants are ravenous and my butt's about to burst," replied Luke reaching towards her bags in the back of the four wheel drive.

"Don't you touch my books!" stormed Lucy running over to her bags before Luke could get to them. "I'll get some paper for you."

Arthur and Simon were watching the game. Each wore an enormous grin on their face enjoying the entertainment. Heidi and Glenda stopped talking and started giggling.

"Hurry up, Lucy," cried Luke, jigging about and holding his buttocks, "I'm about to explode!"

Lucy tore some pages from one of her less-than-interesting books and handed them over. Luke ran off towards the toilet block nearby. They could hear his deliberately loud groans of satisfaction.

"Boys!" sighed Lucy.

"Mum, how come Luke's feeding the ants Christmas pudding?" asked Annie again, trying to work out what was so funny. Then her eyes lit up and she cried out, "He's doing a poop isn't he! That's not pudding that's pooping!" and she squealed in delight at having broken the boys secret code.

"Lucy!" cried Simon getting in on the act. "I've got some ginger bread men in my oven, I need some of that paper too!"

"Oh! Simon!" squealed Annie. The little girl had become fascinated by these two uncouth teenagers ever since they'd arrived at her house. Arty was quiet and subdued compared to these two wild boys.

Arthur couldn't stop laughing and opened his mouth to add to the madness but he stopped when he saw Heidi's fierce frown and sighed softly to himself.

"Simon! Are you going to do a poop too?" Annie squealed even louder, her face wreathed in smiles.

Grabbing at his butt Simon yelled in fake anguish, "Annie, you'd better tell your mum to hurry with the paper because my ginger bread men are just about to jump out of my oven." The girls giggled and Annie squealed again in delight.

All of a sudden Lucy stood completely still, a book in one hand and loose pages in the other. The sunrise had tinged the clouds in the east with pinks and reds making her face glow in an ethereal light. Her body twitched and from somewhere deep inside she began to laugh, a long genuine laugh. It was the first real laugh she'd had since the apocalypse, since she'd lost her joy for living. She could no longer hold herself back at the silliness of these two boys - but just a moment later she burst into tears.

Charlene was watching the show and enjoying the entertainment. When she saw Lucy crying she hurried straight over and hugged her friend.

"Those boys make me want to cry too, Lucy. Silly beggars aren't they," she said awkwardly pulling Lucy to her with her one good arm.

Lucy leaned back and looked into Charlene's eyes. "It's the silly things the boys do and say that remind me of Tony. He liked to tease me like this. I really miss him." She buried her head in Charlene's chest and sobbed even harder.

"Mummy," Annie pulled at her mothers t-shirt, "Luke said I could feed the ants too if I wanted!" She squealed yet again with glee. Lucy pulled herself away from Charlene and bent down to hug her daughter to her breast.

"It's just one of those silly things boys get up to, Annie. And yes, you can make ginger bread people and feed Christmas pudding to the ants if you want to." Lucy chuckled, wiping the tears from her cheeks. "Those boys are silly aren't they?"

Simon called from the bushes, "Annie, when you feed the ants just be careful they don't bite your bum!" and the little girl squealed once more relishing the joy of being with these wickedly funny boys.

Soon after sunrise Nulla arrived whistling cheerily as he walked into the camp. Phil was boiling the billy on the camp fire as Nulla strode past not even noticing him. Phil noticed though. Nulla's body language exhibited a carefree happiness he'd not seen before. It must be more good news he thought.

Nulla went straight over to Glenda who was washing the dishes outside the vans. He picked her up around the waist and swung her around in the air.

"Love, we've met the Birdsville mob and you know what?"

She smiled up at him as he gently settled her back on the ground. "Do I know what? No, I don't know what," she laughed.

"We're going to make it! Those plans of ours? Of a sanctuary to raise a family? Well, we're heading towards that magical oasis in the desert." He picked her up again and swung her around until they were both giddy.

By now everyone had gathered around to hear the news. Phil called from the camp fire, "Well, come on Nulla, tell us all about it!"

Nulla replied, "As you know, Simon and I met two fella's who belong to the Birdsville commando. They both were wounded fighting the local terrorists around here. They have a family nearby who'll be joining them soon - and we'll be meeting them all in…" he looked at his wrist watch, "about thirty minutes if we can get our fingers out."

Fatima stood up and clapped her hands in delight. "Nulla, pick me up and swing me around too!" she called loudly. Her aged voice wasn't quite the alto it once was but she raised it to the skies and sang one of the songs from her church choir days, "*Onward Christian Soldiers*". Glenda joined Fatima and they sang it loud and strong. None of the youngsters had ever seen the insides of a church but they loved the song and clapped in time.

They drove their vehicles along the dry creek bed dodging boulders and huge pot holes until they came upon Riley's truck and the crowd gathered there. Bongo waved as they approached and pointed to the dogs on the back of the truck. They were jumping up and down on their leashes in excitement.

"Hi, everyone," said Nulla, stepping out of his four wheel drive. Bongo began the task of introducing everyone.

The two Birdsville scouts were sad to leave their horses behind. They'd become mates, but there was no way they would survive the trek through the desert to Birdsville. Riley had said that the horses would soon find the wild brumby herds and live out their days in the rugged Flinders Ranges.

The men now gathered around Bongo and Roo who shared their knowledge of the route they took coming in and the condition of the tracks. Bongo said the vehicles shouldn't have too much trouble getting to Birdsville if they followed the tracks they'd used on the way in.

Roo and Riley had travelled extensively throughout the Strzelecki Desert, and Riley in particular knew every track in the Flinders Ranges. They were confident that they would make it without having to use the Birdsville Track.

As they were sorting out who sat where the sun rose high enough over the hills to shed light on their little group.

Charlene was standing apart from the group embarrassed by her useless arm in its sling. She looked up in the growing light and noticed a tall, young man standing silently off to one side. A sunbeam shone directly on his face and his lithe body was just a silhouette in shadow. He had his arm in a sling much like her own, The young man's facial expression reminded her of a lost little boy. At that moment her heart constricted and leaped trying to get out of her chest. She felt herself pant for more oxygen as she struggled to breathe.

Roo stepped into the full sunlight. He loved the mornings with the sun rising when he could actually see the light beams reaching out to touch him. From the corner of his eye he saw what looked like an angel. Her hair burst into a golden halo as the morning sunlight kissed it into life. He stood stock-still, not sure whether this was an illusion or real. Her beauty was like nothing he had ever seen. Her face oval and pale, the eyes were alive and staring directly at him. Roo stood in shock, his heart beat faster, his throat tightened.

Riley glanced around at his cousin right at the moment Roo spied Charlene. Noticing his cousin's expression he looked across to where Roo was staring and he saw it too – Charlene was simply stunning.

The rugged Flinders cattleman hadn't really noticed the girls, they'd stood in the background allowing the men to talk of travel routes and track conditions. Now he saw there were two young women and one in her early thirties, much like his own wife, Katie.

'Blimey, this makes things interesting,' he thought to himself.

Not wishing to break the spell he eased away from Roo and started helping the others to rearrange their gear ready for the trip.

They only had the three bikes but Arthur was still unable to ride. Roo and Bongo were both wounded as well and had lost their bikes to the Wilsons. That meant there was a spare bike, Arthur's.

"I wonder if Heidi and Lucy would like to ride Arty's bike?" Nulla looked at the two, wondering out loud.

The girls heard him, as he knew they would, and they looked up sharply.

"Nulla, are you serious? We've only been riding since we got to Arkaroola and that's just a few days practice. We might slow everyone down," said Heidi, but he could hear the excitement in her voice. Lucy just stood there not believing her ears.

Nulla called out, "Luke, you've got fifteen minutes to get Heidi up to speed. It'll be Lucy's turn tomorrow. You and Simon are their teachers, got it?" He turned back to his job sorting out equipment for the desert trek.

"Woohoo! Heidi, let's go have some fun!" Luke called, starting to pull the bike off the trailer. He was quite mindful not to upset the chickens and rooster too much.

They spent a little more than fifteen minutes because Phil and Fatima wanted to boil the billy for a final morning cup of tea. It was an opportunity for the smokers to sit and enjoy one more cigarette and for everyone to chat and socialise.

Bongo noticed the older woman, Lucy, and his mind wandered to his own partner, no doubt long dead now. In his mind he saw her again and felt a stabbing pain in his chest. He glanced at the woman and saw someone that might help ease that pain. She was pretty, mature, and looked like she was competent and in command of herself. He thought she might be someone he could get to know better. And that little Annie was such a delight, playing happily with Elle, Harry and the dogs around the camp site.

Nulla recognised that this was a good time to firm the bonds of friendship between the two groups. By the time they'd packed everything away again Heidi could change gears without having to look at her foot as it moved the lever up and down. As long as she followed Luke and Simon's tracks she was told she would be fine.

The three children continued to play while they waited for the adults to stop talking. Annie had shown her new friends the rooster and chickens while Elle had introduced her to the dogs. Lucy, Charlene and Katie sat together chatting, they hit it off immediately.

Fatima watched Lucy closely noticing just how much she had changed since the two groups had come together. Sure, Lucy still doted on Nulla but she had stopped clinging to him like she had for the first few weeks. Instead she smiled more, she even laughed. Lucy was becoming human, she thought.

Charlene was in a quandary, her loyalties were shattered. Who should she love? This handsome new guy or her best friend Heidi? Besides, this Roo fellow did seem odd since he never spoke, he just pointed and made funny sounds like a child. Yet her heart went out to him knowing he suffered like she did.

Before they climbed into their vehicles she'd gone over to Bongo and Roo to introduce herself. She saw the young man's eyes light up and it pleased her. In fact it stirred something primal inside.

Charlene felt good about herself for doing that. Before the apocalypse she was an outgoing and confident woman. Now that her group of dwellers had met Nulla's her old self was pushing through the pain, grief and depression. This new group held possibilities that she was afraid to even imagine.

That first day they left behind the arid, rocky wilderness and entered the desert proper. Despite the rough terrain Heidi only fell off a dozen times. There was no way that Action Heidi would leave the bike to sit in the back seat of the Toyota. Her pride demanded she stay on the bike and push through the pain and frustration barrier.

By evening she'd lost a fair bit of skin from her knees and elbows and she was sore all over. She had sore wrists from the front tyre jamming between the rocks and twisting out of her grasp. Her shoulders ached from wrestling the bike as she tried to control it in the soft sand. Action Heidi may have ached badly when they made camp that night but she glowed within knowing she'd shown everyone she could still cut it.

Katie and Fatima took command of meals on the trek. It left everyone else to work on the vehicles to maintain them in the tough conditions. They only made fourteen kilometres that first day. There were two punctures and Nulla was bogged four times in soft sand.

It became evident that if they listened to Riley and dropped the tyre pressure even further on Nulla's Toyota and the trailer they wouldn't become bogged anywhere near as often. Dragging the trailer was the real problem. It was loaded with food and cooking equipment - along with the chickens. There was no way Fatima would allow them to dump a single item either.

Luke specialised in finding the safest and easiest path through the scrub and patches of sand. Riley followed the bikes and directed them with a toot of his horn. He was an experienced desert driver and advised the other drivers as needed. All three vehicles had snatch-straps to pull each other out of the bogs and they carried a set of portable recovery-mats to help them drive through patches of soft sand.

By driving carefully they preserved their vehicles and the chickens who weren't too put off by the constant jogging. It slowed them down but Fatima's omelets were well worth their weight in gold. Despite the hardship they still had eggs every day.

Evenings in the desert are magical. There is nothing to compare it to in the mountains or on the coast. In fact, only a desert can be compared to a desert.

That night after dinner Arthur asked Nulla what the scars on his back and chest meant. Nulla usually took his shirt off when he worked to dig out the bogged vehicles, his scars were a source of interest to them all.

Nulla looked around the group in the glow of the camp fire and began telling them of his time in the arid regions of Australia when, as a youth, he underwent his initiations into manhood.

"Those scars show that I'm an initiated warrior," he said proudly. "In aboriginal culture it's the uncle who mentors the boy into becoming a man. The first thing I learned from my uncle was to be patient. He'd take me hunting and trapping and we'd wait for hours in the sun. I'm sure he did it on purpose. Many a time he'd leave me in the bush alone, sometimes for days, while he went on tribal business." Nulla looked up at the night sky and watched the now dead satellites coasting miles up in the atmosphere and continued.

"I'll tell you a little about my uncle to give you an idea of what sort of bloke he was. One afternoon we were preparing some turtles we'd caught in a lagoon when he suddenly stopped what he was doing.

"Uncle nodded for me to finish cleaning and to cook them while he went and lay down under a tree. After a while he came back and said that his father had just died and we had to return to where our tribe were camped. I knew our elders had special powers but until then I thought they were the only one's who had it. I was a wild boy back then, I never listened to anyone except my uncle. While we headed back home I asked him how he knew that his father had died. He explained that warriors were expected to dedicate time to their spiritual life, just as seriously as they did everything else."

Nulla stopped because he could tell Luke was dying to ask him a question.

"Boss, how did your uncle do that, you know, talk to his dead father."

"He didn't actually talk to his dead father. His brother contacted him and told him by 'mind talk'. I've been planning to teach you boys how to use your mind much like I was taught but I just haven't had time. I'm hoping we can do some of that when we get to Birdsville." Nulla looked around and saw everyone watching him curiously.

"Roo does weird stuff too, Nulla, so does Sundown and Wiram," Bongo said, he looked at Roo who nodded for Bongo to continue. "Roo lets his dream body travel and watch over him when he goes to sleep. I've seen the results lots of times now. He said he learned it when he was a child."

"From what I've seen, Bongo, there's more to life than we'll ever know or imagine. Life itself is a mystery. My uncle was a man of power. I wish I'd spent more time with him before I had to leave my country." He smiled at the young man across the fireplace and for a second thought he saw Charlene staring at Roo.

'Now what's going on here?' he thought to himself. Then it clicked. Every time they had stopped Charlene and Roo would sit together. He hadn't even realised it until now.

Katie spoke up next. "My dad use to do weird things too. He said that when he lived with the villagers in the mountains of Laos, the people often told him of news from across the mountains days before it arrived in the village. They knew things before it even happened. It wasn't just one person in the village, most of the people were tuned in to these messages. My dad had a way with healing too. He could touch someone and tell what was wrong with them." The stories continued until it was time for sleep.

Next morning they were up before dawn and on their way as soon as it was light enough to see. Lucy had a tough day but it was a little easier than Heidi had the day before. They made sure they stopped for tea several times during the day and a long siesta at lunch time when everyone slept or read a book.

Of course the three children rarely slept in the middle of the day, they were usually too excited. They loved to play chasings and to explore the desert landscape with the teenagers. Sometimes Fatima, Heidi or Lucy would read a book and everyone would sit or lie around to listen as they dropped off to sleep one by one.

Despite many patches and repairs by the end of the third week Nulla's trailer finally broke down within sight of the Birdsville Hotel. Not only was the axle broken but it was broken beyond their ability to repair it. Riley, Phil and Nulla were experts in their own right at running repairs in the arid outback. They knew they'd done well to get to the outskirts of the hotel before it died on them.

Once again Charlene found an excuse to be near Roo. The shy kangaroo shooter was smitten, as smitten as Charlene. When they could they would go off together a little apart from the group. Soon the rest woke to the fact that they'd become very close friends.

It wasn't that they kissed or even touched, and they didn't really talk much either. It was about Roo who was still a fledgling at learning to speak again. He had to pick up where he'd left off twenty years earlier. The two would sit and Charlene would talk while Roo nodded and listened - he stared at her in fascination. Before long Charlene took to teaching him sounds and how to use his mouth, lips and tongue to form words.

Roo wasn't shy or embarrassed either. He had decided that it was time he started talking and so tried his best. After all, he was the commando's elite sniper and head scout, he didn't want Bongo interpreting for him forever.

Within minutes of stopping to unhook the trailer and build the camp fire for tea they heard motor bikes approaching. Simon stood on the truck roof and announced that he could see two bikes on their way towards them.

At the same time Luke was on the CB talking to Beamy and Pellino. When he heard Simon he signed off and climbed out of the cabin to meet them with the rest of the group.

Wiram and Assassin introduced themselves and told them not to worry about the trailer, they would sort that out later. They sat down with them to share a cup of tea and catch up on the news. They then organised one of their own vehicles to pick up the trailer's contents. Fatima insisted that the chickens had top priority.

Simon, Luke and Nulla had spoken many times with the Birdsville commando over the past few months.

"Wiram," asked Simon as they pulled into the hotel car park, "what's all the activity with the heavy machinery, are you building something?"

"We sure are," replied Wiram. "The boys are fixing up the perimeter for security. We're expecting a heavy assault from either Mount Isa up north, or Marree down south. We're building a trench system around the entire caravan park and hotel. We've just begun to build fortified fighting pits to put our heavy weapons in, that's what you can see through all that dust. Sundown's even got us to dig out a few rooms below ground level to keep everyone cool in summer. He and Andy planned all this ages ago but we've only just started. It will make this a decent outpost."

By evening Sundown's Commando and the house rats of Adelaide were finally united in what Nulla had set out to find - a civil resistance. He may not be in command but he was now part of something he knew in his heart was what Captain Ridges wanted.

When Roo walked into the hotel, Dog and Cat raced over nearly knocking him to the ground. Riley's three dogs though, reacted quite differently. Used to doing things their own way they soon had Dog sorted out. Within a few minutes Dog became one of the new Birdsville pack. He was delighted, in his own doggy way, to have some of his own kind to play with. Cat hissed, fluffed out his mangy hair and stood his ground. The three new comers soon learned who the real boss was.

"Glenda?"said Nulla at dinner that night. "I wonder how my old squadron are doing these days. I left a lot of good mates back in Adelaide and I'd like to see them again."

"Love, they're probably thinking the same of you. Maybe you could talk to Sundown and his commando, maybe they'll know. We should go and ask Pellino and Gail." She pointed at a table nearby and waved. "Let's take our plates over and get acquainted," she suggested.

 "Hi, we heard you had a bit of an adventure coming across the Strzelecki Desert. Maybe you could tell us a bit more about your adventures now that we can talk openly and not in that mangled code we've been using on the CB," said Pellino while spooning in a mouthful of camel stew.

"It's been tough hasn't it," smiled Nulla, "we did it though. What I was hoping you could help me with is this: what's happening with my mob in Adelaide, the 1st Armoured Cavalry? Have you heard any news?"

Pellino looked around for Wiram and yelled, "Wiram, what was it the major said about the 1st Cav in Adelaide? Didn't he say they'd preserved their Abrams and they still had enough ammunition to push the terrorists out of the country?"

Wiram nodded and called back across the noisy dining room, "Nulla, we only know what Major Thompson said in passing. He let slip that the Abrams tanks were still in action and would help in the push to clear the country. We don't have any details though, sorry."

"I'll ask Sundown when he gets back from Alice Springs, he might have some news for me. I'd really like to know how my mates are going," said Nulla.

Pellino replied, "We expect him back soon, Nulla. Sergeant Ahmet keeps us informed of goings on, what he's allowed to say anyway. He's commander of the Bushmaster stationed on the roads east and north, just outside Birdsville. Everything we want to say to Third Army goes through him now. They're a grand lot but they won't let us in on their network yet. I believe Sundown will swing something while he's in the Alice though, then things will change."

That evening there was plenty of activity as the new comers connected with Mel and Wilma. They had taken on the admin role for new arrivals while Pinkie was gone. The girls got on well and the children were happily in the care of Lulu and Danni.

Donna spent most of her time as Wiram's assistant. She was kept busy planning and preparing the patrols supplies and equipment. Logistics was critical and she was in her element fussing over the boys and yet still being one of them.

But life never stands still for anyone. The city dwellers had yet to unpack their gear when news came of an assault to the south. Their dream of sanctuary was in serious trouble of evaporating.

At first light next morning, Andy ran into the dining room and found Wiram with a few other early risers having breakfast.

"Sorry to upset you but it seems our Bravo Team and One One Charlie on the Birdsville Track south of Mungerannie are in trouble. Sergeant Doff's radioman said the Stosstruppen might push them out of their ambush position. The Patrol One post has passed on the report and have asked for support in case they're hit too."

Andy then turned and spoke to those present, "Folks, please finish your meals and then wake everyone. This looks serious."

Chapter 14 - Stosstruppen Storm Troopers

Bushmaster One One Bravo commanded by Sergeant Ahmet, and One One Charlie commanded by Sergeant Doff, had remained with Sundown's Commando to strengthen the approaches north and south of Birdsville. Doff's One One Charlie was based on the Birdsville Track to cover the road from Marree; while Ahmet's One One Bravo took up position to secure the north and east routes into Birdsville from Mount Isa and Longreach.

Sergeant Doff's Bushmaster, a 6 wheel drive all-terrain armoured vehicle immediately began a series of hit-and-run patrols on the Birdsville track, a practice the sergeant reveled in. Things got so bad that Major Daniels of the Revelationist's Alpha Army in Adelaide decided to step up the training of his beloved Stosstruppen, storm troopers and hit back at Sundown's Commando - and hit back hard.

The Stosstruppen were first introduced into the German army in the later stages of the 1st World War. They consisted of highly trained soldiers using tactics that incorporated massed grenade attacks to clear enemy strong points. These small squads of elite troops were trained in manoeuvring around strongly held bunkers and cutting them off from their rear support. Rapid assault or 'storms' would out-flank and out-fight their opponents in fixed positions.

Used as shock-troops they were trained to infiltrate against the toughest opposition. Their rapid and aggressive skirmishing could push through defended positions not strong enough or willful enough to hold them at bay.

Chan and John were in the current dirt bike patrol with Halo and Beamy. The patrol began soon after Sundown left for Alice Springs. This was Beamy's first patrol since his injuries. He had to convince Wiram and Pellino that he was not only fit enough but had the strength back in his shoulders and legs to get through a week of hard living and riding in tough desert terrain.

To his credit Beamy worked harder than anyone at his fitness. He had recovered most of his lung capacity, strength and had improved movement in his wounded shoulder. He proved that he could manage himself in the hardest terrain. His demonstration for Sundown was not just good luck, he was a crack shot and proud of it.

Sergeant Doff commanded the armoured troop-carrier, Bushmaster One One Charlie, operating as both stationary and active patrol. He worked in with the mobile bike commando and spent a lot of time with Wiram and Cambra developing strategy for defence and assault. Their orders were to keep the enemy busy chasing their tails. This would prevent them from massing an attack on Birdsville with their battalion strength force which was now based at the Marree township.

By now everyone knew Chan and John were ex-Deaths Head Revelationists. Even though the Alice Springs soldiers weren't too comfortable associating with them they soon learned to respect their skill and acknowledged their deep hatred of their former comrades. To make sure they were accepted as equals the two boys worked harder than anyone else and took on the most difficult and unpleasant tasks.

The plan was to attack every terrorist patrol that set out on the Birdsville Track. The two squads headed down to Mungerannie, a small hot water spring resort complete with hotel, about half way between Birdsville and Marree.

This was Pellino and Mel's hotel which had been their home for most of their married lives. Sadly they pulled up their roots for Birdsville at the start of the apocalypse. By switching ambush sites and style of assault the commando hoped to prevent the enemy from being able to predict when and where they would next be hit.

On this particular night One One Charlie took up a position opposite the track in a particularly scrubby section of road. The bike patrol and Bushmaster laid several land mines in the road surface and selected their ambush behind a set of low sand dunes overlooking the track. In the overcast, pre-dawn morning an enemy patrol was seen travelling at speed towards their ambush site.

"Halo!" called Sergeant Doff, "we have four trucks and one Jeep approaching. ETA two minutes. Prepare for contact and pull back to your bikes as soon as we've done some damage."

The sergeant took command of the contacts now and the boys respected his knowledge of all things military.

Sergeant Doff saw service in Afghanistan and Iraq as well as the Solomon Islands in the south pacific. He was an experienced and gifted strategist and well respected by his men. Most of the Alice Springs Command preferred to serve under Doff than most of the other troop commanders, except Tobi and Ahmet. These three sergeants all had fighting experience and the men's respect.

Chan had his Blaser sniper rifle out and sighted on the last truck; Halo had given his machine gun over to Beamy and was happy to be his number two. John took to the Javelin, after they'd captured more ammunition his accuracy rose with each ambush - he was deadly.

Four of Doff's soldiers remained back at their standing ambush site, Patrol One, on the Birdsville Track near the Cooper Creek crossing. But such was the commando's confidence that they didn't think they needed the full contingency there. They did what they usually did - hit hard then run back to the standing ambush site, Patrol One.

All communication was now in code and Birdsville home-base knew of their every movement. Unless the contact was approved by Wiram, Doff, Ahmet and Andy it was a no-go. No one pushed Wiram to do anything. He was as firm as Sergeant Doff. Together with Sergeant Ahmet they ran the entire patrolling operation like a well oiled machine.

"They're not showing any lights so they must have light-enhanced vision, boys. We'd better be extra careful with this. We hit and then we run like buggery," called Sergeant Doff. He now sensed that things might just turn a little sour if he was right.

He turned to his radio operator, "Ivan, get onto Assassin and tell him there's a good chance we'll be pushed hard at this contact and he had better organise backup asap. We'll meet them at Patrol One on Cooper Creek. I've got a bad feeling about this contact, a really bad feeling." Doff was about to call for Chan and John to remove the land mines when he saw the enemy patrol increase speed as it approached.

"Bastards have seen us!" he yelled.

Doff called out to the biker patrol, "They've got night vision and infra-red boys! Get your heads down and only come back up when you hear the land mines explode." He saw them nod to acknowledge that they'd heard him. "Then we hit and then we frigging run. Got it? Fire two full magazines then grab your bikes and get going. One One Charlie will stay to finish off any survivors. I don't want any bikers staying back."

The four bike patrol boys nodded as they eased their blackened faces below the sand dune.

The convoy quickly approached possibly hoping to race past as fast as they could. The Jeep in the lead hit the first landmine and flew into the air. The four trucks behind skidded trying to avoid the debris of the jeep and the other land mines that were sure to be there.

Beamy opened up with his machine gun raking the trucks to keep any organised resistance in check. The Bushmaster 7.62 mm machine gun was working the trucks over killing and injuring the terrorists as they exited. But in the heat of the battle no one noticed the second convoy approaching.

John was searching for a suitable target for his Javelin, anti-tank missile, when he noticed another set of trucks pulling up not one hundred metres away. Out jumped a platoon of Stosstruppen and they began to skirmish forwards. As one squad ran forward the other provided covering fire. John knew that when they got to within grenade throwing distance the commando would be in big trouble.

"STOSSTRUPPEN! Sixty metres south! Doff, time to move!" John knew it was too late to find a target so he quickly disarmed his Javelin and began to pack it up. Incoming fire began to scream off the Bushmaster's armoured sides. The ambushers did what they had done in every ambush – hit fast then move back to their bikes.

The Bushmaster began to back out of it's hull-down position when a missile slammed into it's armoured side and exploded. Pieces of metal and vehicle parts flew through the air. It hadn't penetrated but it shook everyone. The concussion shattered the fuel pump and the engine died.

Doff knew his beloved Bushmaster was stuffed so he bashed open the rear hatch and helped his mates stagger out. Their ears bleeding and their heads reeling from the concussion. He couldn't hear a thing but his instincts told him he had but seconds to get out before a second missile slammed into his beloved Bushmaster. This time it would surely penetrate and shatter anyone left inside.

He reached back and gathered an armful of ammunition and a bag of water bottles. For a second he considered going back for food but he thought better of it and ran. He only just made it to the bikes when a second missile hit the Bushmaster and it exploded in a roar of heat and flames.

"Strewth!" he cried looking around frantically, "where's Ivan?" Screams rent the air and then he knew where his crewman was. Doff went cold inside. Specialist Ivan Luddin was one of his best mates, a great card player and one of the personalities of the cavalry squadron. Sergeant Doff deliberately closed his mind down, down, deep down, then he turned to join his remaining troops.

Four bikes and eight men. John had the good sense to destroy his beloved Javelin. Chan hurriedly placed each Bushmaster crewman with one of the bikes and amid the incoming bullets and grenades they took off to the north east.

It was not their best retreat but they'd had close calls before and survived. But they didn't see the third convoy arrive and spew out another platoon of Stosstruppen who quickly moved forward into a second skirmish line. They too opened fire at the retreating bikers.

Bullets thudded into bodies and Beamy felt his crewman fall off his bike. He immediately pulled up and grabbed at his machine gun to run back to his mate. But it was too late, the enemy had taken up position and were firing into the scrub towards him. It was way too hot to get back on the bike to escape. Beamy gently put his hand on his mate's throat and checked his pulse, he was alive but it wasn't good.

"Shit, Danny! Move, mate!" But Danny could only groan in reply, bubbles of blood foamed from his open mouth.

Beamy positioned himself and his machine gun on the sand dune in front of Danny and began firing at the dark heads he could see bobbing as they ran towards him in the pale, dawn light. He could hear the sounds as his bullets hit their mark in the bodies of his enemy but there were too many of them. His ammunition ran out and he grabbed another belt, fed it through, it took too much time. The silence of his machine gun encouraged the Stosstruppen to push forward and they began encircling Beamy's position.

He opened fire again forcing some of the enemy to drop to the ground. The Stosstruppen began calling out to each other, pinpointing the machine gun's position. Within seconds four grenades were in the air heading towards Beamy and his mate lying on the side of the sand dune. Beamy knew he would die but continued firing, he would never leave a mate. It was an unwritten law now, no commando left their mates behind.

Poorly made in a factory outside Adelaide by inexperienced slaves, one grenade exploded prematurely as soon as it left the hand of it's thrower. It knocked three Stosstruppen to the ground. The second landed on the front side of the dune, it's explosion showered sand over the two commandos.

When Beamy leaned over to shake his mate there was no response and he put his hand on his throat again to feel for a pulse, there was none. The third grenade landed four or five metres in a hollow to the left of him. The last grenade didn't explode, it was a dud.

Beamy held the machine gun in his hands, ducking down as low as he could he raced back to his bike. Bullets zipped past his shoulder and head as he picked up speed and headed in the direction of his retreating squad. He felt tears streaming down his cheek knowing he had left behind a mate and every lost mate was one less to protect those he loved.

He swore as he skidded in the soft sand and almost stalled. The desperate commando put his foot down and pushed hard spinning his back wheel raising a sheet of wet sand. Bullets continued to zip past him. He knew that if it wasn't such an overcast dawn he'd probably be dead by now.

The rest of the ambush squad were several hundred metres away. They pulled up on Sergeant Doff's command. Three bikes and six men, the two wounded could barely hold on and

Doff had another serious problem: Beamy and his crewman were missing.

"Listen, that's Beamy firing! Shit! We've got to go back!" Halo stood his bike up and kicked it alive but Sergeant Doff put his hand on his shoulder.

"Halo, they've planned this and they now out-gun us. We're badly outnumbered and we need to get these wounded back to the standing patrol. Beamy will have to..." he stopped talking because he couldn't say it.

"Fuck that, Doff! He's my mate!" Halo jammed his wrist around the throttle and sped back towards the ambush. Chan and John looked at each other then spun their bikes around too.

"Doff, we have to go back, he's our mate and we don't leave our mates behind," called Chan as the two boys dropped their passengers to speed after Halo.

The big sergeant nodded, he was both glad and horrified at what had happened. He'd seen many a fire-fight, some were very close calls but this one shook him up. He knew that if a soldier couldn't rely on his mates to go back for him in a crisis then they were all lost.

Sergeant Doff helped his wounded crewmen to sit comfortably. Using his pale red-light torch to see their wounds he began to patch his comrades up. Behind them came the growing roar of battle.

Halo could see the tracers of Beamy's machine gun smashing into the bushes and scrub around the ambush site. *'That's where the bastards are coming from'*, he thought. Although he couldn't see anything in the dawn light he knew to follow the sounds and origins of the tracer. He stopped to get his bearings just as Chan and John pulled up next to him. Halo turned to them, nodded then pointed to Beamy's position but the tracers stopped and they heard three grenade explosions.

John called out, "We might be too late!" He opened his throttle and sped forward, the other two right behind him.

They stopped once more on a tall sand dune to look across the battlefield to get their bearings. In the pale light they saw Beamy on his bike riding towards them. His head was down and he skidded and ploughed through the wet sand and scrub.

"Quick, covering fire!" cried Chan as he unhitched his sniper rifle and began firing at the muzzle flashes. The enemy were forming ready to assault Beamy's position from front and both sides. John and Halo opened up with their AK's and although the range was a bit too far for accurate sniping they were experienced enough to accommodate for the distance and scored enough hits to slow the advance.

Beamy hadn't seen his friends yet and was still swearing to himself at his precarious situation. He was also terrified of being hit again. His insides were turning to mush and he felt he might soil himself. He tucked up his sphincter muscles as tightly as he could then crouched even further down over his handle bars to make himself as small a target as possible.

Even so he was hit again and it hurt worse than he ever remembered being hurt before in his life.

The young biker only had another ten or more metres to go and he would have been hidden by the sand dune which Halo and his ex Death's Heads friends were firing from. They were providing covering fire with all they had in them. The bullet went through his side, hit one of his ribs and continued along it to finally exit from his chest just under his collar bone.

"You frigging bastards!" he grunted as he collapsed over his handlebars. It felt like someone had held a flaming brand against his rib cage and chest. He lost control of the bike tumbling face first into the sand.

"Beamy! Beamy! Are you OK?" he heard the voices calling from only a few metres away. The young rigger looked up to see his rescuers, his mates, and he was overwhelmed.

"You damned idiots! You should've kept going!" he sobbed almost unconscious from the shock and pain.

John ripped his throttle open and pulled up next to his friend. "Beamy, climb on! Leave your weapon! Just climb on and hold tight!"

Halo and Chan continued firing until they saw John and Beamy had started back towards Doff then they too stopped firing and took off after them. John paused to put a burst of fire into Beamy's bike so the terrorists couldn't use it, then he raced after Chan.

'*This is a disaster, a complete bloody disaster,*' thought Doff as he watched the boys riding back noticing only three bikes with one passenger. He did the maths and knew that one of his boys was left behind, he hoped he was dead. He also figured that someone would be walking back to Birdsville.

The boys pulled up beside Doff and the two wounded soldiers breathing hard. Chan looked around at their enemy and assessed their situation in those few seconds. He said, "We double and we triple. We're not leaving a single man behind. Got it, sergeant!" He looked directly into Doff's eyes.

The kindly sergeant saw the frightened and exhausted look painted on the boys faces. '*We really are in deep shit,*' he thought once more to himself.

"We've just lost Danny," sobbed John, "I'm not going to let us lose any more. Chan, you're smallest, put Mugga in between you and Doff. It might be slow but we'll make it to our number one supply cache in a few hours." He was sweating hard as he tried to fix his mental map of where the cache was hidden.

"OK, John, you'll have to put Stan in front of you and hold him. He won't fall off but it'll be slow going. Beamy, are you OK like that?" asked Doff, his mind too was working overtime.

"I'm fine. I've done this before you know," said Beamy, his voice slurring as Halo wrapped a large bandage around his chest. Doff knew that Beamy was in shock and had no doubt lost a lot of blood - it was all down his shirt front and side. They had to get the wounded moving and treated as soon as possible. Enemy rifle fire continued to zip around them but in the overcast dawn light none of it was accurate. They had to get moving even if it meant slow going.

They stopped well in front of the Stosstruppen just as it began to rain. A steady downpour that made riding difficult. The drizzling mist shifted and they could see the Stosstruppen trucks moving slowly towards them.

John said they had another hour before they made the first food and fuel cache, he was quite certain he could locate it. He stood looking at his map and compass working out the route. But the desert, flat and featureless without any visible landmarks, made navigation in these cloudy conditions very difficult. His training included orientation and he had been carefully noting the distances on his bike's speed dial. He'd topped his classes in orienteering but was anxious that he might fail to find the cache in this rain and mist.

"We know home base received our message before the fighting started. I told them I didn't have a good feeling about the contact so hopefully they'll have a patrol on its way. It's a bugger losing Danny, Luddin and the Bushmaster." He stopped for a moment, pushed his feelings back down, then spoke again. "Patrol One on the Cooper should all be on full alert now too." Doff took a drink from the water bottle thrust into his hands. Something was wrong, he looked at his hands and they were shaking.

"We were set up by these Stosstruppen, three convoys? Really? They've never done anything like that before. This was deliberate." Again he stopped to drink deeply using both hands to hold the precious bottle of water.

"Sarge?" called one of the wounded crewman, Mugga. "Our boys should be on their way by now but it's gonna take them hours to reach Patrol One's position." He coughed up blood and had to stop talking for a moment. "I don't know if I can hold out that long. My guts feel bad and I have trouble staying on the bike."

His sergeant nodded. He knew they might lose both his crewmen before they could get them to Birdsville, and it hurt to think of it. Again he pushed it down, deep down.

"Boys, we just ride, that's all we can do. Get to the fuel dump and rest up, patch up, then get to Patrol One. Chan, how long will that take?" he asked the young man.

"I think…" Chan looked upwards as he thought, "another hour to the cache. Take a half hour rest then another two hours to the Patrol One site. If we don't have any more contacts with the Stosstruppen we should be there by mid afternoon," he replied, rechecking the kilometres in his head and the hours it should take in this rugged desert country.

"John, is that what your calculations give you?" Doff asked their point man.

John nodded. "Yep, that's about right. Just follow me fella's, I've got this. Thankfully it's getting lighter and that should make it a little easier. Just stay on my six."

They all turned as they heard the sound of vehicles behind them. There were a half dozen Revelationist trucks now only a hundred metres behind slowly approaching their position.

"They just won't give up will they," grunted Halo.

"Do you think you could stay back and put several magazines into them before you head off after us, Halo? It'll slow them down and give us a few minutes head start. We'll need that later on," said Doff.

"I'm on it, Doff," he said. Turning to his mate propped painfully on his bike behind him he said, "Beamy, you'd better prepare for another screaming mad escape." Beamy just nodded.

"OK, let's do it, fella's." Doff helped the wounded onto the bikes and they headed off again at a slow pace. Stan was bleeding internally and would probably have to be held in place by John, an almost impossible task in the rough, rain sodden terrain.

A minute later they could hear the sound of gunfire.

While the bikers engaged in a fighting retreat, Patrol One on the Coopers Creek crossing had it's own problems.

Chapter 15 - Patrol One

Major Daniels the Stosstruppen commander, knew that he had to do something creative and impressive. His battalion was taking a beating and morale was low. With the constant pressure created by Sundown's hit-and-run tactics his battalion was becoming a joke with the rest of General Himmler's Army Alpha. He knew what Sundown's Commando were doing but lacked the military skill to do anything about it.

Daniels was another one of those leaders handed command because of his position in the church. The major liked doing things which he knew he shouldn't but rather than hand him in to the police his superiors simply passed him from one parish to another. This continued throughout his professional career until he discovered the Revelationist church had a degree of tolerance for predator-sized appetites like his. He was good at blackmail too. When he uncovered a weakness in a superior he used that as leverage to work his way up through the hierarchy of power.

Major Daniels loved the Nazi regime and like his commander General Himmler he had a smattering of knowledge about German warfare strategy and could fool most people. He had a lifetime of experience doing just that. It was his second in command, Captain Burgess, who had the extensive experience in the military he needed to play this game successfully.

Captain Burgess returned from a stint in Afghanistan just days before the apocalypse. He came from a family of professional soldiers and military historians. As a member of the church he was a much sought after authority on military matters. His knowledge was exactly what Daniels wanted and he got it, in spadefuls.

While Burgess had few weaknesses he did like to dress up in women's clothing and very much liked to be called 'Mary'. When Daniels discovered this fact he took full advantage and proceeded to blackmail him.

That was all it took to create the Stosstruppen. Captain Burgess was a brilliant strategist with hands-on experience and a lifetime study of all things military. A sensitive man Burgess knew that as long as he performed his duty he was safe from exposure and humiliation. Daniels knew that as long as he held tight control of the captain he was worshiped as one of the foremost military leaders of the Revelationists in Australia.

At one time they were neck to neck with the Deaths Heads for position as the top battalion. But after the shattering losses at Marree and Birdsville, Major Lunney's elite company was all but disbanded and Daniels took first place.

"Burgess, did you get that order through?" asked Daniels over breakfast that morning.

Burgess was bleary eyed after a night drinking himself into oblivion. "Yes sir, we've rounded up all the children you asked for. They should be here in a few days for you to choose from." How he hated the major and his sexual excesses, it made him want to puke.

Craftily Daniels enabled the captain's own excesses, bringing him new dresses and women's underwear whenever he came back from a trip to the city or interstate. In a strange way Captain Burgess worshiped Daniels while daily plotting his demise. Daniels, on the other hand, simply played the game, the game of power.

"Did you make sure Linda and Phillip had enough soap and shampoo for them? You know I don't like dirty little boys, Mary. 'Cleanliness is next to Godliness' is the saying and it's so true of pretty little boys." He enjoyed these little games and his use of the endearment '*Mary*' was as strategic as Burgess' ambush this morning when his Stosstruppen knocked out Doff's Bushmaster.

"Yes sir, it's all done just the way you like it," answered Burgess who at the same time fantasised another way to poison his superior.

Burgess still had work to do but his head was heavy and throbbed. He had no choice but to stall the next move in his game of chess with Sundown's Commando. His scouts knew of the Patrol One stockade, they couldn't miss it. The stockade was built across the road completely blocking any movement north or south. Unless he was prepared to bush bash through soft sand and thick scrub it had to be breached. In reality it proved to be a formidable barrier and they needed to knock out that stockade.

His next move was to be there to direct their assault of Birdsville itself but he just wasn't up to it today. Lieutenant Donata was out there now and reported that the position fell within a few minutes of his assault. They took two prisoners and two enemy were killed. Burgess was disappointed, he expected a force of at least half platoon size holding the post, not four piddling defenders. One consolation was that they were regular army and cavalry at that.

He ordered Lieutenant Donata to hold the position, beef up it's defences, and send out day and evening patrols for several kilometres up the road. He also wanted his lieutenant to set up listening posts closer to Birdsville. If only his head wasn't so sore he would be out there now giving orders but it would just have to wait another day.

Lance Corporal Poole sat with his hands tied behind his back and his wounded comrade lay beside him at the Patrol One site on the Coopers Creek crossing. He was thinking how unprepared they were. They simply had no chance against the full force of a platoon strength assault by the storm troopers.

'These Stosstruppen are good,' he reminded himself. They came right on dawn when the rising sun normally slanted into the stockade blinding them. But with the early morning rain they were completely invisible, they didn't need to have the sun in their enemy's eyes.

It began with snipers firing through their loop holes, the cavalry machine gun was put out of action in the first few seconds. All four troopers were awake, two up top and two below making a brew of black tea to have with their breakfast. They were ready though. There were personnel mines laid on their perimeter but none went off until the fighting actually started.

Poole recalled how he was sitting with his cup of tea in his fist. A lazy cigarette was in his other hand while he waited for his breakfast to warm on their little wood-fired stove. He carelessly stared out of the slit in the stockade wall. Above were his two mates on duty talking softly in the pale dawn light. He sat up in confusion when he heard the 'splat!' of a sniper's bullet striking a human body.

There was an expletive from one of his mates above followed by another 'splat!' The swearing stopped. Poole heard the second body collapse to the wooden floor above him. That was when he knew they were in trouble.

Fighting from a strong defensive position is the best way to reduce your body count. That is, unless the surroundings are perfect hiding places for snipers and a well trained enemy. They can see you, clearly, from a distance too. But you can't see them. Even though Poole and his mates had cleared most of the scrub from around their stockade for twenty odd metres it clearly wasn't enough. A well camouflaged sniper could easily crawl into a position twenty metres away and snipe at their leisure without being detected.

When the two guards went down Poole recalled how Slimmy Lahotski stood up and knocked his head on the low roof and swore. It should have been funny but humour was not on anyone's mind at that moment, just tension and raw fear.

"For crying out loud, Slimmy, get your head down! They've got snipers and we're sitting ducks," he'd said.

Slimmy ducked down and looked across their tiny enclosure and asked in a small voice, "What are we gonna do, Poolie?"

There came explosions as two of the mines went off followed by a hail of bullets, machine guns and then grenades. It was pandemonium and all directed at their post.

Poole knew they were screwed. He didn't even think, he just ducked down below their sandbagged parapet and pulled out his handkerchief. It was off-white, good enough for a white flag of surrender. Wrapping it around a stick he poked it out of the slit and waved it frantically.

"We surrender!" he called over and over but the bullets kept coming. Slimmy tried to crawl out through the exit at the back of the stockade but one of the Stosstruppen was waiting for him. He shot Slimmy in the stomach. When Poole heard the shot he increased his shouting.

Finally the soldier outside called loudly, "Cease fire!"

He could hear Slimmy groaning as he crawled out with his hands over his head. The lance corporal saw his mate lying with his back against the sandbag wall, his hands covering his bloody stomach.

The Stosstruppen NCO searched them then told him to take care of Slimmy. Poole watched as they went through their position searching for weapons and anything they could take of value. They took his watch too, which seemed to be the usual booty of every victor since wrist watches were invented.

"Get your mate bandaged, buddy, because we'll be sending you two back to Marree where you'll be processed," said the NCO as his lieutenant approached. "We'll do what we can for you now, but once the priests get hold of you not even God can help you."

Lieutenant Donata introduced himself and began his interrogation. He ordered food and water then called for his medic to see to Slimmy, but only after he'd treated his own wounded.

There was not much else really, thought Poole. He tried to avoid answering the many questions but his mind was shattered. He stammered awkward replies and couldn't even remember what he'd said, everything happened too fast. And now here he was waiting for the bastards to take him to their Marree camp. He heard they didn't get many regular army prisoners these days because there were so few left after the apocalypse. That made him more depressed than he already felt. It meant not only was he an oddity but he would receive special attention. He could only imagine what that meant.

One scene stuck in his mind as he was walked outside to pee, and that was the miserable state of their stockade. It looked like it would fall apart any moment. Although it weathered the grenade attack the storm of bullets had split the sand bags right open. It looked like the aftermath of a tornado.

'At least it stayed together long enough to save Slimmy and me,' he thought.

There was one thing that stuck in his mind like a stomach ulcer though - he'd forgotten to destroy the radio and code book. Prized possessions that could easily compromise the entire commando.

That morning the new arrivals from Arkaroola were up ready to have breakfast with the locals. They already felt part of the community. All through their trip Bongo spoke of what they would find at Birdsville and how friendly everyone was. They were so excited to have finally arrived at 'sanctuary'. But news of the patrol contacts had broken and now they were subdued and nervous.

"Wiram! Wiram!" called Andy, peering into the lounge where the community usually met for breakfast.

"Over here, Andy!" replied Wiram, he stood up so the old man could see him.

Andy walked over, his limp more pronounced than usual. "Wiram, I think we've lost the Patrol One position as well. We can't get them up on the radio and that's never happened before. Cambra and Pellino are trouble shooting the electronics. They might have been hit by the Stosstruppen just after Doff and the bike patrol were hit." He sat down, his breath came fast and he wheezed as he spoke.

"Hey, slow down, mate," said Wiram steadying their chief administrator. "OK, let me get this straight. First of all we hear that Doff and our bike patrol is hit and on the run. OK, we're covered for that, Assassin should reach Patrol One's post in a couple of hours and he'll let us know what's happening. We're just about ready with Alpha team and they should be gone in a half hour. But now you're saying we've lost contact with the Patrol One post at the Coopers Creek crossing?"

"Yes, we chatted about a half hour ago. Doff said he had bad feeling about their contact on the Birdsville Track near Mungerannie. It is most probable they have wounded but Patrol One have no further information. I'm worried, if the Stosstruppen hit Doff and our bikers then it makes sense for them to take out our Patrol One at the same time, don't you think?" asked Andy.

Wiram nodded. "Yeah, I just wish we had the numbers to have manned Patrol One better, we should have beefed it up a bit, somehow. I knew that it was always a stop-gap measure but now we're paying for our mistakes, we've let our men be caught in something we didn't properly prepare for. We're gonna have real problems if our front line post and ambush patrols have been hit simultaneously. It's possible they've been scattered all over the desert." The giant aboriginal put his face in his hands and tried to calm his racing mind.

Chapter 16 - Prepare and Retaliate

Sundown stood up and was heading towards the door when the general called out.

"Sundown, wait a moment, you can't get there without the aeroplane and if this rain breaks it'll take you a week to cross the Simpson by vehicle. Please, sit down and let's consider our options." Sundown stopped and thought that maybe the general was trying to reconcile?

"Corporal, thank you, please wait here for your orders." Turning to his attentive staff officers he called for their thoughts.

"Thompson?" he asked, nodding towards the newly appointed Colonel.

"Sir, Charlie are a tough lot. Sergeant Doff's seen action in three conflict zones and can handle the situation. I trust him implicitly. Sundown's boys know the country and are hardened warriors experienced in hit-and-run patrols in the desert." He summed the men up perfectly. "I think they'll head deeper into the desert and just melt away. They have procedures for just this event and they have caches of food, fuel and water everywhere. I think Ahmet should run down with Wiram and check the situation, but not compromise the approaches from the north."

"Captain McFly, your thoughts please?" continued the general.

"Sir, I agree with Colonel Thompson, send the Bravo armoured crew with Wiram to investigate," he said.

"Major Lewis, what's the intelligence status of the Mount Isa and Longreach Revelationists, are they in a position to assault Birdsville from the north?" General Hughes asked each of his staff for their assessments.

"Sir, the hit they took from us knocked them backwards. Intelligence reports we shouldn't be too worried about them until their leadership regain control of the rank and file. Seems the fear of a Tajna Služba retaliation has made them a little nervous. We don't expect either battalions to unite, they're back to fighting each other. At the moment the situation appears to be safe for Bravo to head south with Wiram's patrol," came the newly appointed major's response.

"Sundown, what are you thinking?" the general came to him at last.

"Sir, if the terrorists ambushed our patrol that means something is afoot and I'd like to be there to direct our men, but I can't. I trust Wiram to take control and do what needs to be done. He's my second in command for just that reason, he thinks like I do." Sundown sat back down and ran his hands through his thick, greying hair. "It worries me though. The enemy are thinking for a change and that's going to put real pressure on us. We have so few resources and theirs is immeasurable. If they have armour we are well and truly screwed. In short, general, I'm very worried"

General Hughes sat back down and adjusted the height of his chair so he could look down on his staff. Sundown saw his muscles twitch as each mood and emotion conflicted with each other for space on his face.

In his conversations with Blondie he knew that General Hughes was a political appointment. It was a favour for managing a very awkward and embarrassing situation for the government. This occurred when the Minister for Defence was caught in bed with a senior member of the Tajna Služba, a gorgeous blond model.

From Brigadier General he was promoted to full General after the suicide bombing at the start of the apocalypse decimated the high command killing the Chief of Defence. The Governor General had no choice but to promote him further, as Chief of the Australian Defence Force.

Sundown realised, as he watched the general's comical behaviour, that this man was more Dad's Army than Thompson could ever be.

"Thank you corporal, please relay to Sergeant Ahmet that he is to stay put at his post north of Birdsville. He is not to engage unless absolutely necessary. We've just lost an armoured personnel carrier and that is one too many for my liking. They don't grow on trees any more you know," General Hughes said firmly.

He knew his decision would be poorly received so he added, "Commander, your boys are hardened warriors, they'll manage as they've done countless times against these inferior terrorist forces. I'm of the opinion that one lost armoured Bushmaster is enough for one day. We need to protect our most precious resource and that's our armour." Hughes then went back to finish his meal, a smug satisfaction glowed inside him.

Sundown stood and made his way to the radio office next door. He spoke to Wiram. "Can you get on to Assassin? Tell him what we know and to report back as soon as he knows what's going on at Patrol One. Then send him to check out the hidden caches in case Doff and the bike patrol are headed there. Better tell him to hang about for a few days to see if any survivors turn up at the closest cache to the ambush site,"

"Tell Ahmet to do what his conscious tells him to do, I trust him. He was with Cambra and Halo at Mount Isa, he's one of ours now. And Wiram, I've got some good news. Tell everyone, especially Fat Boy, that Pedro has recovered and is making a bloody nuisance of himself in hospital. He's fine except for his hangover. OK, good luck, keep in touch. I'll do what I can from this end but it's now up to you to save our community."

Wiram stood and left Sergeant Ahmet's Bushmaster to walk back to the hotel lounge room, now a hive of activity.

Nulla and his group watched with some concern. Simon fingered the pistol in his shoulder holster nervously.

"Wiram, Sundown's in Alice Springs right now and all we have to protect our community is what's sitting here, plus the girls. I think we need to pull everyone out and send them to the safe house," said Cambra, the entire lounge was silent and everyone heard.

The only Alice Springs Command fighting force left in Birdsville was Sergeant Ahmet and the five crewmen of One One Bravo. They were now stationed at the junction to Longreach and Mount Isa, five minutes away. There were also these new arrivals from Adelaide via Arkaroola. But Wiram wasn't completely certain of their quality, he'd not had time to get to know them.

Wiram worried about bringing Lulu and Danni into the fight. He knew that every soldier counts in situations like this but those too teenagers were barely old enough to hold a gun. He knew Halo had trained the girls well, they could '*shoot the eye out of a frog*' he'd once told Sundown, but…

"Donna, better call Lulu and Danni in, please, I think they need to hear this. Can you also get Tricia but leave Gail on the CB, thanks."

He paused then announced in a loud voice, "Everyone, we'll start with some good news for a change. Sundown just informed me that Pedro is now safely in Alice Springs Hospital and will be fighting fit once he gets over his hangover. He's doing fine." There was a cheer and a rumble of voices.

Fat Boy was still helping the girls prepare breakfast. When he heard the news he came out of the kitchen and hugged Wiram, almost breaking the giant man's back.

"Thanks for the spinal adjustment, Fat Boy," Wiram grunted. "OK, now it's back to the issue of our survival. So please, everyone, settle down while we go through our battle plans. The ladies will bring in some breakfast as soon as it's ready." The creases on Wiram's forehead made him look both worried and angry.

The battle hardened aboriginal warrior was silent for a moment while he ran his thoughts through his head. Fat Boy and Blondie were civilians and he didn't expect them to fight. Besides he thought, Fat Boy might drop dead of heart failure if he had to run any distance. Harry was a civilian and his accident some years ago meant he simply couldn't participate. Besides he needed him to arrange ordinance, transport and run things behind the scenes, as he'd done since that first day at Marree.

The others, Gail, Tricia, Jeda, Jenny, Mel and Wilma were all civilians and there was no way he could put a rifle in their hands. They were needed to look after the only surviving oldies, Polly and Granny, the two tough old birds from Marree.

Wiram looked at Nulla, warrior to warrior, Nulla smiled back and nodded. That reassured the tough aboriginal veteran and he calmed a little.

"OK, this is what we'll do. Nulla, I'm sending you out to the Patrol One site with your boys on their bikes, I'll send Pellino and Cambra with you. They know the set up and can take the dual cab with supplies and extra weapons." He saw Andy writing it all down and felt comforted by the old man's composure in a crisis.

Wiram thought for a split second, turning back to Nulla he said, "Sergeant Nulla… sorry, it's an old habit." He smiled and started again. "Nulla, have your boys recovered from their trip and are they ready to fight?"

Nulla nodded. "Yes, they are. I'm going to leave my girl warriors, Lucy, Glenda and Heidi here but I'll take the three lads." Nulla looked at Arthur. "Arty, are you well enough to ride and fight? And don't bullshit me because this could mean life or death for those who might have to stop and help you if you're not."

Arty turned to Luke and Simon who both nodded. "Yes, I'm ready. I've been riding on and off on the way to Birdsville and I've been working out with Luke and Simon. I'm fine to ride, my arm is heaps better and although my leg does get stiff if it means riding an all dayer I can do it. And don't forget boss, I've had nearly three weeks sitting in the car as a passenger most of this time. Yeah, I'm ready to do my part."

As would he expected Heidi wouldn't let anything pass without her input. "Nulla, you said if we did our training you'd let us help with the defences. Well, now is the time for us to help out," the attractive teenager said with a pert smile at Nulla. Lucy nodded in agreement.

"Heidi and Lucy, I love you girls like my sisters and even though you know how to fire a rifle it doesn't mean you can ride three hundred kilometres, fight a battle and then escape through the desert by bike or on foot. That takes a lot more training than shooting at bottles in Arkaroola. Do you understand?"

He held up his hand to quieten Heidi when she protested. "Another word Heidi and I'll take your rifle off you." Heidi immediately stopped arguing and sat back down with a grumpy look on her pretty young face.

Bongo sat in one of the lounge chairs next to Roo and Charlene. He looked happy and contented with Cat sleeping on his lap. Charlene was sitting beside Roo but she didn't have Roo to herself. There was stiff competition from Dog over who could get closest to the wounded sniper. Roo's pets hadn't moved from beside their master since his return.

Bongo said, "Wiram, there's Riley and his family here too. Riley fought off the terrorists in the Flinders with us, he's a skilled bushman and tracker, like Roo. But even better is that he knows how to kill Revelationists." Riley was sitting with

Katie while their children were outside playing with Annie and Jenny's kids.

Wiram nodded in recognition of their new friend. "Sorry, Riley, it's been such a mad morning. OK, you'd better go with Nulla on the bikes." Before Bongo could say anything else there came some heart lifting giggling in the hotel foyer that broke the seriousness of the morning.

"That sounds like my Lulu and Danni," announced Cambra with a big smile.

Wiram called for the two teenage girls to join him. They stopped giggling over whatever it was they were giggling about and stood quietly beside Cambra.

"Girls, we've got problems and I need every fighter I can muster. Front line troops will be needed to cut the Birdsville track and stop the terrorists from reaching us here. We've begun setting up defences with the bulldozers around the hotel complex but it would only hold them back for a day at the most." Wiram stopped to let this sink in as Tricia and Donna walked in to join them.

"That's why I need you to run shotgun with the families we have here, the oldies, the kids and the other civilians. That means you two, along with Lucy and Heidi, will be responsible for defending everyone. Getting them to our safe house out in the bush, setting up defensive positions, manning the CB radio for us, and keeping up communications between our teams and coordinating everyone."

Wiram now turned to Tricia. "Tricia, can you please ask Gail if she would be willing to stay back as my communications coordinator? And Tricia, I need you to organise transport and logistics with Harry. You'll have to run the show at the safe house while we're gone."

Glenda had remained quiet throughout the meeting but soon decided that she might be left out. She gently elbowed Nulla beside her. "Love, what am I going to do?"

Nulla looked at her and thought for a moment, "Glenda, you'd better go with the girls and run defence as well." He called across to Wiram, "I've got another shot gunner here. Glenda can ride with your girls as protection for the civilians if you like."

Wiram rubbed his face to focus his mind a bit better and nodded, it had been a very long morning. "Thanks mate, I was wondering where that girlfriend of yours had disappeared to." He chuckled lightly. "Glenda, thank you and can I ask that you go with your friends Phil and Fatima. Pack as much food in your vehicles as you can carry."

Wiram was back in management mode now. "Danni? Can you and Lulu take a truck each and fill them up with supplies? Jeda, I need you and Wilma to load up another truck, one of the Deaths Heads' trucks and put as much of our ammunition and weapons in as you can fit, thanks. The rest I'll leave to you, Harry, to sort out."

"Wiram, Sergeant Ahmet is here!" cried Donna with a joyful shout.

The smart Bushmaster commander now walked in and immediately set about getting his piece of the action. "Wiram, what can I do? I can get my Bushmaster up to a hundred k's on that track and into the enemy quick smart." he said in his accented rapid-fire speech.

Wiram thought for a moment. "Sergeant Ahmet, I was wondering if you might need to stay at the cross roads where you are now. We don't know if this is a coordinated attack from both ends or just a local affair. Do you have any updates from your intelligence?"

"Negative, Wiram. Our boys in the Alice have heard zero communication between the Mount Isa, Longreach and the Marree army. They believe they're all feuding with each other again and not talking. It appears that we should be free from any infiltration from the north for the time being. Fat Boy's and our own assault on the Mount Isa force has upset them and they won't be massing for an attack on Birdsville for some months yet."

"What are your orders then, Sergeant Ahmet?" said Wiram, wanting to force his friend into making a decision on where his loyalties lay.

Sergeant Ahmet thought for a moment then looked up with a bright smile. "Alice Springs Command ordered me to maintain my position at the cross roads like you suggested. In a pig's arse, I say! Headquarters can go and get knotted. I'm one of Sundown's Commando now and I'll do what's best for my people."

Everyone stopped muttering among themselves and stared at him.

"Strewth," whispered Pellino, "are you sure about that, Ahmet? That's mutiny."

"No, not at all, this is extenuating circumstances and sometimes the commanding officer in the field, that's me, has to call the shots and act as he sees fit. If these terrorists get through to Birdsville my boys will be left like a shag on a rock. We might as well go home if that happens." He smiled again. The pride in his voice was enough to show just how well Sundown's plan was playing out.

"You know they probably took out One One Charlie don't you? Your boys at Patrol One have stopped all communications…" Wiram didn't have a chance to finish what he was saying when Ahmet cut him short.

"Yes, I heard all that too, Wiram. All the more reason for us to act with swift and shocking retaliation." Ahmet almost shouted, his face grew red, his Afghan warrior blood aroused. "If they've hurt any of my mates I'll kill them with my bare hands." He looked around the packed lounge room. "Are you with me on this or do I have to go it alone?"

The girls shrank back in their seats at Sergeant Ahmet's violent and passionate outburst. Nulla decided that now was a good time to step up as senior non commissioned officer. He stood and grabbed the cavalry troopers hand in his.

"Sergeant Ahmet, I'm Sergeant Nulla, 1st Cav. You mightn't remember me but I attended a course with your boys a few years back. I can see you lot are tough and pissed off, welcome aboard." The atmosphere suddenly cleared as the two cavalry sergeants shook hands.

"Hey! I didn't see you there Nulla. How could I forget you? You're the one who stepped in to flatten that idiot at the bar in Broome, remember?" said Ahmet warmly.

"Yes, I remember. That one I got away with. The next idiot I knocked out I lost my stripes over." Nulla smiled broadly and the two sat down together knowing they'll have time to reminisce after things settled down.

Luke and Simon shared a look and chuckled. Luke said loud enough for most of the group to hear, "That's just typical, boss. I can see why you need Simon and me to look after you, it's to stop you getting into fights all the time." Glenda snorted and giggled out loud. The commando members smiled seeing their new arrivals genuine friendship for the first time.

Wiram addressed Sergeant Ahmet. "Thanks Ahmet, if you don't mind I'll send Donna with you as guide. She might help man your radio to keep me informed back here in Birdsville."

Donna looked up on hearing her name but knew better than comment. She would have preferred to stay with Wiram as his assistant but it would be interesting to be with those rugged army boys in their Bushmaster too.

"Right everyone, here are your orders: One One Bravo to take Donna as liaison officer and to escort Nulla, Luke, Simon, Arty and Riley to our Coopers Crossing Patrol One position. They'll be accompanied by Cambra and Pellino in the dual cab. There they will set up and ambush the enemy, to fight a withdrawal, by stages, to Birdsville and from there to our safe house. At the safe house they will establish a defence holding it at all costs." He paused to think of anything he may have forgotten.

"Um, Gail, you and I will stay here at Birdsville with the CB, we'll coordinate everything until Nulla and Sergeant Ahmet return. Then we all fall back on the safe house. Did I forget anyone?"

Glenda put up her hand slowly. "What about us new comers? We don't know where anything is yet. Can someone help us?"

"Tricia and Harry will look after you. Our safe house has a special name too, it's a little oasis in the desert the locals call the 'Christian Palace', you'll like it." Bongo coughed and Wiram now saw Roo sitting beside that pretty young blond with her arm in a sling, Charlene. He noticed that they both had matching slings.

'*That's strangely funny*', he thought unconsciously.

"Bongo, you and Roo are out of this fight. You've done your bit and deserve some time to recover from your wounds. You both go with Harry and Tricia and beef up the support with the girls if the enemy get past us. Got that?" The two scouts nodded their assent.

"Anything else?" he asked the room. His voice was met with silence, a readiness and an urgency to just get on with it.

Wiram looked out of the window, it was dawn and the sun was just a dull glow in the winter sky. He noticed that dark clouds had arrived with the rising sun.

"It's going to be a busy day, hmm, might rain. Well, we've got our work to do so let's get to it," he said to the room. "Donna and Gail, on me. The rest of you better get moving. And for the new folks, please go and see Harry for weapons, ammunition and anything else you need. Sergeant Ahmet, I want you ready to head out within the half hour. Nulla, you and your boys can see Cambra and Pellino, they'll show you where to find fuel for your bikes."

It was sunrise and everyone was nervous yet they were also excited. Over the next few hours the comforting sounds of Fat Boy, Harry and the older ladies fussing over what should and should not go into the trucks, made it appear more like preparing for a holiday than for an escape from danger.

Chapter 17 - Ancient Sparta

Just as the commando began to leave Nulla stood and called for everyone to wait a moment. "Wiram, if you don't mind I'd like to have a word before we head off."

Wiram nodded wearily, he welcomed any opportunity to ease the load on his shoulders right at that moment. Sergeant Nulla appeared to be someone he could rely on.

"Folks, I'm just a newcomer to Sundown's Commando, but I've been fighting the enemy since the apocalypse too. Before we head off to battle I'd like to tell you a story, a story of the ancient Greek city state of Sparta. It has a special meaning for us today."

Simon and Luke looked across at each other and shrugged, wondering what Nulla was up to now.

"The Spartans trained to fight from childhood. They were hard men, experienced and ruthless fighters. They were also honourable, respectful and devoted to the worship of their Gods and Goddesses. On the eve of battle each man would find a stick and carve his name on it. Then he would break it in half. One half he gave to his officer and the other half he bound to his arm. The half he kept represented his warrior spirit, that part of him that showed no mercy. It was aroused when faced with injustice and an enemy who tried to kill him, his mates and his family. This half would kill and keep on killing, it was like a demon that possessed him. With this spirit he would do terrible, unimaginably cruel and vicious things." Nulla paused allowing his story to sink in.

"The half he gave to his officer represented his gentle spirit, his loving, caring side that would be horrified at what the other half would do. This gentle side was kind and merciful, it was what he showed his wife, his mother and his children." He paused again noticing that each person present appeared to be deep in thought as they listened to the story.

"At the end of battle the Spartan soldiers would collect their dead. The officer would then call out the names of his troop and hand back the sticks to those who survived. Some of the dead might be unrecognisable only identified by bringing the two halves of their name-sticks together. This allowed them to be buried according to their rituals. It was only right that the dead were shown the respect of their names being passed on with their spirit to the next world."

Nulla stopped and looked around at everyone again, his voice rose as he came to the crucial point of his story.

"Handing the name-sticks back to the survivors, represented their return to the world of the living. It gave them back their humanity. Battle is evil, we do and feel things we would be ashamed of in any other situation. Soldiers have to live with their actions, their acts of bravery, their acts of cowardice and their fears. The Spartans recognised that battle could send good men crazy, into a spiral of depression and remorse – we call it Post Traumatic Stress Disorder, PTSD. The ritual of returning their gentle and caring spirit to them at the end of battle was a way of recognising that we must do evil things to save our loved ones. When it is over we must come back to our caring and gentle selves, to be part of our family and community once more."

The commandos listened, recognising their own fears in Nulla's story. He softened his voice as he continued. "When we head out to engage our enemy today we will each do evil things that we'll have to live with. But when we return we need to let it go, somehow." His voice grew louder. "Sundown's Commando will head out and engage the enemy today. We will kill or be killed, witness our enemy and our friends killed. But we do it for a purpose, not just for our family and loved ones but for humanity itself."

The solid aboriginal warrior then stood up straight and waited a few more seconds before finishing his speech. "Good luck and may the Gods and Goddesses, or whatever you believe in, watch over you today."

Each of the commando secretly wondered if they would come back to their caring and gentle selves - or would the experiences of battle send them mad?

There was a rumble of scraping chairs and muffled voices as everyone stood to leave. Breakfast was still being served as Ahmet politely asked Jenny if there was enough for his men as well. Jenny nodded brightly. She liked this fast talking, generous soldier who volunteered to protect her family even though it might end in his court martial.

The girls now needed to prepare extra meals for the patrols in record time. They then needed to pack up everything they could for the retreat to the safe house on the edge of the desert.

"Donna, can you please stick with me for a moment?" Wiram bent down to her ear and spoke quickly. "I need you to keep me informed of all activity. Record everything in your mind and be prepared to recall it for me when I need it. And be careful, love."

He flushed a little as he reached across to squeeze her hand. Donna noticed his flushed face and smiled inside. That was the closest they'd come to a kiss in all their time working together.

"I will, Wiram, don't worry about me. Besides, I've got the entire commando plus six handsome army men to look after me." She giggled and left to gather her weapons and gear from Harry's shed.

"Hurry up with your breakfast boys. We've got an army to kit out and families to place on their transports," called Harry to the lounge room at large. Wiram noticed his furrowed brow, he looked stressed, as would be expected.

"I'm sorry, Harry, you've got a big job ahead of you. All I need to know is if you can get our weapons packed into the trucks in time?" asked Wiram.

Harry thought for a moment. "It's going to take some time, but if I can have the girls I'll make sure it's all done. OK, yep, the girls know what to hand out, consider it done, bro." He walked out calling for the two giggling teenagers.

Blondie held back while everyone else left to get on with their preparations. Fat Boy was already in the kitchen doing what he could to help prepare the meals and food parcels for the fighting patrol. The kitchen had become his new home since they arrived and it was noticed that not once did he lament the loss of his Harley-Davidson.

The blond model walked over to Wiram and asked if she could talk to him alone. They moved a few metres away from the crowd to gain some privacy. Nulla waited some distance away and busied himself rolling a cigarette. He wanted to have a quick talk with Wiram.

"What can I do for you, Blondie?" asked Wiram. He'd heard a little of what had happened in Mount Isa but no one really knew the truth. Wiram was aware that there were many unanswered questions regarding Fat Boy and his partner. In fact, Donna said she didn't believe they were lovers at all.

"Wiram, your people have been good to us from the day we arrived. Pedro in particular has given Fat Boy a reason to live. My poor…" she paused trying to find the words, "my poor… Fat Boy, has been sad and withdrawn since the apocalypse and well, Pedro and everyone here have helped him come out of his depression. We're grateful but no one really knows us, who we really are and what we've done in the past. Just know that we will do what we can to help. I can fire a weapon, I can kill, I can go under cover and do things that would make even you shudder. I don't say that to be prideful, Wiram, but I'm not a nice person under this skin you see. I may be nice on the outside but underneath I'm rotten."

Wiram leaned back a little when she said this then rocked forward again. "Blondie, we've all done shit we aren't proud of. I don't give a rat's you-know-what about your past life."

"Thanks, Wiram," but her eyes said she wasn't finished.

"What job can I give you?" he asked realising she was serious about offering to help.

"I'm an under cover agent for the Revelationist church. Not even Fat Boy knows how deep I am. The truth is he's my brother, but don't tell anyone here. Only one other knows, Sundown, and now you." She spat it out at last and it felt better. Blondie stopped talking to see what impact it had on him. It had no obvious affect at all so she continued. "Wiram, I can infiltrate the church, I'm Tajna Služba." That got his attention she noticed.

"Now it all makes sense. Tajna Služba, huh. Go on," said Wiram rocking back on his heels again. He reached into his pocket for his own tobacco, he needed a cigarette right now.

"So you see I can help from the inside. Just give me the word and I'll be heading south to escape these evil Sundown's

Commandos, ready to provide information to my beloved church leaders."

"Blondie, you've already sacrificed enough, please, go with the girls and support them. But... can I ask that you tell Tricia what you just told me?"

"I will, Tricia knows some of it, just a bit, but the offer stands. If you ever need an infiltrator, the Tajna Služba is ready to do her job." With that Blondie left to find Tricia and offer her services there.

Wiram was still slightly shaken as he looked up to find Nulla. There was no one else in the now empty lounge besides the two powerful aboriginal warriors.

"Wiram, what did you want me to do?" Nulla asked meeting him in the middle of the room, cigarette in his hand and a plume of smoke escaping his nostrils.

Shaking his head to clear it a little, Wiram brought his own cigarette to his lips but grimaced when he tried to draw on it, it had gone out.

"Ah, Nulla, thanks mate," he said as he accepted the lighter. "I first wanted to say how sorry I am that you got caught up in this mess on your first day with us. I'd also like to say 'Thank God' you're here today. We've got real problems and I need you and your boys to go in with the Bushmaster and help Cambra and Pellino to harass the enemy as you withdraw."

Wiram stopped talking to relight the cigarette and handed the lighter back to his new friend. They both drew smoke deeply into their lungs and relaxed a little.

Wiram continued. "While you're out there I really need you to hook up with Assassin. I'll try to contact him and let him know you're on your way. You had better send one of your boys with Assassin to check up on our bike team."

The two stood silently for a few moments enjoying their cigarettes as though it was the last smoke they would ever have. Wiram looked into the eyes of his fellow warrior and saw a reflection of himself, he felt reassured.

"Sergeant Nulla, just get my boys back safely."

Chapter 18 - Lovers Fantasy

The radio and codes the Stosstruppen captured were proving to be very important prizes. The church leaders in Adelaide desperately wanted them. One thing the military excel at is codes and code breaking, but no one had a computer. Without electricity, electrical appliances were dumped, trashed and generally allowed to deteriorate. You can't eat a computer and without electricity no one played computer games, wrote invoices, sent emails or texts. Some people had calculators, some still had DVD players and wrist watches were popular; but mobile phones and computers were worthless.

The church was incredibly ill prepared for the aftermath of the apocalypse. It seemed they could plan the massacre of the entire world's population but the following day...? The intelligence staff had to do everything by hand and there were very few Einstein's in their ranks.

Major Daniels switched from elation to despair and back again. Not only did they knock out one of the Bushmaster armoured transports, obliterate the Patrol One stockade but they captured prisoners and the Third Army radio code book. Daniels had his captain on pins and needles trying to keep up with him.

Captain Burgess was a brilliant strategist but not the greatest mathematician and an absolute failure at code breaking. He did, however, have a genius, a budding Stephen Hawkins-like mind in his personal retinue.

"Private Little!" he yelled, "get in here now and stop stuffing around with that bloody sticky-tape dispenser!" Burgess always became aggravated by the youngster's annoying idiosyncrasies. "And put that blasted box of tissues down!"

Little by name, little by stature but broad of girth, Private Little scampered into his superior's office as fast as his legs and width allowed. He tried to stand at attention but his head lolled to one side. Little stood sniffing a glob of mucus in and out of his nostrils. At first Captain Burgess tried to ignore him but finally he exploded.

"For fuck-sake, Little! Wipe your bloody nose with the back of your sleeve like everybody else!" he roared.

Private Little did as he was told leaving a long slimy line of snot on his shirt sleeve. The captain gagged, he felt an insistent urge to call his duty NCO to take this moron outside and shoot him. But he resisted the urge, he needed Little's brains.

"Little, Lance Corporal Jaina will drive you out to the Patrol One site where you'll take possession of the enemy's radio and code book. You will, with Jaina as escort, return to Marree and reproduce copies for our own intelligence boys before passing the code book on to the Priests. Do you understand that?" His face turned beetroot red when he noticed a splotch of snot on the floor at Little's feet. As he looked up he was just in time to watch as another drop fall off the end of his nose.

Little was terrified of this man, in fact he was terrified of just about everything to do with the military and the church. He'd not joined up willingly - he had no choice. His parents were devoted church members, so, without a friend in the world to advise him otherwise he went along with their wishes.

When the church found out that he was a genius with numbers and just about any problem put to him, they ensconced him into their intelligence section. To their dismay he proved to be a complete failure as a soldier. The closest he ever made it to soldiering was to wear a uniform.

Major Daniels once said that Little wore his uniform as though someone had poured him into it and forgot to say *"when"*. He looked like a combination of sumo wrestler and geek. And geek he was with a mind worth a million useless computers to Daniels. Every time Burgess tried to send him away Daniels stepped in and stopped him.

Daniels enjoyed teasing Burgess, deliberately involving the young man in their conversations. Watching Burgess trying to control himself in the presence of this young man was a sheer delight.

"You will return to Marree and bring the two prisoners back with you as well as the code book and radio." Burgess closed his eyes so he couldn't see the disgusting creature in front of him. "Now get out of my sight and don't come back without everything I've asked for."

Private Little stood there uncertain. He sniffed a long fluid stream of mucus back into his nose and Burgess exploded.

"Didn't you hear me, Little? Get the hell out of my sight you damn little shit!"

On the drive out to the Patrol One site, Lance Corporal Jaina kept up a light conversation with the wretched soldier. They'd worked with Daniels and the church for the past few years and this was the first time she had been alone with him, really alone. Right now her mind raced between high anxiety, dread, then thoughts of raw, adolescent lust.

Jaina kept a special image in her mind of the time, two years ago, when she saw his enormous erection. It was while they were working together for the regional High Priest. Like everyone else in college she treated Little as if he were an insect, a disease. She felt so ashamed now thinking of how she'd treated him so badly, but back then, everyone did.

That special day the large breasted teenager had worn a revealing low-cut top. She soon noticed that Little kept staring at her cleavage. To make a boring day interesting she kept pulling her top lower every time he turned away. She enjoyed not just the nastiness of it, but the teasing seemed to take control of her, amazingly it aroused her.

On that special day Little was standing on the desk in front of her as she handed him some papers to place in the top shelf of a bookcase. Right at that moment his groin was directly at eye level. His trousers were always too tight for his girth and the bulge in his pants looked just like a salami. It reminded her of the salamis hanging in the butcher's window at Hahndorf.

Jaina felt her face flush, then suddenly she felt her whole body shudder in an ecstatic spasm. She couldn't control her arousal on seeing his erection, her physical response took her completely by surprise.

From that moment on her opinion of him changed and she began to look forward to his company. She would often wear provocative clothing just to watch him stare at her. Jaina lived with the anticipation of seeing that magical bulge once more, and she did, several times.

Since that day the teenager spent most of her time daydreaming erotic fantasies of how she would take hold of that salami. She never had the courage to tell him though. Today was the day she decided, she could no longer resist the nagging hot passion blazing inside her loins.

Jaina drove slowly past the ambush site at Mungerannie where the Stosstruppen had destroyed the Bushmaster and forced the bike patrol to escape into the desert. The soldiers waved at her as they cleared the dead bodies away for burial. That was just a mild distraction. Eventually her lustful thoughts were so strong she was forced to pull over into a secluded creek bed just before they arrived at the Patrol One site.

"Little, it's hot isn't it?" she panted in excitement as she pulled her shirt up over her head to expose her pale, ample breasts.

Little ogled. He quickly covered his face in his hands and a squeaky noise escaped his lips.

"It's OK," she said soothingly, breathlessly, "I've been wanting to do this for ages. Here," and she gently placed her fingers on his hands and pulled them down to touch her nipples. "You're allowed to touch and look. Just pretend we're married, it'll make it easier," she said softly, gently, seductively.

Little opened his eyes then shut them again, but after some gentle persuasion he stared at what was definitely the most fascinating objects he had ever seen. He fixated on the round breasts he'd wanted to touch for ages. Jaina could tell Little had never seen a set of well developed breasts up close before.

"Th... th... they're nice, Jaina," Little eventually stuttered, not really knowing what he should say. He wanted to say something appropriate for the occasion but that was all that came out.

Jaina leaned across his enormous girth, straddled his waist, then gently leaned forward allowing her breasts to softly brush his face. She now entered an erotic trance as she played out her fantasy in real life. Lance Corporal Jaina was in heaven, and before too long, Little's salami was in her hands. Her fantasy was now a genuine reality.

When they reached the Patrol One site it was impossible for Little to focus on his task. What was it that Captain Burgess had ordered him to do? Every time he tried to think of his job his mind wandered to other things. His stiffness was uncomfortable and he was embarrassed someone would see its bulge and make fun of him - everyone did. Lance Corporal Jaina on the other hand was all smiles, charming the platoon commander she easily took command of the situation.

"Here, give it to me," she suggested to the lieutenant when he brought out the radio and codes. "Let me keep an eye on it for Private Little. As you can see he's not feeling too well today."

Lieutenant Donata, knowing enough of Little to wonder why he was even ordered to retrieve the codes, agreed and handed everything over to her.

"The prisoners would be best left to the troop carrier, Jaina. One's wounded and in a bad way. You might want to follow behind them on their way back to Marree. I've got a few of our injured fellows that need to go with them. We had a bit of a tough time with their land mines," explained the lieutenant.

"Yes, I could follow along behind, but our orders were to take the prisoners ourselves, immediately. Here's the orders, lieutenant." She handed over the letter with Burgess' signature reciting in detail exactly what he wanted Little to do.

"If you would allow us, we'd better go and check the prisoners ourselves, at least then we can say we met them before they were sent back." She motioned for Little to follow her. With the lieutenant politely in tow they walked to the damaged stockade where the prisoners were held.

"Strewth, lieutenant! That poor man's going to die if he isn't removed soon. How long before you're ready to send your wounded to Marree?" she asked, brushing at a swarm of disturbed bush flies rising from the dead Patrol One soldiers.

"I was thinking maybe this afternoon when we've finished with the truck. It's busy transporting our scout squad up north a few kilometres setting up a listening post. It won't be back for hours yet," he said apologetically. A drop of rain fell on his head and he looked up at the clouds.

"That's not good enough, lieutenant. Major Daniels will eat us alive if we lose one of these prisoners. No, sorry, we're taking them now." Her demand was so confident that the lieutenant was caught unawares. "I don't want to carry the can for you or anyone else, you've already jeopardised yourself by waiting this long. If that prisoner dies it's on your head." She looked into his eyes and saw fear. *'Good'*, she thought, *'now we might get somewhere.'*

"I never thought of that, sorry." He called to one of the men working to repair the stockade. "Corporal, help Little and Jaina to get these prisoners into their Jeep. Make sure you see Poole is properly secured." He stood to one side as the corporal and two others entered the stockade. They gently moved the wounded soldier and placed him in the back seat of the Jeep.

"Lance Corporal, you don't need to mention this to the major or the captain. I'd appreciate if you just went now. Drive safely." He immediately swung around and walked away.

"Little, get into the Jeep. No, not in the back seat, next to me in the front." She turned impatiently to the soldiers escorting the prisoner. "Corporal Bead, be gentle with the prisoners. The last thing we want is for them to be incapacitated when the Priests interview them. We don't want to be the ones in the torture seat now do we?" She lifted the corner of one eye and Corporal Bead winced, imagining just what they might do to him.

"Not at all, Lance Corporal Jaina," he snarled back in retaliation. "You will note that the prisoners have been well cared for. We've fed them and they've had plenty of water. I don't need to remind you that we all work in the same army, and if you want to play games with us then we'll certainly play games with you." He tried to intimidate her but Jaina was not going to be bullied, she was on a mission.

"Corporal, I have noted you have done a reasonable job, thank you. I suggest you all pray we make it to Marree safely and the wounded prisoner doesn't die on the way." With that she jumped into the Jeep and headed back the way she'd come.

The corporal turned to his superior and said, "What's up her arse, lieutenant?"

Lieutenant Donata smiled. "Wouldn't you be terrified of getting the goods back in one piece if you had Private Little with you? Did you notice he had a hard-on? The idiot must have thought he was in heaven with a sweet girl like Jaina asking him to sit in the front seat with her." They both laughed at the joke, Little was a joke to everyone but Jaina.

Blondie couldn't stop her mind racing after her chat with Wiram. She wanted to do something now that her new friends were probably all spread through the desert running from Major Daniels' Stosstruppen - her new-found paradise was all going to hell.

Besides, Blondie had a particular dislike of Major Daniels. At eleven years of age he raped her while the Wilson boys cheering him on. It wasn't just the rape, it was the violence, the total domination and humiliation. He enjoyed inflicting pain on people and he enjoyed brutalising and dominating her and her brother. In her mind's eye she could still see her big brother, Fat Boy, tied naked to a tree. She had been forced to watch as Daniels and the Wilsons brutalised him too.

Every weekend was hell after their father died leaving them at the mercy of their cousins. These thoughts flooded her mind over and over until she thought she would explode if she didn't do something. Jumping to her feet she sought out Wiram once more.

"Wiram, I'm going to Marree. Don't try to stop me." Wiram stood with his mouth open about to deny her but she bulldozed ahead. "I need a bike and I need you to understand that this is personal. The Stosstruppen are led by a personal enemy of mine, a Major Daniels. He's long forgotten who I was. He's brutalised so many people that the little blond Wilson girl would be just a blur to him." She thrust out her chin and continued. "They've no doubt taken prisoners and I know what Daniels will do. He'll send them to the Priests where they'll be tortured. I know because I've been part of that circle."

Wiram's eyes reflected concern but then his face cleared and he nodded. "Go on, I'm listening."

"Thank you. One of the girls that works in his office is one of ours, a Tajna Služba. We planted her there years ago. We've supported her family through thick and thin during her apprenticeship. She's been asleep for the past year, since the apocalypse, but it's time I woke her up and called in a few favours. You need me out there, you need me in the Revelationist's camp. If they have prisoners they'll talk and then the Priest's will find out about our Christian Palace safe house." Blondie stopped talking and waited.

"OK," he said slowly, "take whichever bike you want. I'll alert the boys. They'll be heading out soon so you need to go now. I'll hold them back a half hour. You could say you're running from them if you need to. You've got Assassin's codes in your head?" Blondie nodded. "OK, can you conceal a CB radio in your kit? But don't carry anything else…" he saw she was losing patience. "Sorry, old habit. Blondie, this is not what I wanted for you, it's dangerous, but good luck and please stay safe."

Wiram spoke with Ahmet and Nulla then went in to speak with Fat Boy.

"Hey, Wiram, Blondie's been working the church for years now, she knows what's she's doing. If she says she needs to go then let her go." He slapped Wiram on the shoulder and went back to his packing.

"Wiram, we'll hold for a half hour but I don't want to put it off any longer," said Sergeant Ahmet. "We've made contact with Assassin while you were talking to Blondie. He's been held up with heavy rain on the track. He's also reported enemy movement a few kilometres north of the Cooper Creek crossing. I told him to mark the track for us and then head off into the scrub to find the Bravo boys and the food cache. He said he'll report back on the hour."

"can you run over and tell Blondie, she needs to know this." Wiram then went back to Donna to continue his preparations for the coming patrol. *This is getting worse by the minute,*' he thought.

It was raining in Alice Springs as Sundown spoke with General Hughes and Colonel Thompson. He made sure they left their staff officers outside the room.

"You've got nearly twenty more Bushmasters and ASLAVS and you won't release them? Why didn't you tell me about this, Colonel?" yelled Sundown. He could now feel the heat of his demon below the surface, but he pushed it down - *'not now'* he told it.

"I was ordered to keep everything secret until you joined us, Sundown. Seems pointless now. If we lose Birdsville and the commando then we're up shit creek," replied Colonel Vic Thompson. He turned to watch the general's response to Sundown's outburst.

"You fellows seem to think the war will be lost in this insignificant contact. Calm down, this is a local skirmish and your commando will just walk all over them. I know it," said General Hughes as though he was talking about a local football match.

"General, those are my people out there, they need our backup. This is not a game we're playing, this is for real. If we lose we lose everything," returned an irate Sundown. "Not to mention they're my friends, my family."

"Commander Sundown, you are becoming hysterical. May I remind you that you are an officer of the Australian Government, that I am your commanding officer and you will do as you are told." The general tried to physically stand over

Sundown but the only way he could do that was if he stood on his chair.

"There is no government!" Sundown yelled back, saying each word slowly, forcefully.

The three were quiet for a moment, then Thompson spoke, "Sir, may I suggest we send a section of Bushmasters across the Simpson. That should stiffen the commando and prevent an enemy force pushing into Birdsville itself."

General Hughes sat quietly and appeared to be thinking. His fingers made triangles and pyramids until Sundown realised he was playing for time. He wasn't thinking at all.

'This bloody stuffed up puppet has never had to think for himself in his damned life.' Sundown thought to himself. *'Is it time to make my move? Will Thompson and Lewis' boys step up to the mark and support me?'* he wondered.

"I've made up my mind. I'm now sorry I promoted you, Sundown." The general stood on the top rung of his chair which raised him up a little. "All you've done is complain and make unprofessional suggestions beyond your military capacity. I have no recourse but to break you to the ranks for insubordination. Private Sundown, you are dismissed!"

With a childish smile on his rotund face the general rocked back and forth as he called for the guard outside his office. Major Hughes had just made the worst decision of his life.

Chapter 19 - Coup

It had been raining for some time as Blondie rode her trail bike along the greasy dirt road. She made sure to take care not to come off on the bends and to avoid the many treacherously deep pot holes. She sped past where Assassin had stopped, she didn't notice the secret signs he'd placed to warn the commando of the enemy just up ahead.

It was most fortunate the enemy didn't see her approach either. The noise of their bogged truck revving to get out of the muddy verge was enough to drown all sounds. Blondie fortunately saw them and skidded to a halt removing her helmet in one smooth movement. The soldiers stood in amazement.

"Who the hell are you?" asked the sergeant in charge as he wrestled with the rifle on his back.

"I'm Blondie. I've ridden all the way from Mount Isa and I'm exhausted. You boys don't happen to have any food or water with you? I'm dying for a cigarette too." She flicked her hair and the effect was as if a beam of sunshine burst forth from behind her. The four men in the squad immediately reached into their tobacco and lighters to do her bidding.

"Sorry, Blondie is it?" said the sergeant recovering enough to take command of the situation. "What on earth are you doing out this way? If you were here any earlier you would have been caught in a fire-fight." He lit her cigarette and joined her while his squad turned back to wrestle with their bogged truck.

"I'm escaping the Birdsville people," she said and noticed how his body tone dramatically changed. "I pulled in there last night, on my way to Adelaide to find my children, and they were really rude. The men tried to hit me up all the time, in the end I had to flee for my life." She blew smoke from her mouth up into the air to expose her throat and she could almost hear the sergeant groan with desire.

"Yeah, Blondie, they're bad people. We're fighting them right now. We're trying to rid the planet of pigs like that, evil satanic bastards." He glanced at the progress, or lack thereof, and invited Blondie to sit inside the truck to get out of the rain.

"This is bloody miserable. I'm supposed to set up an ambush out here but look at it, there's no way we can do that now. If this rain sets in we'll need to pull back to Marree in case the Cooper Creek floods." He glanced at Blondie and suggested she shack up with him tonight. "You'll be safe and dry out of this rain, then you can be on your way south tomorrow morning." But Blondie had bigger fish to fry.

"Thanks, but I want to get as far south as I can before dark. I've got my wet weather gear, I'll be fine," she said and the sergeant didn't push. Whereas before he was attracted to her now he began to fear her. There was something dark, something sinister about her that he couldn't quite put his finger on.

"Sure, well, I'd better get back to the boys and see if we can get back ourselves. Good luck and be safe on these wet roads. I don't want to be scraping you off with a shovel on our way back to Marree."

As Blondie went to pull on her helmet the sergeant walked over to her. She paused wondering what to expect.

"Be careful. South of here is our platoon, they're set up at a stockade." He had to yell now as the rain came smashing down. "Make sure you have your headlights on and flash when you see them. We don't want you filled with bullets now do we." He smiled and waved her off.

'Funny man,' she thought to herself then sped away as fast as the rain and the mud allowed.

Blondie pulled into the Patrol One stockade only minutes after Lance Corporal Jaina and Private Little left with the prisoners and the captured radio and code book. The rain had eased off just enough for her to speak with the lieutenant at the stockade. The lieutenant came over to greet her.

"Hello, Blondie isn't it?" he asked and shook her hand. "Sarg radioed in to warn me you were coming and asked me not to shoot you."

"That was good of him," she replied dryly.

"Off to Adelaide then are you? Nice place, I've family there too. I'm sorry but I'll need to have you escorted to base camp to be processed."

Blondie stared at him and the lieutenant started to feel uncomfortable.

"You've been through Birdsville and met with Sundown's Commando? We'll need to ask you some questions that might help us eliminate them from the face of this earth, the heathen scum," he said with some passion but his eyes began to show he wasn't as confident as he was moments ago.

Blondie's eyes bored into him. "Lieutenant, Stosstruppen aren't you? Major Daniels and Captain Burgess?" She stopped, now she had his full attention.

"Do you know who you're talking to?" He shook his head slowly. "No? Did you wonder why I'm travelling along these roads unescorted, through enemy territory, and how I made it through the Birdsville people unscathed?" She moved closer, menace in her voice and posture as she stepped into his intimate space. The lieutenant didn't step backwards, he had frozen.

The Tajna Služba had done this a thousand times intimidating a thousand people. To the Tajna Služba domination and control weren't words they were a way of life.

"If I told you I was Tajna Služba, on a mission, and I needed to know what you are up to and what information you have on our enemy... and what information you have withheld thus far, what would you say to me?" came the menacing voice from this beautiful woman.

"I, I... madam Tajna Služba." Donata regained control of himself as he came to attention. "I would tell you to continue your journey at your leisure. There is a vehicle containing prisoners and captured radio and codes which left a few minutes ago. Madam Tajna Služba, sir, Major Daniels has asked that he see the prisoners and captured equipment immediately. We have nothing else of value or information that we haven't already relayed to Major Daniels." He remained firmly at attention.

The soldiers who gathered to watch now realised something was up. They knew better than to hang around and be noticed. Each made sure to avoid eye contact with their officer and the blond beauty as they slowly wandered off pretending to be busy. Rain started to fall a little heavier and Blondie thanked the officer as she replaced her helmet. He saluted as she rode off.

Lieutenant Donata motioned for his NCO to radio Marree and warn them to expect a special visitor in a few hours time.

Blondie had no idea who had taken the prisoners but she did know that she had to make up time and catch them before they got to Marree. Prisoners, radios and code books were all extremely valuable items that the church would exploit to destroy her new-found friends.

Not far ahead Lance Corporal Jaina was pulled over in the same sandy creek bed where she had enjoyed her lovemaking on the drive in. Poole and his wounded mate were stranded in the Jeep while Jaina took a ground sheet into the bushes and slid back into her real-life fantasy. Little may have been awkward, unattractive and geekish but he made up for it with his enormous sexual apparatus.

"Poolie, can you tell them to shut up with it already?" groaned the wounded Slimmy. Poole was struggling to escape the zip-lock plastic ties securing his hands to the Jeep. It was useless. To make things worse they could now hear a bike approaching from the north.

"Shit, there's more of the bastards coming," said Poole, struggling even harder.

The Jeep was pulled up just within sight of the road. Blondie saw it as she rounded the bend and silently rejoiced at her luck. She pulled her bike over next to the vehicle and immediately recognised Poole and Lahotski. As she took her helmet off she placed a finger to her lips. They both saw her at the same time and remained silent.

"Poole," whispered Blondie, "where's the driver? What's happening?"

"There's two, male and female, youngsters. They're screwing in the bushes over there," he said softly, pointing with his chin.

Pulling her pistol from it's holster inside her jacket, Blondie walked towards the sounds of lovemaking. She saw Jaina, her protege, mounting a fat boy that she recognised as Little.

'Well I'll be. This is just perfect,' she thought. Blondie watched curiously, not with sexual interest but as an entomologist would study an insect's mating. Eventually, with loud grunts of pleasure and relief, Little climaxed and Jaina lay on top of him breathing heavily.

Blondie stepped into the clearing, her pistol pointed at the two.

"You've had your fun. Stand up, both of you, put your hands in the air." With a scream Private Little pushed Jaina off him and struggled to get off the ground. As he stood at attention his enormous, limp penis failed to follow suit.

"Sir, I was…" Little stopped talking and looked at his assailant. "It's you, Tajna Služba, you could have warned us." He realised how rude that sounded and stood up straight again not quite realising he wasn't wearing any pants. Jaina swung smoothly into a standing position, she reached for her clothing then calmly began dressing.

"Hi, Blondie, it's been a while. Have I got something for you!" She smiled delightedly as she handed Little his trousers, motioning for him to dress. "I've got two prisoners, a captured radio and their code book. I've got the grand slam!"

"Jaina, look at me, darling," said the Tajna Služba smoothly. "This is that time we spoke about, it's time for you to come with me." Blondie put her pistol back into it's holster and walked with Jaina to the Jeep.

"We're not going back to the base camp we're going to join Sundown's Commando. Are you with me?" She looked at Jaina seriously and saw her look at the private, now walking towards them, head downcast like a naughty boy. Blondie didn't expect what came next.

"Can I take him with me?" Jaina asked softly, almost intimately as she gazed at Little with what Blondie believed was love.

"Little? You want me to take Little with us? Is that what he wants?" she asked incredulously.

"Jason, we're not going back to the church any more, we're going home with Blondie. We've just switched sides and are going to join Sundown and his commandos. Don't worry, we can trust Blondie..." Jaina paused, her face suddenly blushed bright red. "I love you, Jason, I want you. Will you stay with me even though I'm going over to the enemy side?" Jaina asked with a warmth and compassion that even touched Blondie's stony heart.

"No more church? Are you fucking kidding me? If you said you were going to the moon I'd go with you. Yes, Tajna Služba, if Jaina goes I'm going too," he said with an enthusiasm neither Blondie nor Jaina had heard from him before.

'Well well well, sex doth maketh the man,' thought Blondie with a wry smile.

Sundown kept his demon in check but right now his resolve broke and he opened the door. Now he saw his demon's vicious plan: *a flash of movement as Sundown jabbed his rigid fingers into the general's voice box crushing it against his vertebrate. The fragile bones and cartilage struck the bones in his neck and stayed there, a shattered mess of blood and jelly. The general clutched at his throat and collapsed to the ground, a strangled wheezing sound escaped his blue lips as he died.*

"No!" Sundown shouted loudly to his demon. "I won't let you do that!"

The general blanched and stared at him in shock. "You will do what I say!" shouted the general in response. "Besides, it's not the end of the world you know, a simple court martial and demotion. My goodness man, you rose from nothing and now you're going back to being a nothing."

"No!" shouted Sundown again, but this time it was directed at the general himself. "It's you who are under arrest for withholding vital armourments and equipment necessary for the safety and security of the Australian people. You have failed in your duty to serve those you have sworn to protect."

Sundown looked at Thompson calmly. "Can I rely on your support on this, Colonel Thompson?"

"All the way, Commander Sundown," Colonel Vic Thompson replied. "I guess we'd better get those ASLAVS and Bushmasters out of storage now then, eh?" Vic smiled not bothering to even look at the now stuttering general. He walked to the door and called for the guards to arrest the general.

"I say! This isn't how these things are supposed to happen. I say! Guards! Arrest these two! Not me you pair of buffoons!" He stood and stared as the two guards, both from Vic's own cavalry section, grabbed him by the arms. They lifted the general off the ground and carried him towards the door.

Sundown walked around the desk and called for Corporal Hassam, the duty NCO.

"Good morning, Corporal Hassam, I see your wounds are healing well. The general is to be placed under house arrest. Please search his house for weapons and anything that may harm him. Would you kindly find the medical orderly and ask him to attend the general. And please, send Sergeant Tobi to gather Headquarters staff here for a meeting in five minutes." Sundown rubbed his chin for a moment, "and I think a general parade in one hour would be appropriate as well. Thank you, Corporal." He was calm, focused and hid the excitement he felt deep within.

The corporal saluted smartly and said, "Yes sir. I gather you will be taking command of Third Army now, Commander?"

"Yes, that's correct, Corporal," was Sundown's dour reply.

"Thank goodness, sir. I shall pass the word around. The boys'll want instructions for our upcoming offences now, sir." The corporal had a huge smile on his face as he saluted once more and went off on his errands.

They could hear him as he walked past the duty clerk's desk, "General Sundown's now running the show, he's called the command to parade in one hour. Now we're going to see some action!"

Corporal Hassam pulled on his water-proof cape as the heavens opened and the rain came down.

'Blast.' Hassam said to himself, *'just when we get to see some action this has to happen. It had better clear up by this afternoon or we might get rained in.'*

But what was annoying for the Alice Springs Command and the Revelationists bogged on the Birdsville Track, was a God-send for Chan and John's patrol stuck in the desert fighting for survival.

Chapter 20 - Relief and Rescue

The bike patrol were on their stomachs watching the Stosstruppen empty from their vehicles. Two squads of what appeared to be about twenty soldiers each immediately went into skirmish formation. They quickly spread out and rushed forward under the covering fire of their comrades behind them.

"Forward, they're just over that sand dune," came the cries from one of the officers directing the attack.

The rain fell in spits and spurts not quite knowing what it wanted to do. The terrorist's four wheel drives were heavy and sunk into the boggy sand. Every time they were ambushed it took them an hour or more to catch up to the commando bike patrol.

Chan's hand was bleeding from a gun shot wound so John took over as their 'sniper master'. He was just as good as Chan anyway, he said.

John had his scope on the officer's heart and pulled the trigger. The shot echoed in the morning light and the skirmishers all dropped to the ground.

Chan stood with Halo and Doff as they emptied their magazines into the scrubby desert where the terrorists were skirmishing forward. John fired again and followed it with a third shot. He ducked down below the level of the sand dune they were hiding behind.

"Damn, they're good," John said as he adjusted his sights. "I should know, I trained with this lot."

"Did you hit any, mate?" called Halo slipping the last magazine into his AK. He checked to his left making sure no enemy came around their flank as he did so.

"What do you think, smart arse. Three shots three kills, you bastard," said John, a grim look on his dirty face. "I bet you couldn't do any better."

"Wanna make a bet on that?" came back Halo. Just then there were more shouts and a grenade exploded a few metres to their left.

"Skirmishers, left flank!" shouted Chan. He had already pulled his last magazine from his webbing pouch and placed it within reach. "I didn't think they had any grenades left, looks like they do."

 There were noises front and left. Doff lifted his head then quickly raised his assault rifle to fire short bursts which kept the enemy from pushing forward too quickly. Halo joined him. There came screams of pain clearly audible in the grey light. Incoming fire forced the two commandos to crouch back below the fragile sand dune.

"The bastards will be surrounding us soon. That's when they'll grenade our position but I don't know why they aren't pushing forward as aggressively as they did before," mused Doff softly. "Hey, Chan, I'm empty, hand me your spare magazine, mate, I'll put it to good use."

John looked through his scope and fired again. "Four shots four kills."

"Sarg, they were trained for rapid assault and success not to fight a long drawn-out action like this. Remember, the Deaths Heads had never fought a pitched battle until we met Sundown's mob. The Stosstruppen have never known defeat, no one has ever stood up to them like this before. They're like, you know, robots."

John fired again. "Five shots five kills." He kept score for Halo's education. "Put that up your butt and smoke it, Halo," he said a bit too brightly for their precarious situation.

The hit-and-run bike patrol had been forced into a fighting withdrawal to this, their forth fuel and food cache. A running rearguard battle that had lasted since their dawn contact took out the Bushmaster. The wounded soldier on John's bike died during the withdrawal leaving Beamy, and the other soldier, Mugga, still in dire need of medical attention.

Chan and John had made up wooden stretchers, like the American Indian *travois*, for their wounded. One end tied to a bike the other end dragged on the ground behind. It was a nightmare for both rider and wounded. The travois caught on every bush and clump of sand.

The bike patrol ambushed the enemy countless times but when they thought they'd knocked out the trucks on they would come once more. Doff finally realised the Stosstruppen had armour plated their truck engines. It explained why the

Blaser sniper rifle fire had no effect. The enemy were slow but they kept on coming at them.

If it wasn't for the rain turning the ground into a boggy mess, the Stosstruppen would have easily overrun them. Carrying their two wounded mates compromised them to the point where each stretch was slower than the one before. None of them thought to leave their wounded behind, it just wasn't an option.

Their first cache stop was supposed to be a place to rest up and see to the wounded. Instead, a half hour after they'd sat down they saw the enemy four wheel drives approaching along their tracks. At each rest stop they would fill their fuel tanks, load up their bikes and fire off a salvo or two. They set booby traps while they still had explosives and headed deeper into the desert.

While they were resting Doff had their mobile radio out, he got Halo to stand on the seat of his bike with the wire aerial held above his head. They finally contacted Assassin and planned to meet him here, at cache four. With their position now compromised they feared that he would ride into the ambush and get himself killed in his attempt to rescue them.

The rain came down heavier as they prepared for their final battle. One of the bikes had a rip in its front tyre, it was useless. There was no way they could fit all six of them on just two bikes. They agreed that they would stay put and fight it out, to the death if they had to.

"One in all in," said John who had guided them with pinpoint accuracy from cache to cache. "We can't go any further like this. One bike for three in this slush? Nah, it's not going to happen is it guys. Well, it's been a short but good time knowing you all, I'm ready to die today." He looked at his pale faced, exhausted friends gathered around him. "Anyone with me on that?"

Exhausted, Chan and Halo grunted assent, Doff nodded and Beamy and the other wounded soldier followed suit.

"You can leave us behind you know," said Beamy, but Halo and Chan looked at him in such a way that Beamy had to give in to them. "Well give me an AK, I can shoot from down here." But they had no ammunition to spare, they were all down to their last magazine.

John pulled the pistol out of his holster and handed it over. "Beamy, shoot the first two that come over the dune then shoot Mugga and then yourself. If they take you prisoner they'll hand you over to the Priests and those shit-heads'll torture you." Beamy took the pistol and nodded in response.

Halo had his trophy Deaths Head SS knife stuck in the ground beside him now. "I'm almost empty. I've got my pistol and my knife so I guess I'm ready enough."

John sighted his sniper rifle over the top of the sand dune once more but before he could pull the trigger he was flung savagely backwards onto the sand. The hole in the side of his head slowly oozed black-coloured blood. His body stiffened then rolled face up - he was dead.

Halo and he had become close friends. They were always arguing over who was the better soldier - and now his mate was dead. The commando's weapons master felt a sudden pang of loss rip into his chest and he let out a scream of anguish.

A blast of blind grief filled Halo and he started to stand up. Doff quickly grabbed him by the shirt and pulled him roughly to the sand. He had to forcefully hold him down. A spattering of sand cascaded down on them as the terrorists fired at the movement.

"Halo, get a bloody grip! It's shit, I know, but now you have to get back to cover your sector and make the bastards pay for it!" Doff had seen mates killed in action, he'd just lost three that morning, he knew what Halo was going through. He also knew there was only one thing to do, fight back with vicious savagery until the pain eased.

"You pricks!" roared Halo with such venom that Doff suspected that he was going to be OK. It didn't really matter, it wouldn't be long before they joined John anyway.

Halo crawled to the edge of the flank position and peered through the scrubby bushes. His rifle was at his shoulder and every time he saw movement he fired.

"Six bullets six kills," he whispered to John's ghost. They were now down to firing single shots and Halo knew he only had about five rounds left before he had to resort to his pistol, then they'd be throwing rocks.

The patrol were at a stand-off, neither side had the advantage. Their defensive position was well selected. Doff had arranged his men well and they had taken a heavy toll of the Stosstruppen since the initial assault.

They were backs-to-the-wall though, fighting for their lives and the lives of their wounded friends. The rain began to fall, heavier than before, a curtain of rain now hid their enemy. It didn't stop them calling out, the sound ethereal under the blanket of rain.

Chan was fighting back his own tears. He'd spent years in the church with his best friend, John. They'd done everything together since high school. Each time he saw movement he fired, it only took a few rounds and he was out of ammunition. Chan pulled a grenade from his webbing, their very last one. His pistol was in his good hand and his other wrapped in a bandage ready to grab the grenade.

"Chan, why haven't they tried to grenade us out of existence?" asked Doff as he removed the 7.62 calibre bullets from John's half empty magazine.

The ex-Death's Head soldier sniffed back his tears and replied. "Could be they've run out, Sarg. Don't forget the slave factories that make the church's bullets and explosives haven't produced anything of quality all year. The armoury depots are probably exhausted by now too. The church armies fighting in the cities were first in line and the desert armies came last."

He wiped the sleeve of his shirt across his eyes, it made no difference with the rain falling so hard. He sniffed again and shook his head to clear it angrily.

"Another thing Doff, we had to pay for uniforms and equipment out of our own wages. The city churches had millions of worshipers donating millions of dollars. The country regions had nothing like that. That's why we didn't have many grenades and no armoured cavalry, it was too expensive. That Bofors was a gift from a private collector in Peterborough and the machine guns and other weapons we had to trade, borrow and prostitute ourselves to get. Some of the poorer kids could only afford a sling-shot."

Doff nodded but didn't laugh at the joke. "Yeah, makes sense. So... they can't push us out of this defensive position. They've tried frontal, they've tried flanking. I don't think they've got enough to surround us, that leaves, what, ten or so out there?"

Chan thought for a moment and nodded while keeping an eye on his quarter. "I think they'll pull back and tell their commanding officer they've killed us all. The whole company have done well against us, Sarg. They took out the Bushmaster and half our guys. With luck they just might leave."

"I sure hope so," groaned a wet and uncomfortable Beamy. He was lying on his side next to Doff listening in on the conversation.

There was a sound of firing to their left flank and Halo looked across the sand dune to see who it was. He saw two terrorist soldiers rise and run back towards the vehicles. Then another two ran. A whistle blasted and the rest of the terrorists began to withdraw. More gunfire came from that same direction.

"Hey, someone's firing at them from out there in the bushes. They're retreating back to their trucks," called Halo.

Doff and Chan peered over the same dune and watched like spectators at a tennis match. Halo stood and fired at the disappearing enemy but they were too far away for accurate assault rifle fire and the heavy rain now hid them. His rifle clicked empty, he'd finally used his remaining bullets.

"Hand me the Blaser, Chan. I might be lucky and hit someone."

He grabbed at the sniper rifle without moving his head and pulled the stock into his shoulder. 'Bang! Bang! Bang! Click!' it too was now empty.

"You get stuck into them, Halo," said Beamy softly.

"Three shots… no kills. Sorry, John," he reported as they heard the enemy vehicles engines start up. The sound suggested that they were withdrawing.

"Halo, can you see where that fire came from?" asked Sergeant Doff, his bare head was dripping rain water onto Beamy's face. Beamy had his hand up to stop the drops and remained quiet, it was just too tense to say anything.

Halo grabbed at his binoculars from his webbing. "It's Assassin!" he screamed out loudly at his mate in the distance: "ASSASSIN! OVER HERE, MATE! OVER HERE!"

Through the misty rain he could just see Assassin wave and then disappear for a moment only to reappear on his bike riding towards them. As he pulled in to their position he looked at the two wounded, then at John's still body. There were dozens of empty cartridges lying on the sand, obviously things had been hot for them.

"Been pretty bad has it then, eh?" he stated more than asked. Assassin looked at John's white face covered in rain drops, his eyes open to the black skies above. "I'm so sorry, Chan. I liked John, he was a damn good bloke."

After a few moments he came out of his reverie to look down on his rigger mate, Beamy.

"Is that you hiding behind everyone, Beamy? I'd hide you too, you're a damned bullet-magnet, mate." Assassin bent over and looked at his bandaged chest. "That's nasty, I bet that one hurt." He smiled but it wasn't a funny smile, more like a *you poor bastard'* smile.

"Get stuffed, Assassin, you prick. Next time we go on patrol I'm standing behind you," moaned Beamy. But talking hurt so he finished with, "It hurts just as much as last time."

"At least you'll get to play with Lorraine in the first aid room again. Just imagine snuggling up to those lovely tities, it'll make you feel better," said Halo, trying to cheer Beamy up a bit.

"Don't worry, I tried thinking that already, it doesn't work." His eyes closed as he eased himself into a more comfortable position on the wet sand.

Assassin walked back to his bike and pulled up the aerial to his CB unit, he began broadcasting.

"Sarg, it's been a big day for you boys, for all of us. Patrol One is gone and Wiram is sending One One Bravo down there with a bike patrol and Cambra with the FN Mag." He stopped talking and put his hand up to show he'd made contact. "Hang on, I've got Birdsville."

"Base two, Assassin. I have our Bravo boys, they've been fighting a withdrawal to cache four. We'll be pulling back for home in an hour. Might take us all day to get back though. We have heavy losses and two badly wounded. It's raining and boggy. We'll call you on the hour, out."

He looked back at Beamy and the wounded private. "Chan, how are the boys here?" he asked of their medic. Chan had trained as a paramedic and was again tending to the two wounded as best he could in the rain.

"They'll live. A bit shot up and they've lost a bit of blood. If we just keep it slow and steady, stop every hour for ten minutes, they'll be OK," he replied.

"I've got no medicines, sorry, I had to travel light. OK, lets get some food into us, fuel up and get moving," said Assassin.

Doff and Halo checked their weapons and filled their empty magazines from the enemy dead. There were no grenades on any of the bodies.

While his friends collapsed with exhaustion, Assassin set to preparing them a decent meal. He hoped that it would provide enough energy to sustain them for at least part of their return trip through the sodden desert scrub. It was difficult trying to manoeuvre his frying pan under the piece of plastic he always carried with him. By the time they were ready to go home the rain was falling heavily again.

The small sombre group stood around John's grave while Chan gave the eulogy.

"Our dear friend and comrade." Chan choked back a sob for a second, then continued. "You're now with your God, not that arse-hole of the Revelationists but the proper one."

Halo opened one of his eyes and saw Assassin doing the same. They looked at each other grimly.

"We are sad to say goodbye but we can proudly send you on your way with 'five shots five kills'." He paused. "You got us to safety and found every cache, and in the rain and mist too. You were a miracle worker. It was you who broke their back today with your accurate sniping. You stopped them massing for their final attack that should have wiped us out." He choked back another sob and was silent for some seconds. "Oh yeah. John, you don't need to wait for us, we'll be there with you soon enough. And don't use up all those virgins in paradise either, save some for us." Chan gave a bitter laugh. "OK fella's, let's go home."

The rain didn't ease up at all which just made them feel more depressed and miserable.

While the bike team were battling the boggy terrain heading back to Birdsville, Blondie closed down comms with the Alice Springs Command.

"It seems Assassin has found the bike boys and they're heading back to Birdsville. Our plan is to wait for Bushmaster One One Bravo and the rest of our commando to take back the Patrol One stockade, just up the road. We're to stay here. This track to Birdsville is still held by the Stosstruppen, as you know, but Sergeant Ahmet's patrol should be here soon to clear it. We need to listen and be ready to pull out and meet them."

Blondie looked at everyone jammed together in the Jeep. The rain continued to smash into the earth and with the windows wound up it was hot and stuffy inside. The small group had no choice but to wait for the command to move from where Jaina had parked it in her haste to return to her lovers fantasy.

"This is no fun, Blondie, it's boring. You know, we might have another few hours to wait. What are we going to do?" complained Jaina. She was sitting in the front seat with Little. Her hand on his thigh stroked what appeared to be an over-sized sausage inside his trousers.

Blondie decided to ease the couple's obvious distress. "All right, Jaina, grab your ground sheet and take Little with you. Don't come back until I call you. And can you get that smile off your face?"

Lahotski was in a bad way and she knew it. Blondie had helped many a wounded Tajna Služba operative to live, or die. She made him lie back so that she could look at his wound. Pulling off the pathetic excuse for a bandage she saw a single hole in his stomach. A stomach wound generally meant a slow and painful death unless treated properly and promptly. Even if he received medical treatment tonight there was a good chance infection would kill him within the week.

The secret agent thought quickly, *'do I execute him and save us watch him suffer, or should I just wait and see?'*

"How are you feeling, private?" she asked, still unsure.

"Like shit, Blondie. I'm not sure if the bullet went right through or not," Slimmy grunted. "Their medic was useless, he just put this pissy pad on and walked away. I've got pain in my guts and back. If you roll me over you might see if there is an exit wound. If the bullet has exited then I might stand a chance. I worked as a wardsman for years, I know what to expect." He groaned and his face contorted as he fought back spasms of pain.

Lance Corporal Poole helped Blondie lift and roll the wounded Slimmy. Despite his courage the wounded soldier cried out. His stomach was reddish purple and inflamed but the pain was worth it, he sported an exit wound in his back. Poole told him the good news.

"But now I have to survive whatever damage it's done inside me." Slimmy caught his breath and continued, "Oh well, that's life in the army. I've already lost my wife and kids. I'm not afraid to go and meet them." He closed his eyes and suffered in silence while the lovers made love for the fourth time that day.

'*Perhaps I'll wait and see how he manages tonight,*' thought Blondie as she settled down in the vacated front seat and fell asleep.

Chapter 21 - Sundown's Command

"You can't just take over command of the Third Army, Commander, not like that. You need a formal court martial and that means a hearing with lawyers and adjudicators," snapped Major Louie Lewis. He was in the process of taking command of the armoured cavalry troop from Thompson and was very much on edge. He felt out of his depth right now.

"Major Lewis, we are the government," replied Colonel Thompson emphasising exactly who they were. They were not just an army but the only force capable of controlling the destiny of the entire Australian mainland. "There really is no Government of Australia any more. General Hughes was holding everything together by default. It was smoke and mirrors and now the smoke has cleared and the mirrors broken." He stopped when he saw everyone at the table squirm uncomfortably.

"Excuse me, sirs, do you mean to say this room is basically Parliament House?" asked Lieutenant Shadow. Her uniform was a little large for her but she wore it with pride.

Colonel Vic Thompson smiled and answered softly, "Lieutenant, yes it is. We are it and we are the law, military law. What we say goes and we can override any jurisdiction until an act of parliament, which is us, revokes it."

"That means we command all of Australia?" asked McFly.

"Yes, Captain, it does," Thompson replied comfortably. "The general and I have been playing this game since martial law was pronounced nearly a year ago when the apocalypse began. Government control broke down within days of the apocalypse, by the end of the first week we began to collect what was left of the Third Army in Darwin escaping south and anyone else in the central regions. Alice Springs turned into the centre of government overnight, so to speak."

Sundown leaned forward for a second then adjusted the height of his seat, he just couldn't get it right.

"We have to decide on our strategy. As the acting representatives of the Australian Government we have responsibility to the people of Australia, to protect them. General Hughes failed those he was duty bound to support and protect. When I heard he had twenty armoured cavalry carriers in storage and refused to use them to protect a community on the verge of destruction, I removed him. He gave no qualified reason why and refused to budge. The general placed our people at risk of murder, torture and slavery to the enemy. He knew that, yet failed to act."

Sundown looked at each face in turn and asked, "It was my duty as the next highest ranking officer to replace him. If anyone thinks I did wrong, please speak now, this is the last time we speak of it before the court martial."

No one moved, no one spoke.

"Right, Major Lewis, you will act as prosecution and McFly, you went to university I believe, you'll defend the general. We don't have time right now, we have a convoy to assemble and some Revelationists to exterminate. We'll hold the court martial when we're ready. Anyone not with me speak now or forever hold your peace."

Shadow chuckled. "Sundown, that's a wedding vow, you knuckle head."

Sundown went slightly red in the face when he saw the others at the table smiling. "What? Shoot me! Let's see, speak now or… um, bugger it! We have work to do. Vic, will you assist Major Lewis here to arm and prepare four ASLAVS and six Bushmasters to cross the Simpson Desert for Birdsville? Louie, your orders are simple: exterminate, with force, any terrorists you find on your way to Birdsville. Secure the township of Birdsville, hold it until our community has been restored to normal. If need be patrol down the Birdsville Track to maintain security at your discretion."

Major Lewis' face lit up, he smiled and his voice broke. "Commander, do you mean I'll be running this show?"

"Yes, Major, do you doubt your ability to command our armoured cavalry in action?" asked Sundown patiently.

"Sir, you can count on me. I have the men and the armoured carriers already picked, just give me an hour." Major Lewis' face beamed.

"Colonel Thompson, you will remain at Alice Springs Command, run headquarters here and monitor all communications with your staff as…" He was cut off by a disturbance in the corridor outside the meeting room.

"Bloody boofheads! I'm the bloody general's bloody best mate! He just bloody sent for me ya damn boofheads! Now get out of me way and let me in the bloody room!" The group could clearly hear Pedro yelling and swearing in the corridor. Sundown quickly jumped up and opened the door.

"Hey, Sundown, matey! What took ya so damn long, ya boofhead! I've been waiting in that bloody hospital with all them mean, ugly nurses for you to come and get me."

He turned to look at Lorraine and Pinkie who were standing beside his wheelchair. "Ah, sorry ladies, I forgets me manners when I gets warmed up and passionate like. You pair are the only pretty nursies in Alice Springs I've decided."

"Come on, Pedro, sit here next to me - and promise to behave or I'll send you to stay with the general and he isn't pretty either," said Sundown with a twinkle in his eyes.

He turned to Pedro's escort and said, "Thanks, girls, please, if you could wait outside we'll be finished in only a few minutes... um, ah, and Pinkie love, a cup of tea is something I would die for." He smiled his 'love you' smile then looked at the faces surrounding him at the meeting table. "Anyone else want a cuppa?" he asked.

"Oh, why yes, I do," said Thompson.

"Me too, strong and black," said Lewis and the others put in their orders.

"Love, some sandwiches wouldn't go astray." He smiled again and watched as the two girls walked out. Pinkie turned at the door and stuck her rude finger up at her husband.

"Sundown, dearest, one day you're going to…" she didn't finish because Lorraine grabbed her and pulled her away. They could hear the two women giggling as they closed the door behind them.

"You deserved that, princess," said Shadow, knowing just how hard Pinkie worked to keep her husband from having to deal with the mundane chores of daily life while he protected their community.

"Very nice missus you've got there, matey. Reminds me of that girl in Vietnam, you know, the nice girl what had the husband with the gun. Better watch yerself then," chuckled Pedro.

For a moment Pedro sat quietly thinking. Everyone at the table had stopped what they were doing and continued to watch knowing he was up to something. Pedro leaned towards his friend and spoke softly as though he was talking to a fellow conspirator.

"Sundown, matey, am I right in thinking that you've taken command of Third Army and imprisoned the general?"

"Yes, Pedro," replied Sundown speaking as though to a child, "that's correct on both accounts. Didn't I tell you I wouldn't allow anything, or anyone, to harm my family? Well, I had no choice, just ask Vic here." Colonel Vic Thompson nodded in the affirmative.

Pedro sat back, a smug look on his face. "I knew you would matey. Now we can get on with this bloody war and shift them arse-wipes off the face of this planet!" he said with conviction.

A sigh of relief could be heard around the table as everyone sat back and waited for Sundown to continue.

"Right, now, where was I?" he asked his adjutant who was supposed to be recording everything.

"Lieutenant Shadow, where was Commander Sundown up to?" McFly turned and asked his partner Shadow.

"Smart arse," Shadow said and poked her tongue out at him. "Commander Sundown was just ordering Major Lewis' cavalry troop to form a heavy fighting patrol to secure the township of Birdsville."

"Good work, Lieutenant Shadow. McFly, you boofhead, you'd better pay attention otherwise Sundown might switch your positions," interrupted Pedro. He thoroughly enjoyed being back with his friends.

"Jehoshaphat, I don't believe it! I've just taken command of Sesame Street!" snapped Sundown. "For crying out loud can we get back to work now?"

"Sorry boss, it's my fault. I'll chastise myself for goofing off after we finish here." McFly smiled, he just couldn't help himself. Shadow and the others chuckled softly.

Sundown put his face in his hands for a moment and sighed. He opened his eyes when Corporal Hassam entered to hand him a piece of paper.

"This is just in from Sergeant Ahmet. We've got losses at Patrol One, the entire squad was taken out. Blondie reports she has one wounded and one other with two intelligence staff from Marree. It seems the terrorists were about to get their hands on the radio codes at Patrol One. She's managed to intercept and meet up with one of her Tajna Služba and a willing intelligence staff member. We'll interrogate them when they come in, but if Blondie says they are kosher, then they are kosher."

He stopped and thought for a moment. "Wiram has taken command of Sundown's Commando and One One Bravo, he's sent them down to the Patrol One site. Sergeant Ahmet's orders are to knock the enemy out of their positions and then fight them to a standstill to allow Blondie to bring her group out of hiding and back to Birdsville. When that occurs they are to withdraw back to the safe house."

"Sir?" said McFly. "Wiram has new arrivals doesn't he. Are they involved and what numbers?" Most of this news was new to Sundown's staff.

"Yes, there's five new fighters and they're part of Ahmet's patrol. We've been chatting with them for months on the CB but not everyone knows that. They just got in last night and now they're in contact with the enemy. The poor beggars are probably exhausted. They've been fighting the Revelationists in Adelaide all year and escaped through the Flinders Ranges. They had a few contacts with the terrorist supporters there too.

"They've brought back Roo and Bongo and more survivors from the region. Roo and Bongo are both out of action though." He stopped and asked his 2IC, Thompson, to continue.

"Thank you, Commander, yes, Birdsville have new additions, five active fighting age men experienced in battle. They also brought back your two from the Flinders who were wounded fighting the Revelationists there. Your Roo and Bongo, as Sundown said, they're both recovering well. Sergeant Ahmet has gone as support with Cambra and Pellino, plus the five extras on bikes. It's going to be an interesting contact in this rain." They all stopped to listen to the rain falling heavily on the tin roof just as Pinkie and Lorraine brought in trays with sandwiches and pots of tea and coffee.

"Colonel Thompson, sir, any news on the bikers and Assassin? We know the Bushmaster One One Charlie and bike patrol were knocked out but we've been kept in the dark by the general's staff here," inquired Shadow.

"They're on their way home. Seems they've had a hell of a time but should be back at Birdsville by evening. They've had serious losses." Thompson stopped to consider what to say next.

"The Stosstruppen ambushed both of our patrols. Their tactics appear to be somewhat different to previous contacts you lot have had and they've been successful in knocking out both Sergeant Doff and the bike patrol as well as Patrol One on the Cooper Creek crossing. It also helped that they had Javelins and overwhelming numbers. They took advantage of our complacency. We need to smarten up or it'll happen again." He turned to Sundown. "Sir, I think it's now time to eat our sandwiches then speak to the men. I can see they've formed up and are waiting."

'You may look like you've stepped straight out of Dad's Army, Thompson, but you're a fine officer,' Sundown thought to himself at that moment.

Pedro wheeled himself over to Sundown's chair and chatted with Pinkie and Thompson. A few minutes into their sandwiches Bill arrived, his arm in a sling and a uniformed officer in tow.

"Good morning, Sundown, hi everyone." Bill smiled around the table noting how everyone looked so formal in their uniforms. "I thought you should meet Captain Walker. He's interested in helping scour the countryside for survivors once I'm able to fly again. I've also found a half dozen pilots who know this place like the back of their hands. There's a few planes and helicopters hidden away out there that we can call upon as well."

"Thanks, Bill, good work. I've heard of you Captain Walker, nice work on the retreat from Darwin. I believe you single-handedly rescued the armoured corps, thank you." Sundown invited the two to sit and eat with them.

After their hurried breakfast Sundown inspected his command with Colonel Thompson and Major Lewis. It continued to rain but no one cared. Sundown noticed their bright, expectant faces as he quietly performed the inspection. He then announced that they had their own flag and there arose a spontaneous cheer as Colonel Thompson brought it out.

Thompson was clearly moved as he held up the replica Lulu and Danni made for his ASLAV. Alice Springs Command, Third Army now had their own flag and the *Mount Isa* battle honours sat proudly at the very top.

"Gentlemen and women, this is the start of something special. You will have noticed that this is just a replica, the original rests on a wall in Birdsville which I promise you I'll bring back to its rightful home, Alice Springs Command," announced Colonel Thompson proudly.

Major Lewis and his company worked furiously to get their armoured carriers ready. Even though they were in storage he, Walker and Thompson had continued to service them on a regular basis for such a day as today. It wasn't until the next day that the convoy was ready.

If the rain cleared just a little and everything went according to plan it would take them three to five days to get to Birdsville across the Simpson Desert. But they well knew that this might be too late to save Sundown's community.

Chapter 22 - The Christian Palace

The commando's safe house was a luxurious cattle station a few hours out from Birdsville, an oasis in the middle of the desert. The money that must have gone into what was known as the 'Christian Palace' defied description. The new arrivals were amazed and spent their first few hours just walking around admiring the artworks and the opulence of the forty bedroom mansion.

"Why didn't we move in here in the first place? We could have been living like royalty all this time," Lulu cried out when she saw that each bedroom was like a luxury apartment each with bathrooms fitted with gold plated taps.

Wilma explained that the 'Christian Palace' belonged to a church leader, not one of the Revelationists though.

"You know, those blokes on TV, they sing and dance and get up to all sorts of things with people they shouldn't." It didn't matter who built it everyone was just grateful to have been handed such an opulent safe house. Nothing could go wrong now, even the rain that threatened to bog their trucks couldn't dampen their spirits.

The children were in their own piece of heaven. Due to the rain the children were kept indoors which meant that they ended up annoying everyone with their play. That is until they were shown the games rooms. The dogs had free run of the palace too, but when Mel caught them pooping on the expensive rugs she chased them out, everyone was fed up with them by then anyway.

Eventually Sundown's Commando settled into their new home. The ladies were all experienced in running motels, hotels and caravan parks, they had the organisation side down pat. They even put Fat Boy in a room nearest the kitchen.

When Roo arrived he carried what gear he could in his one arm and insisted he sleep outside in his swag with Dog and Cat. Jenny made him choose a room in the staff quarters instead. These opened to the back of the house where they overlooked the work sheds. It made him feel a lot happier than having to stay inside the big house.

Charlene noticed and told Mel that she wanted to sleep in the staff quarters too. Her excuse was that she needed solitude to continue her healing. Mel knew it was really so that she could be close to Roo.

The pretty young woman with the frozen arm asked Lenny if he would help her and Roo move their gear from the trucks into their rooms. Charlene's room was conveniently next to Roo's.

Lenny and the children were all smiles, they helped the two wounded heroes and were particularly chuffed when Roo let them play with Cat. Cat had a reputation for cussedness and would only let 'very special human slaves' touch him. He put up with the children's attention because it allowed him to stay with Roo.

Dog on the other hand was more interested in Red Dog. It turned out that Red Dog was on heat and much preferred Dog's attention to her brothers Black Dog and Blue Dog. The dog's behaviour perplexed the city kids but simply amused the country ones, they'd seen all kinds of animals in the act of mating, wild and domestic.

It was Katie who helped Fat Boy set up the kitchen. Between the two of them they managed to work their way through the many spacious cupboards and pantries making a list of what they needed to bring back from Birdsville.

In between rain squalls Fatima was outside with Phil and Andy pegging down the slightly damaged Christian Palace chicken pen. It was strongly built obviously to withstand the dingoes, wild dogs, foxes and feral cats. Fatima was adamant that no animal could break in and kill her precious chickens.

"They're my pride and joy," said Fatima. "We've kept these poor birds alive through a whole year of terrorist hell followed by a thousand kilometre drive with them stuck on the roof of the trailer. It's amazing they're still alive."

Phil added, "It's amazing Nulla's driving didn't blow their feathers off."

Fatima ignored him as she continued with what she wanted to say. "Andy, did you know that blasted rooster nearly cost us all our lives?" Andy looked at the scrawny thing and shook his head. "Well, we pulled into a motel not realising it was right next to the terrorist's road block. The blooming thing wouldn't stop crowing so they came to investigate. That's when Arty got shot, poor boy, he was so brave."

Phil cut in. "Arty saw them and fired at the same time they fired at him. He knocked one down but one of their bullets sliced his arm from elbow to wrist, nasty it was. He'd only just recovered from being shot in the leg and blown up by a grenade. He's a great kid, he's our good luck charm," said Phil with a proud smile.

Bongo was the only one who couldn't help, he felt completely useless. With his still very tender leg he spent most of the time sitting, watching. He peeled potatoes for Fat Boy; spliced some rope ends for Phil and Andy; he packed pots, pans and food into the cupboards, all the while moving awkwardly on a foot stool around the enormous country kitchen. Eventually he gave up. Not even Roo was available for him to sit with, his best friend was always with Charlene these days.

Bongo's leg was swelling up again so he asked Katie to put some of her magic mixture on it. It helped ease the feeling of biting ants. The wounded scout then climbed up the stairs to sit in an enormous covered patio and watched the rain. He was pleased when Cat jumped into his lap and began to purr.

He thought of Lucy again. During the desert trek to Birdsville they'd only spoken a few times and that was about the food or the weather or some other mundane subject. He tried but every time he got near her he was struck dumb. He even stuttered a few times when he tried to speak about how he liked her, and he had never stuttered in his life. So he gave up. In the final week of their desert trek he just said hello not bothering to go near her, she didn't even notice the difference. He now felt miserable - and the rain didn't help.

Floating up to him came the comforting sounds of ducks on the lagoon, children laughing and the noises in the rooms below reminded him of families sorting out their holiday lodgings. So he eased into a lounge chair, patted Cats tangled fur and fell asleep to the sound of rain. An unfinished game of solitaire lay on the table beside him.

Heidi, Danni and Lulu weren't idle either. When they arrived the first thing they did was put on their rain gear, take their assault rifles and patrol the palace perimeter. Tricia asked Lucy to stay inside the building and guard the house itself while the three warrior girls were having fun patrolling in the rain.

Tricia noticed Lucy was acting awkward and lost. The poor woman couldn't hide behind Annie because her daughter was busy running around with the other kids. Despite repeated attempts to draw the newcomer into conversation Tricia eventually gave up.

The more Tricia observed the newcomer the more she sensed that there might be trouble if the woman didn't settle in soon.

Lucy occupied her mind with thoughts of Nulla. His strong arms, his manly scent and his deep brown eyes. It wasn't that she'd fallen in love with the aboriginal soldier, rather, thinking of him made her feel safe, safe from harm, but more so safe from the gnawing loneliness that had been threatening to overwhelm her ever since Tony died. It didn't occur to her that Glenda would be jealous. Glenda was so… she thought for a moment, Glenda was always so comfortable just being Glenda.

The Christian Palace was enormous. There were machinery sheds; quarters and outhouses for the stockmen and house staff, and plenty of livestock yards. There was excitement when the kids discovered an outdoor cinema and a swimming pool. The pool was kept to capacity by a pipe pouring artesian water in at around thirty degrees Celsius. Lulu, Danni and Heidi reported that they had discovered a garden maze of native bushes complete with statues of the Greek Gods and ponds filled with water lilies and fresh water fish.

None of the commando had been out to the Christian Palace for months. When Bill and Pellino visited they hadn't done any serious patrolling, they had just walked in through the front door and out through the back. The warrior girls were warned to be on their guard in case there were residents hiding out somewhere.

Before dinner was called the three girls returned to see the children playing by the lagoon and sat with them for a few minutes to enjoy the scenery.

"Will ya look at that. Beautiful ain't it?" said Lulu. "But them bloody dogs, weren't they suppose to come with us and help patrol?"

Heidi was excited to be part of this little group of lively, like-minded teenagers. "Yes, but all they've done is chase that poor Red Dog."

She could now see Roo's Dog and Red Dog, it looked like they were getting overly friendly with each other. "What's going on with them? They're acting really strange," Heidi asked.

The two aboriginal girls laughed delightedly. "City girl, don't you know what dogs do? They're getting ready to mate, you know, make puppies!" squealed Danni. "When Red Dog has puppies we're going to have so much fun with them." The three girls laughed with the sheer joy of being young and alive.

That evening Tricia, Harry and Andy sat everyone down as they sorted out the rosters and routines. Everything went through them, they said, any decision that impacted on the community was their jurisdiction.

"Why the hell do we have to go through you lot? Who put you in charge then?" was Lucy's contribution after a horrid day managing Annie, four dogs and Jenny's three kids. Lucy was frazzled and stressed and that put her in a dark mood.

Tricia certainly wasn't going to let this attitude continue. She knew it was now or never to establish the order necessary to maintain harmony in the commando.

Running the wing of a busy city hospital taught her a lot about diplomacy and communication. She rarely needed to assert herself these days because everyone in the commando pulled together. But here was this rude new arrival with a divisive attitude.

"I'm sorry? Lucy, isn't it?" she said politely. "Where you came from I guess no one bothered to pitch in to help?"

"Where I came from they murdered my husband and I live to see every Revelationist pay for it with their lives. I didn't sign on to be told what to do by the likes of you three either. I'm an adult, I have a child to care for and I'm not going to kowtow to you," Lucy spat back.

Lucy knew that she was being unreasonable but she had no control over herself. The feelings of loneliness and loss placed her on the edge of panic.

Nulla had come into her life at her lowest point, just when she needed someone to make her world whole again. He'd even made her leader of the group that day in Arkaroola. He trusted her and believed in her and that had struck a chord deep in the core of her being. The handsome aboriginal warrior was the solid rock she could lean on. Now he was gone to battle, just as Tony had, and she feared he would never return. Lucy was frightened and had been close to breaking down in tears all day.

"I'm sorry, lovey," said Tricia smoothly, "but you don't have to be here if you don't want, no one is forcing you to stay. If you decide to stay then please accept that we need to do things for the safety and harmony of our community." Except for the 'lovey' slip Tricia felt she had handled this quite well.

"Well screw you and your 'community'! I wasn't brought up to…" Lucy was just standing up when Glenda quickly stood and forced her back into her chair with a gentle hand on her shoulder.

"Sorry, Tricia, Lucy's had a hell of a time. Let me look after her." Glenda looked towards the three at the end of the table and then down at Lucy.

The fragile lady with the fiery temper sat silent for a moment, the sudden sounds of her choking back wet tears made everyone shift uncomfortably in their seats.

 Lucy wiped her sleeve across her eyes. "I'm sorry, I have to go now." She stood quickly and strode off to the front door and down the steps. Glenda limped after her.

She met Lucy at the duck pond which was once a beautiful, manicured lagoon. Now it was unkempt and neglected. Unconsciously Glenda noted that the potential to bring it back to it's former glory was still there. The two dwellers sat down in a covered picnic setting and stared at the ducks floating quietly on the pond surface as the rain came sheeting down once more.

It was quite surreal, until Black Dog and Blue Dog came racing over. Thinking it was their right to chase everything in the vicinity of the palace they ran into the water barking at the wild ducks.

"I'm sorry, Glenda," said Lucy. "I'm scared for Nulla. I know he's yours and all but he's my closest friend. I love him… but not in that way, you know what I mean." She felt awkward and vulnerable right then so Glenda just sat quietly and listened.

"I'm a moody bitch when I want to be, you know, just ask everyone. But until Nulla comes back I don't know how I'll be able to cope." She started to tear up and that started Glenda feeling miserable.

They sat there crying on each others shoulders until little Annie breathlessly came running over to her mother. Liam, Danielle and Lenny were running behind trying to keep up with her. The rain had stopped but rain or shine nothing stopped the children having fun that day.

"Mummy! Mummy! You've got to see this!" she yelled. "Roo's Dog was pushing Red Dog and now they're stuck!"

Lucy and Glenda turned to see what she was talking about. Looking across the lawn she could see the two dogs.

"What on earth?" she mouthed softly her face a perplexed frown.

Lenny helped them out. "Miss Lucy, me mum usually throws water at them. That sometimes makes them unstuck," he said, laughing at Annie and Lucy's reaction.

"I think we might just leave them alone for now, Annie," said Glenda trying to calm Annie down a little. She'd seen the same thing as a kid in Malaysia, she knew that they were just doing what dogs do. "Just don't go near them, they might bite you."

Annie was the happiest child now she had friends, not just friends but friends who loved to play with her. She had all the toys she'd brought from Adelaide and they played up a storm in the car trip to the Christian Palace. They were as close as a pack of dingo pups.

"Glenda, do you think we can go for a walk?" asked Annie completely forgetting about the dogs. Lucy noticed that she and Danielle were holding hands. They were much the same age and acted like sisters. The scene softened Lucy's heart and she started crying again.

Ignoring her mothers tears Annie rushed on, "Glenda, can you and mum take us around the property before it gets dark? Please? We want to see the cattle sheds but they look scary. Lenny said there might be ghosts."

"Sure, let's go. But we stick together and no running off without telling us. Got it? That's the commando's rules here, no one does anything without telling an adult." Glenda reiterated the rules the adults had already told the kids a dozen times that day.

"Yes, Glenda," said Annie pulling at her mother's arm. "Mum! Come on, hurry up! Before it gets dark and the ghosts come out!" Then she yelled at Lenny who was wrestling with Black Dog. "Come on Lenny, we're going on a ghost walk!"

Lucy and Glenda headed back to the dining room after taking the children on their walk. The meal was over and everyone had remained comfortably chatting over drinks. Fortunately the palace was well stocked with alcohol. When Lucy arrived back at the table she asked everyone to listen, the conversations quickly ceased.

"I would like to apologise. I'm sorry, Tricia, for being such a bitch. I'll try harder to be part of this community. If you'll all forgive me I'd like to pitch in and help. Please, give me a job and tell me what to do. I need to keep busy." She spoke quickly without pausing.

"Lucy, we've accepted you already. I know you're on guard duty with the girls but Fatima might need a hand with the chickens and the gardens. Would you like to help her?" Tricia suggested. "It'll give you a break from looking after the kids."

"I'm a bit of a fighter at heart, so as long as I get to fire off a few rounds every now and then I don't mind helping." She saw Fatima and waved. "Thanks," she said finally and sat to finish her cold meal.

When Andy saw that things were settled he resumed his story of how he found the palace wine cellar. It was in a tunnel below the main building, an enormous underground complex that went on and on. It was much larger than the house itself. He noticed padlocked rooms going off the main tunnel that looked like it led to the cattle and shearing sheds. The wine and spirits collection must have been worth millions.

Fat Boy said he'd like to go down with a torch and investigate. He was the one who surmised the locked rooms may have been used for purposes other than spiritual. He should know, he said, he knew quite a few church leaders. He said he'd heard of the Christian Palace, he knew of just about every church-run property in outback Australia, but he'd never visited this one.

The commando settled in for the night. The four female guards were split into shifts. Their security for the first night wasn't going to be left to chance, Heidi made sure of that.

The competition between Lucy and Heidi to wrestle control of the 'Girl Guards', as Phil now called them, intrigued the rest of the commando. Heidi eventually allowed Lucy to command midday to midnight guard duty while she took the midnight to midday patrols. Once that was sorted out Andy, Wilma and Tricia eased themselves into the mansion without detection and went up onto the top floor patio.

Those not on guard duty or putting kids to bed were invited to join them under the awnings well protected from the rain. They sat back in palatial chairs drinking three hundred dollar bottles of champagne in candle-lit splendour. That might be the reason why Phil and Fatima woke up the next morning still in their chairs. The sun was way too bright as it broke through the heavy clouds to wake them.

Chapter 23 - The Push

Sergeant Ahmet led the patrol made up of Cambra's four wheel drive and the five bikers from Birdsville with his all-terrain, six-wheel drive Bushmaster. Throughout their trek it rained and for the bikers that meant hours of sheer misery. The patrol finally pulled up at Assassin's 'danger alert' sign on the road just before they came to the Coopers Creek crossing where Patrol One was posted.

"This is where Assassin said we'd make contact with their forward scouts, Sarg. It's going to be hard to spot them though," said Private Julian sitting in the front peering through the mist and rain.

"All the better to shoot the shit out of them," said Ahmet as he searched for signs of the enemy himself. "We really need to get out and make sure there's no land mines here," he hinted.

No one volunteered to check so Ahmet pulled on his poncho and went outside himself. He called for Nulla to walk with him. It was now raining so hard that Nulla slipped and nearly landed in Ahmet's lap. After a hurried chat Nulla suggested he scout forward with one of his boys. Ahmet was grateful, he was starting to think he might have to do it all himself.

Nulla approached his two main men, Luke and Simon. Luke didn't even have the energy to look at Nulla when he asked for volunteers. Simon slid off his bike while he complained that he was too cold and wet to go into the scrub.

"Boss, that's not fair. Look at us, over three hundred kilometres riding in the rain. We're covered in mud and shit, I'm wet, my feet are saturated, my boots are water-logged and my rifle's filled with water right up to its spout. I'm gonna be useless if we get into a fight," he complained as he dutifully followed Nulla into the soggy scrub that led into the river crossing itself.

The Cooper Creek was a series of shallow creeks, in flood they all joined up to become one massive flood. They'd only gone ten metres when Nulla waved frantically for Simon to get down. They lay in the water now an inch deep covering the sandy river bed.

Nulla crawled over and whispered in Simon's ear, "They're just there, sitting in the truck. Four of them." He wasn't happy. He'd just led his young off-sider right into the giant's cave and there was no beanstalk for them to climb down to safety.

Simon peeped through the leaves and there, above him not a metre away, was the door of the truck. As the rain slackened off he heard music and talking, he could also smell marijuana smoke.

"Nulla, what now?" he mouthed the words too afraid to speak out loud.

In answer Nulla rolled onto his back and cocked his assault weapon, full automatic, and indicated for Simon to do the same. He put up his hand in a 'stop' sign and mouthed for Simon to wait while he crawled to the back of the truck. Nulla indicated for Simon to cover the front cabin in case he was discovered. Simon watched as his leader carefully stood and peered over the truck's tailgate. Satisfied no one was there or on the other side Nulla crawled back.

The cavalry sergeant held up three fingers and indicated, *'on the count of three we stand up and hit them.'* He used his hand to indicate he would stay at the side door while Simon was to walk around to the front window to fire.

'One, two, three!'

They stood together and opened fire. Simon walked his Steyr's bullets along the bench seat of the truck. He could see the devastation of his gunfire from just three feet away.

The firing was over in seconds. Nulla threw the door open and bloodied bodies spilled out onto the side of the road. Simon watched as the rain washed fresh blood off the terrorist's pale, dead faces.

There was a sudden roar of engines as the Bushmaster came forward out of the rain and mist. Simon nearly crapped his pants when he heard the armoured vehicle come right up behind him without warning.

Ahmet jumped out along with three of his men, all armed ready for a fight. Running behind the Bushmaster were the four other bikers and Cambra and Pellino. All were armed and ready to do their bit to protect their friends.

"You bastard, Nulla, we were supposed to get here first," called one of the crewmen as he went through the bodies to collect weapons, ammunition and information.

Ahmet sent his other two men to the back of the truck to watch for any enemy approaching from the Patrol One site. The bikers came up next and everyone could see they looked wet and miserable. Riley was probably the only one to have managed to keep his poncho on in the rain, but even he was covered in mud from boots to breastbone.

"Hey, boss," called Luke looking like a blob of cookie dough. "Is this enough rain for a 'desert bunny'?"

Nulla looked at his bikers, what a sorry lot they looked, he thought. "This is just perfect, Luke. Where I was born water came out of the ground not the sky. This is like…" he thought for a suitable word. After five hours of riding this amount of rain and mud needed something special. "It's like paradise but wetter."

Luke looked at him and twisted his head to the side. "Nulla, that is the lamest description I've ever heard. I think I'd better start teaching you 'prose appreciation'. I think a few lessons on the metaphysical poets would be good for your education. I'll ask Charlene and Lucy if they have any Donne, Hopkins or Marvell, maybe even some Shakespeare."

Simon wiped mud off his face as he listened to the conversation. "You're kidding aren't you, Luke? Nulla and

Shakespeare?" He started to laugh and that took effort in this misery of fatigue, mud and rain.

"Right, we've still got the main stockade at Patrol One's position just down the road from here," called Sergeant Ahmet. "Nulla, do you think your boys are up to it?"

Cambra and Pellino had returned to sit comfortably in their four wheel drive as Nulla looked at his four warriors. He decided it was time to make a few changes. The bikers were wet, cold and downright miserable and in no fit state to fight.

Nulla looked across to his friend, Ahmet. They were both proud of their cavalry heritage and remained staunch in the face of such minor tribulations as the weather. They also recognised that the bikers were absolutely exhausted and needed to take a break.

"Cambra, do you have room for a few of my boys? We're about as wet as a drowned platypus. How about squeezing Arty, Luke and Simon in the back with the machine guns and we'll pick up the bikes on the way back?" he asked.

Cambra was snuggled comfortably inside the four wheel drive cabin and had to turn to peer across the back seat.

"Yeah, it'll be a bit tight but good enough for you poor bastards to keep warm and maybe dry off a bit."

Luke, Simon and Arty didn't argue. They pushed their bikes into the scrub, marked the trees for their retrieval on the way home, and one by one climbed into the back of the dual cab.

"Arthur," said Luke like a kindly professor, "this is an opportunity to take a leak or a dump in the bush if you need to. And we'd better eat something then check our boots and gear. We might not find a chance later on so we'd better do it now."

Arty did as he was told drying and checking his equipment thoroughly. He took his boots off to check the condition of his feet while eating some kangaroo jerky.

Cambra was watching in the mirror and commented. "What's this then, eh?" he asked. "Are you boys getting ready to go to the movies or something?"

Luke explained while pulling his Steyr down and blowing forcefully to remove moisture from its firing mechanism. "It's from the Japanese army field manual, during World War Two, Cambra. If you've got time to sit, then you've got time to piss, and if you've got time to piss you've got time to crap, and if you've got time to…"

"Yeah, yeah, I've got it, you've got time to change your underwear. Where'd you learn that?" stirred Cambra.

"Nulla told us, he's been teaching us all about the army from the time of Alexander The Great." Luke worked the bolt action back and forth. "Did you know warfare is all about resources? Whoever has enough resources generally wins. And if you're rich enough you can buy resources, like soldiers and weapons. That's what they did back in the days of old and they still do it today."

"Yep, that Nulla of yours is spot on, Luke. I liked his story of the Spartans going into battle with their sticks tied to their arms. Makes sense it does," added Pellino as he checked his own weapon making sure moisture hadn't found it's way inside, accidentally, while it sat safely in their dry cabin.

"Well how about that, the things you learn in the front seat of a Toyota." Cambra said as he climbed out of their vehicle. Hunched over in the rain he relieved himself against the nearest tree while he had the chance.

"Riley, you and me get to warm up and dry off in the Bushmaster, come on." Nulla went over to Ahmet to discuss strategy. The three of them climbed in and sat to roll a cigarette each.

"Damn, my fingers are shaking too much, Ahmet. Would you mind rolling me one as well?" asked Nulla. Sergeant Ahmet recognised Nulla's delayed stress reaction to their firefight but kept his mouth shut. The last thing Nulla needed was to be told he was under stress.

"No more running off like that either, Nulla. I know you didn't have much choice but it worries me. Cavalry boys like us need to look after each other. I can't watch your back when you're out acting like an infantry grunt." They smoked quietly for a few minutes as the rain thundered against the Bushmaster's roof.

"Listen to that, no wonder we came up so close to them without being detected. There's no way they'd hear us in this rain," said the cavalry sergeant. He called across to his gunner. "Gunner, ten minutes smoko then we push forward to the main Patrol One site. Pass it on will you."

Gunner Wilmott nodded and pulled on his poncho before he got out. Rifle in hand he went out into the rain to tell his forward scouts and then ran back to tell Cambra and the lads parked behind them.

"Ahmet, we might be better off dropping in on them just on dark. We've got night vision goggles and I'm pretty sure they won't have any. These boys don't seem to be very well trained or resourced," said Nulla.

"Hmm," mumbled Ahmet. "They just pushed our best scouts into the desert and took out our Bushmaster. Every mob we've hit have been trained extremely well. Don't let an ambush in the rain fool you, mate." He got out his tobacco pouch again and rolled another two cigarettes, he absently handed one to Nulla.

"It's only going to take us a few minutes to get to the Patrol One stockade. Blondie said they were rebuilding it. She said she heard the lieutenant mention land mines. I bet these blokes here were supposed to lay mines in front of their position. We didn't hit any so I guess they spent all their time trying to get the truck out of the bog. I'm buggered if I'll send anyone forward to check for mines so close to the enemy though." Ahmet wiped the sweat beading on his forehead. "If Cambra can drive way back from us I'll drive ahead. If we hit a mine the old girl should be fine for at least the first one, then we'll know won't we."

Donna was acting radio operator for the trip, she now whistled and turned to the group behind her. "Holy shit! Ahmet! Sundown's taken command of Third Army and General Hughes is under house arrest. He's sending an armoured troop across the Simpson to support us and he'll be posting their Bushmasters at road blocks on the Stuart Highway as well as the Oodnadatta Track near Mount Dare."

Nulla looked at Ahmet having no idea what they were talking about. Ahmet saw the confusion on his face.

"It's all right, sergeant," Ahmet said. "Sundown's our fighting commander, and Hughes, well, he was a trumped up idiot. Now we're going to see some real action!" He called to his radio operator, "Donna, luv, send this signal to Blondie: 'we attack just after sunset, at 1830 hours'. Can you let Sundown and Wiram know our current situation as well?"

It had remained wet, gloomy and miserable all afternoon but that didn't stop Lieutenant Donata from forcing his platoon to finish their defenses. He had orders to resist any incursions from the Birdsville commandos until relieved.

Right now he was in two minds on whether to get his men into shelter or to complete their defences. The rain and condition of the road was such that any incursion from Sundown's Commando was highly unlikely.

He'd spoken to Captain Burgess only a half hour ago and learned that the ambush at Mungerannie had finally caught and eliminated the Bushmaster crew and the bikers. His sister platoon reported they'd left not a single enemy alive.

Lieutenant Donata expected a call from the major later that afternoon when Lance Corporal Jaina arrived with the code book and prisoners. Maybe then he would be put on the promotion ladder.

While the lieutenant lay back in the repaired stockade he thought of what he would be doing when he got back to Marree. There were the usual soldier's moles offering sex for food and safe lodging. There was occasion when he slept with the girls but he got bored with them easily. He had holiday leave coming this weekend and he thought he might go into Adelaide and share in some fine dining and the churches up-market entertainment there.

A lot of the farming regions had lost their menfolk to work on the church-run properties. It was much like slavery, he thought. The women not taken in by the church officials and officers went to the NCO's then down the line to the regulars. Those who didn't make the cut ended up with the outposts and out on patrol like this one. No one felt sorry for them, the church fed them and gave them a roof over their heads. As long as they provided a service for God, servicing God's soldiers, they were looked after, in a fashion.

At the moment Nancy was busy servicing a few of the bored men in the stockade beside him. The church accepted sex in any shape or form as long as members paid their dues and worshiped the one God according to the rites and traditions of the church. Free sex was just part of God's gift to humanity for bringing on the apocalypse.

Life had never been so good since the apocalypse, he thought. Previously he'd been a railway worker but now he was an officer in the church army doing what he loved doing. Donata enjoyed leading his fellow soldiers. He wasn't cruel like many others, far from it, he took pride in extending God's mercy to those under him, be it his troops, God's children or the enemy.

Now he was waiting for the truck to return with his forward scouts. He decided not to leave them out there in this rain, they should be back here with their mates. But with this much rain they had become bogged and the last he heard was that they'd managed to push the truck off the road and were waiting for the rain to ease before driving it back.

The lieutenant ignored the gasp of a man in the grips of ecstasy next to him. Nancy was certainly earning her keep today, he thought, as he pulled a book from his backpack, 'Robin Hood'. He'd found it in one of the houses they'd raided last month. He was intrigued by it's theme of robbing from the rich to give to the poor. He fell asleep as the rain drummed monotonously on the tin roof above.

There were over twenty elite Stosstruppen in the Patrol One position. Only ten could squeeze into the stockade so the rest had to set up their tents in the bush a little away from the rising creek. They were still within shouting distance of the solid structure where Lt Donata and the others were resting up.

When the lieutenant woke he began to worry about his squad up the road. They hadn't answered his calls on the CB and it was getting dark. He called two of his men.

"Fella's, check out the scouts position up front and find out what's going on." They nodded, pulled their hats down firm against the rain and huddled into their ponchos, rifles well covered. Mumbling under their breath they set out.

"No use rushing it, the sooner we get back the sooner the bastard will give us another shit job. *'Build the bloody stockade, dig the bloody latrine, bloody do this, bloody do that'*." Corporal Normy moaned.

It was slow going in the mud and they slipped and slid all the way to the forward position. He didn't even realise he was a prisoner until he felt an arm around his throat and a knife pushed into his ribs.

"Quietly now, lads, don't mess about. You're now a prisoner and we've got a nice dry spot for you out of the rain," said Julian. Luke had knocked the other prisoner to the ground, his knife pressed firmly into the man's throat just as Nulla had taught him.

The prisoners told the two sergeants everything. Names, numbers, equipment… the most important information was that there were no land mines. It certainly helped when the prisoners knew that they would be travelling with their captors and a land mine would kill them as well.

Nulla secured them to the inner panels inside the Bushmaster and told Riley to guard them. Riley smiled an evil smile and pulled out his hunting knife.

"Don't you worry, Nulla. If these boys try to escape they'll find themselves gutted and skinned. I've already had practice doing that to several of their friends in the Flinders Ranges." He eyed the two terrorists, they shrank back as far as they could from the wild cattleman with the big knife.

Blondie quickly deciphered Donna's message in her head. "Right everyone, we've only got till sunset to sit in this sardine can and listen to these two love-birds outside." As she looked through the bushes she could see Little lying on his back with Jaina lying beside him in their make-do tent. "My goodness, they might have finally exhausted themselves," she muttered.

"We've only got the one rifle, Blondie. Two magazines, that sort of makes it a bit difficult if we get caught in a fire-fight. What's your plan if Ahmet gets pushed back?" asked Poole. "We can't go back into Marree and we can't stay here. Slimmy's going to die if he doesn't get treatment soon."

Blondie thought for a moment. "If we get stuck here and the fight doesn't swing our way we'll go through them. I'll drive, you take the AK and shoot. We drive fast through the road block - and if we die we die." She stopped then reached across for the code book and radio.

"Poole, take these and bury them over there. Here's my knife, carve a strip in the bark running down the tree. If we don't make it they won't get the codes. If we do make it we can come back later and retrieve it." As she turned to hand him her knife she saw Jaina mount the enormous girth of her lover again, she just sighed in resignation.

"And don't go in that direction, the lovers are at it again. We don't want to make them feel embarrassed now do we."

Lieutenant Donata was getting angry. Those two lazy sods he had sent to investigate what was happening with the forward scouts hadn't returned and it was almost dark. *I should have known better than send that lazy bastard, Normy. He's no doubt sitting inside the truck drinking and smoking joints with the others,'* he thought. Donata was sure that the scout party were deliberately relaxing in their dry cabin while everyone else was working.

With the setting of the sun, or what could only be a suggestion of sunshine in the gloom of rain and heavy black clouds, the giant, starving mosquitoes were out in their millions. Finally he'd had enough and got up.

"Damn it!" he grunted loudly. "Private, grab your poncho and come with me." The two staggered, slid and slipped on the muddy road. As they approached the truck in front of them the lieutenant was surprised by a gruff voice and an arm around his neck.

"Don't mess about, move a little too fast and this knife will cut your guts open. Then they'll spill all over this muddy ground just like Humpty Dumpty's innards," said Julian who'd already done one turn on duty with Luke and the two were now on their second.

Julian and Luke brought their prisoners to the Bushmaster where Ahmet met them with a broad smile. "Well I'll be. Two more little birdies have come along to find the worm. Boys, come inside, it's warm and it's dry." He held the door open while Nulla frisked them for weapons. He found thin-bladed knives in their boots where most of the Stosstruppen liked to hide them.

The lieutenant looked at his two privates and scowled at them. "Idiots! What the hell did you get yourselves caught for. Now look what you've done!"

"Sorry sir, but we're in the same warm truck as you are and it's still raining out there. I suggest you just shut-the-hell up and enjoy it while you can. It seems that this lot want their stockade back and we're now just spectators." Normy smiled smugly at his young lieutenant.

"I'm sorry too, I'm going to have to gag and secure you. We don't want you wriggling about when we head into your position and start killing your terrorist bastard friends. If any of you move, Riley here will cut you with his big knife, won't you Riley?" added Sergeant Ahmet.

"You bet I will, Sarg. I know how to gut a sheep, a kangaroo and even a Revelationist, but I've never gutted a Stosstruppen yet but I sure want to." He smiled his evil smile once more as he picked at his nails with the point of his razor sharp knife.

"I'm such an idiot!" was all Lieutenant Donata said as Ahmet bound and gagged him.

"Julian, you and Luke deserve a medal. Good job, boys." Julian and Luke smiled at each other. They felt quite chuffed about having bragging rights that none of the others had.

"Sarg, I've just picked up Blondie's signal, she's ready. Wiram and Sundown wish us good luck." Donna adjusted the headphones and prepared for the Bushmaster to move.

"Right, driver, time to head off," called Sergeant Ahmet. Cambra was told to stay ten metres behind the Bushmaster. This should allow space for Blondie to pass on the muddy, narrow track. The commandos were to race out onto the flanks beside the Bushmaster and pour fire into the stockade and any enemy they see.

Private Julian roared into the Patrol One position while gunner Wilmott opened fire. Cambra and Pellino quickly set up their machine gun to lend a hand - but the fight had gone out of the terrorists.

First there came the rain then the giant mosquitoes. It made everyone miserable as they set about preparing the camp site ready for their stay. It was more than enough to demoralise the Stosstruppen – elite soldiers or not they had their limits. The soldiers dropped what they had in their hands and put up their hands. There was not one shot fired towards the commando.

Blondie raced forwards, slowed, then stopped when she saw the rout. Catching movement from the corner of her eye she pointed and ordered, "Poole, those three running, take them down."

The terrorists were only a few metres away trying to escape through the scrub. Their clothing was wet, their boots saturated and their feet dragged in the clinging mud, they didn't stand a chance. Poole leaned his whole body out of the window and opened fire. The three terrorists fell to the ground.

The biker boys collected every weapon and ammunition magazine they could find. Anything they could use was fair booty to them. Simon found another pistol to add to his collection and Poole made sure he got his wrist watch back.

"All right, load up the vehicles, we've got a collection of prisoners here and five bikes to bring home," roared Ahmet as the rain once again came down like cats and dogs.

He looked at Pellino and nodded. "You take one of their vehicles and jam some of these prisoners in the back. Luke and Arty, you boys ride shotgun with him and make sure they're thoroughly searched and secured."

Luke and Simon did most of the body searches. They found things no one else would have thought to search for.

"Nulla taught us well," smiled Simon as he stuffed a second pistol into his webbing. He also had a collection of Stosstruppen knives that he could trade for more pistols later. Ever since he had caressed the .38 calibre pistol that fateful day in the Adelaide Hills, Simon carried an extra haversack on his back for just this purpose.

Donna had the honour of reporting their success to both Alice Springs Command and Wiram.

"… and Wiram, not one bullet our way, not one," she said excitedly. He breathed a sigh of relief when he heard the good news. The night battle at Birdsville quite a few months ago had unsettled her, today's successes acted to boost her confidence.

"Well, missus Donna, you have just seen how well the Australian military can carry out a successful assault. Do you think you're ready to take command of a patrol now?" he asked.

"Wiram, seriously, no way. I think I'm cured. I don't want to be a soldier any more. The rain, the mosquitoes, the noise, the boredom. No, if you marry me I might be a good wife though," she said and the CB went strangely quiet on the other end.

Donna could hear Gail's voice in the background, "What was that? Marriage?"

Wiram broke his silence. "Will you have me even if this war lasts forever?" he asked.

"Of course, now where are we going for our honeymoon?" she giggled when he swore. "And you'd better not swear so much, you're getting just like Pedro." She giggled again. Wiram knew that her elevated mood was probably just the release of tension from the stress of taking back the Patrol One position.

"I would be honoured to marry such a beautiful young woman as you. Hurry home, Donna."

"When I get back to Birdsville we'll have a bash-up wedding ceremony at the Christian Palace for the entire commando, what do you reckon?" she added.

Sergeant Ahmet tried not to listen but everyone in the cab could hear, even the prisoners - under Riley's watchful eyes. There came whistles from outside as the commandos climbed into their vehicles and onto their mud spattered bikes, it was time to head back home.

"Congratulations Donna, congratulations Wiram! See you when we get home!" yelled Ahmet into the mic as the Bushmaster roared into life.

The action at Patrol One secured an entire platoon of terrorists, but no one knew what to do with them once they arrived at Birdsville.

The ambushed bike patrol arrived soon after lunch the following day. Beamy and the One One Charlie soldier, Mugga, were immediately taken into the first aid room, Gail and Ahmet's medic did their best to make them comfortable.

Beamy said he was used to getting shot up, and within minutes of arrival was sound asleep. He slept for an entire day and a night. His was a slow recovery this time and he became as irascible as Pedro. When Lorraine arrived she would take on the role of nurse, mother and lover to the twice-wounded Beamy.

Most of the wounded who hadn't returned to Alice Springs with Sundown were recovering at the palace. Slimmy, Mugga and Beamy elected to stay at Birdsville because at least they could feel useful manning the CB with Gail and Assassin.

At dinner on their second night back in Birdsville, Nulla again called the commando to quieten down. Everyone was there, Ahmet's crew along with Doff, the survivors of his crew, and the Bravo bike team.

"Wiram; Sergeant Ahmet; Sergeant Doff; Bravo team," he acknowledged each in turn and then faced the commando. "When we were in Adelaide we often heard reports on the terrorist's radio of their contacts with Sundown's Commando.

Yesterday we witnessed just how tough this commando really is. Sundown's Commando is a tough band of warriors who refuse to compromise under any circumstances."

He stopped to reach into the bag he held in his hands. "I have here the Spartan sticks for our returning warriors to welcome you back to the land of the living. This is a reminder that you are now part of your community. You are encouraged to release your anger and fears and to re-embrace your gentle side. While on patrol we were called upon to do things, vicious and violent things, that we now need to leave behind us."

Nulla then called each name. As they came forward he handed them a stick with their name carved on it. The wounded Beamy was there, in a state of discomfort but he was determined to stay for the duration. It was a sombre and serious affair. No one smiled, no one spoke.

Finally he called John's name. Chan and Halo stepped forward to accept their friend's name stick. Together they took it and placed it reverently on the mantelpiece above the fireplace. It had been cleared to receive the unclaimed sticks. They stepped back, waited a few seconds, turned then went back to their seats.

Nulla then asked Sergeant Doff to come forward and call the names of his crew, those of his Bushmaster crew and the Patrol One troopers. The survivors accepted their sticks silently returning to their tables. He then called the names on the unclaimed sticks and one by one he lay them on the mantelpiece beside John's.

"Sundown's Commando!" Sergeant Doff's voice was firm as he included everyone in the room. "We morn our losses tonight in the traditional manner. When Sundown arrives we'll honour them again, remembering our friends, their funny ways, their bad habits and their courage. We'll tell stories of their acts of bravery and drink to their memories." He stopped and turned to the name sticks on the mantelpiece.

"Commando!" he called loudly in the silent lounge, "Attention!" The assembled men and women stood at their tables. "A minutes silence for our comrades, please." Afterwards they settled back to finish their meal, and thus the wake for their lost comrades began.

Halfway through their meal Wiram stood and called for quiet once more. "Men and women, sorry to interrupt your meal but I need to remind you that we now have a platoon of terrorists to watch over. We'll run interrogations tomorrow and give them jobs around the place. We have gardens to look after, trenches to pump dry and defenses to put up. I think we have enough to keep them busy until Sundown and his troop arrive to take them off our hands."

Looking around he noticed how the commando were different. Something had happened to them over the past few days. Wiram thought of what words would best describe what he saw. He came up with 'confident', 'solid' and 'uncompromising'.

Chapter 24 - Sundown's Challenge

Sundown's convoy of ASLAVS and Bushmasters complete with soldiers and crew, was half way across the Simpson Desert on their way to the commando's safe house, the Christian Palace.

The group had taken a little longer than expected because Billie wanted to stop off to visit his tribesmen in the middle of the desert. By this time they knew of the successes and losses of the commando's patrols, so one more day wouldn't matter now.

Billie didn't invite McFly this time, he wanted to attend to his tribe's secret men's business alone. McFly had a feeling Billie wouldn't be back. It wasn't anything Billie said but it was in his manner and in his eyes. McFly watched Billie say 'goodbye' to the convoy, the people around him and his friends. It was a moment that McFly would never forget.

It was the 'making of men' time and Billie was needed. As one of the elders he wanted to be part of what he felt was his last opportunity to give back to the people of his mother's blood.

When Billie returned two days later his health was failing fast. He said that he didn't expect to make it back to Birdsville and wanted to join his ancestors in his tribal country.

His friends sat with him throughout the night: Lorraine, Pinkie, McFly, Shadow, Sundown and Pedro. They sat together, talking quietly, discussing the future and reflecting on the past.

An hour before dawn Billie called McFly over and whispered in his ear, "The spirit mother and father told me you'll be comin' out 'ere one day. They said for you to follow yer path and stick to it. I'm not sure what they mean but they said you should 'ave listened to them and ducked like they told you," he whispered softly.

"Ah, yeah, they did say that. It was when I was in the fight with John and his mates. I stood when I was supposed to duck, I got clobbered," replied McFly with an embarrassed smile.

"Ah ha, that's right I remember now. If the spirit elders say for you to do something then don't muck about." Billie lay back in his swag and closed his eyes. The old warrior whispered that his spirit was happy, it still had some fire in its belly ready for his flight home.

By dawn Billie was gone, gone to walk the stars with his father and mother spirits. McFly sat a silent vigil until he felt a sudden urge to walk in the desert. There was something pulling at him like someone had hold of his belt and was trying to yank him up out of his chair.

"Matty, where are you going?" asked Shadow softly.

"I don't quite know, but I feel an urge to get up and be alone. I need to walk out in the scrub for a while. I guess it's to say goodbye to Billie in my own way. I'll be back in a few hours. There's something I have to do but I don't quite know what yet." He pulled on his pistol belt and slung his sniper rifle over his shoulder then walked off into the desert.

The rain had stopped and the landscape came alive with wild flowers. The large unchanging expanses of sand slowly disappeared as green grasses and coloured flowers started to cover them. The desert plants fought to produce seeds for the next generation before the heat killed them.

After a few hours McFly found that he had climbed to the top of a sand dune that looked down upon the most amazing sight - a lagoon filled with ducks, geese and probably teeming with fish.

"I don't believe it," he sighed, "a genuine oasis in the desert and here's me without my fishing gear."

From behind some low stunted bushes he watched as four aboriginal men came into sight. They carried an assortment of rifles and spears. In their nets were fish, snakes and fresh water tortoises.

"Hey!" called one of them as they walked up the sand dune towards him. It was a well muscled man in his late twenties much the same age as McFly. "I seen you brother. I seen you in my dreams last night."

When McFly looked at him strangely he continued, "My grandfather told me I'd meet you here. He told me in my dreams on his way to be with the ancestors. Will you sit and eat with us? Then we'll collect our grandfather." The young man introduced himself, "My name's Frank, what's your name?"

McFly listened while the men chatted quietly among themselves. Frank was curious as to why he'd seen McFly in his dreams.

"Why, McFly? Why did you come and speak with me? Did you know my grandfather very well?" he asked.

"Yes, I knew Billie quite well. Your grandfather smoked me on our way into the desert country on our trip to Alice Springs. He introduced me to your land and I saw your elders, the spirit man and woman." McFly paused as he relished the sweet tasting fish. The four aboriginal men had stopped talking and were looking incredulously at each other.

"What?" exclaimed the eldest man of the group, a wiry man in his forties with raised scars on his chest and shoulders. "Billie smoked you?" They spoke in their own language for what seemed ages and McFly felt a little uncomfortable, not knowing what they were saying.

"So the spirit ancestors spoke to you?" asked Frank at last, "that's strange, if that happened then you should be dead. We've never known any white fella to be spoken to before. Billie must have known that you were pretty special." The four men looked at McFly and he stared blankly back at them.

"I what? Billie danced and lit a fire and smoke blew in my face and I fell asleep. I thought I saw these two old people." He gave a confused smile. "No one told me I was special. What the hell does that mean?" He felt they were making fun of him, he wanted to get up and leave. But he was also curious because the men were obviously serious, they continued to look at him.

The four men gathered leaves and bark and built up the fire, it smoked horribly. To McFly they appeared to go into a trance. It was uncomfortable to be the centre of attention, especially when he had no idea what they were doing. He felt dizzy and fell into a mild trance as well. After only a few minutes the men came back to consciousness. One by one they opened their eyes and stared at him.

"McFly, we're warriors of our tribe, initiates of our spirit totems. You might say we're 'men of high degree'. Billie was one of our elders, he was one of the highest initiates of us all. We're trained to step out of this world to walk in the other. Ours is a small tribe and we've managed to hold onto our traditions. Now that the world has left us alone we're free to continue in our traditional ways." Frank paused and at a nod from the older man continued.

"We just smoked you and know that you're one of us. Not today, not tomorrow but soon you'll join us. Our spirit ancestors told you to keep going and not look back, well if you did look back they would have killed you for failing the test. You didn't look back, you showed respect. Billie knew what he was doing, he introduced you to the land and we welcome you back."

The four men spoke in their tribal tongue again. When they stopped talking they got up and began walking towards

Sundown's encampment. The older man stayed behind with McFly for a moment.

"Brother, one day we'll come for you, the land will call to claim you. You'll know when and what to do when it happens. In the meantime brother, don't forget to duck." He shook his head and laughed loudly as he walked off to follow his tribal mates to collect Billie and bury him in their traditional way.

McFly stayed there on the sand dune feeding small sticks to the fire while he tried to work out what it all meant. When eventually he headed back to the convoy his mind was strangely calm.

They arrived at the Christian Palace to find everyone in a grand mood, Lorraine said it looked like everyone was on drugs. Sundown called a meeting of the committee and promised everyone they would hold a full commando meeting later in the day. Right now he needed to speak with his administration team.

"Major, your boys can have the sheds for the armour and there's sleep-outs and cabins behind them. The officers and NCO's can have the rest of the staff quarters that face the sheds," said Tricia still trying to get her head around the extra numbers and how they might feed and accommodate everyone.

Andy worried that he urgently needed to send a team to Birdsville to pull down some of the irrigation equipment and rebuild it at the palace. Or should they just go back to Birdsville and re-establish themselves there?

He decided to talk with Sundown but he couldn't get near him. Everyone wanted his time and Andy was too polite to butt in. Instead he spoke to Pinkie and Major Lewis who were sitting under one of the enormous pergolas having lunch.

"Hi, Pinkie. Hi, Major Lewis, and congratulations on your promotion too." He paused then went straight for it. "Major, I need your help and I need it now. We have an extra hundred mouths to feed and I've only got enough food for the commando itself. At this rate we'll be out of food in a week." He saw him nod his heads and was encouraged to continue.

"I need some of your men to go to Birdsville with me and bring back some produce and supplies. We'll need to collect the material to build another set of irrigated vegetable gardens, like we have at home - but it needs to be ten times bigger."

"Whoa, slow down there, Andy," said the major, "ten times bigger? We helped you set up the pump for the sewer line and I still remember what a job that was, can it wait until later?"

"Major," Pinkie spoke before Andy got more flustered. "I know what Andy's on about. We lived on tinned and dried food for months before we had the gardens producing enough food to add to our diet. Andy, how many men, and what gear do you need?" she asked turning back to the aged administrator.

"Well, a hundred blokes with ten trucks, plus earth moving equipment, tractors, back-hoes, pipes and plumbing material, a heap of solar cells and wiring, batteries…" he rubbed his temples and thought for a moment. "If I had your boys for a week we'd have this place running ten times more efficiently than Birdsville." He finished with a hopeful smile.

"Blimey. Andy, we have the enemy at our gates and I'm sure Sundown has other ideas." But when he saw the pained look on Andy's face, and as he turned he saw Pinkie mirror it, he softened. "Yeah, OK, I see, food's pretty important isn't it. We brought enough to last us a while but the sooner we get the gardens going the better I guess. OK, I'll support you on this."

At the meeting later that day it was decided to heavily mine the road and approaches to the Cooper Creek crossing and to continue with the hit-and-run bike patrols. The commando would do the same with the roads to Mount Isa and Longreach.

Sundown explained the current prisoner situation. "Birdsville is over-crowded with prisoners. Sergeant Ahmet and his crew, with the new people that Sergeant Nulla brought with him, have them working in the gardens and general maintenance. But it's tight and we have to process all of them and decide what to do with them."

Sundown gave a brief summary of their current situation. "The fighting on the Birdsville Track has knocked us about. After fierce fighting we've lost Sergeant Doff's Bushmaster and some of his men to the new Revelationist battalion at Marree, the Stosstruppen, Storm Troopers. But we've also held the Birdsville track and taken enemy prisoners.

"Bravo team, our bike patrol, are back and stationed at Birdsville in support of Sergeant Ahmet. They took a beating at Mungerannie too and sadly we've lost another of our friends, John. Beamy has been injured, again, and Gail is looking after him and the other wounded."

Lorraine was doing her best to remain calm and positive but being reminded of her boyfriend's fresh wounds upset her. Wilma placed her arm around her shoulders to comfort her.

"I'm sorry, Lorraine. I know you'll want to go with us when we head out with the relief convoy tomorrow. Beamy said he's looking forward to seeing you."

To the soldiers of Third Army he said, "Boys, we have a lot of work to do. Firstly we're making this our new home base. I like it here and apparently so does everyone else." There were smiles all round at that news. "We have security to run, patrols to organise and we have Birdsville and the prisoners to sort out. Major Lewis will arrange who goes where. As for the prisoners, we'll keep them in Birdsville until we know what to do with them. In the meantime we patrol and strengthen our position here and the approaches to Birdsville."

Before he could continue, Andy coughed. Sundown looked and then remembered his conversation with Major Lewis only a few minutes earlier.

"Oh yes, we'll also be building an extensive garden system here at the palace. Andy said that it will make our Birdsville gardens look like flower pots."

Sundown had previously asked that Polly and Granny be present when he announced Billie's passing on the trek back home. Billie's extensive range of friends and relatives included Lulu and Danni. They had already heard the news but they cried all the same with the two oldies. He told them they would be holding a wake for their lost friends, soldiers, commandos and family, that night.

Everyone was relieved to be staying at the Christian Palace, it was Sundown's easiest decision of the day. It meant that Birdsville would now become an outpost and they would rotate personnel between outposts, the palace and Alice Springs.

The hard work over Sundown left it to Andy to organise personnel with Major Lewis while Harry organised equipment and logistics with his wife, Jenny. Thank goodness there were plenty of big sisters, mothers, aunts and grandmothers to help look after the kids.

Sundown had one more task so he called the Girl Guards together and invited Shadow and McFly over for support. He asked the major to bring his second in command, Captain Walker, to meet the girls.

Captain 'Johnny' Walker was an interesting character. He was regular army for most of his life, retired at forty then came back as a reservist just before the apocalypse.

It fell on his shoulders as the highest ranking survivor to collect what was left of the Darwin military, a motley band of soldiers and ten times as many civilians. He led a fighting retreat to Alice Springs bringing most of the armoured cavalry with him. It was still spoken of in the mess nearly a year later when Sundown's group were in Alice Springs. Captain Walker was a well respected officer and a welcome addition to the commando.

"Sir!" snapped the captain when he arrived at Sundown's table. "You sent for me." Walker saluted and waited to be invited to sit.

"Captain Walker, for God's sake cut the saluting, my arm hasn't stopped quivering since I met you," said Sundown. "Do you think you can manage the guard duty rosters for the palace?" he asked as the girls ogled the new officer. "These are your Girl Guards: Lucy, Heidi, Lulu and Danni. They're our very best," he added as he introduced them.

The girls were smitten by Captain Walker's good looks, charm and manners. The middle-aged soldier was tall, dark and ruggedly handsome.

"Sir, it would be my pleasure." He sat without being asked this time because Sundown refused to tell him one more time to *cut it out with this bloody army bulldust'*.

Captain Walker smiled for the girls. "I heard we had some rather attractive girls they call the Girl Guards and I was hoping I'd get to meet them. I can see that I wasn't ill advised."

When Pedro discovered that Sundown had asked Captain Walker over to meet the Girl Guards he had wandered over to join them. As usual he just could not stop himself from commenting.

"Captain Walker, they say you can leap tall buildings in a single bound, is that correct?" One of the old man's eyebrows slowly lifted as he waited to see if the captain would step up to the challenge.

"Pedro, not only can I leap tall buildings but I can run faster than a speeding bullet and snatch it out of the air with my teeth." He smiled delightedly. The two had enjoyed variations of this same conversation while on their way across the Simpson Desert.

"I'm going to enjoy this, ya boofhead," Pedro laughed. "From what I can see right now these girls will devour you and spit you out within the week, matey!"

Captain Walker was quite prepared to meet any challenge. However, neither he nor the others had met the two cocky newcomers from Adelaide. None were ready for the onslaught to begin quite so fast.

"Mr Walker, the Girl Guards, that's us... there's four of us and... well, we've already arranged our roster... but you might want to have a look and check to see if it's all OK." Heidi breathlessly passed him a sheath of papers covered in lists. Of course Heidi had an agenda, she always did. As she leaned forward her breasts strained against the thin cotton shirt she was wearing its buttons threatening to pop. Sundown winked at Pinkie, they could plainly see what Heidi was up to.

"Well, ah, nice work, thank you. I see you've split the duties into, ah, two well defined, um, sections. Yes, I see, we can certainly work with this." Captain Walker placed the sheets of paper down on the table and reached for some food to gain some time to compose himself. He needed to prepare for battle, to battle the exuberant Girl Guards.

"Captain Walker, if you don't mind, can you tell us what we might expect to do while on guard duty? I mean, I've never done this sort of thing before and your tuition will be, um, really useful." Lucy was making sure she got her bid in as well. Although not as young as Heidi, Lucy had '*I'm available and more experienced than her*' written all over her face.

Sundown and Pinkie continued to watch the newcomer's performances with fascination. Major Lewis completely ignored it, he'd seen it so many times before.

"Yes, um, Lucy isn't it? Of course I can take you on your rounds with your partner." Captain Walker saw he had to take the initiative before these voracious girls swamped him.

"In fact I've decide that we'll all be doing guard duty training starting right now, if Sundown is fine with that." He twitched the corner of his eye at Sundown and without the girls noticing he rolled his eyes and made a face. Sundown fought not to laugh but Pinkie couldn't help but let out a tiny giggle.

"Girls, it's time to gather your gear together," he barked in his officer's voice. "I want all four of you back here in ten minutes. I want you fully prepared to undertake an armed guard patrol of the property. I want full kit, webbing, backpack, weapon, spare ammunition, boots and caps."

He noticed Black Dog and Blue Dog wandering among the tables eating the scraps. He decided on the spur of the moment to make things even more interesting for the girls.

"And I want those dogs on a leash because you'll be responsible for training them as guard dogs. They'll come with us today. You have ten minutes, now move!"

The group at the table were amazed to see the four girls leap from their seats and race off to do their hero's bidding.

"Wow, Captain Walker, what is it about you? We nearly had to pull them girls off you," McFly chuckled and poked at Shadow. "You never acted like that with me," he teased.

Before Shadow had a chance to deliver a caustic reply, Sundown added, "no one's ever run that fast when I've given them a job to do either."

"Guys, I don't even like girls. I mean, I like girls but sexually, nah, they do nothing for me." He too had a grin on his face. To Captain Walker, the hero of the Darwin, Alice Springs and Stuart Highway retreat, the silliness of sex appeal was real, he had to put up with it on a regular basis.

"OK, I'd better grab some gear too. I'm going to work those girls so hard they'll come back begging to be taken off my team." He smiled brightly but Pedro and Sundown knew he just might have met his match.

Dog and Red Dog were now exhausted after their romantic encounter. It helped when Jenny poured water over them and chased them with a stick. Lucy called the children together and explained they needed to round up the dogs to go on patrol with them. Annie and Danielle caught Black Dog and Lenny brought over Blue Dog. The dogs panted in joy, they just loved the attention.

"Mummy," said Annie, "Lenny said we better leave Roo's Dog and Red Dog alone for now. He said they'd be too tired to do any work today. Is that all right for the captain?"

"Darling, anything's all right for the captain," she sighed in reply. "Tie the dogs to Sundown's table and wait for me, I won't be long. And if you see Captain Walker make sure you tell him who you are, that you're my daughter, and be on your best behaviour too." Lucy quickly had a splash-bath and freshened up, she was a girl on a mission.

The commando were given the rest of the day to sort themselves out because tomorrow they were to relieve their comrades at Birdsville. Most of them would then be sectioned off to start building the Christian Palace vegetable gardens.

In Birdsville Wiram was readying the hotel to receive their relief. Sergeant Doff and the Bravo bike team were still recovering from their ambush and Gail was kept busy tending

Beamy and the One One Charlie wounded. Sundown also wanted to speak to every member of the commando, to thank them personally.

Then there was Blondie and her gang of misfit intelligence staff, Jaina and Jason Little. Sundown asked if she would remain with the Birdsville commando's and help debrief the prisoners. Wiram, Nulla and Blondie had done one set of interviews and they now waited for Major Lewis to arrive with support. No one knew what to do with the prisoners.

All through their desert crossing Wiram kept Sundown up to date of events. Sundown felt just as upset as Wiram with the loss of John and the One One Charlie soldiers. At the same time he was elated that Blondie had rescued the two Patrol One boys and captured the two intelligence operators.

Captain Walker was up to his armpits trying to manage the enthusiastic ambitions of the Girl Guards. Major Lewis's transition to Sundown's Commando, however, was straight forward. He took command of all military operations from the capable hands of Wiram and Donna.

With the situation seemingly under control Pinkie and Sundown decided to take some time off to explore their new home and headquarters.

Pinkie grabbed Sundown by the hand and like two excited children they went exploring the Christian Palace. They were both appalled and amazed at the display of expensive paintings and sculptures. The sheer magnitude of wealth soon filled them with disgust.

"Was this all built from the hard-earned money fleeced from the church's followers?" wondered Pinkie as they paused at a painting by one of the old masters.

Sundown mused that the wealth on the walls alone was enough to challenge the Vatican.

An enthused Fat Boy saw them walking outside his kitchen and decided to take them on a tour of the palace. But what he really wanted to do was show Sundown the underground network of rooms and tunnels.

The commando's head chef was desperate to get inside those locked rooms. Despite his pleas Sundown told him to wait until he got back from Birdsville.

"Fat Boy, I don't want to miss seeing inside these rooms myself. Besides, we've got way too much work to do right now without creating more work."

By the end of the day anyone who didn't have a job took their drinks to the roof top and watched the sunset. It hadn't rained for a while and the clouds were gone.

"You know what, Sundown," said Pinkie, "I think we've found our little slice of heaven at last."

Sundown looked into her eyes and saw that she was as tired of the fighting as he was. "Love, tomorrow we'll have most of our commando back together. We've still got to sort out the prisoner problem and it worries me that we've had those serious losses. But you know what, we have the most incredible friends we could ever ask for, right here with us tonight."

Little did they know that something nasty was brewing in Birdsville.

Chapter 25 - Epilogue

Lieutenant Donata felt strangely complete. He loved working in the gardens and managing his men in their imprisonment. At that moment everything felt right. Unfortunately there were some elements in his platoon that he didn't trust but if that was the only fly in his ointment then he could cope, he thought.

Donata had strong morals, he loved to lead. He always strove to be the best leader he could be, someone the men and women in his platoon respected. The ex railway worker was well known for doing the right and honourable thing. Sadly there were some who didn't share his aspirations.

Every night they planned their escape. Despite the soldiers careful handling and watchful eyes the Stosstruppen were soon ready to make a move. Corporal Normy was a born leader, some would say he was just a conman. He knew how easy it was to mould the minds of his fellow worshipers to his will. His group sat apart from the lieutenant and his supporters.

"Tonight we make our move," he said quietly to the platoon members sitting around him, their heads bent as though in prayer. "I've got the keys to the four wheel drives, they'll get us to Longreach. Heffo's given extra special attention to the other vehicles." He grinned slyly and his friends nodded, understanding exactly what he was hinting at.

Nancy was the only one who had any uncertainty. Should she stay with the nice lieutenant, or go with Normy and his group to Longreach where she had family.

"Why Longreach, Normy? Why not back to Marree?" asked one of his group.

"Because the Birdsville Track's mined and heavily defended. I'm not going to tempt fate with my life. Besides, we have church folk in Longreach. The Crusaders of Light run the place, they'll treat us like long lost heroes," was his confident reply.

Wiram, Ahmet and Blondie knew their prisoners were planning a break out. They hadn't managed to find out how, where or when despite Blondie's Tajna Sluzba expertise and Chan's Death's Head cunning, they were still in the dark.

In the early hours of the morning, Normy and his group broke out through the wall of the shed they were housed in. They had gagged and bound Donata and his supporters then quietly pushed the wall apart where they had broken through the rivets that held the corrugated iron sheets together.

It was incredibly easy. They had five days to collect the tools had they needed to break out and five nights to separate the wall sheets. They timed their sawing to the snores of one of their platoon and other odd noises. The wall panels now parted and they crawled out of their prison.

The guards were standing in their hastily thrown up stockade smoking and chatting, oblivious to the terrorists moving quietly towards the vehicle shed. Normy had his troops sorted into vehicles and their engines roared into life.

"What the hell!?" cried private Wilmott. It wasn't one vehicle it was many. Before he had a chance to grab at his Steyr or nudge Halo the vehicles had roared out of the shed and onto the road heading towards Longreach.

"Holy crap!" cried Halo who just stood there in shock, watching.

As one, the two guards leaped into action grabbing at their weapons and calling loudly for the commando to wake up. They put their heads down and raced towards the vehicle shed.

Suddenly Wilmott stopped and stood dead still. As the cavalry squadron's go-to man for explosives he knew a bit about setting up simple trip mines.

"Hold it! Halo!" he yelled. "Don't move! Walk slowly back towards me, and do it very very slowly."

Halo stopped, he entered a state of heightened awareness as he took one slow step at a time back to Wilmott.

"What is it? What did you see?" Halo whispered.

"Booby traps, one right in front of you, at the shed door. See that wire? Little trick of ours, a trip wire attached to a grenade, when you walk through - kaboombah!" said Wilmott as he pointed to the trip wire right where Halo had been about to walk.

Halo felt a wave of recognition sweep over him. For a moment he was back in Marree and he held four sticks of sweaty dynamite in his hand placing detonators and trip wires around the door. He felt nauseous and dizzy remembering the smell, the sounds and the sight of body parts in what was left of the laundry on that eventful day.

The morning was spent cleaning up the damage the Stosstruppen did to the remaining vehicles. There was no way they could follow, not for days.

Within minutes Wiram had Lieutenant Donata in Sundown's office with Ahmet, Blondie and Chan. "I'm not sure what to do with you Donata, you've been dumped by your own kind you know. What does that mean for you?" asked a tired and irritated Wiram.

"I guess it means they think I've turned traitor. I can't go back to the church now. I know what they'll do to me and those who were tied up with me. Wiram, I've always followed my heart and my Lord's teachings. Just let us continue our work here with you that's all I ask," Lieutenant Donata replied.

The commandos grumbled among themselves and sent the lieutenant back to his shed. There wasn't much more they could do. Wiram turned to his fellow committee members and shook his head.

"We've lost the prisoners and the vehicles are trashed, Sundown's gonna be pissed." He wasn't sorry the prisoners escaped, it solved one of the problems he had. What he was sorry about was the damage they had left behind, that would take ages to sort out.

It was a fine morning at the palace when Sundown and Pinkie woke to the news of the breakout. He called his officers and administrators together. Over breakfast they watched the sunrise over the lagoon while discussing the breakout and what they needed to do next.

They could hear the rooster crowing from the chicken pen, the ducks were settled on the lagoon in front of them, and the children were already awake and playing with the dogs.

Sundown settled Cat in his lap and looked at his team and smiled. "You know what? It's going to be fine. I've told Wiram we're on our way in a few hours, we'll be there for lunch. First we set up patrols north and south. Over the next few days we'll transport the gardens, irrigation gear and solar panels from Birdsville to the palace. Then we finish the defenses we've started to build at Birdsville.

"Major Lewis, give your mechanics extra staff and we'll support them to fix our vehicles. We'll use everyone else not involved in fixing the vehicles or patrolling, to work on the garden systems here at the palace. We keep busy and by the end of the week we should be set up. We'll have an oasis in the middle of the desert right at our doorstep to rival the other marvels of this Christian Palace."

Sundown looked around at the lagoon and lawns as he saw the world waken anew. "We might have lost prisoners but we appear to have gained four experienced patrol members and two intelligence staff. Remember how valuable John and Chan have been, my hope is that we'll attract more ex-Revelationists to our cause."

Captain 'Johnny' Walker now asked to speak.

"Sure, Johnny, what is it? And you'd better not be asking to be relieved from your Girl Guard training program," said Sundown, knowing exactly what Walker was about to say.

"Ah, Sundown, yeah… well, it's those girls, they're driving me crazy but I guess I'll just have to stick it out. Just make sure you leave a few of my boys behind. I need all the support I can get." His face appeared to have aged since their arrival.

Major 'Louie' Lewis laughed as he put down his piping hot cup of tea. "Johnny boy, you're doing fine, mate. Pick two men to help you with the girls and I'll see that they're placed with you. I'll go with Sundown and leave one of the Bushmasters for you. After we leave you are in command here."

The convoy arrived at Birdsville with most of the Alice Springs Command. It was lunch time and people were starting to wander into the lounge room for their midday break. Wandering over to the fireplace, Sundown noticed a row of sticks and idly picked some of them up.

'*Crikey*,' he whispered to himself, *'these are our troops who have died in battle.'*

Sundown quietly read each name to himself so that he could send his personal thanks to them in spirit - but there was one name that stood out.

'*Who the hell is Private Brinley?*' Sundown asked himself.

THE END

Glossary of Australian Words

ASLAV– Australian Light Army Vehicle, armoured cavalry troop carrier with mounted 7.62 mm machine gun and 25 mm cannon.

Alice – Alice Springs, affectionately called 'the Alice'

Billy – tin to put on the fire to boil water in, for tea making and heating water

Blimey – crikey, strewth, darn, damn

Bloke – man, male, fellow or fella

Bloody – damn or darn

Blowed – confused, no idea, can also mean exhausted (out of breath)

Boofhead – meat head or beef head

Brumby – wild horses

Bullcrap – bullshit, not true

Bushmaster– six-wheeled cavalry armoured personnel carrier with 7.62 mm machine gun.

Cobber – friend, mate

Comms – communications, radio operator

Crikey – strewth, blimey, darn, damn

Dingo – Australian wild dog

Duffel bag – all-purpose canvas bag

Fellas – fellows, people

Flaming – bloody, damn, darn

Flinders – Flinders Ranges

Football – rugby, like gridiron without a helmet

Four wheel drive – SUV's designed for travel in the desert, all four wheels engage for better traction

Fussed – bothered, worried

G'day – good day, hello

Mate – friend, buddy

Men of high degree – fully initiated aboriginal men with elevated status in their tribe – some would have nangarri, sorcerer or 'medicine men' abilities and training

Mob – mobs, a lot of, usually associated with a group of people and of kangaroos

Nangarri – aboriginal medicine man or sorcerer – see also 'men of high degree'

Needy – horse

Noogy – rubbing the knuckles briskly against the scalp of a friend in fun

Outback – the desert country

Salt-pan – salt covered plain, flat as a saucepan, also called salt-flats because it's flat – the desert has many such salt covered plains

Sod – slang for 'bastard' or 'ratbag'

Stations – property or large farm in outback Australia, some larger than Texas

Strewth – damn, darn, crikey, blimey

Stuffed – exhausted

Swags – bed roll, blanket or sleeping bag wrapped in a waterproof canvas

Walkabout – aboriginals would 'go bush' to get back to their roots, sometimes it involved spiritual works as well as for a vacation

Wallaby – small kind of kangaroo

Whacked – hit, smacked

Willy-willy – dust devil, mini desert tornado, whirlwind

Yabbies – fresh water crayfish

Characters in Book 3

Revelationists: Marree Stosstruppen: Major Daniels, Captain Burgess, Lieutenant Donata, Corporal Normy, Nancy, Corporal Beade

Revelationists: Mt Isa Raven's Claws: Private Brinley

Bikies Mt Isa – Iceman Ed, Smiley

Flinders Ranges: General Russell Himmler, Colonel Rommel

Wilson's of Flinders Ranges: Kelvin, Jack, Greg, Joey

Alice Springs Command

General Hughes, Major Vic Thompson, Captain 'Louie' Lewis, Sergeants Tobi, Ahmet and Doff, Corporal Hassam, Captain 'Johnny' Walker, Noddy, Parsons, Lance Corporal Poole, Slimmy Lahotski, Gunner Wilmott, Driver Julian

Sundown's Commando

Sundown, Pinkie, Andrew, Wilma, Pellino, Mel, Harry, Jeda, Lenny, Danielle, Liam, Donna, Lulu, Danni, Wiram (Wirrie), Halo, Assassin (also called Creed), Beamy, John, Chan, Cambra, Shadow, McFly (also called Matty)

Scouts: Roo, Bongo,

Arkaroola: Riley, Katie, Elle, Harry

Adelaide: Nulla, Glenda, Luke, Simon, Charlene, Heidi, Lucy, Annie, Arthur (Arty), Phil, Fatima (Fati)

Tajna Služba - Lance Corporal Jaina, Private Jason Little, Blondie, Fat Boy

Reviews

"… readable with some well developed characters that you can't help but root for." D

"Leo Nix has a real winner with this series. 'Homeland Defense' continues the story of the three groups of survivors from the overthrow of the Australian government by what he characterizes as neo-Nazi religious fanatics. In this book, these survivors now all in the far reaches of the Australian outback come together and begin the process of laying the foundation for an organized resistance. Nix continues to develop his characters while adding new faces into the mix. Great writing, realistic action (people are lost, mistakes are made); but the overall focus remains positive. This was a good book and advanced the story considerably. Again, highly recommend the series, one of the better ones out there." M

"Sundown Apocalypse 3: Homeland Defense is a great read and I heartily suggest you pick it up. The dialogue is fresh and colloquial, and though the Australian dialect is used throughout the book. It is not a distraction, though not always knowing the colorful Australian slang caused a quick look at a Google, it added to the story-telling of the adventure." DC

Sundown Apocalypse series is now in audiobook

www.ingramcontent.com/pod-product-compliance
Lightning Source LLC
Chambersburg PA
CBHW071143100726

47908CB00002B/231